For

Fraser Robert McIntyre
and
Matilda 'Tilly' Scott McIntyre

Two bright lights in the gloom of 2021

Best
DEFENCE

Twelfth in the
Best Defence/Robbie Series

William McIntyre

Honesty is the best policy, but not always the best defence.

'Delightfully upbeat and utter fun'
Andrea Grossman - Writers Bloc Los Angeles

ISBN-13: 978-1-9998133-8-3

www.bestdefence.biz
wm@bestdefence.biz

More Best Defence/Robbie Munro Thrillers

Relatively Guilty
Duty Man
Sharp Practice
Killer Contract
Crime Fiction
Last Will
Present Tense
Good News Bad News
Stitch Up
Fixed Odds
Bad Debt

Chapter 1

'In a way you killed my client's mother, wouldn't you agree Mr Gleddoch?'

The Sheriff didn't allow the witness to answer. He waved Hugh Ogilvie, the Procurator Fiscal, back into his chair. The man had been on springs all morning.

'Mr Munro. The witness did not kill your client's mother – not in any way whatsoever. Now, you've been warned about this line of questioning several times already. It's not the witness who's on trial, it's your client, and this is not a murder case, but it is developing into something of a farce. I want no more of it.'

I hated to break it to the sheriff, but there was a long afternoon ahead.

'Members of the jury,' the sheriff continued, 'you will disregard that last question. Continue, Mr Munro. Carefully.'

Before I could put the same question into different words, my client shifted in the dock and muttered, 'murderer' under her breath so quietly only the whole courtroom could hear it.

'And that goes for your client too,' the sheriff said. 'Any more outbursts from her and she can cool off downstairs in the cells.'

Isabella Ewart's knuckles whitened as she gripped the edge of the dock, and I was pleased to see sympathetic looks in her direction from one or two of the jurors. Most people in West Lothian knew Isabella Ewart; most people in Scotland did. Six feet plus tall, and with more muscle than the Mafia, she was hard to miss. Big Bella had once represented Great Britain at the Olympics, where her bronze in the discus would have been gold but for a couple of eastern European rivals with more steroids in them than the average dairy herd. Nowadays Isabella was better known for her charity work, and there was seldom a local fundraiser where she didn't appear. My daughter and Isabella's niece were in the same class at the local primary school. Between them Tina and Florence Ewart usually scooped most of the sports day prizes. This year Flo's famous aunt had come along and closed the event with a stirring speech. Although Tina, along with most of Primary 4, hadn't a clue who Isabella was; nonetheless, my daughter had spent that evening in the back garden seeing how far she could fling the lid of a biscuit tin.

That had been a few weeks ago, in June. What had taken place nine months before was the reason we were now in court. At the start of October last year, when the weather was taking a turn for the worse, or, since this was Scotland, the even worse, Isabella's mum had been persuaded by local contractor Tam Gleddoch that her roof needed seeing to. For what was little more than an afternoon spent replacing a few missing slates and some aluminium ridging, Gleddoch had charged the old lady eighteen thousand pounds; a sum he preferred paid in cash to avoid overburdening Her Majesty's Revenue & Customs officers. Such was his largesse that, at no extra charge, he'd even chauffeured Isabella's mum to the building society so she could draw the money from her savings account. Whether the loss of a large portion of her life savings had anything to do with her demise, the old lady's health had deteriorated rapidly thereafter. Isabella hadn't found out what had happened until after her mother's death, but when she did, she'd put two and two together and come up with one baseball bat.

In hindsight, and from what we lawyers like to call a medico-legal point of view, the whole situation could have been handled so much better. Medically speaking, Gleddoch should have started out of his blocks the moment Isabella's shadow fell across his work-yard. While, legally speaking, if Isabella felt she had to repeatedly strike Gleddoch about the body with the aforementioned baseball bat, she shouldn't have done so in front of Gleddoch's entire workforce of six. Add their boss to that number of unskilled chancers and you had enough cowboys to defend a Mexican village from bandits, far less build a prosecution. It was viewed as such a magnificent Crown case that Hugh Ogilvie, the Procurator Fiscal himself, had been unchained from his desk to appear for the Prosecution.

When Isabella had come to me for advice all those months ago, I'd listened to the tragic tale and agreed what had happened to her mother was enough to make anyone angry. It was my opinion that the whole set of circumstances made for the sort of mitigation a defence lawyer could only dream of; however, as a complete defence, it was more of a nightmare.

But Isabella didn't want to throw herself on the mercy of the court. She wanted to go to trial and for me to put Gleddoch through the cross-examination wringer, no matter the cost. What could I do? I'd learned from experience that arguing with women - never mind women who can hurl a lump of metal seventy metres down a field - was a risky business. I might weigh a lot more than a discus, but when I'd consulted with Big Bella I'd not been sitting all that far from my office window. The laws of physics if not the law of the land told me I should shut up and accept her instructions.

So, Isabella pled not guilty, Gleddoch and his crew duly took to the witness box, and after two days of evidence the trial was set to conclude on the third with speeches from prosecution and defence followed by the sheriff's charge to the jury. First to address the jury was Hugh Ogilvie, and when a tedious twenty minutes had dragged by and Ogilvie returned to his seat, the Sheriff looked down at me.

'Mr Munro?' he enquired, as though so hopeless was my case there was a good chance I might not even bother to

3

address the jury. To be fair there wasn't a lot I could say. Even had my client's *he deserved it* approach to justice amounted to a defence or, at a push, to provocation, which it didn't, I'd had a great deal of trouble leading evidence of Gleddoch's eighteen grand bill because his Lordship thought it irrelevant. Sheriffs tended to find a lot of evidence irrelevant, or, as they liked to put it, collateral and thus inadmissible. Strange that most of the time it was the sort of irrelevant evidence that might assist the defence. Sometimes it seemed to me that a judge's job was to make sure the jury heard the truth, just not the whole truth. I'd lost count of the number of times Hugh Ogilvie had objected during my cross-examination and of the number of times those objections had been sustained. That said, losing to an objection is not always a bad thing. Sometimes it's the only tactic available to the defence. Watch the proud faces of the jury when, before the trial, the judge tells them how important their role is. Then watch those same faces during the trial as the judge tells them they can't be trusted with certain pieces of evidence. It's never easy to read a jury, but I could feel a certain uneasiness as time and time again the Sheriff ordered me to withdraw a question and asked the jury to ignore it. Judges are always keen to advise jurors that a question is not evidence, but if a witness is told not to answer a particular question, certain inferences are capable of being drawn - no matter how many times a Sheriff tells a jury not to. Like men in dirty raincoats, once it's out it's out and difficult to forget.

I rose to my feet and glanced over at my client. She gave me the same steely gaze I'm sure she had shared with her fellow medallists on that performance-enhanced Olympic podium all those years ago. 'Ladies and gentlemen,' I began, only to be interrupted by the loud clearing of a throat from on high.

'*Ladies and gentlemen*? Mr Munro, you forget yourself,' the Sheriff said.

'I placed both hands on the front of the jury box. I must apologise. I forgot that the law says you are no longer ladies and gentlemen.'

'That's not quite what the law says, Mr Munro,' the Sheriff chimed in. I didn't mind. The more often he butted in, the more victim cards I was being dealt, and the public loved an underdog. 'Ladies and gentlemen is no longer seen as an inclusive means of addressing the... the members of the jury.'

'Perhaps I could ask for a show of hands,' I said. 'To see if there is anyone present who is neither a lady nor a gentleman.'

'Enough, Mr Munro! Just get on with whatever you think can be said for your client.'

I was happy to see a few disgruntled expressions on the otherwise generally confused faces of the former ladies and gentlemen as I carried on. '*Members* of the jury, not only must I apologise for mis-addressing you, I also have another apology to make. You will undoubtedly recall that during my cross-examination of the Crown witnesses, I asked if it was true, that they had defrauded Isabella Ewart's elderly mother out of her life savings.' I shook my head with sincere regret. Something that gets easier with practice. 'I think I may even have suggested their actions contributed to the late Mrs Ewart's untimely death.'

'Mr Munro, you've been warned,' the Sheriff said.

'And his Lordship quite rightly held that in law such matters are irrelevant and not for you to concern yourself with. So, I say to you, put out of your mind anything I may have unsuccessfully tried to introduce as evidence to suggest Mr Gleddoch cheated my client's mother out of thousands of pounds and may very well have been responsible for the death of the elderly lady...'

Ogilvie was on his feet to object. The sheriff beat him to it. 'Mr Munro!'

I pressed on. 'That's not something his Lordship says you should hear, and his Lordship will decide such matters because he is the master of the law in these proceedings.' I looked up at the bench and received a stern and almost imperceptible nod of approval. 'So, with that apology, there is no need for me to take up more of your valuable time.' Folding the few sheets of blank papers I'd brought with me for show, I started towards my seat on the far side of the table, stopping halfway to turn and face the jury box again. 'But, of course, while it is his Lordship's job to say what the law is - what justice is, and always will be ladies and gentlemen - is your decision. And yours only.'

Chapter 2

'Not proven? I suppose you're pretty pleased with yourself?' Joanna said over the breakfast table next morning. We were both standing, me cramming toast into my mouth, my wife trying to push mashed-up Weetabix and banana into young Jamie's though with less success. Jamie had survived our attempts at parenting thus far, but then babies are really only flesh and blood Tamagotchi. Once you've mastered the eat, sleep, poop, regime there's not a great deal to it. Now a toddler, things had changed. Jamie was already well ahead on the terrible-twos graph, and we were hoping he'd emerge at the same speed as that which he'd entered.

Meanwhile, Jamie's half-sister, eight-and-a-don't-forget-the-half-year-old Tina, was sitting at the other end of the table multitasking by eating a bowl of Cheerios while doing yesterday's homework.

Joanna had taken on Tina as part of the Robbie Munro package deal after my daughter's own mum had died. A mum who'd neglected to inform me I had a child until after she'd left this world and me with a four-year-old.[1] Eighteen months into our marriage and along had come wee Jamie, an object as perpetually in motion as the laws of thermodynamics would allow. Finding ourselves with two children, Joanna and I had decided that someone should be promoted to principal carer. My wife's former career with the Crown Office & Procurator Fiscal Service had been high pressure. She'd constantly been at the beck and call of less competent senior management who nonetheless dictated what she should and shouldn't do. For that reason, we

---

[1] Crime Fiction – Book 5

decided she was better suited to the demands of childcare. In corroboration Mother Nature had even supplied her with specialist equipment, albeit no longer in use - hence the Weetabix and mashed banana.

So, for the time being it was mainly down to yours truly to keep Munro & Co. ticking over while Joanna spent most of her days with the kids. I say most of her days, because she still occasionally helped me out, especially when it came to High Court work. During her tenure with the COPFS, Joanna had qualified as a solicitor advocate. It meant that whenever the firm needed junior counsel, she could step in, and if it meant her working for a few days, or even a week or two every so often, we could always call on my dad to help out with babysitting.

'It's justice,' I told Joanna. 'As a former procurator fiscal depute you may not like it, but as a partner of Munro & Co. - defence lawyers to the stars—'

'Isabella Ewart?' Joanna said. 'A star?'

I thought my wife's tone a trifle unfair. Isabella might not be Alpha Centauri, but she was definitely to be found twinkling in one of the galaxy's lesser constellations. 'It's great publicity for the firm. Did you see the bit about it on the BBC website?'

'It was hard not to see it with you shoving your iPad under my nose every five minutes,' Joanna said. 'And I'm not complaining about the result, Robbie. Or the fee. It's just that you can get into trouble putting forward those kinds of spurious defences. You're lucky it wasn't Sheriff Brechin on the bench. He'd have had you up for contempt. In fact, you could still hear more about it. The Crown might appeal.' Is what I think Joanna said, because I'd slammed on the ear brakes and shifted into reverse at her "spurious defence" remark.

'*Spurious defence*? Was any evidence I tried to lead untrue?'

'Well... Probably not... But—'

'There you are then. I was merely attempting to relay the facts.'

'But those facts you were intent on relaying were irrelevant and inadmissible.' My wife had the annoying habit of bringing the law into our legal debates.

'I think what you mean,' I said, 'is that I sought to introduce certain evidence that the legal system, and I say legal system because it's not much of a justice system, didn't want the jury to hear because it assisted the defence.'

'And if the Crown had tried to lead inadmissible evidence that was detrimental to the defence. What then, Robbie? I'll tell you what. You'd be objecting like crazy. It's hypocritical. There are laws and we're lawyers. We're supposed to abide by them. That's how it works.'

My wife is a highly intelligent and cautious individual. I know that. It is she who takes a jug of water to the fridge to fill the ice-tray, rather than fill it from the tap and carry it all the way back to the freezer compartment, spilling water as you go. It's the sort of rational thinking that I have to contend with on a daily basis. To make matters worse, I'd noticed that ever since Joanna had been given rights of audience in the High Court, far too much of that, *I'm an officer of the court*, integrity stuff had rubbed off on her. I was sure the training involved brainwashing, or maybe they'd implanted a chip.

'That man...' Clearly my wife wasn't finished with me. 'The roofer. What was his name?'

'Tam Gleddoch.'

'Yeah. What Gleddoch did to your client's—'

'*Our* client's.'

'Okay, what he did to our client's mum, wasn't relevant as to whether or not she was guilty of assault.'

'The jury seemed to think so,' I said.

'Yeah, by a majority.'

'Could have been fourteen to one.' I tore off a piece of toast, laden with peanut butter and dotted with Marmite, and handed it to Jamie. Having long since rejected the highchair as a suitable dining venue, my son was sitting on a cushion atop a kitchen chair. He took the toast and stuffed it in his mouth. I waited for the Marmite to hit. It did. Jamie looked surprised for a moment. Then stuck out his hand for another piece. My boy.

'More likely a majority of eight to seven,' Joanna said. 'And not proven. How many women were on the jury? Nine, wasn't it? Didn't you once say women could never make up their minds what shoes to put on, far less who's guilty or not guilty?'

'I was kidding, and if you're going to resort to unfounded allegations of sexism, I think this conversation is over.' I leaned over and gave her a peck on the cheek, not easy when you're smiling.

Having realised she was getting nowhere with Jamie and the bowl of splodge, Joanna left the room, returning with a piece of stiff paper in her hand. 'Here, this'll wipe the grin off your face.'

Something I'd learned over recent years was that while there are only two sexes there are lots of genders. Or maybe it's the other way around. Whatever, and leaving chromosomes at the side of the park for a moment, I believe it would save a lot of argument if the issue were settled by the means of one simple test: how does a person react to an evening-only wedding invitation? As I saw things, there really were only two camps. One lot started browsing for a new set of heels and wondering if they could get away with the same outfit they wore to Samantha's wedding last year, while the other lot dusted off the Bumper Book of Plausible Excuses and prayed for a sudden, if temporary, debilitating disease.

Though still very much in the formative years of our marriage, when deciding on matters societal we proceeded on the basis that I regarded myself as the boss, while Joanna knew she was the boss. It was a system that had thus far served us well. So, although on the subject of evening-only invitations the Munro household fell neatly into the classic binary penis/vagina divide, it was the vagina-owner who held the casting vote.

Chapter 3

You expect to see ushers loitering at the door of a wedding reception; perhaps some cousins of the bride, or maybe a drunk uncle or two; but not bouncers. For that's what the two gentlemen who met us at the entrance door undoubtedly were, for all their sharp suits, winged collars and green bowties. The smaller of the two was the older and looked like he might try and sell us some life insurance. The other looked like we might need it.

'Do either of you have a camera with you,' Little asked, while Large stared into the depths of our souls.

'No,' I said. 'We're from Linlithgow not the nineteen nineties.'

He smiled, revealing a diamond embedded eyetooth. It was the professional smile of a man for whom dealing with smart arses was all part of the job. 'Phones then?' He had a distinct accent. Italian? French? Spanish? Somewhere they drank lots of wine, and not Greenock.

'Of course, we've got—'

Sensing a breakdown in diplomatic relations, Joanna nudged me out of the way. 'Yes, we both have phones. Is that a problem? I was hoping to take some pictures of the bride and groom.'

Large cleared his throat, the way a Pit Bull clears its throat before ripping yours out.

Little was still smiling, diamond tooth glinting. 'I'm sorry madam. Absolutely no photographs; however, there are official wedding photographs available for guests. Just select the ones you like from the display in the corner, leave your email address and the hotel will do the rest. There is no charge,' he added, sensing my impending cross examination on the matter.

From there we followed the sound of music and found ourselves a table dangerously near to the dance floor where we made awkward talk with total strangers in between decibels. I was about to make a move for the bar, until Joanna beat me to it. I might have lost the war over whether to go the reception, but I'd won the battle on who was driving home. Joanna set a glass tumbler down on the table in front of me.

'Maybe that'll stop you sitting looking like someone's stood on your sandcastle,' she yelled in my ear over the sound of *Teenage Kicks*. And while it is true that whisky does tend to cheer me up – the occasion would require more than a single measure of a single malt that really wasn't old enough to be up this late. I raised the tumbler and sniffed the amber dribble inside. Joanna put a hand on mine as I put the tumbler to my lips. 'That was seven-fifty. Make it last,' and lifting her own glass of soda-water and lime, advised that she was deserting me to go and say hi to the bride, adding, ominously, 'When I come back, we'll have a dance.'

Dancing and weddings. They go together like love and marriage or, in my case, car and crash. At every wedding there's a bloke who's never off the dance floor. By the end of the night, he's got a tie around his head, hands in the air and is surrounded by women cheering him on. That bloke is not me or anyone I am related to. The Munro men don't cut a rug, we chew up the carpet with a chainsaw. Don't get me wrong, I'll slow dance with my wife all night, but up the tempo and I have all the poise and rhythm of a cow on cobblestones.

Sensing some reluctance on my part, Joanna clamped a hand on my shoulder. 'Yes, we will.'

'Okay, the first slow one,' I said, as she scanned the gathering for signs of the walking wedding cake whose friendship with my wife was the reason we were spending

Friday night surrounded by strangers in a posh hotel, listening to a six-piece band bashing out hits from the 70s and 80s at volume 11.

Beverly, or Bev, had been at University with Joanna, and on graduation moved down to London. Armando, the bridegroom, was a semi-retired, asset manager and now a consultant to the firm where Bev's first-class honours had secured an internship after graduation. Though he had seen many more tax years than his bride, neither the considerable age difference nor Armando's immense personal wealth had been an obstacle to Bev. These days the couple spent summers in the country and winters in the town. The town alternated between London and Madrid, the country between a small estate situated not far from Linlithgow, and a larger one at La Mancha, in south-eastern Spain. A year or so back we'd been invited to Armando's and Bev's Scottish residence for dinner. West Hope House was situated not too far from our own home, nestling somewhere between the House of the Binns and Hopetoun House, bounded to the north by the Firth of Forth. It was the more modest of Armando Diaz's estates, still I'd bought a tank of petrol to be sure of making it the length of the driveway. The house itself was a mansion, with more rooms than Radisson, and it was in that cosy abode where Bev could be found writing books on the patriarchy and veganism, while her husband was off hedging funds in the city or whatever he did. Leaving Bev and Joanna to do some catching up, Armando had given me a tour of the property, ending up in his study; a room not quite large enough to stage a rock music festival. In his spare time, semi-retired Armando liked to shoot things. Feathery things that didn't shoot back preferably. Stuffed game birds adorned the furniture, and discretely fixed to the far away wall was a shotgun cabinet with a solid oak facade, home to a fine collection of weaponry, some old, some new, all very expensive.

14

Despite his keenness for blood sports, Armando and I had got along fairly well. We'd got along even better once I'd discovered my host's collection of rare single malts; some admittedly a lot rarer after I'd left.

Later, having joined the ladies, the conversation moved onto Bev's latest book and Armando's thoughts on the world of high finance. It was then, with a few geriatric whiskies under my belt, that I'd felt the urge to express my views on extreme feminism and bankers' bonuses, which, as it happened, didn't coincide seamlessly with those of our hosts. Suffice to say the invitation to the post-nuptial celebrations had come as something of a surprise.

So, my plan on Bev's and Armando's wedding night was to drink whisky, have one or two obligatory dances with my lovely wife, and then head home as soon as was socially acceptable, and before my eardrums perforated.

The hand on my shoulder tightened. Joanna sat down again. 'Don't look. I think he's coming over,' she hissed. 'No, I said don't look!'

'Who are you talking about?'

'You know.'

'How can I know if you won't tell me and I can't look round?'

'Mario. Or Dannyio or… You know… The footballer. I'm sure it's him. Handsome, isn't he?'

'Mario? Do you mean Dario? The *actual* Dario?' Now I had to turn around. It was him. The great Dario. A man born so cool his parents hadn't even bothered with a surname, had been scouted by Glasgow Rangers as a sixteen-year-old kicking a cabbage around the streets of Cali. He'd stepped off the plane from Colombia and into the Rangers first team for a couple of glorious seasons before Real Madrid swooped on him like a seagull on a seaside sandwich. For a time, the world's finest central defender, Dario, nicknamed El Mejor by the adoring fans at the Santiago Bernabéu Stadium, had lifted

15

more silverware than the butler at Downton Abbey, and finished an illustrious career with a move to the States and a transfer fee that had more numbers than The Beatles back catalogue.

Now, as he had during his football career, the Great One eschewed publicity. He didn't give interviews or sign autographs and there were more photographs of Count Dracula sunbathing than of Dario in a social setting. Suddenly the welcome party on the door and no photos policy made sense.

'I wonder if his wife is with him,' Joanna said, looking about. 'She's supposed to be gorgeous. Where do you think she is?'

'I don't know,' I said. 'Look around for the second prettiest woman here.'

Joanna gave me a kiss and a little hug that turned into more of a squeeze. She tugged at my arm. 'Quit gawping.'

'I'm not gawping, I'm smiling,' I said, through clenched teeth.

'Then stop it.'

'I can't. He started it, and now he's waving at me.'

It was true. He was smiling. At me. Smiling and waving. Now he was coming over. What could The Great One possibly want with me?

'Malky?' he said, hesitatingly. The smile thinning as he neared, peering at me through the gloom and the beams from the laser show. 'I am so sorry,' he yelled over the top of *Come on Aileen*. 'I thought you were—'

'Malky Munro?' I yelled back. It was a mistake a lot of people made, even though we looked nothing alike. 'He's my brother.'

'That explains it,' he said. 'You look just like him.' He came closer and riffled my hair. 'I thought maybe he'd had a haircut at last.' He patted my stomach. 'And put on a little weight. How is Malky? I've not seen him in a while.'

Sometime around the end of my brother's illustrious footballing career, the one he'd be happy to tell you all about if you bought him a drink, in fact, even if you didn't buy him a drink, Malky had been brought in as part of the training staff at Ibrox to teach the young Dario the finer arts of defending; something the young central mid-fielder had excelled at, while also finding time to nod in twenty or so goals a season.

'He's doing fine,' I admitted. 'He's a football pundit now on TV, telling everyone what they're doing wrong.'

Dario laughed. 'He always did. Especially the referees. Which means you must be his brother the lawyer. He told me about you, but he cannot have been right because you have with you such a delightful companion.' While Dario was infusing the surroundings with his charm and wafts of expensive cologne, the bridegroom appeared by his side.

'You two know each other then?' Armando said.

'Mistaken identity,' I replied.

'Then let me introduce you. Dario, this is Roddy—'

'Robbie.'

'Of course, Robbie. And this delectable creature is Robbie's wife, Joanna, a friend of Beverly's.'

Dario took a hold of Joanna's hand and stepped back. 'Let's dance.'

Watching the two of them join the gyrating mass, I downed my whisky before it evaporated, like Armando seemed to have done. Could I make it to the bar and back again before my wife returned?

Nothing ventured, by the time the closing fiddle strains of Dexy's floor-filler segued into the opening keyboard swipe of *Dancing Queen*, I was back in my seat - similar glass, bigger and better whisky. But there had been no need to rush. Joanna was showing no signs of leaving the dance floor. Sensing we could be in for a long night, I necked the drink and sashayed over to the bar again, gripping a shell-shocked credit card.

The world seemed a better place as I leaned my back against the counter, rolling a Benromach Batch 4 around a chunky tumbler. Inhaling the peat and sherry aromas, I rehearsed my plea in mitigation for the next credit card bill post-mortem. Yes, darling, it did cost nearly twenty pounds, but it was a double and cask strength. Which meant some water was needed, therefore by volume of liquid it was the best value. I was actually saving us money.

Dancing Queen dissolved into something I'd not heard before, quieter and a lot slower. Whatever it was, it was popular. I sat it out. Like buses and global pandemics there'd be another along in a minute. There was, *Home to Donegal*, and as even more couples flocked to the dance floor, I realised I could no longer see Joanna. Taking my drink with me, I skirted the edge of the throng, eventually catching a fleeting glimpse of a red dress, except it couldn't be Joanna's red dress because there was a hand on its bottom. The dress, hand and bottom went out of sight momentarily, to reappear seconds later through a gap in the dancers, and, while I might not have been able to pick out either hand or dress in an identification parade, I would have recognised that bottom anywhere. Joanna reached down, removed the hand and placed it on her waist, only for the hand to return. When it happened again, I sconed the whisky and began to swim through the dancers like an Olympic spermatozoon in search of an ovum playing hard to get. This time it was me who removed the offending hand from my wife's rear-end. Armando's hand. He must have swapped partners with the Great One.

'Mind if I cut in?' I shouted in the bridegroom's ear, in a manner which I hoped made it clear I could've cared a lot more whether he minded or not.

18

He pulled away from me, whirling Joanna off, hand clamped to her bottom. Barging my way through the dancers, I caught up with them and tapped the bridegroom on the shoulder. He didn't respond. I tapped again, harder. He turned, an angry expression on his flushed face. 'Will you leave us alone, Roddy?'

By this time some of the dancers closest to us had slowed to watch. Not far away Dario was swaying elegantly, a beautiful woman in his arms. I reached out for Joanna's hand, forgetting I was still holding the whisky glass. Armando batted my hand away. The glass flew out of it, fell and smashed, scattering shards of glass and nearby dancers. The band stopped playing. I sidestepped, took my wife's hand and pulled. Armando had the other hand and wasn't for letting go. By the way Joanna was glaring at me, I had the feeling the cost of whisky had dropped down the list of immediate topics for discussion once we'd returned chez Munro.

It was Dario who amongst the faces encircling us was first to recognise the absurdity of the situation. He left his dancing partner and came over, the man with the diamond tooth materialising by his side.

'Boys, boys. Play nice,' he said.

Armando threw his head back and laughed. Letting go of Joanna like a wine connoisseur letting go of a lukewarm Chablis, he held up both hands, fingers spread wide, and dusted them off above his head.

Dario stepped between us, a wide smile on his face. 'Let's go, Armando,' he said, and taking a hold of the bridegroom's arm, his bronzed face still smiling, the Colombian turned on a Cuban heel, skidded on a fragment of glass and, flailing helplessly, fell backwards dragging Armando with him. The pair of them, not blessed with the same natural posterior padding as my wife, landed with quite a bump.

Joanna looked down at the sprawled bridegroom and his guest of honour, and then up at me. Her face matched the colour of her dress.

I tried to help the pair of them up, but Diamond Tooth placed a hand on my chest. 'I'll get your coat, sir,' he said.

Chapter 4

'I never thought there'd be so much blood.' Malky stared down at our dad, bent double, clutching his hands to his stomach.

I had to agree. Covid 19 had a lot to answer for. My dad's lockdown woodturning hobby, or finger reduction programme as some people called it, being one. When my brother and I had chipped in to buy him a lathe and set of chisels for his birthday a couple of years back, somehow we'd expected more bowls, spindles and peppermills, and fewer trips to A&E.

Tina came running into the shed carrying the Walker's shortbread tin that had long since been pressed into service as a first aid box. Over the woodturning months my daughter's vocabulary had been considerably extended. 'Is Gramps still swearing?' she asked, voice muffled by a dust mask and the full-face visor my dad insisted she wear when watching him in action, while thinking an old pair of NHS specs and scarf wrapped around his nose and mouth were sufficient PPE for himself.

'The swearing has stopped, the bleeding not so much,' I said. Taking the tartan tin from her, I approached with the bravery and caution of Androcles. Fortunately, this old lion's wound wasn't too bad. Which is not to say I'd have liked it, but at least there was a full complement of digits even if the index finger on his right hand didn't look too pleased with life.

'You need to run that under a tap and get some pressure on it,' I said, taking him by the elbow.

He yanked his arm away. 'It's only a flesh wound.'

'I know, Dad,' I said, 'but you're made of flesh.'

Once again I took hold of his arm. He shrugged me off. 'I can manage,' he said, and injured hand under his armpit, he cupped the other behind his granddaughter's head and allowed her to lead him away.

'Where were you last night?' I asked Malky after the pair of them had left. 'You look like something the morgue's been defrosting.'

He stared over the top of a pair of sunglasses at me. Perfectly normal in July, just not July in Scotland.

'Had a bit of a night last night,' he said, not narrowing things down much. Most of Malky's Friday nights were bits of a night, and a lot of those bits he had trouble remembering in the morning. In the past a normal Friday for my brother had been spent, early evening, taking calls on a radio football phone-in, before driving through to Linlithgow to overdose his favourite nephew and niece on sugary snacks. After that he'd head off with his mates for their weekly five-a-side game, before disproportionally replacing the lost sweat with pints of beer and returning in the early hours to crash at my dad's. Now that he'd been promoted from Friday afternoon radio to Saturday evening and Sunday afternoon TV, he occasionally broadened his Friday night horizons.

'I was at the opening of that new nightclub in Edinburgh. You know, the one Addo, Stevey and Taiters bought over. All the boys were there. Never put my hand in my pocket once.'

Most of Malky's former teammates had nicknames ending in O, Y or occasionally ERS. The aforementioned Addo, Stevey and Taiters being three who, unlike my brother, had, after their retirement from the beautiful game, spent their money on nightclubs rather than in nightclubs.

Malky's mobile rang. Today's ringtone was Simply the Best. 'Dario, how's it going?' he yelled into it.

I felt my heart sink. Dario? What did he want?

Malky put the mobile to the side of his leg. 'He's looking for a lawyer.'

22

Oh, no. He'd been injured in last night's fall. That had to be it. He'd pulled a moisturised muscle, and now, unable to clotheshorse his latest range of ludicrously expensive underpants, was coming after me for damages.

'No, no, there's no need to go into detail on the phone, Dario,' Malky said, phone back at his ear. 'I know. Tell me about it. Women, eh? Yeah, I can give you the number if you like.'

Malky returned the phone to his thigh. 'Dario's having women problems.'

The only problems I imagined Dario had with the opposite sex was fighting them off.

'Where is he?' I asked.

'Edinburgh. He was at a wedding last night.'

'Really?'

'Yeah. He's in Scotland. He's written a book.'

By which my brother meant Dario's soon to be released life story, modestly entitled, 'El Mejor'. I'd read an excerpt in one of the newspapers. As autobiographies went, it couldn't have been better if he'd written it himself.

'He wants your office number so he can arrange an appointment,' Malky said. 'Will I tell him you don't do that kind of law?'

Dario wanted an appointment with *me*? Was he really looking for legal advice or just to come around with Little and Large and wreak revenge? He couldn't be genuine. He must have a team of lawyers. In fact, his team of lawyers probably had lawyers. What did he want with a High Street solicitor whose idea of legal advice on relationship strife was, have you tried a bunch of flowers and some chocolates? And yet, in his playing days Dario had earned more in a month than I'd earn in a lifetime, and that included my old paper round. If he really did want to consult with me, it was too good an opportunity to miss.

'Tell him any time, any place,' I said.

Malky returned the phone to his ear, listened for a few seconds more and then said, 'Sure, eleven o'clock tomorrow would be fine. The Newberry? No problem. I'll tell her to be there. No, happy to help. Let's catch up. Yeah, arrivederci or ciao or… see you.'

'Her?' I said, after Malky had ended the call.

He grimaced and put a heavy hand on my shoulder. 'I don't think you're going to like this.'

Chapter 5

Sunday morning, I was in the kitchen watching Jamie slide toy cars across the lino while Joanna tried to steer a bluebottle out of an open window. Funny how a fly can slip into the house through a crack in the door but can't find its way out again unless you take down a supporting wall.

'Are you still in the huff?' she asked. 'There's no need to be like that, Robbie. Me and Dario, we just sort of hit it off. I was telling him how hard it was to be a lawyer and have kids and he started telling me all about the problems with his marriage. In confidence, of course. He was going to ask us to join his table before you started coming over all caveman with Armando.'

'Oh, was I supposed to stand back while a rich Spaniard groped your backside, just because an even richer Colombian wanted to tell you how much his wife didn't understand him?' I asked, not taking my eye of the bluebottle.

'You behaved like a jealous idiot,' Joanna said.

I swung at the bluebottle with a rolled-up copy of the Law Society Journal and missed.

'Admit it. You liked it,' I said. 'Two men fighting over you.'

'No, I did not.'

The next swipe also failed to connect.

I gave her a cuddle. 'Not even a wee bit?'

She kissed me, then pushed me away. 'Just get rid of the fly.'

The insect had made the fatal error of resting overly long on the window ledge. This time I hit a bullseye.

'Hey!' Joanna, took the rolled-up magazine, rubbed the dead fly off on my trousers, and smoothed it out. 'That's my journal.'

I'd assumed it was Joanna's. She read hers. I treated mine as collectors' items, but the collectors weren't due to come for the blue bin until the end of the month.

I took the magazine from her. A corner of one of the pages was creased. 'Recent developments in Family law? You're suddenly an expert because you've read up on the subject for five minutes?'

'Maybe not, but it's five minutes more than you. Possibly six minutes more than you.' She stroked my head. She was loving every moment of it. 'Don't forget, it was you who said it'd be a good idea if we diversified the type of work we took on.'

Which was true. After I'd been acquitted of a murder charge, I'd attracted quite a lot of quality, private-paying work. Plenty of lawyers fell afoul of the law. Some did jail time. Who better to defend you than a lawyer who'd been there, done it and, most importantly, taken a walk? Although, to be fair, what set me apart from most of my new clientele was I hadn't actually done it. Still, private clients in criminal law were not that thick on the ground, and so with Legal Aid largely ditched, apart from a few dripping roasts, and although we'd had to pay an extra whack more professional indemnity insurance, Munro & Co. had moved into new and hopefully more lucrative fields of law. Which was to say any field of law that didn't have the tattered old Scottish Legal Aid Board scarecrow standing in the middle of it.

'Anyway...' I said, having graciously accepted a conciliatory peck on the cheek. 'Why would I be in the huff? It's all grist to the Munro & Co. mill. It's not like I want involved in the sordid world of family law. I've got more than enough good clean crime to be getting on with. Do I have to refer you to this again?' I got out my phone and brought up the BBC Scotland news page and scrolled to one of the minor headlines: *Discus Thrower's Charge Thrown out.* 'When word gets around about my famous victory for Isabella Ewart, the clients will be queuing round the block.'

'Of course they will.' Joanna planted another kiss on my cheek. I was moving in to reciprocate when she froze. 'Where's Jamie?'

'He'll be fine,' I said, drawing her to me. 'He's through the room, playing with his cars.' When it came to child-rearing, I'd developed what my wife called a policy of benign neglect.

'He was right there a minute before you started on about Dario,' Joanna said.

'*I* started on about—?'

She gave me another shove. 'Don't argue. Go find your son.'

And so I did, and he was exactly where I'd said he'd be: in the livingroom, except he'd moved on from the world of toy cars and was doing what all two-and-a-half-year-olds like to do, that is seek out new and evermore dangerous pastimes and boldly go where their parents had told them not to go. I dispossessed him of the crayon he was trying to plug into an electric socket and carried him wriggling back to the kitchen.

'Did you tell the Great One that you knew as much about family law as the average ex-procurator fiscal depute who's spent Saturday night reading a magazine article on the subject?'

Joanna shrugged. 'I can learn on the job. It's not rocket science. It's all about emotions. We women are good at those. We're born with it.'

'And what if he wants more than your female intuition?' I said. 'What if he actually wants some legal work done? There's bound to be documents or writs or.... stuff to be drafted. A separation agreement maybe,' I said, dredging up something from a long-ago family law lecture that I must have attended by mistake.

Joanna pinched my cheek. 'I wonder how much he'll pay me to sort it out for him.'

'Pay us,' I reminded her. 'You work for... I mean, with me. We're a team.'

'And don't you forget it,' Joanna said. She looked down at the squashed bug on the floor and grimaced. 'Now, get rid of that.'

Chapter 6

Joanna's consultation with Dario was to take place at, where else but, The Newberry, Edinburgh's most exclusive hotel. The Newberry didn't advertise its presence. If you didn't know where it was that was because they'd rather you didn't. With nine outrageously decadent suites and hosting the city's finest restaurant, if you had to ask the tariff you couldn't afford to stay there. I'd previously been allowed entry to investigate the sudden death of one of its guests, Hercule Mercier, multi-millionaire paramour of my former fiancée Jill Green[2]. Jill was not so much a bullet I'd dodged, as a bullet that had deliberately swerved around me and hit some other poor sod. It was a long story from what seemed like an even longer time ago.

Joanna and I caught the mid-morning train and walked along George Street to the hotel. It was the last Sunday in July, and the weather was making a better-late-than-never appearance. Strictly speaking, I hadn't been invited to the consultation, but someone had to carry Joanna's briefcase.

'Mrs Munro?' enquired the doorman of Joanna. My wife having confirmed her identity, the man in the tartan trews turned to me with a slight lift of his nose like a Presbyterian catching a whiff of incense. 'And?'

'And Mr Munro,' I said, striding past him into the grand lobby. I had been about to add, 'to see Mr Dario,' but I could already see Mr Dario. He was standing straight ahead on the middle landing of the great staircase. He was dressed in a white silk dressing gown held at the waist by a gold satin sash, gesticulating frantically at us. When the gesticulations

---

[2] Stitch Up - Book 9

showed no sign of reducing in vigour, Joanna and I hurried up to meet him. There was no time for polite reintroductions.

'What are you doing here?' he asked me. 'Never mind. Salome is supposed to be staying with friends, but she is downstairs in the bar right now.' The extreme urgency of the situation creased his otherwise wrinkle-free bronzed features. Joanna had told me nothing about Dario's marital strife, and by the time my razor-sharp legal mind had concluded that Salome might very well be the reason the Great One was in need of a family lawyer, he had seized Joanna by the arm and was dragging her up the stairs. 'Talk to her,' he said, shooing me off. 'Do not let her know why you are here.' Sounded easy enough. I didn't know why we were here. 'Under no circumstances allow her to come up to my room.'

With that, he and my wife rounded the sweep in the staircase and disappeared from sight.

Fortunately, bars and the finding of them has never been a problem for me. Although to describe the opulent surrounds of the cocktail salon at the Newberry as a bar was a bit like calling the Garden of Eden a nice spot for a picnic. I looked about. In the far corner beside a window draped with extravagantly embroidered curtains, a pianist caressed the keys of a highly polished mini-grand. To my left, in an armchair, someone was hiding behind a copy of The Financial Times, and at a table to the right, two couples, Americans. The women with that look of perpetual surprise that only the surgeon's knife can inflict. The men all gut, thick limbs and voices not adapted for built up areas. I walked on following the marble of the bar top around the corner until I came across a woman sitting on a bar stool reading a hardback. A cup of black coffee sat at her elbow, next to a tiny, sequined handbag. She was dressed in a plain lilac dress with a scoop collar. Her only jewellery a gold chain and tiny gold crucifix. As I neared, she closed her book and picked up her handbag. She stood, ready to leave. I stepped into her path.

'Are you Salome?' I asked.

She tossed a tress of long blonde hair to the side, looked up at me and smiled. She was gorgeous. Involuntarily I let Joanna's briefcase drop to the floor.

The woman looked down at the fallen briefcase and then up at me. 'What is it you want?'

Tell the truth I hadn't really thought much further ahead than the initial, 'Are you Salome?' line. 'Er, I'm Robbie Munro,' I said, eventually, holding out a hand that she didn't take. 'I know Dario. Sort of.'

She frowned. 'Yes, I saw you talking to Dario at the wedding before... before you had to leave. How is it you know my husband?'

'I don't. Not really. He saw me at the wedding and thought I was my brother. They used to play football together a long time ago. Malky Munro - you might have heard of him?'

She hadn't. 'But you do know Armando?' she said.

'Again, only sort of. My wife was at University with Beverly. We don't live far from them actually.'

She nodded as though to confirm this was an acceptable answer and continued her interrogation. 'You say you are here to see Dario. So why are you not seeing him? Why are you speaking to me? Where is the woman I saw you with through the window? Is that your wife?'

'Yes,' I said, casual as you like. She's here to speak to Dario about some...'

'Some what?'

'Oh, just some legal matters.'

She sensed my casualness was starting to wear off. 'Really? What kind of legal matters?'

I'd already said too much. I tilted my head and squinted at the spine of her book. The title was in Spanish, but I recognised the author's name. Joanna always made lots of

New Year's resolutions. Most of them were for me, but this year she'd made one for herself, and that was to read the top fifty novels of all time as decided by some book-blogger or other. I'd tried to support her, and after the shock of discovering there were no Iain M Banks or Kinky Friedman books mentioned, I was going through her cast-offs, avoiding the ones where the protagonists wore petticoats and took a lot of afternoon tea.

'Gabriel García Márquez. One Hundred Years of Solitude. Great story,' I said.

'You don't have the Spanish,' she said with a smile. 'This is *El Amor en los Tiempos del Cólera*. Love in the Time of Cholera. Very sad.' The smile vanished. 'What legal matters did you say?'

'I'm not really sure. I'm just tagging along. Any excuse to visit the Newberry.'

She raised an exquisite eyebrow, 'What kind of lawyer is your wife?'

'Same as me,' I said. 'A criminal lawyer. Defence work.'

She squinted one eye in suspicion.

'Have you heard of Isabella Ewart?' I asked.

She hadn't. 'The Olympic discus thrower?' Still no signs of recognition. 'She had a court case recently. I was her lawyer. She was found not proven - that's the same as not guilty in Scotland.'

'What had she been accused of?'

'Hitting a man with a baseball bat.'

'Why did they think she did this thing?'

'Because she did it.'

'Then why was she found not guilty?'

'Not proven, and it was because of what the man had done.'

'And what had he done to her?'

'To her? Nothing.'

'Then why did she hit him?'

32

'She thought he deserved it.' I could tell Salome was having difficulty understanding. 'It was in all the newspapers.' I glanced over at a silver rack at the far end of the bar. Washington Tribune, Die Welt, La Monde. The closest to home was the Sunday Telegraph. No sign of a Sunday Post anywhere. 'Maybe not all the newspapers.' I pulled out my phone and showed her the online article on the BBC website, scrolling down to where I received a name check. Yes, it was boasting, but all in a good cause.

Salome glanced at my phone, smiled politely, and began to look around for the best means of escape. She took a step to the right which I mirrored with a step to the left. 'When I say he hadn't done anything to her, the man had defrauded my client's elderly mother of her life savings. I managed to persuade the jury that he deserved all he got.'

'Do you think he did?'

'In court it doesn't matter what a lawyer thinks. It's what the jury think.'

'But do you? Personally speaking?'

'I suppose so, but in court you just try your best anyway, no matter what you actually think.'

'But you try harder if you believe in something. Yes?'

'Subconsciously maybe,' I conceded.

She sat back down on the stool. 'What has Dario done this time? Has he not paid his tax? Again?' She turned, took a sip of coffee and dabbed at her cupid's bow with a cocktail napkin. 'The pretty woman with you. You say she is your wife?' Salome cocked an exquisite eyebrow.

'Yes, sometimes I don't believe it myself,' I said.

She laughed. 'I saw her at the wedding in the red dress. She was dancing with Armando. You didn't like that? You smashed a glass. Dario was very angry afterwards.'

I looked around. 'This is a great place, isn't it? What's that tune he's playing? Chopin?' I asked, Chopin being the only virtuoso pianist of any era whose name I knew.

'Yes,' she said. 'Nocturne number nine, I think.'

I was coming to terms with having correctly guessed the provenance of a piece of classical music when she asked again. 'Why is it you say your wife is here to see Dario?'

'Honestly, I've no idea,' I said, nearly honestly.

'But he has sent you to come to see me and how do you say? Chat me up?'

'Not so much chat you up. Just to…'

'Keep me talking while he speaks to your wife. In his suite. This woman you don't like dancing with other men?'

'This is business,' I said.

'What kind of business?'

I gave her my best helpless smile.

'How old are you?' she asked.

'Thirty-nine. No. Forty,' I said. 'Very recently. Practically still in my thirties. Give or take.'

She brushed a hand across my forehead. 'So many lines. Dario has a range of products that will help you.'

'Products? Oh, you mean like moisturiser and lotions and all that stuff?' I said, unable to avoid a smirk, as though my usual morning routine was a splash of kerosene after a quick scrape with the business end of a broken bottle.

'You think it's funny for a man to look after his appearance?'

'No. But…'

'A beautiful wife like that… Maybe you need a little help to keep her.' She moved closer and gently stroked the corner of each eye with a finger. 'You laugh too much, I think.'

'Have you seen the legal aid rates?' I said.

She moved even closer, placed her fingers either side of my forehead and pulled the skin taught. She smelled wonderful. 'A little rejuvenating formula in the morning and at bedtime and—'

'I hope I'm not interrupting anything.'

I started backwards almost tripping over a stool.

34

'Joanna,' I said. 'I'd like you to meet Salome. She was j—'

'So I see.' Joanna took my hand, and, throwing Salome a tight little smile, led me away like I was a toddler who'd strayed too close to the fire.

'How'd it go?' I asked. 'I thought you'd be longer.'

'Thought or wished?'

We didn't speak again until we'd left The Newberry and were on George Street heading for the train. Joanna pulled up. 'Okay. What exactly was going on in there?'

'Your client told me to go and talk to his wife. That's what I was doing.'

'And the face stroking?'

'She thought I had too many wrinkles for a man of my age. I told her I put it down to married life.'

'What else did you tell her, Robbie?'

'Nothing?'

'Robbie…?'

'Okay, I told her we were lawyers.'

'Robbie!'

I had to say something. Anyway, she recognised you from the wedding. She wanted to know why you were visiting her husband after what happened.'

Joanna sighed. 'What else did you say?'

'Just that you were here to see Dario on some legal matters. Don't look at me like that. Dario must have tons of legal matters, contracts and… things. He's got his own line of make-up or something. He'll be seeing lawyers all the time.'

'And that's it? You never mentioned…'

'What?'

'D.I.V.O.R.C.E?' As a parent you fall into the habit of spelling out words you don't want certain others to hear.

'Whose?'

'His.'

'How could I mention it? I only knew he wanted to ask you something about family law. I wasn't even sure if he was married until I was hurled into the clutches of his wife.'

'I'm so sorry, Robbie,' Joanna said, her sarcasm knowing no bounds. 'It must have been horrible for you.'

'Hey, don't get on at me. I wasn't the one alone in the hotel suite of a strange Colombian man.'

'And I wasn't the one having my face caressed.'

'Caressed? Pawed you mean. I'm not a piece of meat, Joanna. You and the Great I Am, pimping me out so that the two of you can talk about his problematic love life in his three-grand-a-night bedroom.'

Joanna linked her arm though mine and we started walking. 'Salome is very pretty, though, isn't she?' she said after a while.

I shrugged. 'I suppose, but not like you.'

'She's pretty, but not like me? You mean I'm not pretty?'

I noticed we'd stopped walking again. 'What I mean is that she's pretty in a dead obvious sort of a way.'

'Then I'm not obviously pretty?' Joanna looked at her reflection in the shop window.

'She wears a lot of make up,' I said.

'I've got some make up on.'

'I like you better. Your face… Your… everything.'

'But you do like her?'

'Well... It's...'

'You like her and yet you've only just met her?'

'What I mean is... I don't' like her —'

'You just said you did. Are you going back on that?'

'No, but yes. You see...'

Joanna punched me on the arm and laughed. I'd tear you apart in the witness box, you know that?' Fortunately, she was still laughing as I hurried her along past her favourite dress shop. 'One place I never want to see you,' she said, 'is giving evidence in court.'

36

Chapter 7

Someone who would be giving evidence in court was medical student Marc Traynor. He was standing with Joanna and me outside Edinburgh High Court on Monday morning, the first day of August. Yesterday's reasonably good weather was now but a fond memory, and the weather was closing in like shades of the prison house about our twenty-three-year-old client.

'Are you telling me the jury won't be allowed to hear any of that? I don't understand.'

It seemed to me that young Marc had understood well enough what I'd just told him. I'd previously gone over things with him at length to warn the young man of the likely outcome of today's Preliminary Hearing and the chance the defence's application under section 275 would be rejected. What he actually meant was he couldn't believe it.

'Me and Kirsty had been going out for months. We'd had sex tons of times. Kirsty didn't go to the police for a week. Not until after I'd dumped her.'

Kirsty was my client's ex-girlfriend, now complainer in the case HMA -v- Marc Traynor, who hadn't reported the alleged rape until she'd discovered her boyfriend texting another woman, upon which she stormed out of his life and into the police station.

Whereas in the prosecution of 'stranger rape' cases, the conviction rate must have been approaching 100%, difficulties for juries arose in what were often referred to as 'date rapes', where there were no injuries, no screams, no allegations of violence and only two people who actually knew the truth. For this reason, in order to secure more guilty verdicts, the rules of evidence were changed many years ago.

Now cross examination of an alleged victim that dared to challenge their good character or past behaviour, sexual or otherwise, and that might suggest they were not a credible or reliable witness, was not permissible without prior sanction of the court. And yet rape myths still abounded in the minds of the general public. The uninitiated believed that a witness could expect to be asked about previous relationships, the length of their hemline or what kind of underwear they had on at the time. Not a chance.

'I'm afraid these are the rules of the game, Marc,' Joanna said, 'and we have to play by them.'

'But it's not a game. Not for me.'

'Listen Marc,' I said. 'I've told you before that the rules on evidence in sex cases are very strict. There are certain questions we can't ask Kirsty.'

'But she can say whatever she likes?'

'You'll get your chance to tell your side of the story,' I said.

'And when you do,' Joanna butted in. 'Don't say you dumped her. Say you told her the relationship was over. Something that sounds less like you've taken out the trash.'

'But that's what happened. She kept snooping at my phone, I told her we were finished and the next thing I was being hauled away by the cops.'

Joanna stretched out the palm of a hand and caught a drop of rain. 'Marc, now isn't the time and it's definitely not the place to discuss this.'

'Well, I want to discuss it,' he said.

I led him away from the big bronze front door of the Lawnmarket building and into the relative shelter of David Hume's statue. Hero of the Enlightenment, Hume's unenlightened 18th Century views now threatened to have him removed and replaced by someone whose own credentials were no doubt currently being vetted.

'Marc, I've told you. The law says that unless we have the permission of the court the defence is not allowed to lead evidence of any sexual behaviour on the part of Kirsty other than what is set down in the charge.'

'So, the jury won't hear that we had sex the day after the party? Why would she consent to that if I'd raped her the night before?'

I shrugged. 'Marc, I don't make the law, but we've got to abide by the rules. Joanna, that is Miss Jordan...' Joanna retained her maiden name for court purposes, 'knows what she's doing. She's going to do everything she possibly can to make sure you're acquitted.'

'And how's she going to do that if the jury only hear one side of the story?'

'They won't. They'll hear yours too,' Joanna said.

'Not all of it. Not if I'm not allowed to say we'd been at the party, had a lot to drink and she was all over me. Or that the next time I saw her, after I'm supposed to have raped her, we'd had sex too.'

Joanna set him straight. 'The law is only interested in whether Kirsty was too drunk to give her consent on the night it's said to have happened.'

'But I'd had as much to drink as her. More in fact, and I was okay. Tipsy maybe. How come she gets to say she was drunk, but I don't? What if I say I was drunk and she raped me?'

It was a topic of conversation I'd had many times, and at least once before with my young client, though in slightly dryer conditions.

'There are two things wrong with that, Marc,' I said. 'Firstly, only someone with a penis can rape somebody else, so I'm assuming that rules Kirsty out. Secondly, legally speaking, a man can never be too drunk to consent, only his alleged victim.'

'And what about the fact that she made a false report of rape against her last boyfriend? Is that just brushed under the carpet? Those investigations you made, Mr Munro. My mum and dad were paying you to do that and now you're saying they were all a waste of time?'

I put a hand on the young man's shoulder. 'You saw what happened in there just now. Miss Jordan tried her best, but the judge is letting none of it in.'

He birled around and kicked the stone plinth of the statue. Scotland's greatest philosopher didn't seem to mind. Maybe, like my client, he suspected his days were numbered and was making the most of his time in the fresh air.

'I take it things went pretty much as expected?' Grace Mary said, when Joanna and I arrived back at the office. My secretary was opening the morning mail that never arrived until the afternoon, setting in about it with a letter-opener like she was gutting fish.

I threw my briefcase onto the reception desk. 'Lord Birkenside kicked the s.275 application straight into touch. Apparently, it's all extraneous and irrelevant that my client and his ex-girlfriend were at it like honeymooners before and after the alleged rape.'

'What about the girl's conviction for making a false report against her last boyfriend?'

'That's out too. It would tend to show that the complainer was not of good character, therefore, under section 274, not the sort of thing the jury should get to hear about.'

'Them's the rules,' Joanna said. 'What's important is what happened at the actual time. Not before or after. If his girlfriend was too drunk to consent then that's rape. Her pal says she'd had a full bottle of Mad Dog at the party.'

Mad Dog or MD 20/20 was a favourite tipple of the youth. It came in a range of flavours from Blue Raspberry to Dragon Fruit and the only advantage I could see in it was that it probably tasted the same when you vomited it up as it had when you drank it down.

'It's 13% proof,' I said. 'That's the same as a bottle of wine. How drunk could she have been?'

Joanna sliced the top off an A4 envelope. 'Maybe she's not used to strong drink. Her friend's statement says she seemed drunk when she left the party.'

'What does she look like?' Grace Mary asked, bringing us back to basics. 'I mean I've seen him. He's quite handsome. What about her? I don't suppose —'

'She's got two heads and a hairy wart on one of her noses?' Joanna said. 'I'm afraid not. In the beauty stakes I'd say it's pretty much neck and neck.' She set down the letter-opener, unlatched my briefcase and removed a bundle of papers. 'I'd better go home and relieve your dad of Jamie. I'll read the brief over again.'

'Good,' I said. 'Maybe you'll be able to find something to cross examine the complainer on, apart from what the weather was like that night.'

Chapter 8

I left the office early. Mondays were long enough already without any help from me. I got home around half past five. Joanna had given the kids their tea, much of which was on the kitchen floor, Jamie's face and Tina's T-shirt. My dad had stayed for food too. I was sitting in the livingroom when Malky showed up.

'What are you doing here?' I asked, when he'd returned from having unburdened the fridge of my last bottle of beer.

'I've messed up big time, Robbie.' He was going to have to narrow it down. 'Did you watch the match yesterday?'

I had to confess that, thrilling though a Dunfermline Athletic/Ross County fourth round cup tie sounded, I'd decided to miss it in favour of absolutely anything else that was on telly.

'Did you see the penalty?'

'Did I see the penalty in the game I've just told you I didn't see? That one?'

Malky wasn't listening. He dropped into an armchair like he was testing the springs, and the house foundations. 'I still can't believe it,' he said, voice muffled by both hands over his face. 'Can you believe I could be so stupid?'

I was preparing to give it a go, when Tina came charging into the room and, ignoring her parents, threw herself on top of my brother and started hunting in his pocket for sweets. Malky didn't respond. Head still in his hands.

'What's wrong with him?' my dad asked, coming into the room after a toilet trip with Jamie.

'We're still trying to work that out,' I replied.

Malky looked up. 'Dad, did you see the game yesterday?' he asked from between his fingers. He was on safer ground there. My dad would watch a jakey kick a beer can between two wheelie bins.

'Aye, what about it?'

'The penalty. That's what about it.' Malky lowered his head again to study the red wine stain on the carpet that Joanna had wasted a glass of white wine on trying to clean up. 'Did you hear what I said about it?'

'You said it was soft, didn't you? But that's how it is these days, son. The game's full of sand-dancers. You could knock some of them over with a warm gust of air.'

I could only agree. It was a well-established fact that the modern-day footballer's sense of balance deteriorated the closer they came to the penalty box. Simulation was what the producers on Malky's TV show had told him to refer to it as. Not diving or cheating which could lead to litigation. My dad continued his line of thought. Like on most of the world's great problems, he had a theory on the subject. A theory based on his own footballing career, which, if you believed him, was spent playing with a brick-hard, moulded-rubber football on frosty mornings on shale pitches littered with broken glass, dog shit and the fractured bones of the competition. If, or so ex-Police Sergeant Alex Munro's theory went, a tackle wouldn't cause you to fall over onto a pitch strewn with broken bottles, there was no excuse to throw yourself onto the velveteen playing surfaces installed in the stadia of today. It was a fair enough point, if one largely ignored by professional footballers the world over. Even his most ardent admirer would have had to concede that during his illustrious career, the great Dario had taken more dives than a scallop fisherman's flippers.

'You're right, Dad, I did say it was a soft penalty,' Malky said, 'But there was more. Did you not hear what I called the Ross County centre-forward?'

'Dempster? No. What did you call him. A diver or something?'

Malky took his hands from his face, looked up at us all and shook his head.

Tina's search for sweets was fast becoming the sort of thing she should really have had a warrant for. Joanna lifted her off my brother. 'Just tell us, Malky. What could you have said that's so bad? It's a football game. You didn't insult anyone's haircut, did you?' But my wife might as well have tried to vaccinate a rhino as attempt to inject some humour into the situation.

'I'm not supposed to say it again.' Malky glanced around as though a TV sports executive might be hiding behind the sofa.

'You've not to say what again?' my dad asked, looking at his watch and no doubt realising that Monday night there might be some football on a telly somewhere.

Malky sighed. 'The N word,' he said at last. 'I've been suspended pending a disciplinary hearing.'

Joanna took a step back almost dropping Tina in the process. 'Oh, Malky. You didn't.'

I was as surprised as she was. My brother had played for Glasgow Rangers. Wherever he went the chances were that someone would shout things at him that were thought best left out of the Good Friday Agreement. Although I'd heard him respond ungraciously, I'd never heard him make mention of somebody else's colour. Not even when he himself was being called orange.

'The N word, Malky. What got into you?' I said. 'You've had tons of teammates over the years who were persons of colour, you've got plenty of friends who are—'

'The N word?' my dad butted in. 'What's that?' I went over and whispered in his ear.

He nodded. 'Oh, I see. What did you go and call him that for, Malky? I mean if you're going to be racist you might as well—'

'What, Dad?' I said. 'If you're going to be racist, do it properly?'

'Dempster's white,' my dad clarified.

'White?' Joanna and I said in stereo.

'As the driven,' my dad replied. 'Billy Dempster's a Dingwall hometown boy. Pride of The Staggies. He's got ginger hair and freckles. He needs to put on sun cream before he blows out the candles on his birthday cake.'

Malky's ringtone-of-the-day was the opening riffs of *Pick Up the Pieces*.

'Not that N word,' Malky said. Exasperated he got to his feet, pulling his phone from his trouser pocket. 'The other N word. Actually, not the other N word, I've already been warned about that one. The other, other N word.'

How many N words were there?

Malky put the phone to his ear, listened for a few seconds then covered the phone with his hand. 'It's Dario's wife for you, Robbie.'

'For me? What does she want me for?'

By the look on Joanna's face, she was wondering the same thing.

'You'll find out if you take the call,' Malky said. He held the phone out to me. I took it from him. It was Salome. And she wanted to see me. As in right now.

'I've got to go,' I said. 'It's some kind of emergency.'

'Maybe she's got a new face cream she wants to try out on you,' Joanna said.

'It's not funny. She sounded scared, Jo.'

'It doesn't matter how scared she is. You can't go. If she wants legal advice then there could be a conflict of interest seeing as how I've already spoken to her husband about the...' She looked from me to Malky and back again. 'The you-know-what.'

'It can't be anything to do with that,' I said. 'She knows I'm a criminal lawyer.'

46

Joanna got to her feet. 'Then if you're going, I'm coming too.'

'You can't,' I said. 'One of us has to stay and put the kids to bed.'

Joanna turned to my dad, who, having lowered Jamie to the ground, was making moves in the direction of the door. Malky held up his hands. 'Don't look at me. I have difficulty putting myself to bed.'

I gave my brother his phone back. He took it with a wink. 'Don't do anything I wouldn't do.'

But by the look on Joanna's face that was giving me far too much leeway.

Chapter 9

The directions I'd been given were not to the Newberry but were equally familiar and made for a much shorter journey. Fifteen minutes after ending the call I was winding my way down a long driveway, eventually coming to a halt on the gravel courtyard in front of West Hope House, home to the newlywed Armando and Beverly Diaz. It was the sort of place where you half expected the staff to come out and greet you. No one did.

I alighted and walked up a few stone steps to a landing the size of a bandstand. The front door was ajar. There was one of those bells you pulled, and as I did so I heard it sound around the house. When after a minute or so no one had answered, I stepped inside and into the hall. A moment later Salome appeared. She was wearing sunglasses. Strange, when the sun had taken the afternoon off. Even stranger indoors.

Why was I here? Come to that, why was Salome here, when I assumed the married couple would be on honeymoon?

'What's going on?' I asked. Salome didn't reply, just kept walking across the hall towards me, the only sound her footsteps on the fine Italian marble beneath her feet, echoing around the high walls and vaulted ceiling.

'Come with me,' she said, and I followed her across the hallway to what I knew from my previous visit was Armando's study. Home, as I fondly recalled, to a rather splendid whisky collection.

The room was just as I remembered; the whole of one side lined with books, on the wall opposite a glass unit displayed a who's who of single malt whiskies, on another wall a cabinet contained Armando's collection of firearms, while on the far side two large windows looked out onto the garden. The curtains were partially drawn and the light in the room was poor. It was actually the shot gun cabinet that first attracted my attention because its doors were wide open. Then through the dimness I made out the figure of Beverley sitting hunched in the same armchair I'd sat in months ago when sampling her husband's rare malts. As I walked further into the room the smell hit me. Not the sweet smell of vintage single malt whisky, the smell of gun powder mingling with the metallic stench of blood. Lots of blood.

I stepped back. Salome took a grip of my arm and tugged at me, drawing us level.

'Over there,' she said softly, tilting her head towards the corner of the room, where below the window I could just make out an upturned armchair and a dark bundle beside it. Salome cleared her throat. 'Something terrible has happened,' she said, I thought a little unnecessarily.

She ushered me forward. I took a few hesitant steps. They were all I needed to realise the bundle was Armando, or rather what there was of the former financier that hadn't been splattered across the heavy drapes. Next to him was a toppled side table, a smashed glass lamp and, on the wooden floor beneath him, a pool of sticky, wet blood. A few yards away beside a footstool embroidered with some crest or other lay a shotgun in a V-shape, the barrel broken.

'Has an ambulance been called?' I said. Not that a fleet of ambulances would have made any difference.

I rushed over to Beverly. 'Are you all right?' She didn't answer, just sat staring at the far wall. 'What happened? Why aren't you on honeymoon?' But I'd have been better off talking to Armando.

'We need to get her out of this room,' I told Salome. I gently levered Beverly from her seat. In a daze, she allowed herself to be manoeuvred to the door. Closing it behind us, together Salome and I took the newly wed widow upstairs and laid her on a bed. Satisfied she was safe enough, I called 999 and Salome and I went downstairs to the lobby to wait for the police. 'Why isn't she off sunning herself somewhere exotic with him?' I said, jerking a thumb at the study. 'And what are you doing here? Did Beverly call you?'

Salome pressed the fingers of both hands against her forehead and took a moment before replying. 'Beverly was visiting her mother. She is ill. She left last night and came back today, just after… just after…what happened to Armando.'

I had so many questions.

'Why did you call me?'

'I am scared,' Salome said.

'Scared? What are you scared of?' I asked. 'Why are you even here?'

Salome took a deep breath. 'Armando helps Dario with his money. We come here sometimes. Dario was angry when we got back to the hotel after the wedding on Friday night. We argued a lot on Saturday. We were supposed to be going to our holiday home on Sunday afternoon. I called Beverly and she said I could come and stay here for a few days. They were not going on honeymoon right away because Beverly's mother is so ill. When I saw you on Sunday I had returned to the Newberry for some things.'

'Salome, who else is in the house apart from you and Bev?'

'Nobody.'

'You said that when Beverly arrived back from her mum's, you were already here?'

She nodded, took a paper tissue from the pocket of her designer jeans and wiped away a tear from under her sunglasses. 'Who else knows about Armando apart from you and Beverly?'

'Nobody.'

'You called me and didn't call the police? Where were you when Beverly came home?'

Salome pointed at the study door and then started to cry again, wiping the tears from her cheeks with the tissue. I pulled a handkerchief from my pocket, inspected it and tucked it away again. 'Salome,' I said, recalling how far the shotgun was from Armando's body. Too far. 'Will your fingerprints be on that shotgun?'

'I don't know,' she said, still sobbing.

It wasn't the answer I'd been hoping for, but it would have to do for now.

Chapter 10

Detective Sergeant Russell MacGillivray was a large man who looked to have fallen out with his barber. He was accompanied by Detective Constable Lynn Swan who like him was in plain clothes. Beverly having remained in her bedroom, we were in the drawing room of the big house where I'd already spent a long hour providing what was a short witness statement.

MacGillivray ran a hand through the entanglement of hair that looked to have once been ginger but was now mostly grey. 'So, just to recap...'

Cops love to recap. What they mean is, let's go over everything again in detail, but in reverse order this time so that we can test if you're lying or not.

I preferred to start at the beginning. 'As your colleague has already noted, I was at home shortly before 6pm with my wife, my father and my brother.'

MacGillivray leaned back in his chair, took off his thick rimmed, black spectacles and used his tie to polish the lenses. 'Oh, yes, your brother. Malky Munro. Saw him play for Scotland. When was that? Must have been—'

'A while ago. And yes, it was on Malky's phone that I received the call from Salome to go and see her.'

'Salome. You keep calling her that. You must be on friendly terms.'

The fact was I had no idea what Salome's full name was. She was married to Dario and as far as I was aware he didn't have a surname.

'I take it you mean Mrs Ramirez,' DC Swan assisted. 'So, you got the call. What did you do next?'

'I entered my vehicle and proceeded in an easterly direction,' I said.

The DC allowed herself a little grin. MacGillivray looked at her until the grin had disappeared and then back to me. 'This is no laughing matter.'

'I'm not laughing. I've already told you. Salome, that is Mrs Ramirez, phoned me. She said it was urgent. I got in my car and drove here. When I arrived, she showed me the body in the study. Mrs Diaz was there too, sitting in a chair. We took her up to her bedroom, and after that I called you. There's not that many more ways I can explain it, and I think your colleague is tired of writing the same thing down.'

MacGillivray let my remarks sail over his head. 'You say Mrs Ramirez is a client of yours. You're a criminal defence lawyer aren't you?'

'Not exclusively. My firm has provided legal advice on various matters to Mrs Ramirez and also to her husband.'

'Her husband? Dario? The footballer? Why'd he want you for a lawyer? No offence, obviously.'

'Obviously,' I said. 'And just as obviously, what my firm advises its clients about is strictly confidential.'

MacGillivray smiled unconvincingly. 'Confidential like your client's surname seems to have been? How long did it take you to get here?'

'It's about a fifteen, twenty-minute drive.'

'The CCTV at the front gate shows Mr Munro's car arriving at ten past six, Sergeant,' his colleague said.

'If you think it's a fifteen-minute drive, you must have known where you were going,' MacGillivray said. 'As we've just found out for ourselves, there are a lot of twists and turns, country lanes and wrong turnings to take if you don't know your way here.'

'I've been once before. My wife is a friend of Beverly... Mrs...'

'You're not great on surnames are you Mr Munro?'

'I know Beverly as Beverly Groome. She was married very recently. I don't know whether she took Armando's—'

'Armando? You mean the victim?'

'No, I mean the deceased, Armando Diaz,' I said. 'And when I arrived here, Mrs Ramirez showed me immediately to the study. I went in, saw Mr Diaz, saw the shotgun, tried to console Beverly who we took upstairs to her bedroom and then I called you. That's it. That's all I know.' I made to stand up.

MacGillivray didn't. 'Why do you think Mrs Ramirez called you first and not us?'

'Because she was in shock, I suppose. Anybody would be traumatised by an experience like that.'

'Like what?'

'Like finding a dead body. Especially the body of a friend in that condition.'

'Not sufficiently traumatised to call her husband for your brother's phone number so she could pass a message onto someone who just happens to be a defence lawyer. Would've been a lot easier to call 999 don't you think?'

'Inspector, I appreciate Mr Diaz's won't be the first dead body you've seen, but I've been a defence lawyer long enough to know that where there has been a suspicious death the police often like to find a culprit and then find the evidence, rather than the other way around.'

'You think the death is suspicious, then?'

I did. Highly. And when it came to murders in the home, the police started in the middle and worked their way out. If Armando's wife had some sort of an alibi, that pretty much left the only house guest right in the centre.

'In my opinion,' I said, 'calling me before you was the best thing for Mrs Ramirez to do.'

'Really, why's that then?'

'Well, for a start, and without any evidence to back it up, you've already described Mr Diaz as the victim.'

54

'A slip of the tongue.'

'And a slip of the tongue by my client given her current emotional state is what I'm trying to avoid. She needs to get over the shock of things. Which is why I've advised her not to speak to you at this time.'

'But she will speak to us?'

'That depends,' I said. 'But if she's to be questioned as a suspect, and I'm present, I wouldn't bet on her saying anything.'

This time I did get up. By the time I'd left the drawing room, the number of police vehicles parked outside the front door had grown considerably, and the entrance hall and study were taped off with a couple of officers in fluorescent yellow bibs directing traffic.

Salome was standing in the hallway with a uniformed officer. The cop distanced herself when I went over. I was explaining to Salome what had happened so far and what she could expect to happen later, when DC Swan appeared at the drawing room door.

'The Inspector would like another word, Mr Munro, if you don't mind,' she said, in a manner that suggested that she didn't mind if I minded or not. 'With your client.'

'You'll appreciate I am going to have to interview your client at some point,' MacGillivray told me when we were gathered. 'If necessary, I'll do it today under caution, but that would mean I'd have to arrest her now, take her to the police station, process her… Well, you know the procedure. I'd prefer to do it later once we have a better idea of things. So, until then I'd like her to… What is your home address Mrs Ramirez?'

'We are here until autumn in our home near Eastruther.'

'Where's that exactly?'

'South. Maybe sixty kilometres.'

MacGillivray frowned. 'I'd rather you were somewhere closer to hand for the next few days?'

'The Newberry, then,' Salome said.

'Where's that?'

'It's a hotel in Edinburgh,' I said.

'Never heard of it.'

'You wouldn't have. It's a high-class establishment,' I said. 'No offence, obviously.'

MacGillivray grunted. 'Okay, your client can go to this Newberry place for the next few days, but I'm going to have to ask that she leaves her passport with me for the time being. Do you know where it is?'

Salome's passport was back at the Newberry. I undertook to collect it and hold it in my safekeeping.

MacGillivray reluctantly agreed. 'And I'm going to need your mobile phone and the passcode, Mrs Ramirez.' Salome looked at me. 'Or we can make other arrangements to obtain it,' MacGillivray said, before I could offer any advice. 'But that would involve me placing you under arrest.'

The average mobile phone is of course the prosecution's best friend. It's a tracking device as much as a means of communication. Real criminals never carry one or they have someone else carry it for them while they're off somewhere miles away up to no good, in which case it can also serve as an alibi. 'And I'll have to ask you to leave your car and the keys here so we can look it over,' MacGillivray said. 'Just a box we have to tick.'

Whatever grey matter was lying under that mop of grey hair it wasn't cold porridge. MacGillivray clearly suspected Salome, but he'd be in no hurry to arrest and question her until he had a lot more information. By seeming to be terribly reasonable he could obtain the right to search her phone and car for evidence on a voluntary basis. Her refusal to allow it would only look even more suspicious. On the other hand, calling the DS's bluff could very well lead to a long night in the police station while evidence was ingathered, and Salome

56

interviewed under caution a long time later. All the while her phone and car would be taken as evidence anyway.

'Good,' he said, after Salome had nodded her consent. 'I'll have someone drive you back to your hotel. Don't change address without having your solicitor notify me first. Do you understand?'

Salome flicked a grim smile at him and turned to leave.

'Before you go,' MacGillivray said, 'DC Swan will take you somewhere and you can change out of those clothes. I'll need them as well.'

I was about to protest. MacGillivray was way ahead of me. 'Voluntarily or at the police station, it makes no difference to me,' he said.

Salome placed a hand on my arm. 'It's okay. I am happy to help in any way.'

'Good,' MacGillivray said. 'Could you please remove your sunglasses?' It wasn't a question. He nudged his colleague who stepped forward and reached out to Salome's face.

'This has gone far enough,' I said, stepping between them.

MacGillivray held out his hand. 'The sunglasses, Mrs Ramirez. Please remove them.'

Chapter 11

'Nancy?' On my secretary's return from Sandy's café next morning, I told her all about Malky's plight. 'They've sacked your brother for calling someone Nancy? There's a woman at our bridge club called Nancy. What's wrong with calling someone that?'

'The woman at your bridge club is a woman, Grace Mary. The centre-forward for Ross County isn't. And it was Nancy-boy, not just Nancy. Anyway, Malky's not been sacked. Not yet. At the moment he's suspended. He's already had a warning for calling someone a big girl's blouse and another time he said niggle. Yeah, I don't understand that last one either.' I turned my attention to the crispy bacon roll Grace Mary had brought back for me. On the days Joanna was a stay-at-home mum, second-breakfast at the office was the most important meal of the day; however, this Tuesday morning things were terribly wrong, and not just Malky's use of the other, other 'N' word. I opened the lid of my roll and confirmed my suspicions. 'Did Sandy forget to put HP on this?'

I could tell by the way Grace Mary was muttering she was still trying to work out what was offensive about niggle. Like me she gave up and took a sip of the extra-hot latte I'd apparently bought her for going. 'Sandy was busy. It was his new girl who served me.'

'And you didn't think to tell her?'

'I'm your secretary, not your waitress. Next time go yourself. Now, what are you going to do about Malcolm? You'd better think of something fast. You don't want him to lose his job, do you?'

This was what I'd come to call the Malky effect. Women liked him. Even women like my secretary who thought men were put on earth to teach woman-kind patience and loosen jar lids. A flick of Malky's overly long hair, a flash of the boyish grin and the opposite sex were ready to die for the cause. Meanwhile, mortal men like yours truly had to put up with a reluctant tolerance of our existence and the sort of dereliction of secretarial duties that led to under-sauced breakfast comestibles.

'He's not had a date for his disciplinary hearing. I'm still giving it some thought.' I searched in my desk drawer for a sachet of brown sauce and came out with ketchup which, of course, simply wouldn't do. Not on bacon.

'Disciplinary hearing!' Grace Mary snorted. 'For calling someone a wimp? These footballers are always rolling about pretending to be injured.'

'Times have changed, Grace Mary,' I said, deciding that eating the roll without brown sauce was preferable to taking it all the way back to Sandy's for a squirt. 'He didn't call him a wimp. He called the player a Nancy-boy and, well… people are more sensitive these days. Certain words trigger emotional responses.'

'Nancy-boy,' she scoffed. 'Can't you call someone a big softy anymore?'

The answer to that was probably not and certainly not if there was any correlation, intentional or otherwise between big-softiness and sexual orientation. It was difficult to see how Malky's outdated quip wouldn't be viewed as anything other than a career ending faux pas, and that would mean my brother's lucrative TV punditry contract being offered to someone a lot more reconstructed. From my experience of footballers, that was going to be a small pool to fish in. The only reconstruction most footballers of Malky's vintage had gone through was to their knees.

The phone rang and my secretary took her paper cup and righteous indignation through to reception to answer it. I had barely swallowed my next bite of roll when she buzzed me. 'There's a woman on the phone wondering if we do no-win-no-fee on accident claims.'

Munro and Co's recent widening of the scope of its practice had resulted in lots of new business inquiries, not all of which I felt able to deal with. Normal clients were so much more demanding than criminal clients, and without the same sense of humour I found.

'What's the story?' I asked, hoping her car had been rear-ended or something like that where liability was unlikely to be an issue.

'It's a slip and trip.'

From my limited knowledge of delict, the law on pavement trips had largely been decided by Lord Denning in a series of House of Lords' judgments back in the 1970s, possibly after he'd read and taken inspiration from Catch 22. So far as I could make out, according to the former Master of the Rolls, we the people were not to view public footpaths like bowling greens. Paving slabs upraised by less than one and a half or two inches were to be expected, and not the local authority's fault. Defects over that size were large enough to be noticeable and members of the public only had themselves to blame if they weren't looking where they were going. For no guarantee of a fee, it was a lot of work dealing with the local authority's loss-adjusters who replied to correspondence every lunar eclipse.

'She didn't trip over a pavement,' Grace Mary said, when I'd asked her to gently get rid of the caller. She wants to sue Sainsbury's because she slipped on a grape in the fruit aisle.'

'Fruit? Why didn't you say so? Tell her that we don't deal with those types of cases. She'll have to find a lawyer who deals with fruit.'

'You mean a lawyer for fruit cases?' Grace Mary said dryly.

She'd got the message and so I replaced the receiver and ignored the next twice the phone buzzed, which it did in quick succession. 'What's the panic?' I said, polishing off the last bite of bacon roll and strolling into reception to collect my court files for the day. Grace Mary had not quite finished her coffee, and the empire biscuit she'd bought to accompany it had somehow turned into an iced fly-cemetery.

'Professor Bradley's trying to get hold of you,' she said, scooping a sugary raisin from her lip and into her mouth with a finger. 'You wanted to know as soon as the post-mortem had been done on that Diaz guy. Well, it has.'

Professor Edward Bradley had recently gone from regius to emeritus professor of forensic medicine at Edinburgh University. No longer a forensic medical examiner to Police Scotland, he'd set up his own business and was these days a lot keener to speak to defence solicitors than in the days when he was mainly instructed by the Crown.

'Well get him back on the phone, will you?'

'I can't. He's going away somewhere. He'll phone you later. He's got your mobile number.'

'Try anyway.' She did, but the Professor's phone rang out.

Typical. I'd told Salome that I would let her know as soon as there was any news, and the most important news was the Crown pathologist's opinion as to cause of death. Prof. B wasn't carrying out the autopsy, but there was only a small body of forensic pathologists in Scotland, and Bradley, being a major organ in that body, had trained most of the current generation. He was bound to have the kind of inside information I needed to justify the ludicrously large retainer Salome had paid me. It was a lump sum that was keeping the lights on at Munro Towers and why I could afford to shower my secretary with carry-out vanilla lattes and baked

61

confections, instead of telling her to stick the kettle on and crack open the Rich Teas.

I packed the files in my briefcase. There wasn't much in court that morning. With a bit of luck, I could track down Prof Bradley as soon as I was free, hear what he had to say, break the news, good or bad, to my client late afternoon, and be home in time to put the kids to bed.

The phone rang. Grace Mary picked up. 'Munro and Co. Yes, he's here,' she sang into the receiver, despite all my shaking of the head and pointing at the wrist where I didn't have a watch. 'Yes, he'll take the call.' She put the phone to her chest. 'It's the police. They have Mrs Ramirez in custody and she'd very much like to speak to you.'

Chapter 12

As I was soon to learn, the police had gone to the Newberry at crack of dawn and dragged Salome from her bed without even allowing her time to change from her night attire. Dawn raids and humiliation are all part of the process. It helps disorientate people. As does a four-hour stew in a cell while the cops pretend to have problems contacting your solicitor. Salome had been fingerprinted, photographed and swabbed for her DNA. Kitted out with baggy jeans and a red sweatshirt from somewhere, as well as a pair of socks, but no shoes, hair tousled and face devoid of makeup, she still looked gorgeous. What slight bruising there had been when DS MacGillivray had asked her to remove her sunglasses the day before was much less pronounced.

I was given a chance to speak with my client before the interview and made it very clear to her that she was to make no comment to every question. That included the introductory soft questions that were designed to get a suspect nice and relaxed and chatting away, before they were hit with one that wasn't quite so easy. If a suspect started answering questions and then made no comment to the first tricky one that came along, it didn't look good. It was a chink in the defence's armour that your interrogator would happily spend the next few hours trying to pry open. Not that police interviews had ever made any sense to me. The law said that a suspect was entitled to legal advice before interview. That legal advice was invariably to make no comment. Why then did Police Scotland - the very people tasked with ensuring the law was upheld - insist suspects should ignore the very advice that Parliament had thought it so important they should have?

Salome's interrogation was no different from most. It took place in a stuffy, windowless room with me sitting beside her opposite a couple of plods - in this instance DS MacGillivray and his colleague, the young DC Swan. Supposedly to put us at ease, my client and I had been provided with complimentary coffees in cups made from the world's thinnest plastic. The lightest of squeezes was enough to send the scalding contents spilling onto the table; which is the best place for police station coffee. You wouldn't want to go drinking the stuff. I'd always harboured suspicions surrounding the froth.

But, refreshments to one side, the big waste of time was that the cops knew that unless my client was going to go completely against legal advice, she wasn't going to speak up. Only the stupid ones did, and it was probably best they went to prison in order to increase the average IQ of the public at large.

So, if the cops knew my advice to the suspect was to say nothing, why bother with an interview at all? My being called away meant that I'd had to ask my pal Paul Sharp to cover my cases in court, which in turn meant I'd have to reciprocate in due course, and no doubt receive a poisoned chalice of a case he'd been dying to give a body swerve.

'What is your full name and address?' MacGillivray asked, once DC Swan had booted up the recording equipment.

'No comment.'

'I'm only asking for your name and address.'

'Why do you want it?' I said. 'Do you think you might have dragged the wrong person out of her bed this morning?'

MacGillivray sighed. 'If you don't mind Mr Munro, please don't intervene. You're here to see that everything is done fairly, not to answer questions on behalf of your client. If Mrs Ramirez needs to consult with you further, I'm sure she'll ask.' He turned to Salome with an innocent smile. 'Do you need more time to consult with your solicitor about what your name and address is?'

'No comment.'

MacGillivray cast a glance at me. My turn to smile.

'I think you are Salome Ramirez and that your current address and other personal details were given to the custody sergeant on your arrival at the police station at...' The DS checked his notes. '6.05 this morning?'

'No comment.'

'Okay. Tell me this. Security footage from the home of Mr and Mrs Diaz shows your car arriving in the courtyard at about ten past five yesterday afternoon. Is that correct?'

'No comment.'

'Mr Diaz and his two dogs are seen on the security camera walking through the courtyard, heading to the rear of the house at five twenty-two. You sat in your car until around twenty-five past, before entering the house. You must have seen him. Did you?'

'No comment.'

'Were you waiting for Mr Diaz?'

'No comment.'

'Why else were you waiting all that time in the car?'

'No comment.'

'Were you aware that Mr Diaz was carrying a shotgun?'

'No comment.'

The security camera also shows Mrs Diaz's car drawing up outside the house about ten minutes later, at five thirty-five. Do you remember that?'

'No comment.'

'Your phone records show that you put a call through to your husband at five thirty-eight and another call this time to a different number three minutes later. Who did you call?'

'No comment.' Salome's initial confident approach was showing signs of deterioration as she sank further in her chair.

'Our records show that the second number you dialled was that of the brother of your solicitor Mr Munro. Is that why you phoned your husband? To get his number?'

'No comment.'

'Don't you have your solicitor's number on your own phone?'

'No comment.'

'The security camera shows your solicitor Mr Munro, arriving around about six minutes past six, yesterday afternoon. Why did you summon him?'

'No comment.'

'By the time Mr Munro arrived, according to his statement and that of Mrs Diaz, Mr Diaz was already dead. Will you admit that much?'

'No comment.'

DC Swan slid a sheet of paper in front of MacGillivray. He picked it up and asked, lightly, 'Do you know of any reason why your fingerprints would be on Mr Diaz's shotgun?'

Although the DC gave me a smug sideways glance, I dead-panned her while my brain screamed, 'They were what!'

'No comment?' Salome said after a worryingly long pause.

'Did you attempt to wipe your fingerprints from the gun?'

'No comment.'

Raising both hands to either side of his face, MacGillivray removed his glasses and carefully laid them on the table. He studied them for a while and then quickly looked up, eyes fixed on my client, leaning in. Here it comes, I thought. 'Did you murder Armando Diaz?'

Salome's face set firm. Then her nostrils twitched and her lips began to quiver. 'He… He…'

It was the work of a moment for my brain to decide that the phrase no comment, did not begin with two he's, not even one. We needed a time out, and fast. 'I think my client wants to consult—'

'She's given no indication of that, Mr Munro. Now, if you'd let us continue.'

The accidentally-on-purpose spilling of coffee during a police interview is not a manoeuvre you read about much in legal textbooks, but I'm not the first lawyer to have employed such a diversion when the cheese started to slide off the cracker.

DC Swan leapt to her feet to avoid the mini tsunami that was heading her way and rushed from the room.

'My client would like to take time out to consult further with me,' I said. I gave Salome a nudge. 'Isn't that right?'

She nodded.

MacGillivray, who had remained seated, pushed his notes to safety. 'That won't be necessary,' he said, as his colleague returned with paper towels to mop up the mess. 'I think we have enough.' He turned to Salome. 'Mrs Ramirez I am charging you with the murder of Armando Diaz. The video equipment is still running and although you are already under caution, I must remind you that anything you say will be recorded and may be used in evidence. Do you understand?' Salome nodded. 'Do you have anything to say in reply?' MacGillivray asked, when he'd finished reading out the wording of the charge in full.

I really hoped she hadn't. Salome turned to me as though she was going to ask me something, and then threw her head back. 'Se lo merecía.'

Chapter 13

They put Salome in an adjacent interview room so that I could have a word with her before she was banged-up for the night. It was the usual layout of two bolted down chairs each side of an equally bolted down table. She lifted her head from the tabletop when I came into the room and rushed over. She'd been crying.

'*Se lo merecía*?' I said. 'Where did that come from?' My Spanish being restricted to a few essential phrases, most of them to do with cerveza, I'd had to Google translate, and, as I feared, it didn't mean no comment. '*He deserved it*? What made you say that?' It was hard to keep the anger out of my voice.

Salome stood up, walked over and stared at the far away wall. Not that far away walls are all that far away in a police interview room.

'What if I go back and tell them I killed Armando?' she said.

I wiggled a pinky in one of my earholes. 'Sorry, I didn't quite catch that. No, no need to repeat yourself.'

She turned, took a step towards me, pulled my hand from my ear and pushed her face into mine. 'I said, what if I tell them I killed him? That I took his shotgun and I shot him for what he did to me.' Like all defence lawyers my hearing is highly selective, but from a matter of inches away, even I couldn't pretend that she wasn't coming across louder than a bad neighbour's TV.

The door was slightly ajar. I walked over and pushed it shut. 'You're really going to have to stop saying things like that. It could mean I can't be your lawyer.'

'But Armando did deserve it, and I want you do to what you did for that other woman. The one who hit the man with the stick.'

Why had I mentioned Isabella Ewart's case? I could have talked about anything in the Newberry on Sunday. The weather, the price of paella, beach resorts in Colombia... But no. Faced with a beautiful woman in a bar, I'd started bragging like a schoolboy on his first date.

'That other woman's case was different,' I said.

'How was it?'

'Because that other woman gave someone a few nasty bumps and bruises. You're here because a man is dead.'

'That other woman, she only lost some money.' It had been Isabella Ewart's elderly mum who'd actually lost the money, but now wasn't the time to go into that. 'What Armando did to me...' She stabbed herself in the chest with four fingers. 'Was much worse.'

'What are you talking about?'

Salome took a deep breath, the better to glare at me through red-rimmed eyes. 'When Beverly was away, Armando raped me. Is that not a good reason for me to kill him?' There were more tears. She sniffed and wiped her eyes with the hanky I'd dug out of my pocket. I ushered her over to one of the bolted down seats and gently sat her down on it.

A woman killing a man as a last resort to prevent rape is a valid defence in Scots law. Not so where a man is trying to rape another man, but in Scots law it's different for girls. I could see the green shoots of a defence starting to appear. 'Tell me what happened.'

'Early on Monday morning, Armando came into my bedroom. Beverly was away. I said no. Armando was a big man. A strong man. He pushed me on to the bed. He hit me. See?' She pointed to the mark on her face.

'He came into your bedroom in the morning? Don't you mean the study, sometime late afternoon?' I asked, hopefully. She didn't take the hint.

'No, my bedroom. Get my night clothes, the bedsheets for proof if you need them,' she said, spraying weedkiller all over the green shoots of her own defence.

I sat down opposite her. 'Salome, don't think I'm trying to play down what happened to you. It was a terrible thing, but if Armando wasn't shot in your bedroom...'

'I don't understand.'

'Well...' I said slowly, 'it's like this. A woman can claim self-defence for killing a man who's attempting to rape her, but not if she kills him after it's happened.'

I could see Salome was confused. 'What you are saying is that if I killed someone to stop him raping me, that would be okay?' I nodded. 'But it's not okay for me to kill someone who *has* raped me?'

When she put it like that, I could see how it might seem illogical. Not that it's ever a good idea to conflate logic with the law.

'I don't think the law says it's ever okay to kill someone, Salome. But, yes, if you'd killed Armando when you say he tried to rape you, we could argue it was because you were defending yourself.'

'I didn't say he tried. I said he did.'

I wasn't sure how much of what I was saying was getting through to her. 'It's to do with timing, Salome. One is a necessity in the heat of the moment. The other is more like an execution, and we don't have capital punishment in Scotland, not even for rapists.'

There was a knock on the door and DC Swan poked her head into the room. 'Everything okay?'

No, I thought. Everything is very much not okay.

70

Chapter 14

After I left my client tucked up in a police cell for the night, I returned to the office and worked late. The kids were in bed, and Joanna was sitting in the livingroom reading a book in the company of a glass of white wine when I got home.

'I take it the interview didn't go too well then?' Was my wife's accurate take on things once I'd thrown my briefcase into a corner and dropped onto the sofa beside her. She closed the book, set it down on the arm of the sofa and took a sip of sauvignon blanc. 'How not well?'

'I wouldn't say she confessed,' I said. 'Not exactly. But—'

'What did she say?'

'She was doing so well.'

'What did she say?'

'It was no comment all the way. Right up until the very end.'

'Robbie,' Joanna thumped me on the arm. 'Tell me. What did she say– exactly?'

'That he deserved it. But in Spanish.'

'Oh.'

'She was upset. Something must have got lost in translation. English isn't her first language.'

'What else have they got? What about the murder weapon?'

'Some of Salome's fingerprints are on it and probably enough of her DNA to put on a sandwich.'

'I see.'

'And, at the time of the... let's not call it murder. At the time of death, there doesn't appear to have been anyone else in the house apart from Salome.'

'And?'

'One possibly good thing - she had a black eye.'

'How did she get that?'

I wasn't going to bring Joanna in on the rape/the bastard deserved it defence. Not at this stage. If ever. 'It could suggest some kind of scuffle,' I said. 'A struggle for the gun perhaps?'

'Self-defence?' Joanna grimaced. 'Somehow I don't see petite Salome overpowering six foot two Armando in a fight to the death. Never mind, at least you know what you're up against. Any thoughts on other lines of defence?' She elbowed me in the ribs. 'Come on. It's not like you not to have some cunning plan marinating.'

'Could've been an accident,' I said. 'Salome. A woman unused to firearms. Curious and unaware that Armando has foolishly brought a loaded shotgun into the house. She accidentally discharges it... Why are you screwing your face up?'

Joanna reached for her glass. 'How does oops it was all an accident tie in with the whole, "I'm glad he's dead" thing?'

'She's Colombian. Maybe it means something different where she comes from.'

'And then there's the black eye.'

'It's not that bad really. More of a scuff.'

'It's still an injury. Bit suspicious don't you think?' Joanna took a sip of wine and smacked her lips. What else you got for me to tear apart?'

I stood up. 'Armando's wife—'

'Bev, yes, go on.'

'She was away visiting her mum—'

'I know. Poor Bev. Her mum took a funny turn the day of the wedding, and now her husband gets killed with a shotgun by Miss Colombia in the drawing room.'

It was the study, but I did have to admit it was more like a bad game of Cluedo than an ideal start to married life. I tip-toed softly into a possible line of defence. 'What if Armando had been trying it on with Salome...'

'Armando? He wouldn't do something like that. Anyway, is this all supposed to be happening on Monday? The man only got married on Friday afternoon.'

'And by Friday evening he was busy groping your bum.'

'It was his wedding reception. He'd been drinking,' Joanna said.

'And whose bum was I groping on *my* wedding night?' I asked.

'It better have just been mine.'

'Precisely, so just drink your Tuesday night wine...' I thought the day of the week needed highlighting, 'and listen for a moment. You never know what a man is capable of.'

'You mean like the Marc Traynor case?' Joanna said.

'That's different.'

'Why? We've had two consultations with him and you think he's innocent. You've met Armando twice. On one of those occasions he put his hand on my bum, and that's enough for you to form an opinion that he's some kind of molester.'

'I didn't say that I thought Marc Traynor was innocent. I just don't like that the jury won't hear the whole facts. Anyway, where was I? That's right, Salome's in the study,' I said, getting us back on track. 'Armando tries it on. Comes across a bit heavy. Salome decides it's not happening. Armando, who's been away shooting things, has left the gun lying about.'

'A shotgun? In the study?'

'Yes. That's where his shotgun cabinet is. He showed me it that time we were at the house. As I was saying, he's not put the gun back. Salome picks it up and points it at him not realising it's loaded—'

'Why would she point it at him then?'

'To keep him away.'

'But in the wonderful world of Robbie Munro's imagination she doesn't know it's loaded? Why would she think an unloaded gun would keep him away? Also, pointing a gun at someone not knowing if it's loaded or not is highly dangerous. Not much of an accident. More like culpable homicide.'

'Not self-defence, then?'

'No, Robbie. If women were allowed to shoot men every time one of them tried it on with us, we'd all be walking about like Mexican bandits, with six shooters in our handbags and ammo belts strapped across our chests.' I didn't think Mexican bandits carried handbags, but let it go as my wife continued her thoughts. 'Why not sound out the Crown and see if they'll take a culp hom? If there has been some kind of indecent assault, maybe get some women's rights groups involved...'

Perhaps there was something in that. If I launched Fiona Faye QC at the judge with all sails unfurled, armed with a report from Women's Aid or somewhere, Salome could be out in no time.

'What's wrong with that for a suggestion?' Joanna asked.

'Culpable homicide is what's wrong with it,' I said. 'You never know what sentence you're going to get. It could still be life.'

'More like eight years, I'd say.'

'Not long if you say it fast,' I said, 'but I was thinking more along the lines of not guilty and take it to trial.'

'Robbie—'

'Do you remember the Isabella Ewart case?'

'You mean your famous defence that the bastard deserved it?' Joanna had been about to take another drink but was laughing so much she had to place the glass on top of the book to steady it. 'He made some amorous advances and so I blew him away with a twelve gauge? This is the High Court, Robbie. Good luck finding a QC who'll lead that defence.'

'What if he was trying to rape her?' I asked, warming to Salome's theory that if it was okay to kill a man who was trying to rape you, what was so wrong with killing one who had? Would it harm to massage the timing a little?

'Self-defence?'

'Ties in nicely with the black eye and what she said to the police don't you think?'

'You know what I think, Robbie? I think you should go and ask your client what really happened and take it from there. Joanna's re-opening of her book signalled the ending of that topic of conversation. She held it up so I could see the front cover. It had a shattered glass effect and was entitled, Smash 'n' Grab. 'It's one of Bev's. She gave it to me ages ago. It's a signed copy. I haven't got round to reading it yet.'

I took it from her and began flicking through the pages. 'There doesn't appear to be any ripped bodies on the front cover, are there any ripped bodices inside?'

'It's non-fiction,' Joanna said, 'and the smashing in the title is a reference to the glass ceiling. You know - the patriarchy.'

'Come off it, Jo. There's no glass ceiling. Not these days. When I started my own business, nobody said, *okay Robbie, you can go ahead and have a huge overdraft but only because you're a man.*'

'That was different Robbie. You had to go out on your own...' she snatched the book back from me. 'Who in their right mind would employ you?' It was a harsh opinion, but one hard to argue against. 'And then there's also your deep-rooted problem with authority.' There was that as well. 'And also—'

'Okay, okay, I get it. You see, Jo, what people like Bev—'

'You mean women?'

'No, I don't. Not the one's I know anyway. I mean women like Bev. What they seem to want is for a man to start up an organisation and then make them the head of it. That's not business. That's marriage.' Joanna's smile was more a warning than an appreciation of my attempt at humour. The ice creaking under my feet, I ventured on. 'Proper businesswomen take a risk. They go to the bank, put their house and savings on the line. They don't wait for a man to do it and then whine when he won't give them his job. I'm not trying to criticise women.'

'You could have fooled me.'

'No, really, I admire women. I'd say, as a rule, they are more sensible and take fewer risks than men. Take you for an example. You're an excellent lawyer, but you joined the Fiscal service straight from Uni, and why not? Reasonable salary, holidays, flexi-time, pension, paid maternity leave. The COPFS even paid for you to do the solicitor advocate training. It was the safe and sensible course for you to take. A lot better than doing what I did: hung up a sign and hoped some paying clients came to see me before the Sheriff Officers took the office furniture away.'

'You think I'm some kind of career coward, then? Is that what you're saying?' Joanna shifted in her seat, moving noticeably further away from me. 'I left the Fiscal service to join Munro & Co. That was a risk, wasn't it? It certainly wasn't a step up on the pay scale.'

I sat down beside my wife and attempted in vain to put an arm around her. 'I'm not saying women are inferior. Of course they aren't. I'm saying it's only some women who are stopping themselves. Take Bev. What did she do? Got a law degree then promptly married Armando the ancient financier. She's never done a hand's turn and now she's writing books wondering why no one's asked her to be CEO of General Motors yet.'

'The CEO of General Motors happens to be a woman,' Joanna said.

'There you are. I rest my case.'

Joanna braced herself with a glug of wine. 'Perhaps I should resign from Munro & Co. and go on to greater things.'

'You're well capable of it,' I said. 'Be all you can be. There's nothing in the legal world you couldn't do if you put your mind to it.' Perhaps it was my words or the sauvignon blanc, but this time Joanna allowed me to slip an arm around her shoulders. 'You're a solicitor advocate and yet you've hardly set foot in the High Court apart from a few pleas.'

'I'm doing Marc Traynor's rape trial am I not?'

'Yeah, okay, but there are bigger cases out there than a he-said-she-said rape indictment. What's stopping you? You've seen some of those counsel, haven't you? Half of them went straight to the Faculty of Advocates because Daddy didn't send them to Fettes College to be a shiny-suited solicitor or they like strutting about Parliament Hall dressed like Bonnie Prince Charlie. Put some of them in a trial situation and they couldn't fight sleep. Take this case for Salome Ramirez for example. It doesn't matter what anyone says, she wants to plead not guilty and that's her inalienable right. What I'm looking for is an advocate to take on her defence. A fighter. Not some Q.C. who'll dial in a defence and do their best not to upset the judge. I need someone whose been in the trenches. A person with lots of Sheriff Court experience - preferably one whose worked both sides of the fence. Someone unafraid to put their client's interests above everything else. Someone...'

Joanna laughed. 'Where do you think you're going to find a person like that?' She went to take another drink and realised the glass was empty. I found the bottle by the side of the couch and topped it up.

'I don't need to find a person like that,' I said. 'I married them.'

Chapter 15

Fortunately, white wine doesn't stain. When I left for work next morning, the best that could be said was that Joanna was not yet fully onboard with my suggestion. In fact, she was standing on the platform with a hanky waving it off down the track. The big issue she had with my proposal was the conflict of interest aspect. Her argument being, how can you represent the person charged with murdering your friend's husband? I'd countered that with the fact that Beverly wasn't a particularly close friend. If Joanna remembered, she was an evening-only wedding invitation friend. A much closer acquaintance, I reminded her, was our bank manager. He contacted us a lot more frequently and often in red ink. Then there was the presumption of innocence. Joanna shouldn't look at it as representing the person who murdered her friend's husband. She should view it as representing the person who was, in law, presumed not to have murdered her friend's husband. But even such a solid jurisprudential argument wouldn't sway my wife, and, as I left for the office that morning, Joanna remained a work in progress.

Salome's Petition case was supposed to call at Livingston Sheriff Court, but for some reason best known to the Crown was set down for Edinburgh. I used the change of venue to arrange a consultation on the autopsy findings after the case had been dealt with, which it eventually was around three o'clock that Wednesday afternoon. The case was to be continued for further examination, so it was merely a matter of me seeking bail. Applications for bail in murder cases, though competent, were routinely opposed by the Crown. Salome's was no different. According to her schedule of previous convictions, Salome had skipped bail several years before, when charged with drink driving, and more recently been fined for bringing some personal use cocaine into the country. Those previous convictions and the fact that she didn't hold a UK passport were enough for the Sheriff to consider her a flight risk.

I told my client we'd try again at the full committal hearing in a week's time, and I waved her off on a seven-day -lie-down. Outside the court I pushed my way through a disappointed ambush of reporters on Chambers Street, walked up George IV Bridge, and took a left as I neared the Royal Mile to wind my way down Victoria Street, probably the city's most photographed thoroughfare. The Bow Bar is situated around halfway down the street on the left as you head for the Grassmarket, and at four o'clock on a Wednesday afternoon is usually to be found populated by tourists sipping whisky flights and wondering when it's going to stop raining.

'You're late.' Professor Edward Bradley held up a pint glass to admire the contents. 'And why do I have a feeling that us meeting here has less to do with it being handy for the court and more to do with it being one of Edinburgh's better whisky bars?'

'Two birds,' I said, and ordered a half pint of whatever he was having, with a measure of something peaty to keep it company. 'Well?' I asked, waiting for my drinks to arrive. 'How did it go?'

'It was certainly a messy one,' the professor said, lifting the glass in the direction of his beard. He took a long drink and wiped froth from his whiskers.

'Single round to the upper thorax, from what I understand was a twelve bore, resulting, as you'd expect, in massive damage to the lungs, heart and just about every thoracic blood vessel of any importance. You'd need to consult a firearms expert if you were really interested, but the spread pattern is fairly tight, around four inches. It would suggest a shot from close range.'

'Another thing we found which you'd expect at close range was the presence of debris in the wounds.'

'Debris? What kind of debris? Fragments of clothing?'

'There was that of course, but I'm talking about the fibrous wadding from the shotgun cartridge itself. And I know what you're going to ask. Could it have been self-inflicted? I don't know. Possibly. What was the length of the barrel? Was it shortened at all?' The weapon I recalled lying on the study floor a few metres from Diaz's body, was definitely not a sawn-off, but it had seemed shorter than normal. 'Well then there's that, but a great number of other variables: cartridge type, choke, were there powder stains on the clothing…? I can't really say much more.'

'And that's it?' I said. 'You've charged two grand for, *he was shot at close range by a shotgun and died?*'

'If you're asking me for a definitive answer, I can't give you one, Robbie. If you want my opinion, from what I know so far, I'd estimate that when your girl fired the shot her victim was less than six feet away. That's two metres to you. I haven't tested the theory, but it may have been possible for him to shoot himself. Don't see why not, he was a big man. To be certain you'd need to ask a firearms expert to do some test firing and then send me their report.'

'But suicide is a possibility?'

'I can't rule it out at this stage.' That was good enough for me. Professor Bradley sank the rest of his pint and with the help of the counter levered his bulk from the stool and onto his ox blood brogues. He was all set to leave while the barman was still getting my change. 'I don't propose to prepare an autopsy report. I wouldn't be saying anything different from the Crown pathologists, and how interested are you really about the state of health of his internal organs - those that your client didn't turn into Pâté?'

80

'Nothing's been proved yet,' I said.

He laughed. 'Not what I've heard.'

'And what have you heard?'

'That your client was the only other person in the house and why would the newly married Mr Diaz go and shoot himself?'

The thing I've found with forensic experts, of whatever kidney, is that they are always tremendously pro-Crown and love nothing better than to jam a stick between the spokes of the defence case.

'Tell me this,' I said, as the professor showed me his back and took a step towards the exit. 'Have you received my cheque for this consultation yet?'

He slowly about-turned, stared down at the stool I was using the sole of my shoe to push towards him, and sighed.

'Right,' I said, once he had regained his seat and I'd refreshed myself with a drink. 'Never mind suicide, consider this hypothetical scenario. A woman is staying with friends, a married couple.'

'Newly-weds by any chance?'

I ignored the interruption.

'One afternoon while his wife is away visiting her sick mother, the husband is out taking pot shots at the local wildlife. He returns and goes into the study where the woman is—'

'Is this the woman who didn't call the police but phoned her lawyer instead?' the Professor said, I thought a little tetchily for someone who was expecting me to shove 2k in his waistcoat pocket any time soon.

'He comes on heavy with her. She repels his advances—'

'What is this Robbie, a Victorian melodrama? Should I be twiddling my moustaches?'

'She picks up the shotgun he's left lying around—'

'Careless of him.'

'Not knowing it's loaded - just to make it clear she doesn't want anything to do with him,' I said, cutting off his next question at the pass. He had another.

'Why would the husband bring a loaded shotgun into the house with him in the first place?'

'That's the point. He wouldn't. It was an oversight. Which is why the woman wouldn't think the gun would be loaded. In any event, she hasn't the first idea of how to use it. He laughs, walks towards her. She takes a step back, trips over a footstool and, BLAM!' A few of those sharing the bar with us looked around and then went back to their flights of whisky. 'All a terrible accident. What do you think?'

'I think she would probably have blasted the ceiling if she'd fallen backwards.'

'Let's assume she didn't.'

'Fall backwards?'

'No, blast the ceiling. Let's assume that as she fell, the gun barrel rose, she accidentally pulled the trigger and—'

'I know,' said the professor wearily. 'Blam. What about it?'

'Would it kill you just to listen to me for five minutes and try and see things from the defence point of view? After all, I am the person paying you.'

'Not yet you're not,' he said. 'And anyway, my evidence can't be bought.'

'I only want an objective opinion.'

'Oh, I suppose it's just about possible,' he said, grudgingly. 'Can I go now?'

Possible. That was the second time he'd said that. The word came as music to my defence lawyer's ear. In one of Michael Connelly's books, his fictional US attorney, Mickey Haller, likens a prosecution case to a tree, carefully planted by the State. *No money is spared nurturing the tree, guarding the tree, so that its branches of evidence, motive and opportunity can spread ever wide, inviting those seeking justice to gather in their shade.* According to Mr Haller, people who go to see him are looking for a man with an axe. *Someone who'll chop the tree to the ground and burn its wood to ashes.*

The people who go to see defence solicitors in the real world, usually bring with them a rubber axe and point us defence lawyers in the direction of the Crown's mighty oak. But then in the real world, defence lawyers aren't seeking to chop and burn. All we're looking for are signs of woodworm.

'Great,' I said. 'Consider my cheque to be in the post – along with your witness citation.'

Chapter 16

My motion for bail on behalf of Salome at the full committal hearing a week later was refused. I lodged an appeal that would take another week to be considered, went home and had the kids in bed by eight o'clock, though Jamie was still making the occasional cameo appearance.

By half-eight I was sitting in the livingroom perusing some of the productions in the case that had recently been disclosed via the Criminal Justice Secure Email. It was the usual sort of stuff that comes in the early stages: the Crown autopsy report and photographs taken at the post-mortem examination. These had come along with a request for release of the body to the family. I had no difficulty with that. The PM report was thorough and the photos extensive, not only that, but the defence's own expert in the form of Professor Bradley had been present at the autopsy. Also in the electronic bundle was the firearms report. As I already knew, Armando kept his small arsenal of shotguns in a secure cabinet in his study. What I didn't know, and according to the report, was his ammunition was kept separately in a storeroom off the kitchen at the rear of the house. The report described the shotgun in detail, confirming unsurprisingly that it had been recently fired. More surprisingly, it was a single barrel gun. Upon examination there had been no cartridge in the breech, and one had been found nearby on the study floor. There were accompanying photographs of the shotgun and cartridge in situ and later at various angles on a lab bench, as well as close-ups of each.

I closed my laptop. I'd study the productions more carefully tomorrow, but for now I wanted to go in search of

Joanna who had been lying strangely low for most of the evening.

I found her in the utility room sorting out the washing. Joanna hadn't been her usual self the last wee while. I didn't know why. Every time I asked if everything was okay, she said she was 'fine' - always a warning signal. It couldn't just be down to her reluctance to take on the defence of Salome Ramirez. I'd more or less resigned myself to looking elsewhere for counsel, but I really needed someone I could… manipulate was such a strong word, persuade to see the defence my way - whenever I had worked out what the defence was. I took a pair of Tina's muddy jeans from her and threw them back onto the pile next to the washing machine.

'We can deal with the laundry later,' I said, guiding Joanna through to the kitchen and sitting her down at the table, where the crusts from my daughter's supper of roasted cheese were still tucked in either side of her plate. How the girl had ever managed to get curly hair and white teeth, I had no idea.

'What's Salome Ramirez saying about it all?' Joanna asked, while I placed a mug of tea in front of her. 'Taken any instructions yet?' My wife put a lot of store in taking clients' instructions.

'Still building up to that,' I said.

'Then how did you get on with Prof. Bradley? You consulted with him last week didn't you?'

'The good news is he seems pretty much onboard with both suicide and the trip-over defence.'

'Trip over defence? What happened to the scenario where Salome's presenting the gun at Armando—'

'I think you mean picks up the shotgun to keep it out of his reach, slips and accidentally shoots Armando,' I said.

'Accidentally? That's new.'

'More a refining of an earlier position.'

'I'd say it was more of a contortion of an earlier position,' Joanna said. 'And you're saying Prof. Bradley agrees to *both* scenarios?'

'He said they were distinct possibilities.'

Joanna's raised eyebrow sought clarification.

'Maybe not distinct. I asked him if they were possibilities and he agreed.'

'Robbie, me buying a lottery ticket and winning ten million pounds is a possibility.' She took a sip from her mug. 'You making a cup of tea that doesn't taste like you've been stewing pennies, might even be a possibility, but—'

'What more do you want?' I said. 'Sorry I can't come up with CCTV evidence of our client having lunch with the Archbishop of Canterbury at the time of the murder, but at least it's something, isn't it?'

Joanna shrugged. 'It's definitely something. What it's not is a complete defence. You can't point a shotgun at someone and then complain if it goes off and kills them even if you do slip.'

'Did I say she was pointing it at him? What if it was by his side, and she was taking it away from him so that he wouldn't do anything stupid with it and then she tripped up?'

'Is that what happened?' Joanna asked, always a stickler for details.

'I don't know what happened.'

'Well, is that not sort of your job? You know, ask the alleged murderer what happened, see if it amounts to a defence and then check that what she's saying ties in with the actual evidence?'

'Teach you that at prosecution school, did they?' I said. 'Was that before or after the course on how never to tell when a cop is lying?'

'Robbie, if you're still trying to win me over to represent Salome Ramirez, you're not making a very good job of it.'

Win her over? There was no winning with some people, my wife being one of those people. First of all, she'd given short shrift to my *he deserved it* defence, and now when I was presenting her with possible alternatives, she was coming over all self-righteous.

'I'm not being self-righteous, Robbie. I'm being ethical. And you can't have more than two alternatives. It's one or the other. If, and I do mean if you want me to represent your client—'

'Our client.'

'And if she has an actual defence, I want it laid out in front of me clearly. Not some would've, could've, possibly might've. Come back to me if and when you have a defence I can present with confidence. So that means no Isabella Ewart *he deserved it* stuff. No High Court judge is going to let that go to the jury.'

Otto Von Bismarck famously said it was better not to see how laws and sausages are made. To that list it appeared Joanna had added Robbie Munro defences. Thinking it was about as good as it was going to get, I let it rest, and as we drank our tea the conversation moved on to other things; the kids mainly and then eventually Malky's plight.

'Are you going to help him?' Joanna asked.

'He's my brother. What else can I do?'

'I don't know.' She wrinkled her face. '*Not* help him?'

'Yes, that would be the alternative,' I said. However, can I refer you back to my earlier answer? He's my brother.'

Joanna still wasn't entirely happy. 'But *should* you actually help?' I didn't understand. My wife explained. 'Isn't there a slight possibility you might… you know?'

'What?'

'Make things worse?'

I didn't reply. Just dabbed a strip of kitchen roll at the tea I'd spilled down my shirt.

'I'm not suggesting you're homophobic—'

'Oh, really? Thanks for that,' I said.

'Because I know you're not. It's just that…'

'Go on.'

'Well, people take these things extremely seriously nowadays.'

'What things?'

'Certain words.'

'And?'

'Well, you don't. Not always. If you go into that disciplinary hearing with Malky, I'm scared you'll make a big joke out of it. Try to make the panel see the funny side of things, how ridiculous it all is… Except it'll be you they'll think is ridiculous.'

I had to admit that, although I hadn't yet drafted my address to the disciplinary panel, something along the lines of: 'It was all just a bit of banter,' was formulating in the back of my mind.

'You see, Robbie. It's no longer a matter of what you mean when you say something. It's what other people think you mean, and a lot of those other people are—'

'Stupid? Petty?'

'Two words you must never use if you do take on Malky's case. My advice is that he apologises profusely—'

'Throws himself on the mercy of the court? A court full of irrational people who think niggle is a bad word because it begins with the same four letters as a certain bad word? How merciful are they likely to be?'

'It's the culture we live in,' Joanna said.

'Then it's no culture for old men like me, and I'm only thirty-nine.'

'You're forty.'

'And I suppose I should be thankful I'm not Marc Traynor. His trial is next week. Twenty-three, waiting a year for his case to come to court, career on hold and not knowing if the next six years will be spent sewing up patients or mailbags…'

'Don't forget, he could very well be guilty. In which case he deserves what he gets,' Joanna said. 'I mean, how would we like it if, years from now, Tina was going out with a boy, had too much to drink and… well you know.'

'And how would we like it if it was Jamie facing a rape allegation from a girl, the only reason being he'd dumped her?' I said.

'We're not saying dumped, remember? Anyway, I'd expect Jamie to have more respect for a girl who'd had too much to drink.'

'Joanna, she'd had the equivalent of a bottle of wine. They had sex again a few days after the alleged rape. She didn't show any signs of distress until he broke up with her. And, as we know, she has a previous conviction for making a false allegation.'

'So? Doesn't mean it's false this time.'

I was beginning to wish we'd never taken on the case. Or that I'd thought it such a great idea to ask Joanna to act. She seemed to be bracing herself for defeat.

'Are you worried about this case?' I asked.

Joanna took a long drink of tea and winced. 'What am I supposed to cross examine her on? Obviously, I can put it to her she wasn't so drunk as to have been unable to consent. She'll say she was, and then what do I do? Sit down again?'

'You'll think of something.'

'I half hoped someone at Crown office would take a proper look at the case and mark it for no prosecution.'

'Come on, Jo.' You worked for the Crown long enough to know that never happens in a sex case where there's a sufficiency of evidence. He doesn't deny having sex with her.' Like a lot of people who think they are innocent, Marc hadn't thought he needed a solicitor present at his interview and fully cooperated with the police. 'That's the first crucial fact proved. She says it was without her consent. and the Prosecution have a witness saying the alleged victim looked very drunk when she left the party. That's enough for a conviction. What is it you always say to me? We don't make the laws - we just have to work with what we're given.'

'And when do you pay any attention to that, Robbie?'

'That's me. This is you, and we've both been given section 274 of the Criminal Procedure (Scotland) Act.' I put an arm around her. I didn't remember my wife getting so cut up about similar cases when she was a prosecutor. But then, as a prosecutor it's not your client, the person you've got to know, whose version of events you've listened to and possibly even believed, who's in danger of spending the next half-dozen or so years in jail followed by a lifetime as one of society's outcasts if you fail.

'It's not too late to back out,' I said. 'We can instruct someone else. You can concentrate on Salome Ramirez's case.'

'Nice try,' Joanna said. 'But as for Marc Traynor, the trial is only days away. How would it look if I chickened out at this late stage and had to drop it in someone else's lap?'

The door from the livingroom creaked open and Jamie toddled into the kitchen. His wee face was all crumpled with sleep and he was followed in by Bouncer the dog.

'Finish your tea,' I said. 'Things will look better in the morning. I'll let Bouncer out the door and put the wee man back to bed.'

But Joanna was already on her feet, and by the time I'd put the dog out and come back to the room, she had our son in her arms and was hugging him tightly.

Chapter 17

'What's wrong with what I'm wearing?' Grace Mary looked down at herself and then back up at me.

'Nothing's wrong with it,' I said. 'It's just that if you're going to court, you need to wear something... more official looking. You'll need to lose that cardigan for a start.'

'First of all,' Grace Mary said, lifting the mug of tea I'd made her in an attempt to lubricate proceedings, 'why am I going to court? You're supposed to be his lawyer, not me. And, secondly, what's wrong with this cardigan? I knitted it myself.'

The trial of Marc Traynor was due to start, and I'd decided I couldn't go. Joanna was more than capable of dealing with the case herself. All she needed was someone to note her cross, which, although I had the speed of hand to cope with, only I could translate afterwards. There was also the fact that I couldn't ask Paul Sharp to cover my Sheriff Court cases that Thursday morning. Not again. Plus, I had other clients, ones who wanted me to act and wouldn't take kindly to being represented by a 'fire-in'.

'The cardigan's lovely, Grace Mary, but you just don't see too many auburn mohair cardies in the halls of the High Court of Justiciary. Or tartan skirts for that matter.'

My secretary narrowed her eyes. 'Has Joanna told you not to go?'

Not in so many words she hadn't, but there had been certain vibes come floating my way over the breakfast table that morning. 'It's the complainer's evidence today, and... well, Jo and I have, let's say, differing views on strategy when it comes to cross examination. She finds my approach—'

'Annoying? Unethical? Just plain wrong?'

She looked like she could go on, so I brought the conversation back to the subject of acceptable clothing for court. 'Can you not sling on a white blouse and something dark on your bottom half?'

'And when am I supposed to do that? It's gone nine o'clock. I'd have to go home, change and catch the train. I'd never be there by ten.'

'That's perfectly all right,' I said. 'The jury isn't coming in until eleven so you've plenty of time.' I walked around behind reception and tried to pull her chair out to let her stand up.

Grace Mary clung onto the edge of the desk. 'Will I take the taxi fares out of petty cash?'

'It's a ten-minute walk to the Lawnmarket from Waverley Station,' I said.

'Yes, uphill all the way, and hundreds of steps.'

'You don't have to take the steps to the High Street. Walk up Cockburn Street, look in the shop windows on the way.'

'Cockburn Street? It's like the north face of the Eiger with nothing but tourist-tat and hippy shops.'

Tempus was very much fugiting, and I had to make it to Livingston Sheriff Court by ten. 'Okay, take money for a taxi.'

'And lunch?'

'Go with Joanna. She'll buy you something.'

'Joanna will probably take a sandwich with her and eat it with the other lawyers. I'm not hanging around court listening to all the boring legal chat. And anyway, if I'm having to go to Edinburgh, I've got a pair of slippers to take back to John Lewis and could have something to eat while I'm there.'

If some of the major Trades Unions ever got wind of Grace Mary and her negotiating skills, I'd have to find myself a new secretary.

A day of trial at the High Court generally starts at ten o'clock and is finished by four, with a fifteen-minute break for coffee in the morning and an hour for lunch. I assumed Grace Mary would catch the train back to Linlithgow and go straight home, but when I returned to the office from the Sheriff Court at the back of four, she was sitting in reception, typing.

'What are you doing back so soon?' I asked. 'Was there a problem with the Traynor case? Did it not get started?'

'No, it started all right.' Grace Mary printed off the letter she'd been typing and slid it across the desk to me. 'Sign.'

I signed whatever it was and shoved it back to her. 'Then why are you here?'

'Well, they empanelled the jury and put in the first witness who was the wee girl that got—'

'The complainer. Go on.'

'Well, she was quite good at giving evidence, I thought. Very confident. Apart from when she cried.'

'How did Joanna get on with the cross examination?'

Grace Mary made a face. 'She tried her best... In the circumstances.'

'What do you mean?'

'Well, the judge, Lord Barchester or Birkfield or...'

'Birkenside?'

'He hardly let her get a word in edgeways. Just about every time Joanna asked a question the AD objected, and each time the judge sent the jury out so the lawyers could argue about it. One time Joanna asked the victim—'

'You mean the complainer.'

'Joanna suggested that the bottle of alcopop she'd had to drink hadn't made her very drunk, just lowered her inhibitions. There was a legal argument about that for twenty minutes and then Joanna was told she couldn't ask it.'

'What did Joanna do?'

'She didn't do anything. She had to ask a different question. I could tell she was fuming. That, and the clerk reading out a joint minute, took us to about half-two/quarter to three and then the Advocate depute said the next witness was a policeman, but he'd been called away in an emergency. They were going to play the recording of the police interview to the jury instead, but it was two hours long, and, because the first witness had been a lot quicker than everyone expected, they adjourned the case until tomorrow.'

'That means it will definitely spill into Monday,' I said

Grace Mary shrugged. 'That's your problem sunshine. I'm not going again. The client and his parents were really unhappy you weren't there. Gave me a right few hard stares.' She delved into her handbag and brought out a strip of paper. 'That's the receipt for my lunch.'

I took it from her. 'Thirty-four quid?'

'I bumped into Nan Jack when I was at John Lewis's.'

'And so you thought you'd buy her lunch too?'

'What else could I do? I wasn't paying for mine. How could I ask her to pay for her own?'

I was still trying to work that one out, when Grace Mary pushed a fat file across the desk at me.

'If you're looking for someone to get all grumpy with, you can make a start with her,' she said.

I picked up the file. 'Isabella Ewart? What's she done now?'

'It's not what's she's done, it's what she's not done. She's not paid her fee. It came to three and a half thousand and she's paid nothing since you took the initial payment to account of fifteen hundred off her away at the start.'

I stared at the file. How could the woman who had insisted I run her stupid *he deserved it* defence, caused me to trample roughshod over the rules of evidence, almost had me found in contempt of court and then benefitted from my result of the year, not have paid me? 'Get her on the phone,' I said, and marched through to my own room.

'Hi, Robbie.' Isabella sounded light and chirpy for a woman laden down with two thousand pounds of my money.

'Hi Isabella,' I replied as airily as I could through clenched teeth. 'I think there's been some kind of mistake, because Grace Mary tells me you've not paid the rest of your fee.'

'No mistake, Robbie,' she said.

I waited for more words. None came.

'No, I think there must be a mistake, Isabella, because, you see, if there wasn't I'd have received another two thousand pounds from you. I usually ask for payment up front in a criminal trial, but I made an exception in your case because I knew you'd be good for it.'

'I'm not,' Isabella said.

'Not what?'

'Good for it.' This time she did expand. 'I'm broke. That fifteen hundred I gave you was the last of my savings.'

'Why didn't you apply for Legal Aid, then?'

Isabella snorted down the phone at me. 'How would that look? Can you imagine the headlines? Olympic medallist claims Legal Aid.'

'Isabella the only headline I can imagine at the moment is, lawyer's children starve because Olympic medallist didn't pay her fee.'

'You got paid fifteen hundred. For only two days—'

'Two and a half—'

'Okay, two and a half days' work.'

'Two and a half days of trial. That doesn't include my appearance when you first got arrested, the two first diets, the preparation or all the flak I had to take from the Sheriff. Or VAT. And let's not forget the very important fact that you're not having dinner on the Queen for the next few years.

I did what you asked me to do, and I got you the result that you wanted.'

'I wanted a not guilty.'

'You got a not proven. It's the same thing. You got what you wanted and now I should get what I want. How many houses do you own?'

'Do not bring my mum's house into this,' she growled.

'Why not? It's an asset. And the roof's fixed. You're telling me you've got no money and yet you've got two properties?'

'I don't know what I'm doing with my mum's house yet. It's too early.'

'She died last year. It's August now. Sell it or rent it, take out a loan. I don't care what you do, just get me my money.'

'Money. That's what it's all about with you lawyers, isn't it?' was Isabella's unoriginal comeback.

'Look,' I said. 'I'm not asking you to sell your pet cat or go down the docks when the fleet's in town. You're bound to find some kind of work soon. I'll take instalments. Two hundred and fifty. No, two hundred a month. That way you'll have me squared up in ten months. We can set up a standing order.'

There was silence on the other end of the line and then another growl. 'Or what?'

'Or I'll see you in court,' I said. 'See how you like those headlines.'

She coughed up a laugh, like she was dislodging a fish bone. 'Seriously? I can't believe you're being like this, Robbie. All over a couple of thousand pounds. And when you think about all the publicity I got you.'

'Wait till you see the publicity I'll get you, if you don't let me have the first instalment by the end of the month,' I said, and was going to hang up, but she'd beat me to it.

Chapter 18

I was still in a bad mood when I got home and about to go on a rant about it to Joanna until I discovered that she had her own rant all ready.

'Marc Traynor is going down,' she said, bouncing Jamie on her knee.

'Grace Mary did think the complainer was quite good,' I said.

'Good?' Joanna handed my son to me and got up from the sofa. 'She was excellent. She made it sound like our client got her drunk, took her back to his place and had his evil way with her.'

'Maybe he did,' I said, trying to stop Jamie wiping his sticky face on my new tie. 'Stop taking things so personally. You don't know what happened. All you can do is present the best defence you can.'

'And how is it the best if every time I try and ask a question it's not allowed?' Joanna said.

Joanna appeared to have changed her tune on the whole thing about what questions were relevant or not. Life on the defence side of the criminal justice fence was gradually beginning to tell on her. I followed her through to the kitchen and between us we set about making Jamie's bedtime snack: squares of toast on peanut butter and a cup of warm milk. At the tender age of two-and-a-half, my son eschewed non-spillable baby cups and demanded he drink from a particular plastic mug that had a purple dinosaur on the front of it. From outside the back door, I could hear Tina running around, shouting at Bouncer. It was getting near her bedtime too.

'Try not to get too worked up,' I told Joanna, as I opened the door and called girl and dog inside. 'You've done hundreds of trials. You know how it goes. It always looks worse at halftime. Don't worry. We'll take our boy off the bench tomorrow, he'll score an equaliser and you can seal the win in extra time when you make your speech.'

Joanna snorted. 'You're getting worse than your brother for the football analogies. What's happening with him by the way?'

'I've been trying to speak to Colin Lancaster, but he's been dodging my calls.'

'Who's he?'

'The new head of production at Scotgoals. He's the man who decides what happens to Malky. The good thing is that I did a road traffic case for him years ago when I was with Caldwell & Craig. I'm hoping he'll remember how I got him a good result and maybe let this problem with Malky slide.'

I directed Bouncer to a bowl of water and Tina to a schoolbag that looked like it had remained unopened since she'd come back from school.

'I've done my homework,' Tina assured me.

'Better let me check it then.'

'By the way Robbie,' Joanna said. 'You do realise you'll have to be there tomorrow. Marc Traynor's parents were wondering where you were today. It doesn't look good you not turning up.'

Joanna's intervention gave Tina time to skip out of the room with Bouncer at her heels.

'Don't worry, I'll be there,' I said, as we adjourned to the livingroom to watch Jamie demolish the squares of toast and pour most of the milk down his front. 'Did you tell Marc to wear—'

'A blue tie? Yes, I did.' Joanna was usually disparaging about my blue-tie-of-truth theory, but I had the feeling that on this occasion she would take all the help she could get.

'Don't worry. All he's got to do is keep the head,' I said. 'The jury have turned up for a rape trial. They were expecting to hear about a woman walking home and being dragged into the bushes. You've got to explain to them that what they're hearing is a story about two young people who'd been at a party, had too much to drink, gone home and had sex that one of them, for whatever reason, regretted later. There were no signs of any injuries, and so long as Marc doesn't start shouting or coming across as aggressive when he's answering questions, the jury will see two nice people with differing views about what happened one night last year, and end up just as confused as the rest of us are about what actually happened.'

I located Tina's schoolbag and opened her homework jotter. She hadn't lied. Her homework had been done, insofar as all the correct answers may very well have been on the page, they just weren't legible. I rubbed out her efforts, sat her at the kitchen table and, amidst the wails and gnashing of teeth, made her do it all over again.

Later, once the kids were in bed, we watched some TV, and Joanna began to relax. It wasn't like my wife to be this concerned about a case, but her day in the High Court with Marc Traynor and a judge that was giving her absolutely no leeway had really upset her.

We were in bed for half-ten, early for us, both sitting up reading. Me clutching a Tom Holt novel, Joanna still ploughing her way through the next on a list of what the New Year book blogger had declared the fifty books to read before you die. I'd got as far as James Joyce's *Finnegans Wake* and decided it might be preferable just to die.

I was at the point of switching off my bedside light when my mobile buzzed. Private Number flashed up. It would be the police. For most people a late-night call from the local constabulary signals bad news. For a criminal lawyer, no late-night phone calls from the cops is a sign they're going out of business. This one was different I discovered after I'd climbed out of bed to take the call in the hall.

'You're not having to go out, are you?' Joanna asked, when I returned to the bedroom.

I laid my phone down by the side of my bed, rolled over and kissed her cheek. 'Just an intimation,' I said. 'It'll keep till the morning.'

Women's intuition, call it what you will, Joanna must have heard in my voice something I was trying my best to keep out of it. She sat up, switched on the bedside light and looked down at me. 'What is it? What's happened?'

I could have lied, kept the news until the morning. 'It's Marc Traynor,' I said. 'He's… dead.'

Joanna threw back the duvet, jumped out of bed and stared down at me. 'What!'

'His mum found him. Seems that he hanged himself somehow. I don't have any more details.'

Joanna dropped onto the bed and sat there staring at the wall.

I got up, sat down beside her and put an arm around her. 'The case will call tomorrow to be formally deserted I expect. I'll get someone else to cover it. It'll only be a five-minute job. You stay here. Spend some time with Jamie. Take things easy. You've put yourself under a lot of pressure lately. Maybe this High Court stuff is too demanding.'

'Are you saying I can't handle it?'

'No, it's not that. I know you can handle it.'

'Then what?'

'I don't know what to say.'

'Then don't say anything.' Joanna took my arm from her shoulder and helped me to my feet with a shove. 'Get me the Salome Ramirez file.'

Chapter 19

The weeks flew past like the Red Arrows at a Royal birthday party. On a Friday at the start of October I had an early morning prison visit with Salome. She had been on remand for two months and it was beginning to show. Her hair was limp and greasy, her golden complexion showed signs of tarnish, and she looked to have put on weight.

'I know it's difficult for you in here,' I said. 'You just need to hang in there. The Crown has one hundred and forty days to get your trial started.' I didn't tell her that usually either the Prosecution or the Court came up with some excuse why the time limit needed to be extended. It wasn't uncommon for an accused to remain in custody for a year or more awaiting trial. It was no way to treat those presumed innocent.

Salome expected a visit from me once a week, which wasn't so bad because she'd arranged for me to receive a monthly retainer. It would have been better if I had something to report each week, but the fact of the matter was that in most High Court cases very little happens for ages and then everything happens at once very close to the trial. Whether the last-minute disclosure of evidence is down to incompetence on the part of the Crown or a cunning attempt to make the defence seek a postponement of the trial so as to investigate the newly released material, is anyone's guess; probably a bit of both. Salome's case, however, seemed relatively straightforward, and I was determined that for once the Crown would adhere to its statutory time limit.

'There's nothing much new to tell you,' I said. 'We've already been through the witness statements and experts' reports. The next step will be the service of an indictment with the date of your Preliminary Hearing. That's when the court will fix a date for your trial. Until then, you just need to try and keep your chin up and—'

'And what?' she snapped, then apologised. 'What if I put up money? Would I get out then?'

We'd been through this before, many times. There was no money bail in Scotland, but it was possible to put up caution (for some reason pronounced kayshun) as a guarantee of an accused person's adherence to the conditions of bail. 'I'm not saying it's impossible to lodge a sum of money with the court in return for bail, Salome, but it's unusual, and since yours is a high-profile case, the court would be looking for a very large sum so as not to give the impression you were being given preferential treatment.'

'How much?'

I thought a million might swing it. It was the sort of money the High Court wouldn't break its stony heart over if my client jumped a Colombia-bound tramp-steamer and never returned.

'I don't have that kind of money.'

'I'm sure Dario has,' I said. 'I've tried to speak to him, but his people won't let me anywhere near. Why don't you—?'

'Forget him,' Salome said. 'I don't want his help.'

'If he knew what Armando did to you, he might,' I said.

'He would never believe it. I don't want you to say anything to him about it. Ever.'

'Okay, how much can you scrape together?'

'Maybe forty or fifty thousand.'

I didn't think it would be enough. 'The problem is that you've breached bail before.'

'Years ago. For driving after a few drinks.'

'It's not the drink driving conviction that's caused this problem. It was you not turning up for the trial. You gave the court an address in Scotland and then disappeared for nearly a year. It's given the court an excuse not to bail you.' That temporary absconding, her foreigner status and the strength of the Crown case were working against her. Not that the court was supposed to consider the strength of the prosecution case when deciding on bail, but the Crown never failed to drop it into the equation. At both first calling and full committal, the Procurator Fiscal had mentioned how the evidence tended to show there had been no one else but the accused in the house at the time of Armando's death, and that her DNA was on the shotgun. Despite reassurances from the bench that they had no wish to go into the merits of the case, to my mind the Sheriff had decided Salome could start her sentence now and we could have the trial later.

'Salome, the reason I'm here today, is so that we can try and get a handle on your defence once and for all. This business about you being raped and shooting Armando in revenge – it's not a defence.'

'But you do think he deserved it?'

'It doesn't matter what I think. In the High Court, the judge will simply not allow that to be put forward as a defence. You can put it forward as mitigation. It would be worth thinking about, especially if the Crown agreed to drop the charge to culpable homicide, but I don't see why they would.'

'What's culpable homicide?'

We'd been over this I didn't know how many times before. 'It's the Scots version of manslaughter. You know what that is? It means you killed someone, but there was no intention or wilful recklessness on your part. That would be hard for the jury to accept since a shotgun was used. Still, if the Crown were to accept that, it would be pretty powerful mitigation.'

'Mitigation?'

'An explanation of why you did something that makes the judge believe he or she can impose a reduced sentence.'

'The prison?'

'Yes, definitely the prison. Even if they drop it to a lesser charge, you've still killed somebody, and it's still prison. Probably prison for a long time.'

She folded her arms and sat back in the chair. 'What do I do then?'

That's what I wanted to know. I had Joanna on board, but hadn't told her what Salome had told me otherwise she'd be insisting Salome plead guilty and there was no guarantee, in fact it was a remote possibility, that the Crown would take culpable homicide; not for what looked like a premeditated revenge killing. That would mean pleading guilty to murder, and who did that?

What I couldn't work out was why Armando had come back from his afternoon's shooting and brought in a loaded shotgun to the house. We sat in silence for a while. I still had up my sleeve Professor Bradley's opinion that it could possibly have been suicide or an accident, but both defences were holed under the waterline by my client's, *"he deserved it"* reply to the police. The more I thought about it, the more I was coming to the conclusion that if Salome wanted to plead not guilty, she should see another solicitor and start from scratch. I couldn't put her in the witness box and ask her to swear under oath that she didn't kill Armando; not after she'd confessed to me that she had.

She listened carefully as I explained my predicament to her, then sat up, lifted her chin and said defiantly, 'I didn't kill him. I made the whole story up.' With a wave of her hand, she threw herself back in her chair, turned her head to the side and stared at the wall waiting for me to say something. It took me a while to find the words. Eventually, having considered this latest development, taken time to mull things over and pondered the legal and ethical issues that arose, I leaned forward across the table and said, 'Eh?'

'I didn't kill him. I just said that because I knew how it looked and I thought it would get me off better than the truth. Just like you got that other woman off when she attacked that man.'

'I'm sorry, Salome. I don't believe that.'

'Why not?'

'Because you've already told me that you killed Armando because he raped you, and now I'm expected to—'

'He did rape me. He raped me like I told you. It had happened before. The first time I threatened to tell Dario. Armando laughed. Said he'd tell Dario the sex had been my idea. So, I said nothing. This time I *was* going to tell Dario. I went to see him and then changed my mind. He'd just have thought I was trying to get his sympathy. I know why your wife was seeing him. He wants to leave me because I don't give him any little footballer children. So, I went back to confront Armando and demand he gives me money.'

'Why would you need money? You've been married to Dario for how long?'

'Fourteen years.'

'If he divorces you, you'll be well looked after by the court,' I said. I didn't know much about family law, but I knew that much.

Salome begged to differ. 'We had an agreement. Before we were married. His lawyers made me sign it. I don't get so much money as you think.'

'That's why you waited in the car? So you could speak to Armando?'

'Yes. I went to see him in the study. He was putting his shotgun away. We argued... I told him I'd been to see Dario, and that I wanted money or I would go to the police. He hit me.'

'Your eye?'

Salome nodded. 'I told him thanks very much. It would be good evidence when I went to the police. I left him and went to the bathroom. I heard a loud bang, rushed back to the study and there he was with the gun lying on top of him. I

105

threw it to the side and then saw I was too late to help. As I ran out of the study, Beverly came into the house. She saw me. I had blood on my hands. I told her there had been a terrible accident. She ran into the study and saw her husband. She wouldn't leave him. She started screaming at me, saying I had done it. She wouldn't listen. I knew how it must look and didn't know what to do. That's when I remembered you and phoned Dario for your number, and he gave me your brother's.'

I was stunned, but, as defences went, this was much more like it. It certainly explained the *"he deserved it"* outburst.

'Why didn't you tell me this before?' I asked. 'This changes everything. What you have here is an actual defence.'

A complete change of tack though it was, it made perfect sense. Salome's injury, the rape, the threat to report what had happened, the remark to the police about Armando deserving it. It had been bothering me why an experienced shot like Armando would bring a loaded gun into the house. He hadn't. He'd brought an unloaded gun into the house, then, faced with Salome's threat to report what had happened, he'd gone back to the ammo store for a cartridge, put it in the barrel and shot himself. My mind was racing. The cartridge. I'd seen the fingerprint and DNA report on the shotgun. Traces of Salome were all over it, but there was now an explanation for that, and also the distance the shotgun was from the body. What I hadn't seen was a forensic report on the shotgun cartridge. An oversight by the Crown? Unlikely. They'd have tested it and if Salome's dabs had been on it, it would have been included in the report. If it was only Armando's, they'd have treated it as a negative result. Negative insofar as it didn't help the prosecution case. If it turned out that Armando's dabs were on it and not Salome's that would tie in perfectly.

'You're smiling,' Salome said.

106

'Sorry, I hope I'm not causing too many premature wrinkles.'

She managed a weak smile.

'Salome,' I said, 'the reason I'm smiling is because what you've told me is not only the truth, but it actually sounds like the truth. There are just a few inquiries to be done to make the defence case watertight.' I couldn't wait to tell Joanna. Then I thought to myself: did I want Joanna to do it now? She was so inexperienced. This was no spurious *he deserved it* defence. This had meat on the bone that someone like Fiona Faye QC could carve into succulent bite-size pieces and serve up to a jury.

Salome must have noticed a change in my expression. 'What's wrong, Robbie?'

'I was just wondering about your choice of counsel,' I said.

'What do you mean?'

'I mean who should talk for you in court. Present your defence.'

'Well, you, of course. Like you did for the big javelin woman.'

'She was a discus thrower, but the fact is that I don't have rights of audience in the High Court. I practice in the Sheriff Court, and although jury cases there can be remitted to the High Court for sentence, they are usually only for cases where the sentence is likely to be five years imprisonment or less. In a High Court case, I prepare the defence and someone else does the talking.'

She understood. I was glad about that. It saved me using the analogy of the solicitor loading the gun and the advocate firing the bullets.

She shrugged. 'Then make sure you choose someone good.'

'I was going to choose my wife. Unless—'

'She can do the speaking in the High Court?'

'Yes.'

'Very pretty and very smart.' Salome wagged a knowing finger at me. 'I think you are very lucky.'

'So people keep telling me,' I said. She smiled for the second time since I'd met her in the bar at the Newberry. 'Salome, I have to tell you that Joanna's not all that experienced, not when it comes to the High Court.' Was I trying to talk my client or myself out of instructing Joanna now that there was an actual defence? 'And as you also know, she gave Dario advice about your separation.'

'Leave Dario to me,' she said. 'I know he still loves me. There are other forces at work, and he is just a little mixed up right now. He'll come back. You'll see.' She reached across the table and took one of my hands. 'Do you trust your wife?'

'Of course.'

'Would you trust her to speak for you in the High Court?'

I could only tell the truth. 'Yes, I would. Definitely.'

'Then,' Salome said, squeezing my hand tightly. 'So will I.'

Chapter 20

A defence lawyer entering offices operated by Police Scotland is usually met with the same sort of warm welcome a Union Jack receives at a Scottish independence rally. Livingston police station was no different. Eventually, after the civilian staff realised that I wasn't leaving until I spoke to someone senior, DI Dougie Fleming dragged himself away from a Danish pastry to behind the reception desk. 'How's your dad doing?' he asked. 'Not spoken to him in ages.' Fleming, the man who put DI into DIY confessions, had been a cadet when my dad was the local uniform sergeant at Linlithgow. Back when the world was young and many a misdemeanour was settled by an extra-judicial boot up the arse. Fleming was a work of art, not only in a professional but also in a Picasso self-portrait sort of a way. All the right facial features were there, just not necessarily in the correct order.

'He's fine. I'll tell him you were asking for him,' I said, coming to the reason for my visit. 'I still haven't seen the CCTV evidence in the Diaz murder case.'

'Speak to the PF's office,' he said, in a manner that suggested that our conversation was officially over.

'I have. They say the evidence is still with you,' I said as he turned to leave. 'DS MacGillivray kept referring to the CCTV evidence all the way during the interview with my client. That was more than two months ago. I'd like to see it. I'm happy to watch it here. I'll even sit at the back and promise not to crunch my popcorn.'

Fleming shook his head and spoke slowly, as though giving a lost idiot directions back to his village. 'It's not as simple as that. DS MacGillivray viewed the evidence in situ at the locus,' he explained, exhausting his Latin vocabulary.

'The original recording has been sent to the Cyber Crime Unit who're going to format it for the court system.'

I didn't bother to ask how long that would take. The Cyber Crime Unit spent most of their time viewing child porn, a duty I felt sure that would result in psychological damage and keep personal injury lawyers busy in years to come. Not that disclosing any evidence that may potentially assist the defence preparations in a murder case was going to be allocated top priority in any event.

'Well, can I speak to DS MacGillivray for more details of what exactly the CCTV shows?'

'Annual leave. Not back until next Thursday.'

'Okay, how about you arrange me a locus inspection?'

'The locus is sealed. Forensics won't want you tramping about disturbing things.'

What could possibly be left to be disturbed? 'Okay,' I said. 'How about you at least tee me up with a meeting with the deceased's wife for a precognition?'

'That's a job for the reporting officer, and that's not me,' Fleming said, smugly.

In a lot of High Court cases the reporting officer is a constable who hasn't a clue what is going on, and is given the role precisely because of that. 'I've spoken to the reporting officer. It was him who said I should speak to DS MacGillivray, but if he's on holiday and you're the officer in charge here today, what's stopping you setting something up? You can send someone with me if you like.'

'Sorry, no can do,' Fleming said, not looking particularly remorseful. 'We don't have the manpower at the moment. Like I said, Russell MacGillivray will be back next week. You can try and get hold of him then.'

This time the conversation was over.

While I was at the Civic Centre, I went up to the Procurator Fiscal's office to collect any disclosure evidence they might have for me in upcoming cases. I'd been attending the same

110

office, collecting disclosure, more or less on a weekly basis for the past ten years or so. Most paperwork was sent by secure email, but there were always USB sticks containing police interviews, photographs, video clips from mobile phones and such like to be picked up. That was the routine. Pick up the USB sticks, take them back to the office and then find out you didn't have the correct software to view the stuff. I was met at the security glass by the same person who usually served me, a small woman who looked like she didn't get enough sleep. She didn't have bags under her eyes, she had luggage.

'What's the name of your firm?' she asked, like she always did.

I told her it was still Munro & Co., and she disappeared through the back to return empty-handed. 'There's nothing for you.'

'Any idea when we'll be getting more disclosure in the Salome Ramirez case?' I asked.

Without a word she disappeared again. This time she didn't come back. Instead, she was replaced by Hugh Ogilvie, the Procurator Fiscal.

'It's you,' he said, keeping the excitement out of his voice. 'What is it you're wanting to know about the Ramirez case?'

'Oh, nothing much, just wondering when the defence can see all of the evidence – or is it all a big secret?'

'You've been sent the crime scene photos, you've got the post-mortem report and some forensic stuff, and you've got most of the witness statements. What more do you want?' he said, as though I'd asked him to throw in some unicorn dung for my roses.

'What I'd like, Hugh, is for you to give me whatever evidence the Crown has. All of it. Not just fob me off with the edited highlights so that you can reveal the juicy stuff five minutes before the trial starts.' Although all witnesses and productions for the Prosecution were supposed to be listed on the indictment and disclosed to the defence, the Crown could introduce additional evidence at the last minute before a trial by way of a s.67 motion. Assuming, of course, they could persuade the court to allow the late intimation. Persuading a judge to accommodate the Crown was a bit like asking Tina if she could accommodate another ice cream.

'You've got everything I have,' he said.

'I don't have the CCTV evidence.'

'Neither do I.'

'Why not? When my client was interviewed a month ago the cops could tell me everything that was on it '

'Then why do you need it?'

'So I can do my job. And another thing. I've got the Firearm Officer's report but where's the one from the Forensic Lab?'

Ogilvie sighed. 'I'll email you the stuff when it's made available to me. Now was there anything else?'

'Yes,' I said. 'I'd like to do a locus inspection and take a precognition from Beverly.'

'Beverly? Oh yes, Joanna and Mrs Diaz are friends. Or maybe I should be putting that in the past tense. After all what's friendship compared to a hefty fee?' I didn't rise to Ogilvie's bait. 'Okay, I don't suppose a site visit and meeting with Mrs Diaz will be a problem. Speak to the police.'

'I have. They say the locus is sealed and they don't want it disturbed.'

'Nearly true,' Ogilvie said. 'The study has been taped off and left as it was in case the jury want to view it. But there's no reason you can't go in with an escort. You can arrange to see Mrs Diaz at the same time. Have you tried the reporting officer?'

'He told me to speak to DS MacGillivray who's on annual leave.'

'Looks like you'll have to make do with the photographs and Mrs Diaz's police statement then,' Ogilvie replied.

'Or I could refer the Crown's lack of cooperation to the court. Seek an order,' I said.

Ogilvie groaned like a fat man's sofa. 'Wait there.' He left and returned ten minutes later.

'Three weeks on Friday. PC Gale comes on shift at two o'clock. He'll meet you there at half past, show you the locus and then you can take a prec from the widow if she's prepared to talk to you.'

I was about to leave when Ogilvie said, 'Is it true that you're instructing Joanna to conduct the defence? Do you think she's up to it? I know the years working with me are bound to have rubbed off, still I'd have thought you might be bringing in senior counsel. You know who's prosecuting don't you?' I didn't. 'Cameron Crowe. Fiona Faye's usually your first choice, isn't she? It takes someone like that to get one over on Crowe.'

'Hugh,' I said, 'I can assure you that anything that you rubbed off onto Joanna has been thoroughly washed off and I have every confidence she can deal with Cameron Crowe.'

Ogilvie held up his hands. 'Joanna's very capable, I know that, but in the Sheriff Court. The High Court is another country. They do things differently there. Take for instance the Marc Traynor case. Didn't go so well, did it?'

'No, Hugh. Our client killing himself because he wasn't allowed to tell the jury the full story does definitely fall into the category of not going so well.'

'I don't make the laws, Robbie, but we both have to work under them.'

'Except the law means the court kicks out a lot of the stuff that helps the defence.'

'No, Robbie. What you mean is stuff the court decides in advance is irrelevant,' Ogilvie said. 'Now calm down.'

I realised I was getting red in the face. Only now was the death of my young client fully hitting home. I wasn't sure if I could take on instructions in another case like it. Ogilvie was quite correct, the law was the law, but my acceptance of it made me feel somehow complicit.

'I'm sorry about what happened to your client,' Ogilvie said. He seemed genuine enough. 'Personally, I thought the case had not proven written all over it. It was Crown Counsel who insisted we proceed. Once we have a sufficiency, that's it. No-one's going to pull a plug on proceedings just because there's no reasonable prospects of success. Not if they want to keep their job. This isn't England. Let it run and let the jury decide. That's what the Lord Advocate says. Or is told to say.'

The woman from the front desk returned carrying something more than the bags under her eyes. 'We were about to send this to you, Mr…'

'Munro.'

'It's the second provisional witnesses list in the Ramirez case,' she said, slipping a sheet of paper under the glass screen that separated the good from the bad.

'There. Don't say we aren't good to you,' Ogilvie said, as his demon returned to her own particular circle of hell.

I looked down at the names on the sheet of paper. The first thing the uninitiated should know about a Crown Witness list is that it's designed to be of very little use to the defence. Don't get me wrong, the list does provide the names of the witnesses, but that's about it, for most are designed as care of Police Scotland. With no other contact address provided, in order to track down a particular witness on the list, there is a set procedure that must be followed. First, the defence lawyer should contact the reporting police officer. To do that requires a call to 101 where a computer narrates all sorts of reasons why phoning this number was a terribly bad idea and politely suggests you stop bothering people and go off and do something more constructive with your time. When eventually you do get through to a human, the chance of them locating the police officer you are after is remoter than some of the tribes in the Amazon basin. But, if by a miracle that does happen, the reporting officer will insist on contacting the witness to see if they will consent to speak to you and promise to call back - much in the same way as a politician in a pre-election speech will promise to lay before Parliament the Free Ice Cream Friday Bill.

Most of the names on this additional witness list were cops, no doubt speaking to the chain of evidence for the various productions. Their evidence would be agreed by a Joint Minute of Admissions to save them from having to spout undisputed information from the witness box. My name was on the list too since I'd given a statement to the police. My evidence would also have to be agreed in advance. I could hardly assist Joanna conduct the defence from the confines of a court witness room. I recognised the names of the two Crown pathologists, but not some others.

'Scientists speaking to the forensic analysis of the gun,' Ogilvie said, when I pointed to a couple of them. 'And, yes, I will remember to email the report to you. The rest are mainly to do with the phone analysis.'

When someone has committed a crime they often panic and start phoning people. The police check who's been phoned to see what can be gleaned from that. In Salome's case she'd only phoned Dario, and then Malky. Dario was already on the original witness list and my brother wasn't on either, probably because they already had my statement to say Salome had called him from her phone to find me.

'How about this one at the bottom? Rosemary Dow. Who's she?' I asked.

'Housekeeper or cook or something,' Ogilvie said. 'She's speaking to the layout of the big house and the fact that she hadn't noticed any dead bodies lying about the study when she'd been dusting that morning.'

I was sure Ogilvie found himself hugely amusing if nobody else did.

I took the list and left.

Chapter 21

'I've got good news and more good news,' I told Joanna,
exactly two weeks later. She was in the kitchen tidying up
after having given Tina and Jamie their tea. Bouncer was
snoring in a corner. 'First of all, Salome's happy for me to
instruct you in her defence. And before you start, she knows
you advised Dario about divorce or whatever, and she's not
bothered. If I say you're the right person for the job, that's
fine by her.'

'You've got her in the palm of your hand, haven't you?'
Joanna said, putting a bottle of tomato sauce in the cupboard.
'Or is it the other way around?'

'Sit down,' I said.

'I can't. Look at this mess.'

'Leave it to me. You've got more important things to deal
with. I cleared a space on the kitchen table and dropped a
bundle of papers down onto it. 'I've spent a fortnight
preparing you a brief based on our new defence.'

'New?' Joanna said.

'New and greatly improved. I've even had Grace Mary
type you up a memorial, just like I would for real counsel.'

Joanna ignored the jibe and began looking around for her
specs. Of late, and to her great annoyance, my wife had taken
to wearing reading glasses, but only when absolutely
necessary, and preferably not in public. Her specs were to be
found left lying all over the house. Jamie had already ripped
a leg from one pair. When she returned to the kitchen with
them, I pushed the bundle of papers towards her and placed
the summary into her outstretched hand. She sat down. I
waited anxiously while she flicked through the memorial like
a schoolboy hoping his mum would like the story he'd
written and maybe stick it on the fridge door.

I'd washed the dishes, fed the dog, wiped the table and put the kettle on by the time Joanna had finished skimming through the papers. She took off her specs, stood up and gave me a peck on the cheek. 'You've been a busy boy, haven't you?'

'Just doing my job,' I said. Being so modest almost hurt. Since Salome had furnished me with her latest version of the truth, I'd visited her another couple of times in prison and been making lots of inquiries, the results of which were now set out in summary and in Joanna's hands.

'You know what this is, Robbie?' Joanna said. She patted the brief, stood up, stretched and yawned. 'This is an actual real live defence. I'm not saying it's a great defence – not yet - but it's definitely the best defence so far.' She walked around behind my chair and started massaging my shoulders like a slow assault. 'And with some more work I think it could be even better.'

Slightly deflated I asked for clarification.

Joanna was happy to explain. 'For one thing, there's the shotgun cartridge. You say it has Armando's fingerprint on it, but not Salome's. That's not what the Crown forensic expert says in her report.'

'That's right. What she says was that the shotgun gave up some fingerprints, several of which could be attributed to Salome.'

'So?'

My wife had spent most of her professional years as a prosecutor. When faced with a Crown expert's report, she took it at face value, not yet having acquired the patina of suspicion that every experienced defence lawyer acquires like green mould on stale bread. While she'd read the Crown's forensic report, she'd not read into it.

'Read it again,' I said. Joanna replaced her glasses and picked up the report. 'It says that tests on the cartridge for fingerprints were inconclusive.'

117

'Yes, it does. But I've precognosced the forensic expert. What she meant by inconclusive is that there are fingerprints and partial prints all over the cartridge, most are unidentifiable, and none are attributable to Salome. The forensic expert claims to have correctly answered the question she was asked, and that was, *"Are the accused's fingerprints found on the shotgun and/or ammunition?"* The report is 100% accurate: tests were inconclusive - for Salome's fingerprints. It completely misses out the fact that the only quality print was a dirty great big thumbprint on the brass head where someone has pushed it into the barrel. Armando's thumbprint.'

'It's the truth, just not the whole truth,' Joanna said. 'Where have I come across that recently?' I knew she was recalling Marc Traynor. She returned the report to the bundle. 'Okay, that's the first thing. The second thing is why would Armando kill himself? He could have simply denied any rape allegation… and…' Joanna tailed off. Marc Traynor had denied the rape charge against him too.

'You're right,' I said. 'We do need to beef that up a bit. That's why there's an article I think you should read on the website for the Department of Psychology at Cambridge University.' I found my laptop and brought up the webpage. 'It's by six UK experts including Doctor Philip Dankworth from the Centre for Suicide Research. The research study concludes that: *most gunshot suicides in the UK are male, middle-aged and living with a partner and involve the use of shotguns.*'

'Could be helpful,' Joanna admitted. 'But do we know if Armando had any mental health issues?'

I continued reading. '*They are less likely to have current or past mental health problems, or a previous act of self-harm than people who commit suicide by other methods, and their suicide is more likely to have been precipitated by a relationship dispute.*' Point made, I closed my laptop. 'Anything there that doesn't fit full square with Armando's profile? Middle-aged, okay

118

slightly older than that, but he's male, no mental health issues that we know of, has a partner, and if someone is threatening to reveal that you raped them in your own house two or three days after your wedding, it might suggest a potential for a relationship dispute. I've already got the lead psychologist on standby.'

Joanna looked only mildly impressed. Then again, her job was not to pat me on the back for my findings, it was to pick at them and locate the flaws a prosecutor the calibre of Cameron Crowe QC most certainly would.

'Okay, there's one final thing we need to firm up on,' she said.

'And that is?'

'Do the post-mortem results tally with suicide?'

I was satisfied they did. Hadn't Professor Bradley said as much? Okay, *possibly* wasn't the same as definitely, but trying to extract a concrete opinion from a medical expert was like trying to extract a mammoth's molar. With all the rest of the evidence supporting suicide now stacking up nicely, I felt sure an *"it's possible"* from Scotland's most eminent pathologist would do just fine.

'Let's leave Prof Bradley alone and not give him a chance to change his mind,' I said.

Joanna squared the bundle of papers in front of her. Jaw set, she stared at them for a while. I'd never seen my wife like this. Marc Traynor's case had really done a number on her. Whether she was convinced of Salome's defence or just wanted to prove she could perform in the High Court, I didn't know. I only knew that for her another defeat was out of the question.

'Tell me this defence is the truth, Robbie.'

'The truth? How would I know that? Only two people know that and one of them is dead.'

'But this defence is based on actual instructions?'

'Yes.'

119

'From the client.'

'Of course, from the client. Do you think I would make up a story about rape and suicide? Is that honestly the sort of man you think you married?'

'No…' Joanna said, removing her glasses again and putting them atop the bundle of papers. 'But did you, though? This business about the rape. You didn't mention that to me before. You only said something about maybe Armando had been coming on heavy with Salome. That was before you had even taken instructions. You haven't simply spiced that up a bit. Have you?'

I put my hands up. 'Okay, I did know about the rape. Salome told me about it, but I shut her up before she could say any more. She wanted to go with a defence of the bastard deserved it. And—'

'You knew no counsel would go with that?'

'Not without a lot of persuasion.'

'But you thought you might be able to persuade me. Is that why you chose me ahead of Fiona Faye? You thought you could manipulate me into leading some—'

'Cup of tea, darling?' I went to fetch some mugs from the cupboard, not looking round to find out if the growling sound behind me was my wife or if Bouncer had heard a noise outside.

'There *is* one small problem I'm still working on,' I said. 'The Crown firearm expert's supplementary report was emailed to me this afternoon. It was after Grace Mary had prepared the brief, so it's not included. The shotgun was a vintage, single-shot Italian model.'

'Single shot?'

Apart from the pump action jobs favoured by zombie-killers in American action movies, I, like Joanna, thought all shotguns were double barrelled, either side-by-side or over-and-under.

'That's not the surprising thing,' I said. 'The spent cartridge was found lying on the carpet.'

'So what?'

'Think about it. How could someone shoot themselves at point blank range in the chest and then break the shotgun open and eject the cartridge? Unless it happened when Salome says she threw the gun to the side.'

'Or maybe after he'd fired it, because obviously the gun would have fallen to the ground, it could have broken open when it landed,' Joanna said. 'Couldn't it?'

'Either way, we have to find an explanation. We can't afford to go into the trial half-cocked,' I said.

'Very funny, Robbie, but you're right. We need to instruct our own firearms expert. I'm not going into this trial leaving a loose thread that Cameron Crowe can get his talons on and unravel the whole defence case.'

Joanna pushed the pile of papers out of reach, raised herself to her feet and cuddled into me. Usually, but not always, a good sign. 'But before we do anything…' she said. 'I've been thinking...' Usually, but not always, a bad sign. 'I'd like you to go and see Beverly.'

'I've got an appointment to precognosce her,' I said. 'A week from now. I'm supposed to go along for a locus inspection at the same time and need a police escort.'

Joanna had other ideas. 'Never mind a locus inspection. You've been in that study twice now, and we have the photographs of it taken from every possible angle. I want you to go and see Beverly.' Joanna took one of my hands in hers. 'Do this for me, Robbie. Go see Beverly and explain things to her. Tell her why we're doing this. It's not about money. It's about getting to the truth.'

I didn't like that idea much. I was no good at all that sweet talking stuff. The Diplomatic Corps' recruitment team had never come hammering at the door of Munro & Co looking for me. Not unless it was to place me under arrest.

'If it's all right, Jo, I'd rather wait until next week and just take a formal precognition,' I said.

'It'll be more informal if you don't have to go there with a police officer.'

Sensing my continued reluctance, Joanna tugged at my arm. 'Let's discuss this further in the bedroom.'

'Okay,' I said, as she gently led me from the room. 'But don't think you can use your womanly wiles to persuade me.'

Chapter 22

A swirl of dry leaves as ethereal as Joanna's new nightie blew across my feet as I alighted from my car next morning and crunched my way across the gravel towards West Hope House. Any police presence was long gone, and on that bright, cold autumn morning the small country estate was once more the very picture of tranquillity.

Beverly came out as I neared the steps to the front door. She was dressed for the weather in a waxed Barbour jacket and jeans. I'd phoned in advance and come in my work suit, not realising Beverly would be disinclined to let me set foot indoors. She walked down the steps to meet me, an excited golden retriever either side of her.

'Robbie,' she said, stiffly.

'Hi Beverly. Joanna's sorry she can't come too, but you'll understand that—'

'I understand that you and Joanna are representing the woman who killed my husband. What is it you want? If it's a statement, hurry up and take it. I'm going for a walk with the dogs.'

I didn't need Beverly's statement. The one she'd given to the police seemed to cover everything. She'd been to visit her mum and arrived back at the house late afternoon. She hadn't heard the fatal shot, but when she'd entered through the front door and into the great hallway, she'd met a flustered Salome exiting the study at speed. Salome had told her there'd been what she'd described as a terrible accident. Beverly ran into the study, saw Armando's body and thought she must have passed out in a chair. She vaguely remembered me arriving and helping her upstairs to her bedroom.

'Joanna would have liked to have come herself…'

'Then why didn't she?' Beverly marched off, grinding gravel under the heels of her Wellington boots, the two dogs running ahead. I had to sprint to catch up.

'She can't,' I said. 'She's not supposed to meet with Crown witnesses personally. Not before they give evidence in court.'

'Really? Good. Whatever she's got to say to me can wait until then.'

'Beverly, Joanna knows how you must be feeling right now.'

'Does she? I don't recall her husband being shot dead,' she replied, with just a hint of more's-the-pity.

Why had Joanna talked me into this visit? Before today, I'd only actually set eyes on Beverly twice in my life, and one of those was a fleeting glimpse at her wedding reception before being shown the door. Consoling widows wasn't what I was used to. Especially ones who thought I was out to deprive them of justice for their murdered husband. Still, I was here now and couldn't leave without passing on the message I'd been told to deliver. By this time we were at the side of the house, where a little further on a rough path led into the woods. It looked rocky and muddy in equal proportions, and I didn't think my footwear would be up to the task. A couple of quick steps and I was in front of Beverly, stopping her in her tracks.

'Joanna wants you to know that she is satisfied that Salome is not guilty... She wouldn't have taken the case on otherwise.'

Beverly's grunt suggested that she wasn't quite so certain.

'I've been making a lot of inquiries and think that Salome's been wrongly accused. Don't get me wrong, I know how it looks.'

The dogs stopped and looked back to see what the hold-up was.

'If that's what you were sent to tell me, you can go back to your wife like a good little errand boy and tell her that I hope

124

the two of you enjoy every last penny of the blood money you'll be charging for this case. But if you expect me to stand here any longer and listen to you tell me that little Colombian bitch didn't—'

'It was suicide,' I said softy. 'Everything points to Armando having killed himself.'

'Killed himself?' Beverly snorted. 'Seriously? Three days after our wedding?'

I wasn't going to mention the rape. I wasn't angling for a kick somewhere soft with the hard toe of a Hunter welly; nonetheless, I felt she should know the truth, or at least some of it. She tried to push past me. I took a step back, still blocking her path. 'Stop and listen for one minute to what I have to say, and then I'll go.'

'One minute?' she said, exasperated. 'Promise?'

A murder defence in sixty seconds. I went for it. 'The pathologist I've spoken to says suicide is possible.'

'Anything's possible.'

'What's Armando's normal routine when he comes back from shooting? You must know what he does.'

The words escaped Beverly's lips like mud through a mesh. 'He leaves the dogs at their kennels by the kitchen door. They're not allowed in the house. Comes in the back door and—'

'What does he do with his shotgun cartridges?'

Beverley looked over my shoulder at the dogs who were sniffing around the trunks of the trees on the edge of the woodland. 'There's a storeroom. He leaves his ammunition in there, then goes to the study…'

She could see where I was going with this. I finished for her. 'To lock his shotgun in the cabinet. That's right, isn't it? Guns and ammo kept apart. Think about it Beverly. You say, why would Armando kill himself. I say why would he bring a loaded shotgun into his study?' She didn't answer. 'According to the forensic scientists the cartridge they found in the shotgun was inserted by Armando. His fingerprint is on the base. There's absolutely no trace of Salome's fingerprints.'

She looked at me properly for the first time since I'd arrived.

'Did Xyenco send you?' Was a question I hadn't been expecting.

'Who?'

'Xyenco Associates. Armando's company.'

'Why would they contact me?'

'Okay, I'll ask again. Has Xyenco been in touch with you?'

'Beverly, I don't know what you're talking about. No one has been in contact with me about Armando. Why would they?'

'Because Xyenco has been in touch with me. The solicitors dealing with Armando's executry say Xyenco won't honour Armando's death-in-service payment. Three years' salary. Do you know how much money that is?' I didn't, but had an idea that if they piled it up I wouldn't want to jump off it without a parachute. 'They don't pay out on suicide. They told me they wanted to wait for the coroner's report. When I told them we don't have coroners in Scotland, but that someone had been charged with murder—'

'They said they'd await the trial verdict?' I guessed out loud. One of the dogs started to bark. Beverley was set to go. 'Look at it this way,' I said. 'What would you rather have? The friendship of Salome, who is innocent of killing your husband, or some money?'

'What would I rather have? I'd rather you didn't suggest something stupid like my husband killed himself. If you say Salome didn't murder him, why don't you find the person who did?'

She made to push past me again, and this time I made no attempt to stop her.

126

Chapter 23

Malky slapped the forehead that had cleared a thousand corner kicks. 'I don't know why I didn't think of this before.' He shook his head in disbelief, took a drink and leered up at me from his bar stool. 'He's got a daughter and I know where she works.'

It was late Friday night. Having played his weekly game of five-a-sides, Malky had spent the last few hours in the Red Corner Bar replacing lost electrolytes with pints of lager. His normal routine around about now would be to have a taxi drop him off at my dad's house where he'd crash, only to wake the next morning with no trace of a hangover. The ability to drink copious amounts of alcohol with impunity was one of my brother's attributes. That, attracting weak-willed women, and football. There was a search party out looking for the others. Modesty had been given up as a lost cause.

Since Malky only called me up to his five-a-side squad if the player with no legs cancelled last minute, I'd spent the evening at home. The reason I was here amidst the hoi polloi of Linlithgow society was because Malky had called to tell me he'd had an idea - and Malky had ideas like J. Robert Oppenheimer had when someone told him all about atoms.

'I met her at a club. Stevie's place or it might have been Addo's,' he said. 'Doesn't matter, the point is she was all over me like pineapple on a pizza. It was a while back. I said I'd call her but didn't. You know how it is.' I didn't really. The only dates women ever wanted me to phone them about was their court dates. 'Anyway, she's a manager at that FastFreez place.'

'Who is?' I thought the obvious question.'

'Colin Lancaster's daughter.'

'The producer of Scotgoals?'

'Yeah, he's got a daughter. Dead sporty. Can't remember her name exactly. Something to do with tennis…'

'Venus? Serena, Monica?'

'No… Hang on. Annette. Yeah, that was it.'

'Where's this going Malky?'

'FastFreez. You know the shop I'm talking about don't you, Robbie?'

I did. Every parent with a daughter had heard of FastFreez. Heard of it and wished they hadn't. It used to be said pop music was just a way of stealing pocket money from kids. That's how I felt about designer brands aimed at children and my wallet. Originating on America's west coast, FastFreez was the latest must-have sports brand for pre-to-early teens girls. They could have sewn their label onto bin-bags, called them training tops and their sole Scottish outlet on Edinburgh's George Street would still have been queued around the block.

The barman came over. 'What are you having, Robbie? You'll need to be fast, I shouted last orders half an hour ago.'

'Nothing for me, thanks, Brendan. I just came for Malky. By the way, how's things going with the big fight night?' I asked, as my brother drained the rest of his pint, burped and went off in search of a urinal. 'Always a great night,' I said, hoping he wouldn't think I was angling for a free ticket, even though I was.

Brendan whipped a nearly clean dish towel from off his shoulder, gave some damp patches on the countertop a wipe, and sighed. 'Tell the truth, it's all up in the air, Robbie. We've had a late call-off and I'm not sure what to do.'

Brendan *'The Linlithgow Lion'* Patterson, former Commonwealth Gold medallist at lightweight, co-promoted an annual Scotland versus England, pre-Christmas boxing event. It was held in a marquee and hosted by the Rugby

128

Club. The occasion had grown year by year, and now attracted TV coverage. To help glamorise things Brendan always threw some tickets at Malky and encouraged him to invite some of his former teammates along to adorn the ringside seats.

'It's still a couple of months away. Surely you can call someone up on short notice?' I said.

Brendan left me and wandered further down the bar, the better to slap a couple of slow-drinkers on the backs of their heads.

'It's not that easy, Robbie,' he said on his return, eyes still fixed on the two who were now tipping pints down their throats. 'We've got this new TV sponsorship deal, but they insist on diversity and equality. Fifty percent black fighters isn't a problem. Finding less than fifty per cent would be more difficult. But I also need a women's fight on the card or they could pull the plug. I've got this heavyweight girl coming all the way from Middlesbrough. Built like the Bismarck and no one to fight since our own girl broke her hand in sparring.'

A hand clamped onto my shoulder from behind. 'Right, as I was saying... You know how Tina is always harping on about getting one of those new tracksuit things from that FastFreez place?'

My brother's grip on the latest fashion trends was almost as insecure as my own. Though with a daughter, mine was showing gradual signs of improvement.

'What about it?'

'Well, you're always telling her you're not forking out that kind of money for a label.'

Which was true enough. I unclamped the hand and turned to look him in eyes shiny with alcohol and bright ideas.

'It's like this.' He looked furtively around, then, with arms outstretched, shepherded Brendan and me under his wing. 'You know this thing with me and Scotgoals?'

129

Brendan didn't, and so I summarised rather than wait for Malky to give us the director's cut.

'Some guy dived at the football when Malky was on telly. Malky called him a Nancy-boy.'

'Was it a Nancy-boy or Big Jessie?' Malky said.

'It was you who told me it was Nancy-boy.'

'Doesn't matter,' Malky said. 'Whatever it was, someone complained saying it was sexist.'

'I think you mean homophobic,' I said.

Malky shrugged. 'We can go into the details later. What Robbie's trying to say, Brendan, is that for some reason the TV folk didn't like it, and I've been suspended pending a disciplinary. It's been months now.'

What that had got to do with him once having met the daughter of the show's producer at a nightclub was thus far unclear. I had the horrible feeling he was about to clarify.

Malky continued. 'The guy who's head of the diss... The dish...'

'Malky's going up before a disciplinary committee,' I explained to Brendan, to save Malky a third attempt.

'That's right,' he said. 'And there's a guy called Lancaster. He's the new boss of Scotgoals and he's got a daughter.' Malky pulled me and Brendan closer. 'And she's the manager there.'

'Where?' Brendan asked. He shot a glance up at the clock on the wall behind him, and yelled, 'Hey, Mickey!' At the sound of his master's voice the six-foot six figure of Brendan's nephew emerged from the backroom through a curtain of multi-coloured plastic strips and joined his uncle-slash-boss behind the bar. Mickey was all muscle and that was just his head. As Brendan's sister's boy, after a six-stretch for a bungled armed robbery, he'd secured work with his uncle whose rehabilitation techniques had put those of the local Criminal Justice Service to shame. Then again, the CJS were less likely to punch your headlights in at any sign of recidivism. 'Tell that lot…' by which Brendan meant everyone not included in Malky's huddle. 'To drink up and get out or else you're going to help them out. Understand?'

It took a moment or two, but eventually, with a nod to indicate he did understand, Mickey lifted the heavy wooden flap in the bar like it was made of cardboard, squeezed through the gap he'd created and began to broadcast the news.

'Okay,' Brendan said, once he'd gone. 'Who works where?'

'Lancaster's daughter. She works at FastFreez.'

'So what?' I said. 'Are you expecting a discount or something?'

Malky wrinkled his brow. 'What don't you understand about the plan?'

'Everything,' I said, and after a moment mulling things over, Brendan tended to agree.

Malky sighed alcohol fumes and released us from under his arms. 'It's simple. If me and this Annette become an item, and I tell her what her dad's doing to me - what do you think will happen?'

'Tell us,' I said.

'She'll make him change his mind of course. Fathers and daughters, there's a special bond between them. Look at you and Tina, Robbie. She's got you wrapped around her little finger. All I need is an excuse to bump into her.'

'Why not just phone her?' Brendan asked.

Malky shook his head sadly. He was clearly dealing with amateurs. 'Brendan, Brendan, Brendan. To phone her after all this time would seem like the act of a desperate man. Burds can smell desperation like a shark can smell a cut finger from a mile away. I need to meet her by accident. Let nature run its course. Problem is, I can't just go waltzing into a kids' clothes shop. So, here's what I do. I take Tina to buy that tracksuit she's wanting, just happen to see her, we get chatting…' He dusted off his hands in a need-I-say-more fashion.

131

'What if she's not interested?' I said. 'She must be a lot younger than you for one thing.'

Malky gripped one of my cheeks between finger and thumb. 'Would you listen to my brother Brendan? What if she's not interested? How could she not be interested? She's a woman. And I'm... Well I'm me. And why would I be interested in a woman my age?' Malky took a step backwards, arms outstretched, awaiting it seemed a round of applause.

'Let's talk about this in the morning,' I said, pulling my genius brother in the direction of fresh air. 'With a bit of luck you'll have forgotten all about it by then.'

I paused on the way to the door, turned and called to Brendan. 'What's the purse?'

'The purse?'

'Yeah, the one for this match between the two female fighters.'

'What's it to you?'

'Just tell me how much and I'll take Malky away so you can close up.'

'It's four grand to the winner, fifteen hundred for the loser.'

'And how long would it take you to train someone to get in the ring?'

'And put on a decent show?' Brendan scratched the greying scrub that grew out the top of his head. 'Depends what I'm working with.'

'A former Olympian athlete.'

'Where are you going to find an Olympian athlete?'

'How long?' I repeated.

Brendan rubbed his chin. 'Six months might do it.'

'You've got six weeks,' I said.

Chapter 24

'Not a chance,' was Grace Mary's verdict next morning after she'd put a call through to Dario's country retreat. 'His staff say he's not speaking to anyone.'

Right from the start of his wife's prosecution, Dario had been keeping a distance. Why, I didn't exactly know, other than with talk of divorce maybe he saw this as the perfect opportunity to offload Salome. Though why anyone with a molecule of testosterone in their body would want to do that, I had no idea. On the other hand, it could have all been part of his publicity shyness; whatever, three months down the line, with the indictment now served and Salome's defence tighter than the UK Overseas Aid budget, I thought it the perfect opportunity to approach Dario about putting up surety for his wife's bail. There was no guarantee the court would accept it, but it was definitely worth a try taking advantage of the vast sums of money Dario would undoubtedly have at his disposal. Maybe his reluctance to engage was because Armando was not just a business contact, but also a friend. If only I could assure him of Salome's innocence he might see things differently, for old time's sake if nothing else.

'Try again and make sure you tell whoever answers that I'm his wife's lawyer,' I said.

'They know that. The chap I spoke to said Dario is speaking to no one about anything, and definitely not about his wife's case. Not even you. Oh, and your brother phoned,' Grace Mary called after me as I left reception for my own room. 'Said he's been ringing your mobile all morning. You better not be ignoring that poor boy.'

That's exactly what I had been doing. Hopefully he'd have forgotten all about the grand idea he'd regaled us with on Friday night, and just wanted to know what I was doing about his disciplinary hearing. The answer was nothing. I'd been too busy in court, not to mention preparing the Salome Ramirez defence, and then, of course, there was the Munro motto of never putting off until tomorrow what you can put off until the day after tomorrow. I punched in the numbers on my phone. After a while I was put through to the office of Colin Lancaster, producer of Malky's show, 'Scotgoals'.

'He's on an outside broadcast,' his secretary said. 'Yes, he does have a mobile, but he doesn't give the number out to just anyone.'

Trying to explain that I wasn't just anyone was like trying to explain to a non-whisky drinker that a 30-year-old Highland Park isn't best served with ice and a slice. I hung up, just in time for my mobile to buzz again. Carelessly, without looking at the screen, I answered. It was Malky and he sounded excited.

'Calm down,' I said, I've been trying to get hold of this Lancaster guy, but—'

'He's at Falkirk Stadium. Right now. For the Falkirk/Dunfermline game. That Gaelic channel has got an outside broadcast unit there, and Scotgoals is going to do the pre-match and full-time interviews with the players because none of them speaks Gaelic.' There was a longstanding rivalry between 'The Bairns' and their Fife rivals from across the Forth, 'The Pars'. Ironic that there were so many nationalities on the pitch and yet the commentary was to be done in the one language none of them or any of their supporters spoke. 'If you get down there you can collar him and put in a good word for me. You said, he owes you.'

It was true, to some extent he did. I'd met Lancaster once before, in my former life working with Caldwell & Craig. If Munro & Co was to the legal profession what the Eurovision

134

Song Contest was to Geopolitics, my old established Glasgow law firm was in the G5 of the legal world. Anyone who could afford their absurd fees went to C&C, and when Lancaster had come seeking legal advice on a no insurance charge, he'd been referred to me as the only solicitor in the place with a working knowledge of the Road Traffic Act. Lancaster had been one of my last clients before Caldwell & Craig had decided crime didn't pay, chiefly because most of their clients were too smart to get caught. It had been easily ten years ago, but I remembered the case and how a young, silver-tongued R. Munro esq. had managed to persuade the Justice of the Peace Court that Lancaster's lack of motor insurance had all been down to a terrible misunderstanding with his broker. There followed a finding of special reasons under s.44(2) of the Road Traffic Offenders Act 1988, and my client's driving licence had swerved around the endorsement of six penalty points that would have handed Lancaster a six-month totting-up disqualification. That had to count for something.

Falkirk Stadium was seven miles away from where I was sitting, with no speed cameras en route. I was grabbing my coat when the door to my office burst open and Isabella Ewart burst in, Grace Mary bringing up the rear. 'Miss Ewart to see you,' my secretary said helpfully, before withdrawing and closing the door behind her.

'I got your voicemail message,' Isabella said, like I'd sent her a bout of botulism in the post. 'You've arranged a fight for me. Is that right?'

'That's right,' I said, 'and it's not happening today in my office with me, so take a seat and listen.'

Isabella looked down at the wooden contraption I reserved for clients as a deterrent for overly long interviews. She assessed the ergonomics and decided to stand.

'Okay, Isabella, here's the thing,' I said. 'You promised to pay me to do your trial. I did and I won and I deserve to be paid. Your answer to that is that you won't pay because you don't have any money and yet you own a house—'

'With a mortgage. What about it?'

'And your mum—'

'Don't bring my mum into this.'

'Your mum,' I continued, carefully. 'She died and left you her house.'

'I'm going to rent it out.'

'When?'

Isabella sniffed. 'I don't know. I'll need to do it up a bit first.'

'And how are you going to pay for that?' I asked. She didn't answer. 'It's six rounds of two minutes each, and you've got a month and a half to train for it. More than enough for an elite athlete like you. Look at you. You're in tip-top condition. You could probably step into the ring right now and win. You only won that gold—'

'Bronze.'

'Medal, six—'

'Ten.'

'Years ago. Step into the ring, beat up this big English girl and they'll slap four thousand smackers in your glove. That's two for me and two for you to redecorate your mum's house. Everyone's a winner. Apart from the English girl, obviously.'

'And what if I lose?' Isabella asked, not unreasonably. 'What if this professional female fighter, who has probably been boxing for years, knocks my head off?'

'That's not going to happen,' I said. 'Have some faith in yourself, and in Brendan.'

'Who?'

'Brendan Paterson. Commonwealth gold winner. He's going to train you.'

'But if I do happen to lose. What then?'

'Then you'll still get fifteen hundred. That'll be enough to pay me what I deserve. I don't mind waiving VAT for a cash payment. Or don't you think that twelve minutes eating leather beats three years eating prison food?'

With a final glower at me she turned on her heel.

'I'll text Brendan your phone number. He'll be in touch!' I shouted after her.

Chapter 25

I don't always leap into action on the instructions of clients, but if I didn't do something I'd never hear the end of it from Malky or my dad or Grace Mary for that matter. The good thing about wearing a suit, especially if it looks like it's not for the first time, is that it, a confident smile and the impression that you know where you're going, will allow you access just about anywhere. Once I'd arrived at Falkirk Stadium I had no idea where I was going, but I was wearing the suit and the confident smile. After scouting around for a while, I found myself walking down the players' tunnel and onto the track at the side of the plastic pitch where I saw a man with a furry microphone on the end of a pole chatting to another man who was holding a clipboard. I had no need of Malky's, *"an arsehole sucking a lemon"*, description for despite the intervening years I recognised the man with the clipboard straightaway. He was tall and skinny and could've looked through a keyhole with both eyes at the same time.

I walked over and interrupted the conversation by sticking out my hand. 'Hello? Colin Lancaster? Robbie Munro.' He looked down at my hand but didn't take it, so I shoved it in my pocket. 'We met a few years ago. That business about your car insurance.'

He turned his head to the man with the furry microphone. 'Mike, do you mind?'

'Mike? That your name? Really?' I said.

Mike with the furry microphone rolled his eyes at me. I guessed I wasn't the first. He turned and wandered off further down the track.

'I was in the area,' I said, which was true, I'd only just driven there, 'and thought I'd take the chance to have a quick word with you about these disciplinary proceedings against my brother,' I said with a light laugh, hoping he'd join in. He didn't. He just stood there, like he was harbouring the uneasy feeling that someone somewhere might be enjoying themselves.

I cleared my throat and battered on. 'Is it all really necessary? I mean, you know what Malky's like.'

Lancaster squared up his overly-trendy, red-framed glasses and squinted at me through them. I could just tell he was the sort of guy who liked to go to meetings and use words like stakeholder and helicopter-view a lot. 'I know what your brother's like, all right,' he said. 'I was warned about him when I took over at Scotgoals.'

'I know, I know, it's true,' I said, as amiably as possible. 'Sometimes Malky doesn't always think before he speaks.'

'Then he should,' Lancaster said through his tight little mouth, the more to corroborate Malky's description of him.

'And we should all butter our toast after we've dropped it,' I said. 'But, come on. Malky's an ex-footballer. Can you not cut him a break? It's only a few years since he discovered his head was for something other than clearing corners. I mean... Nancy-boy or big Jessie or whatever? Did anyone even notice? Or care?'

Judging by the soft choking sound that ensued, I guessed there was someone who noticed and cared very deeply. At least one person on the disciplinary panel would be returning a guilty verdict in due course, and they'd be wearing red-framed spectacles. Still, justice delayed and all that.

'Well at least can you tell me when and where the hearing's going to be held?' I said. 'Malky's been suspended for months. I take it he'll be allowed legal representation?'

Lancaster looked anywhere other than at me. 'There won't be a hearing. Your brother is suspended until the end of his contract. He will be paid in full, and then his contract won't be renewed.'

It made sense, in a weaselly sort of a way. Have a hearing and it would attract publicity. For many football supporters, LGBT was something to do with a dismissal in cricket, and the thought that Malky Munro might be sacked for using language less politically incorrect than they used themselves, would have kept the football phone-ins and red top newspapers in front and back page headlines for weeks. No, far better to do nothing, pay Malky until the end of the season and then quietly let him go. No explanation. No hullabaloo. Just a velvet assassination of his TV career.

The floodlights came on though it was still two or three hours until kick-off, and a groundsman walked past us with some corner flags under his arm.

'Now was there anything else?' Lancaster asked, with an air of finality.

'What if Malky apologises on air? Puts things right with anyone who was offended?' I said. 'There's no need to hold grudges.'

'I'm not holding a grudge.'

'Calling people names is just unforgivable, so he's to be cancelled. Is that it?'

'Save the melodrama for the courtroom,' Lancaster said. 'Scotgoals viewers deserve—'

'Scotgoals viewers don't care. If they did, they wouldn't be tuning into a bunch of ex-footballers chuntering on about how the boys done well. All they want is some people who've been there and done it and can speak to them in a language they understand.'

'Are you having a dig at Gaelic broadcasting?'

'No, what I'm trying to say is—'

'What you're trying to say is that we should excuse your brother's outdated one-of-the-lads language. Well it's not the type of language we want them to hear.'

'And who are you to decide that?'

'I'm the producer of the show, that's who. And I've decided that Malky and his antiquated racist, sexist and homophobic quips are out.'

'But he doesn't mean his words to be any of those things. I mean, *niggle*?'

'My mind's made up. Now if you don't mind, I'm busy.'

The groundsman had reached the first corner of the pitch and inserted a stick with a navy-blue flag. It was time for me to wave my own flag. A white one.

I watched Lancaster walk down the track towards Mike the fluffy microphone man who was loitering a few metres away. There then followed a short but heated exchange with microphone Mike doing most of the talking and pointing frantically in my direction.

I thought nothing of it, but as I was making my way back up the tunnel, I heard footsteps behind me. I turned to see Lancaster. He took out a lens wipe from its foil sachet, cleaned his glasses quickly, folded it, sealed it inside the packet again and tucked it into his pocket. 'I've been giving what you just said some more thought,' he said. 'Mike tells me you're the lawyer acting for Dario's wife in the murder trial of that Spanish financier.'

'You're busy, I'm busy too,' I said.

As I made to leave, he put a hand onto my shoulder in a grip that was too tight to be friendly. His face twitched and puckered, lips not quite achieving smile status. 'Perhaps between us we can reach some kind of compromise over Malky,' he said.

Chapter 26

Surgeons Hall on Nicolson Street is just up the road from Old College where in my younger days I'd slept my way through many a constitutional law lecture. It's home to the Royal College of Surgeons of Edinburgh, and once a year hosts a whisky festival called The Whisky Stramash. The early 19th century building, designed by William Henry Playfair who was responsible for Edinburgh's New Town, also houses a pathology museum; so pickled livers are nothing new to the place.

My dad had been threatening to go to the Stramash for years, eyeing the adverts like a cheetah sizing up a wounded gazelle. Mainly due to high demand, his poor memory and internet ineptitude, he had never managed to secure a ticket; however, on this occasion he'd persuaded Malky to weave his magic. One of the benefits of having a has-been soccer superstar as a son was your off-spring's ability to blag himself tickets to almost any event. The man could have wangled the unicorns a berth on Noah's ark. I met the pair of them outside the Varsity Music Shop where we waited in a queue made up mostly of men, buzzing with excitement and bristling with facial hair.

The Stramash whisky-tasting takes place in two parts of the great building. In the middle is a quad where whisky drinkers can take a time-out from the hard stuff and relax with food and a softer drink, otherwise known as a pie and a pint. And not just any pie and pint: artisan pies and real ale. The main difference between three artisan pies and three normal pies, so far as I could establish, having just shelled out on them, being about a tenner. So, having come through the first session of the venue relatively unscathed, Malky, my dad and I took a break from sampling single malts, and with pies and pints in hand, flitted lightly through the crowds until coming to rest on some rickety garden furniture that looked to have seen more winters than summers.

'This criss-cross stuff is all well and good,' Malky said, studying the lattice effect atop his steak and Guinness pie – even the food here was alcoholic – but it's just an excuse to give you less pastry for the sake of a nice pattern.'

There was more scintillating conversation along these lines until I felt it necessary to bring up my brother's employment difficulties.

'When's it happening – the disciplinary? Will you be there?' Malky asked.

'Of course he'll be there,' my dad said. 'He's your brother.' Why did people have to keep reminding me? 'Where do you think he'd be? Leave it to Robbie. He'll tell them to get a grip and stop being so sensitive. You'll be back on the telly in no time at all.'

My father's unprecedented faith in me was touching, if whisky generated.

'I don't know,' Malky said. 'It's not really Robbie's thing, is it? No offence, Robbie, but you'd maybe be all right if I'd committed a crime or something, but this is different. This is proper law. Employment stuff. I was thinking about throwing some money at it. Getting a big hitter in to do the disciplinary. Someone who really knows their stuff.'

'There's not going to be a disciplinary hearing,' I said.

My dad was aghast, though not sufficiently so to prevent him from taking a large gulp of real ale before responding to the news. 'What do you mean? They can't do that. Every man is entitled to his day in court. What's Magna Carta got to say about it?'

'Never mind her,' Malky said. 'They can't just sack me without a hearing, can they?'

143

'They're not going to sack you,' I told the two bewildered faces. 'They're going to keep you suspended on full pay until your contract runs out.'

'But that's only a couple of months away.'

My dad was still of the view that they couldn't do that, and that I was being a tad defeatist. 'Maybe Malky should get another lawyer. Someone needs to put a stop to this.'

The pair of them were clearly having difficulty understanding the legal niceties of the situation, in the same way Scots don't understand why the English leave the skin on fish suppers.

'Malky's on a six-month rolling contract. Scotgoals will pay him up until it ends and then not renew it. Providing they pay him, they're not in breach and there's nothing he can do. It's all perfectly legal,' I told them.

'So that's it,' Malky said, dropping the last piece of pie crust into his mouth. 'My TV career gone...' He wiped his hands on a white paper napkin, folded it up into the paper plate his pie had come with, and tossed the whole lot in the direction of a large plastic bin. From that range it was hard to miss, but he managed. 'Just like that.'

'Not... necessarily,' I said. 'I spoke with Colin Lancaster. There is a possible compromise deal.'

My dad's smile was not just the smile of a Scots man who finds himself trapped in a venue with unlimited supplies of free whisky. He slapped me on the back. 'Tell us more, son.'

'Well, Malky,' I said, 'the producer has agreed to forget all about the Nancy-boy thing. You can get back on telly, and have a new contract—'

Malky ruffled my hair. 'I knew you'd think of something.' He wrapped an arm around me, squeezed and poked me in the stomach with a finger. 'Didn't I just tell you that, Dad? I told you Robbie would think of something. Remember?'

While my dad tried to recall a moment in history that had never happened, I continued. 'All you have to do is secure an exclusive interview for Scotgoals with Dario.'

The hair ruffling stopped. Malky jumped to his feet, his creaky wooden chair toppling backwards. 'What!'

'That's the deal,' I said. 'You get Dario to give Scotgoals an interview. His first since retiring—'

Malky stared down at me. 'Since retiring? He's never given an interview. There are Papist monks who have given more interviews than him.'

'I think you mean Trappist,' I said.

'Trappist monks are Papist, aren't they?' my dad chipped in. 'Roman Catholics, I mean.'

'Most monks are Catholics, Dad.' I said.

'What about those Kung Fu monks?' Malky wanted to know.

I could see we were starting to stray off the beaten. 'Focus, Malky. It's really simple. You get Dario to do an exclusive interview on Scotgoals—'

'It would have to be exclusive! The man doesn't do interviews.'

'Then talk him into it. Take him out. Get him drunk.'

'He doesn't drink!'

'Think of something. He's your pal,' I said. 'Ask him to do it for old time's sake.'

'Robbie's right.' My dad was fully on board with the idea. 'It's the least he can do considering you made him what he is today.'

Malky sighed. 'We had a few months of training together when he was sixteen. To be honest, I've always thought he was a bit of a fanny. Wouldn't have lasted five minutes back when I was playing. Before they all became ballerinas. I've only seen him a handful of times in twenty years. Robbie, you're defending his wife for murder. If anyone's best placed to talk him into an interview it's you.'

My artisan pie had an artisan chunk of gristle in it. I picked it out of my mouth, wrapped it in a napkin and, collecting Malky's rubbish on the way, put it in the bin along with my dad's leftovers.

'There are two problems with that,' I said on my return. 'Firstly, I've already tried to speak to him. Grace Mary's phoned dozens of times, but his security people have erected a ring of steel. With his wife on remand for murder, the press have been hanging about outside his country lodge for months. He's living like a recluse.'

'Things'll quieten down,' Malky said. 'What's the second problem?'

We were at a wedding a wee while back and Joanna was dancing with Armando Diaz—'

'Who's that?' my dad asked.

'The dead guy,' Malky said.

'Then how could he…' I could see my dad trying to focus through a haze of whisky.

'This was when he was alive, Dad. He had his hands all over Joanna.'

'Okay, hands all over her. So what?' Malky said.

'So, he kept putting his hand on her bum. I didn't like it. I might have waded in a bit.'

'Why didn't you ask Joanna first?' my dad asked. 'It was her bum after all.'

'Yeah, well I'm married to that bum.'

Malky was puzzled. 'I thought you said they were dancing?'

'They were.'

'Then where's he supposed to put his hands?'

'Not on my wife's backside for a start!'

Malky held his hands up. 'Okay, okay. Apparently, hands on arse in a dancing situation is a no-no. I mean, who knew?'

I continued. 'There was a bit of a scene in the middle of the dance floor. A glass smashed. The band stopped playing. Dario slipped. He fell over. People were laughing at him.'

'And then what?' my dad asked.

'Then I was asked to leave,' I said over the sound of Malky's groans. 'Upshot is I'm not Dario's bestest pal right now.'

'But you are still his wife's lawyer,' Malky said.

'He's not talking to her either.'

'She did kill his friend, I suppose.'

'I also think he's wanting a divorce. But don't tell anyone I told you that.'

'If he's a witness, you can make him talk to you,' my dad said. 'Tell his security people that unless he speaks to you, you'll get a warrant to take a precognition on oath about his wife's case. He'll not want to go to all the hassle of an appearance at the Sheriff Court. Can you imagine the publicity that would get?'

It was actually a good idea, just not one I felt would endear me to The Great One sufficiently for me to then persuade him to break his vow of silence and give his first ever interview to a TV channel that had the same sort of viewing numbers as Paint Drying for Beginners.

Fortified, we decided to mull things over with the aid of more single malt. My dad was a great one for independent bottlings. Mainly, I suspected, because they were usually cask strength. We had sampled a few Adelphi editions, followed by some Cadenheads, and it was at the Gordon & Macphail stall that inspiration struck Malky. 'Peter Falconer. That's who you need to speak to.'

'Lang Pete? The man's an idiot,' my dad said, knocking back a Glenallachie, showing it the same sort of respect he clearly held for the sports agent in question. It was an opinion that mirrored my own.

'What about him?' I asked, adding a drop of water to my Glencairn glass.

'He's Dario's agent,' Malky said.

I didn't think it likely. Peter Falconer was regarded as one of Scotland's top sports agents, it was true, but surely Dario's interests were handled by a mega firm with offices in Madrid, London, New York. Not a couple of rooms at the bottom of the Royal Mile.

Malky seemed certain about it. 'No, he definitely is. I was at a dinner with Pete not so long ago, and he was talking about Dario's book coming out. Said he was going to make a killing out of it.'

If that was true, Peter would certainly be the man to approach. The problem was that him and I weren't seeing eye to eye at the moment, and that wasn't just because he was six inches taller than me. 'Me and Peter are not exactly on speaking terms,' I said. 'Remember how he bumped me on my fee for defending his snooker client?[3] No-win-no-fee and then he doesn't pay me because I didn't win the way his client wanted me to win.'

My dad shoved his glass under my nose. 'Take a whiff of that. Connoisseurs Choice. A 1997 Glenburgie. 59.1%, cask strength, unchillfiltered, natural colour, first fill sherry butt, and they're practically giving the stuff away. A hundred and fifty a throw. If we all chipped in we could—'

'Buy a bottle and keep it at your place?' I ventured. 'Somehow I don't see me getting my fifty quid's worth out of that little arrangement.'

Eyes narrowed and moustache twitching, he replied, 'It would be seventy-five between the two of you. I've not got my wallet with me. But if you're going to be like that—'

---

[3] Fixed Odds – Book 10

'Sorry Dad, but I'm trying to talk to Malky about something important.'

'Look about you. *I'm* talking about something important. Whisky. No wonder folk keep on falling out with you.'

'You're never getting that money Peter owes you,' Malky said, as sipping our samples of Speyside we watched the old man turn his back on us and weave his way through the gathering. He was searching for the perfect malt and prepared to put the hours in. 'But, if you can put that behind you, I'll phone and tell him there's no hard feelings and set up a meeting. When I think of all the times over the years I've helped Pete out...'

I trusted Peter Falconer about as far as I could throw him - through plate glass preferably - but what my brother said was true. There was no point holding a grudge, and it sounded a lot better than Malky's other idea.

Chapter 27

Salome Ramirez's Preliminary Hearing took place ninety days to the day after her full committal. The train we'd gone for had been cancelled and the next one delayed. So, on that bright November morning, Joanna and I had to take the News Steps two at a time and fight our way through the crowds on the Royal Mile to the big brass doors of the High Court building on the Lawnmarket. As we passed through security, the Tannoy announced that HMA -v- Salome Ramirez was to be the first of several cases to call. Your case being near the top of the calling list is always directly proportional to the lateness of your arrival.

Running down the slope to Courtroom 1, me helping Joanna struggle into her black gown on the way, Salome was already in the dock by the time we entered the packed courtroom. I left Joanna to take her seat in the well of the court and catch her breath while I went over to reassure our client that everything was all right. 'I need to speak to you,' she said.

At that moment the judge was led on by her Macer, and everyone in the court stood. I turned to look up at the bench to see Lady Carrick, a woman in a horsehair wig, her corned beef complexion contrasting with the white silk gown and matching the red crosses on it. At the end of a vein-burst nose perched a pair of standard issue judicial half-moon spectacles.

'Call the diet, Her Majesty's Advocate against Salome Kristina Ramirez,' the clerk announced.

As everyone sat down again, I could sense the eyes of the court turning from the prisoner in the dock and resting on Joanna who was still standing; no wig and clad in the same black cotton gown her parents had bought her when she'd finished her traineeship. I went over, sat beside her, gripped her hand and whispered, 'You've got this.'

'Who appears?' Lady Carrick asked, not bothering to look at anyone in particular.

Joanna gave the judge a professional smile. 'Good morning M'Lady. Miss Jordan for Mrs Ramirez, who pleads not guilty to the charge on the indictment.' She was about to sit again and let Crown counsel speak first, which was the usual procedure, until the judge had other ideas.

'Is the defence fully prepared, Miss…?'

'Jordan. And it is M'Lady. There are two witnesses cited for the defence, a list has been lodged and intimated. There are no Special Defences.'

Like all judges selected to preside over Preliminary Hearings, Lady Carrick was there to assess the state of each party's preparation while at the same time make life as difficult as possible for all concerned. In Joanna she clearly had the scent of fresh blood in her nostrils. She lifted a sheet of paper from the Bench and read it, eyes screwed up as though the very act of reading what was on the paper was causing her pain. 'Dr Philip Dankworth, psychologist, and Professor Edward Bradley? Professor Bradley is a regular visitor to these courts. Surely his evidence is capable of agreement?' She looked down to her right at the Crown's side of the table where the Advocate depute, the Lord Advocate's representative on earth, was sitting. They didn't call Cameron Crowe QC Nosferatu in pinstripes just because he looked like he slept upside down in a cave. Crowe could bite the neck of a defence and drain every last drop of blood. He might have the social skills of a rotting corpse, but the man was meticulous in preparation, knowledgeable on the law and merciless in cross examination. There was a rumour Crowe had been in the running for admission as a Senator of the

College of Justice, but that Lady Carrick had pipped him at the judicial post.

Cameron Crowe QC hoisted himself to his feet. 'Professor Bradley, if not a regular visitor, is certainly a frequent one, M'Lady,' he said, his renowned pedantry spared no one neither judge nor junkie, not that those descriptions were mutually exclusive. From cocaine to cannabis to caffeine to cocoa beans, everyone has their own drug of choice; Lady Carrick's came in decanters. 'However, as the defence has not lodged a report by either of their witnesses, the Crown is unable to agree any defence evidence, nor has it been asked to.'

With that he sat down again. The decision not to lodge our experts' reports was deliberate, mainly because we didn't want to give the prosecution any idea of the defence until, hopefully, it was too late for them to counter it, and also because in Prof Bradley's case, I didn't have a report; only my recollection of our meeting in the Bow Bar all of ninety days ago.

Like most judges, Lady Carrick was appalled at the thought the defence might not do all in its power to aid the Prosecution and smooth the way to a conviction. 'Is that correct Miss...?'

'Miss Jordan,' Joanna said, 'and that's quite correct, we haven't lodged reports from either Dr Dankworth or Professor Bradley. The defence will be calling the witnesses to answer the questions put to them in the witness box.'

'To what end?'

'The ends of justice I hope,' Joanna said.

Lady Carrick flinched as though her knickers were wired to a 12 -volt battery, but she let Joanna's reply go. 'And Miss...'

Joanna helped her out again. 'Miss Jordan.'

'What are the issues?'

'Sorry, M'Lady?'

'What is the accused's line of defence?'

Defences such as incrimination, self-defence, insanity, alibi, coercion, all had to be intimated to the Crown and lodged in court in advance of the Preliminary Hearing. They called it fair notice, but it was basically to give the Crown time to spike the defence's guns.

'As I've said, there is no special defence, M'Lady.'

'But what is the defence? Your client must have one.'

Crowe rose to his feet again. 'Not necessarily, M'Lady,' he said, surprisingly coming to Joanna's aid. Perhaps it was chivalry, perhaps he recognised Joanna's inexperience and wanted to help, most likely he couldn't resist putting the judge right. 'The accused needs no defence. It's for the Crown to prove its case.'

Lady Carrick looked from Crowe to Joanna, not sure who was irritating her the most.

'Something,' Crowe continued, 'that the Crown will have very little difficulty in accomplishing.'

Somewhat reassured by that, Lady Carrick stared down to her left again. 'Miss…?'

I was certain the judge's inability to recollect Joanna's name had nothing to do with a bad memory and everything to do with Joanna not being a member of the Faculty of Advocates. High Court judges tend to view solicitor advocates the same way an alcoholic views empty beer cans; useless, but handy if you want to kick something down the street.

'Tel her it's still Jordan,' I hissed.

Joanna rose again, stepping on my toe in the process. 'Miss Jordan,' she said with a smile.

'Of course, Miss... er... Jordan, I take it your client has been advised that she is entitled to representation by senior counsel? She is facing a murder charge after all.'

153

'Miss Ramirez is content with her choice of representation, thank you, M'Lady,' Joanna said, a lot more politely than I would have managed.

The judge grunted. 'Is the defence prepared to agree *any* evidence in this case. You do recognise the duties incumbent under section 257?' The judge look down to her right. 'Advocate depute, surely parties can save court time and agree formalities such as the forensic evidence?'

'Indeed, M'Lady,' Crowe said. 'Although, of course, evidence of any type given in court is by definition forensic; however, if your ladyship is referring to the Crown's *scientific* evidence, then, yes, much of that is the subject of a Joint Minute of Admissions currently being adjusted between parties.'

Crowe could have breathed on a mirror and left no steam. In contrast, Lady Carrick looked like steam was coming out of every orifice. With eyes mere slits and face the colour of fine vintage claret she turned her countenance once more upon Joanna. 'Is that correct?'

'It is M'Lady. The defence has liaised with the Crown on certain matters not in dispute. There will be a Joint Minute agreeing the Crown's autopsy report, the fingerprint analysis, and a great deal of other routine evidence concerning the provenance of the Crown productions and labels and such like.'

'In all it should reduce the length of the trial considerably,' Crowe said, not bothering to get up.

'How considerably?'

This time he did stand. 'Comfortably within a fortnight, M'Lady. Six days with a following wind.' With a simpering smile and a swish of his silk gown, Crowe took his seat again.

There being no further interventions from the bench nor requests by either side for a continuation of the Preliminary Hearing, all that was required was for the clerk to fix a date for trial.

In Scotland the trial of an accused who is remanded on indictment must start within one hundred and forty days. The law on the prevention in delay of trials looks good on paper but doesn't translate well to real life. High Court diaries are seldom able to accommodate trials within the statutory time limit, and clerks look for an excuse to postpone trial diets for as long as possible under the pretence that's it's down to somebody else's fault rather than the court's own institutional failings. Which is not to say that delays are never caused by the parties involved. Perhaps an expert report is awaited due to a backlog at a science lab. Another common reason is the unavailability of certain expert witnesses or defence counsel engaged elsewhere. There were only so many QCs who'd take on a murder defence, or, perhaps more correctly, who you'd want to take on a murder defence. Those counsel tended to be booked up well in advance. An accused had to decide whether to remain in prison until such time as their QC of choice was free, or else put their fate in the hands of someone less experienced. Salome Ramirez's defence didn't have that problem. I'd chosen counsel. She wasn't a QC, she was a solicitor advocate, but most importantly she was my wife, and she was primed and ready for action.

The Clerk managed to shoehorn in a diet of trial for the week before Christmas. The date was being read out when my name was called.

'I think your client wishes to communicate something, Miss Jordan,' the judge said.

Joanna nudged me. It's not the done thing for counsel to take instructions direct from a client in court. I went over to Salome and asked her what she wanted. Bail was the answer to my question.

'There needs to be a change of circumstances before I can ask for bail again,' I said. 'We've already appealed, and it was refused. What's changed?'

'I'm pregnant,' she said in a loud voice, and stood up, turning to stand in profile to show an obvious bump in her dress. She was always sitting down at our prison visits, and I'd put my client's weight gain down to lack of exercise, prison food and boredom Mars Bars. She didn't look it, but she had to be over three months pregnant because, though theoretically it was possible these days to conceive while in an all-women jail, I doubted there'd been any prison romance.

No sooner was Salome on her feet than there came a strangled cry from the back of the court and someone in the public gallery stood up. It was Dario.

'Sit down!' the clerk commanded. 'Both of you!' When Dario didn't obey, the Macer marched briskly from the side of the bench, and upon his signal two of the court cops set off in his direction.

I joined Joanna in the well of the court. 'You heard the pregnant lady,' I said. 'Move for bail.'

'M'Lady,' Joanna said. 'The defence has a motion at this stage to request a review of bail. As you may have heard—'

'Your client is expecting a child. Can you verify that?'

'Not medically, M'Lady. At least not immediately, but, perhaps you can see for yourself that—'

'How much!' Dario yelled, the cops either side of him not sure whether to lay hands on The Great One. 'How much to let my wife go?'

'If that's your client's husband he's liable to find himself in contempt of court,' the judge said.

'Offer caution,' I said to Joanna. 'Lots of it.'

'M'Lady, you know who my client's husband is. I'm advised he would be prepared to put up a sizeable sum in surety of bail, and my client's passport is already in the safe custody of her solicitor.'

Surprisingly, despite the outburst in her courtroom, Lady Carrick didn't dismiss the suggestion, and waved away the

AD opposition. The more I thought about it, the more I realised it was a no-brainer from the point of view of the judge. Why not let the accused out on bail for the short time left before her trial? According to the Advocate depute she'd be going off on a life sentence anyway. Until then, with no passport and the wife of one of the world's top footballers, she was hardly going to disappear. Worst case scenario, Salome skipped bail leaving behind a hefty wad of cash. If nothing else, it would make for one hell of a Scottish Courts & Tribunal Service Christmas party. The most likely outcome was that she wouldn't, and the judge could come across as having been sympathetic to the plight of incarcerated pregnant woman.

'Five hundred thousand pounds,' Lady Carrick said. One hundred thousand pounds for every week between then until the trial. It was a lot, but less than I'd expected.

Dario had been ushered into the aisle, with the two police officers still in attendance. From where I was seated, he looked to have tears in his eyes. Without another word he pushed past the cops and out of the courtroom.

Chapter 28

One phone-call was all it took for Dario to arrange the transfer of Salome's bail money. Half an hour later, Joanna and I were standing outside the High Court having waved off our client and her husband.

Joanna flicked a finger at the statue of David Hume, sitting in the off-the-shoulder toga that he would never have worn in real life. Covered in verdigris, he looked more like the incredible Hulk taking a break between rampages than a hero of the Scottish Enlightenment. 'I can't look at that statue without remembering Marc Traynor kicking it out of frustration. I was so impatient with him that day, and in such a hurry to get away just because it was raining. I should have noticed the signs.'

'How could you, Jo, if his own family didn't? A lot of our clients are in a state of distress. That's why they come to see us.'

'Then maybe we should pay more attention to their mental wellbeing.'

'Maybe we should,' I said. 'But we're lawyers, not psychologists. We can't ask every client if they're thinking of topping themselves.'

'Don't, Robbie.'

'You know what I mean. We tried our best. You tried your best. We were dealt a hand—'

'From a stacked deck. Well, I'm not letting anything happen to Salome. Especially not now she's pregnant. Can you imagine her child growing up without a mum?' I sort of could since I'd never known my mum. 'I'm going to show that lot in there what I'm made of.'

'Is this about you or the client?' I said. 'Stop taking things so personally.'

Joanna squeezed out a laugh. 'You're one to talk.'

We parted company at the top of Cockburn Street, Joanna heading for the train back to Linlithgow, me heading for a destination further down the Royal Mile where I met Peter Falconer leaving his office. The sports agent was dressed casually and wearing a pair of very white trainers.

'You're early,' he said. 'It's time for my walk. I'm trying to do six thousand steps a day. We can talk on the hoof.'

I was going to ask him why his target was six thousand not ten thousand steps, until it became apparent that one of Lang Pete's steps was about one and a half times longer than mine.

'Right,' he said after we'd crossed the road and were walking in front of the Scottish Parliament. 'Malky says you're ready to let bygones be bygones and quit harping on about that fee you never got.'

It's not easy to talk while biting your tongue, but I managed it enough to indicate I was prepared to overlook past injustices.

'Good. Now what's this really urgent thing Malky wants you to talk to me about?'

'He'd like you to do him a favour. They're going to cancel his contract with Scotgoals because of something stupid he said.'

Peter laughed. 'The Nancy-boy thing? I heard about that. It was all over Twitter. He should have known better. It's not the first time he's opened that big gob of his and put his foot in it.'

'This is Malky we're taking about,' I said. 'Operating mouth before brain is engaged has always been a problem.'

'And you want me to get him his job back? How am I supposed to do that? I've had dealings with Colin Lancaster before. The face of a dead mongoose, and the personality to go with it. I'm never going to talk him into taking Malky back. I've absolutely no clout with the man.'

We skirted the paddling pools, or whatever the things are that the crisp packets float in outside the Parliament building, and made our way onto Horse Wynd, opposite the gates to Holyrood Palace. I really hoped Peter wasn't planning a walk up Arthur's seat. I was having enough difficulty keeping pace with him on the flat.

'Lancaster wants an interview with Dario,' I said. 'I'd intended to approach the subject more gradually, but my dress shoes weren't made for a route march, and, if nothing else, my words caused Peter to screech to a halt, allowing me time to catch my breath.

'Oh, is that all? Shall I see if I can get the Pope and Elvis to come along too? Make a night of it.'

'Lancaster will renew Malky's contract if Dario goes on Scotgoals for an interview,' I said, adding, while Peter was choking on his next words, 'What's the big problem? He can talk about his book. It could be part of the book tour. You're bound to be lining up a few interviews, chat shows and things to promote—'

'It's not happening,' Peter said. 'Malky's going to have to think of something else if he wants to save his job.'

'Really? Then let me tell you Malky's alternative idea. It's to go to the new FastFreez store where Lancaster's daughter's the manager and chat her up.'

'What good will that do?'

'Naturally she will fall head over heels, and Malky reckons if he can trifle with her affections long enough, she'll talk her dad into forgetting the whole Nancy-boy thing. After that he'll kick her into touch like she's got Mitre written down her back.'

Peter laughed. 'Sounds like a Malky idea right enough. Trouble is it might just work.'

I didn't think so. Best case scenario, Annette Lancaster would tell him to sling his hook, no matter how insane a possibility my brother thought that might be. Worst case he broke the poor girl's heart. Either way I couldn't see Annette Lancaster's father changing his mind because his daughter had the hots for a has-been footballer. 'I'm serious Peter. It's an interview with Dario or nothing. I thought you and Malky were friends—'

'We are. Sort of. More acquaintances really.'

'He's helped you out over the years with events you've hosted, hasn't he?' I said, as Malky had instructed.

Peter shrugged. 'True.'

'He's never let you down when someone calls off from a sportsman's dinner, has he? No, he's always been happy to step into the breach.'

Malky's readiness to accept invitations to a free meal, drinks and the chance to make an after-dinner speech about how great a footballer he'd once been, wasn't too much of a shock to my system, but I latched on. 'And all he's asking in return is that you do him this one small favour.'

'One absolutely, huge, impossible favour.'

'Come on, Pete. You're Dario's agent—'

'I'm not.' The big man started walking again. He crossed the road and I had to wait until a car passed before I could catch up with him.

'Malky told me you were.'

'I'm not, but I am,' he said, not making things an awful lot clearer.

'I don't understand. You either are or you aren't. Which is it?'

'I *was* his agent.'

'Then who should I be speaking to?'

'You don't speak to Dario's agents, Robbie. They speak to you. And if they do, you'd better listen.'

'What do you mean?'

'Colombian neckties is what I mean. You know, where they cut a person's throat and pull their tongue—'

'No way, Pete.'

'Maybe not, but I wasn't going to test the theory.'

We continued through the car park at the foot of Arthur's seat and into Holyrood Park. Some students were playing football, jerseys for goal posts. We took to one of the narrow tracks through the grass worn away by footfall. I'd no idea where we were going but didn't care.

'Are you saying Dario's agents threatened you?' I found that hard to believe. Football agency is a big money business and most of its businessmen didn't go to business school. Where there's millions to be made exploiting young footballers and their families, there's also organised crime in the background. Pete swam in that pool. He knew people who knew people that most people would rather not know. Who was heavy enough to threaten him?

'This is in strictest confidence, Robbie. I mean it. Not a word to anyone. If this ever leaks out, I'll know who it was. When Dario came from Colombia to Glasgow, he was sixteen coming on seventeen. It was a great piece of scouting by Rangers. The boy was always going to go places. I had him signed up on a five-year contract for ten percent of his earnings, and let me tell you, at the start, that was ten percent of not very much. I took care of everything. I found him a flat, gave him financial advice, got him his first car... The time I spent on him, I was actually losing money, but I could see the potential. By the time he'd turned nineteen every big club in the world was looking at him. This was going to be my big pay day.'

'What happened?' I asked, assuming something must have happened otherwise he wouldn't be telling me the story nor would he be looking like someone had stolen his last chip.

'The day the offer from Real Madrid came in, two men turned up at my office. They were lawyers acting for a sports agency that dealt mainly with Latin American sports stars. They said it would be in mine and Dario's best interests if their clients took over control of his affairs. I mentioned the contract I had with Dario. They put a suitcase on the table. It had… Let's just say there was a lot of money staring me in the face, but I knew it was peanuts compared to ten percent of Dario's next move. They said I should take the money and gave me a document to sign. I asked them to leave. They refused. I could have thrown them both onto the street without having to breathe heavy. One of them took out a mobile phone. I still remember it. It was one of those Motorola's with the big silver buttons and stubby aerial. He punched in a number and handed it to me. Someone answered and the next voice I heard was my wife's. She wasn't scared or anything. She said a couple of men were at the house who insisted she call me to find out if I was interested in buying some neckties from Colombia. I told her that she should tell them no thanks and I'd see her when I got home.'

'You signed?'

'Right there on the dotted line. Of course, I got my own lawyer onto it straightaway. You remember him, Gordon Devine?' I did. Devine was also a man with a great many shady contacts. He'd offered me a job once. That was before someone had blown his head off.[4] 'Gordon made some enquiries and told me I'd made the correct decision. It was him who told me about the agency and rumours of torture and murder.'

'Why does Malky think you're still Dario's agent if all this was over fifteen years ago?' I asked, as we took a small flight of stairs onto Milton Street. If we were walking a circuit back to Peter's office, we were around about the halfway mark.

[4] Duty Man – Book 2

'Because Dario's retirement from football has caused certain people a cash flow problem. Also, he's lost a lot of money recently.'

He couldn't have lost that much, I thought. Not if he could dig up five hundred thousand in readies inside half an hour.

'I'm talking big money, Robbie. He was advised to get into shipping, so he bought shares in some boats. And I'm not talking sailing dinghies. This was a fleet of ships, exporting/importing cargo all around the world. Except some of the cargo was seized when it was being loaded in transit by a speed boat from a beach in Aruba.'

'Cocaine?'

'Two hundred kilos. The authorities confiscated the drugs and every ship he, and certain others, held an interest in. It cost him millions in legal fees and, I suspect, bribes, just to keep his name out of it. A lot of people lost a lot of money, and Dario lost more than most. Dario's agents might be serious people, but the Colombian government has the biggest gang. For the time being, I'm allowed to do what I can to bring in some dosh, and they're letting me handle Dario's book deal, at least the UK side of things. You know what Scottish football fans are like.'

I did. Someone plays for their team for five minutes, it doesn't matter where the player goes after that, he still belongs to them.

'Decent bit of business for you,' I said.

'They know I get on well with Dario. He's never forgotten what I did for him back when he was starting out. I even arranged for his girlfriend to be brought over from Colombia with his parents so he wouldn't be homesick. She was only fifteen. You've no idea the problems I had with immigration.'

'Salome Ramirez?'

'Yes, and she's turned out to be a decent bit of business for you, I hear.'

'So how come no mob lawyer has come to see me and asked to take over her case?' I said.

'She's of no interest to them. In fact, they'd love it if she was out of the way. She's always been the fly in the ointment. They think they control Dario, but up until now it's been Salome at the helm. When his agents wanted Dario to leave Real so they could cash in on another mega transfer deal, Salome wouldn't hear of it. She liked Spain and had no wish to move to rainy Manchester. After that, for his last couple of years, the big move was China, but she preferred the States, and you know where he ended up – California not Changchun. What could they do? Threaten Dario's sweetheart? That would be killing the Golden Goose.'

'This is also confidential, then,' I said. 'Did you know Dario was looking for advice on a divorce?'

'Yes, he told me that.'

'When?'

'A few days ago. We were discussing the book launch. He will be doing an interview, by the way, and it is going to be televised live. Tell Malky I'm sorry, but the rights were sold to SKY before a word of the autobiography was written.'

'What did Dario say to you – about the divorce?'

'He loves the girl, but she's mid-thirties. They've been trying for a kid for years with no luck. She's been to umpteen clinics.'

'What about him?'

'Who? Mr Macho? Don't dare suggest he could be shooting blanks. No, leaving Salome will be tough on him, but he's determined to start a football lineage. Hell, his agents have probably had Real Madrid sign his sperm up on pre-contracts. I don't think it will be too difficult for him to find a fertile young thing looking to wed a handsome thirty-six-year-old multimillionaire, superstar.'

'He won't have to,' I said. 'Salome's pregnant.'

The pavement narrowed, and we had to walk single file to the end of the street. When we reached the give way sign and turned left, Peter stopped to look at me. 'When did this happen?'

'The big announcement came this morning.'

'But Salome's been in jail.'

'She says she's twenty weeks and counting. She's been inside for less than fifteen and now she's out.'

'Out of jail? Not guilty?'

'Not yet. We got her out on bail pending the trial in a few weeks' time.'

'I'm glad for her,' Peter said, when we'd started walking again. 'She's a lovely girl, and a good influence on Dario. He's stubborn, but he met his match in Salome. I hope you get her off. How can they think she could kill anyone?'

'The man Salome's meant to have killed, Armando Diaz. Did you ever have any dealings with him?' I asked, when we'd reached the end of Abbeyhill and gone under the railway bridge.

'Never met him.' Peter's mobile phone rang. 'I'm just two minutes from the office, tell them to wait,' he said to whoever was on the other end of the call.

'He was an asset manager for a big firm with offices in London and Madrid. He dealt with Dario's finances. The two of them were pals. Dario was at his wedding. You don't think he'd be mixed up in—'

'Robbie, do not mention anything I've said to you to anyone and never bring up the subject again. You promised to keep this between us. You cannot tell anybody, and I mean *anybody*. Not Malky, not your wife, nobody. Tell Malky I'll phone Lancaster and see what I can do. I can't get a Dario interview, but I've others on the books he might be interested in.' He reached out, took hold of my tie and pulled me close. 'Seriously, not a word. I might not like your taste in neckties, but they're a sight better than the Colombian versions.'

166

Chapter 29

I parked at the front of West Hope House and walked around to the rear of the building that backed onto a small forest. Clearly Armando had held the same view as Lord Rothschild who once said, "*No garden however small should be without at least two acres of rough woodland.*" Immediately outside the back door was an enclosed patio area with sandstone paving, a barbecue grill and some distressed garden furniture that was in need of oiling. The patio was accessed via a small wrought iron gate where I was greeted by Beverly's pair of highly excitable golden retrievers whose loud barking had announced me while I was still a distance away.

The name Rosemary Dow, West Hope's cook/housekeeper, who appeared on the indictment's witness list, had conjured up for me a homely, dimple-faced, middle-aged woman, hair in a bun and clad in a full-length white apron. The sort of person who could whip you up a batch of fruit scones and a Victoria sponge while still finding time to do a spot of ironing. Instead, the person who met me at the back door had to be early thirties at most. She was pretty and slim and dressed in the sort of martial art gear that comes in handy if you're attacked by a person wearing pyjamas. All tied about her waist by a thick orange belt.

'Robbie Munro,' I said. 'I'm looking for Rosemary Dow.'

'That's me,' she replied. 'What do you want?'

This is the awkward part because the person you've come to precognosce has absolutely no obligation to speak to you. The trick is not to let the witness think they have a choice in the matter.

'Miss—'

'Mrs.'

'Mrs Dow, I'm here to ask you a few questions about the murder of Armando Diaz,' I said flashing my Law Society ID Card like it was a detective's gold shield.

The karate cook sized me up, didn't see anything to be unduly worried about, and without another word let me into the kitchen. Leaving me standing on the cold stone flagstones, she shoved the dogs out the back door with the sole of a trainer and closed it behind her. Then she went over to the AGA range, ladled out a bowl of tomato soup and set it and a glass of orange squash in front of a small boy who was sitting at the kitchen table.

'I don't want soup, Mum. I want a piece on tuna,' he said.

The housekeeper skiffed the boy's hair with the flat of her hand. 'Don't say piece, say sangwidge. There's a lawyer here.'

'But it's lunchtime and I'm hungry. Soup's just like hot water, but with stuff in it.'

'I've got one about the same age,' I said. 'A girl. I didn't realise how little I knew about everything until she came along and started putting me right. The trouble with us parents is that we're not young enough to know everything.'

But even my best JM Barrie lines weren't cracking a light. The housekeeper buttered a thick slice of white bread, cut it into two and placed it next to the boy's soup bowl.

'I wanted triangles,' the boy said.

'Triangles are just squares with three sides.' She walked to the far end of the table from her soup-slurping son and gestured to the chair across from her. 'Could you make it quick? My Aikido class starts in an hour. I've got to finish up here and then drop him off at his gran's.' She jerked her head in the boy's direction, like she was sticking the nut in him. 'He woke up this morning not feeling well and then astonished medical science the minute the school bus left without him.'

I sat down at the table, took out my notebook and opened it to a clean page. 'I'm the lawyer for Salome Ramirez,' I said. At mention of my client's name, I could see the excitement flicker in her eyes. 'I take it you've met her?'

'Dario's wife? Of course. She's lovely.'

'How often did Salome come here?'

'Beverly and Mr Diaz have only lived here for three years, but I'd say she's been coming here off and on, maybe two or three times a year. She stayed here for a few weeks before the wedding to help out, but usually Dario comes here more than Salome. He flies in for a day or two, either business or shooting, usually both, then goes back to Spain or wherever.'

'Dario and Mr Diaz were good friends?'

'Yes, they did a lot of shooting together. And Mr Diaz did work for him. Accountancy or whatever. I never really met Dario. Saw him around, but he kept himself to himself. I had Salome have him sign a shirt for my Andy.'

'You a big Dario fan, then?' I called down to the boy at the other end of the table whose poor health hadn't affected his appetite any.

'Who's Dario?' The boy wanted to know.

'Not him,' his mum said to me. 'Andy's my other half and an even bigger wean than that one. As for Salome, I don't know what more I can tell you. I've already given a statement to the police.' I didn't doubt it, but it would be a while before I saw that statement, and if the police had asked the same questions as I intended to, they would only have noted the answers they liked. 'Seems a waste of time if you ask me.'

'Salome was staying here the weekend before... Before it all happened. You know. With Mr Diaz.'

'That's right. Saturday teatime, Bev's mum was ill, and she was going to see her before she and Mr Diaz went on honeymoon. Bev phoned me at home to ask if I'd mind coming in and freshening up one of the guest rooms.' I noticed it was always Bev and Mr Diaz. Possibly reference to the age difference.

'You don't live in, then?' I said.

'No, Blackness. Just down the road. I'm used to working funny hours, and the job comes with a car. I've been here since they bought the place. The previous owner, Mrs Reid-Kerr, put a good word in for me.'

'You'll already have been asked this by the police, but where were you the day Mr Diaz…' I glanced down at the boy who was dipping chunks of bread into his soup and getting most of it in his mouth. 'Died?'

'That was just a usual Monday for me. I don't start 'til half-eight, nine,' she said, getting up from the table to rip off a strip of kitchen roll and stuff it down the collar of her son's jumper as a napkin.

'And what was a usual Monday like when Mr Diaz was still alive?' I asked, when she came back to my end of the table and sat down again.

'I'd usually come in, speak to Bev or Mr Diaz, see what kind of thing they fancied for lunch and dinner that week, and go to the shops if I needed anything. I make the food. I don't serve it. I leave it in the fridge or on the hob. After that I do whatever else needs done: laundry mostly, though a lot of that goes to the dry cleaners. I eat my lunch here. My hours are flexible. I can more or less come and go when I like. The last thing I do every day is feed the dogs, and I try to be finished and home by half three for his lordship coming in from school. I've told the police all this.'

'I know, but it could be a while before I get to see your statement,' I said. 'Did you see Salome that day?'

'Yes, I took her breakfast in bed. Mr Diaz had his downstairs. I went to the shops and when I got back before lunch, Salome was gone and Mr Diaz was out the back. He does a lot of that clay pigeon shooting. He's got an automatic thingummy that he loads up and shoots away. Those clay pigeons look nothing like pigeons by the way. Sometimes he goes after real ones, and I've got to make something with them. Trying to get all the shot out of them is a right bugger. There was this time I missed some, and—'

'You would have heard the sound of a gun firing even here in the kitchen, wouldn't you?'

'If I'd been here.'

'So, Mr Diaz must have died after you'd left at half past three?'

'Not exactly. More like after three o'clock. With Bev and Salome away and not knowing when they'd be back, Mr Diaz told me to make something cold for him, leave it in the fridge and I could go home early. I went to the shops, came back, made a chicken salad and went home. I was giving the boy his tea when the cops phoned and told me to get here pronto.'

'So, you wouldn't know if Salome came back or if she did what time that was?'

'No, I do. It was the back of five. It's on the security camera. There's one at the big gates and there's others at the front and sides of the house. In fact, there's cameras everywhere except outside the back door. I suppose the dogs are a big enough deterrent.' I doubted it. They might do a lot of barking, but I reckoned the two animals I'd encountered would be anyone's friend for a handful of treats and a tummy tickle. 'The security system is in a cupboard in the hall. It's quite old. Mrs Reid-Kerr had it put in after her husband died. I'm the only one who knows how to work it. Mr Diaz was hopeless with stuff like that. The police took a copy of everything that happened that day. I think it only keeps twenty-four hours and then overwrites itself. I showed them where it was, and they made a copy and had me sign some wee brown cardboard things.'

'Labels,' I said. 'For court. They need to keep the chain of evidence intact.'

171

She shrugged. 'They watched some of it before they made the copy. It showed Salome coming back. She parked outside, sat there for a while and then just walked in the door. There's no cameras inside the house, and the alarm isn't switched on during the day obviously. Not if folk are in.'

'And you won't know if Mr Diaz was dead or alive then?'

'What do you mean?'

'If Salome…' I looked down at the table where the boy was listening intently while spooning in soup. 'You know, if she did what they're saying she did, she would either have to have done it first thing before she left or after she came back.'

'He was definitely alive when I left about three o'clock. I could hear him shooting down at the range.'

'Where's that?'

'If you walk down the side of the house for, I don't know, a hundred yards, probably more, there's an outbuilding and a big space for shooting. Bang, bang, bang. Just about every day. You get used to it.'

'It looks like it was Salome who found Mr Diaz in the study. Why would she go in there?'

The housekeeper shrugged. 'Maybe to talk to him. They were very pally. Or just to go somewhere quiet. Salome's a great reader. When she's here and Mr Diaz and Dario are talking or away somewhere or out shooting, and Bev's writing one of her books, Salome sits in the study and reads. If you ask me, when she came back that day she went into the study for a quiet read and found him.'

The boy had finished his soup and bread. He jumped down from the table. 'Can I take the dogs into the woods, Mum?'

'If you're feeling that much better, maybe I should drop you off at school for the afternoon.'

The wee face above the red-spattered kitchen roll fell. He folded his arms on the tabletop and laid his head on them.

Taking the side of the defence becomes a habit. 'Exploring the woods sounds fun,' I said. 'It could be like a nature trip. Learn more doing that than an afternoon stuck in a classroom.'

I hadn't noted anything. The best precognitions are taken when the notebook is closed. Witnesses are more relaxed and unguarded in what they say. I stood up and looked down at the witness.

'Mr Diaz's death. What do you think happened?' I asked.

She snorted. 'Well, it wasn't Salome. I can tell you that.'

'Why are you so sure?'

'Have you tried firing one of those guns? Mr Diaz had guests up here in the summer. I took them out some food, and they talked me into having a go. Nearly tore the shoulder off me, and I work out.'

'So, who then?' I thought was the obvious next question.

'There was no one else here, so I suppose he must have done it to himself…'

This was more like it. 'Why would he do that?'

'Who knows why anyone does anything?'

'Can I ask you something personal,' I asked, and took her silence as consent. 'Was Mr Diaz… Did he ever… With you… Harass—'

'Did he ever try it on with me? He'd try it on with anyone. Couldn't keep his hands to himself. He only stopped his nonsense when I told him I knew Aikido and could break a man's arm in three places. I can't, of course.' She patted her orange belt. 'Not yet.'

'You've been very helpful' I said. 'I'll let Salome know.'

She looked pleased at that. 'Before I go do you think—'

'Down the hall, on the—'

'No, I was going to ask if I could see where Mr Diaz did his shooting.'

She stood up. 'Right buggerlugs.' At his mother's voice, the wee boy looked up from his sulk. 'Half an hour. Then you're going to your gran's. Take the lawyer and the dogs down to the shooting range. It'll save them shitting on the slabs out there, and me having to clean it up.' I wasn't sure if she was talking about me, the dogs or both, but the words were scarcely out of her mouth than the wee boy had jumped down from his chair, yanked open the back door, and me and a couple of overweight golden retrievers were doing our best to keep up.

Chapter 30

Next day, having spent most of the morning trying to persuade Sheriff Brechin it wasn't mandatory to jail all my clients, around about lunchtime I was inside the court café trying to get on the outside of a cheese and ham toastie, when Hugh Ogilvie the Procurator Fiscal joined me.

'Joanna all set for the big case?' He ripped a corner off my toastie, dropped it into his mouth and leaned back in his chair. 'The pair of you must really be raking it in with all your private client work. Who needs Legal Aid, eh?'

'That's right Hugh,' I said, moving my lunch out of reach. 'These days I bathe only in the finest vintage champagnes.'

'Come off it, Robbie. You had that private-paying date-rape a few months ago—'

'Where my client killed himself, and I could hardly ask his parents to stump up.'

'Then there was Isabella Ewart—'

'Who bumped me for most of my fee.'

Ogilvie was laughing so much he almost choked on the piece of toastie. 'I'd say serves you right, but wasn't that your defence? *Served him right*? Seems like everyone got what they deserved apart from your client. She deserved the jail. Still, this case for the footballer's wife...' He put a hand to his ear. 'Is that a cash register I hear in the distance? What's your defence by the way? I'm told it was all very secret squirrel at the Preliminary Hearing. You wouldn't be trying to spring a surprise come the trial, would you?'

I took a bite of toastie to save me from having to reply.

'Suicide's probably your best shot, no pun intended. Old Armando got some bad news, retired to the study to clean his shotgun and took the honourable way out.'

Had I said too much to Beverly and word filtered back from there? Or was suicide really the only obvious alternative if Salome wasn't claiming self-defence or incriminating anyone?

Ogilvie wiped his lips with my napkin, screwed it up and left it beside my paper plate. 'And yet, what news could a multi-millionaire get that was bad enough to shoot himself? No health problems according to his medical records, and he was a private banker, so honourable doesn't really come into it either. I think your best bet would be tragic accident. What's your firearms expert got to say about it all? That's right. You don't have one. Or at least there's not one on your witness list. All you have is Prof Bradley and some psychologist or other without a report between them.'

'I'm in the process of tracking down a firearms expert,' I said. 'Unlike your expert, an independent one. Not a person who's employed by the same police force that's charged my client with murder.'

Ogilvie smiled like an eel. 'Thought there'd be a reason you were hanging about here eating a rubber toastie. You're trying to catch Laszlo Derry, aren't you? No expense spared right enough.'

Laszlo Derry was Scotland's most well-known countryside conservationist, often to be seen on TV burrowing through the brush and branches in search of wildcat lairs, capercaillie nests and red squirrel dreys. Not that all wildlife was safe when Derry was around. Birds of a feather might flock together, but grouse and pheasant quickly dispersed when the man in tweeds came striding through the heather at them. Derry was a firearms' expert, one recognised by defence lawyers as being open-minded when it came to defence scenarios. In fact, it was said the more open your client's wallet, the more open his mind. Most of my cases being Legally Aided, Derry's fee structure was usually well out of reach. 'Is he here?' I asked.

'Don't give me that,' Ogilvie said. 'Derry's here to give evidence in a civil proof. Something about common shooting rights.'

'What can I say, Hugh? You've sussed me out again.' Leaving the OF and the rest of the toastie behind, I wandered across the stone-floored atrium of Livingston's soulless Civic Centre and waited at the foot of the stairs leading down from the Sheriff Court. Ten minutes later, bang on one o'clock, my target arrived.

'Mr Derry?' I said, recognising the man from the many times I'd seen him on TV. The striped tie, that may have borne some old school affiliation, clashed like the Titans with the checked shirt beneath his tweed jacket. He was a lot smaller than I thought. Older too, somewhere in his sixties, but with a military bearing. The sort of person who could wear crimson corduroy breeks in public without anyone questioning his sanity.

'Can I help you?' he said, looking down at me from three steps up through a pair of fantastically bushy eyebrows.

'I hope so,' I replied. 'I'm Robbie Munro. I'm a solicitor, and —'

He held up a hand. 'Sorry, I'm still to give evidence. I don't think I should be speaking to any lawyers.' He walked down the last few steps and brushed past me heading for the exit.

'I'm not interested in the case you're here for,' I called after him. 'I'm looking for an opinion from a firearms expert in a criminal case.'

He stopped and turned. 'What kind of firearms? Who's your client? If it's Legal Aid you can —'

'A shotgun. My client is Salome Ramirez.' The name didn't seem to ring any bells at first and then slowly he nodded his head a few times. 'The woman charged with murdering Armando Diaz?'

'That's right.'

'Shame. Damn fine shot, Armando.'

'You knew him?'

'Knew of him more than actually knew him. I did meet him pigeon shooting at Drumlanrig once. I presented him with a prize. That was years ago. I think Jackie Stewart was there that day. Now, let me see, when was that…?'

My expert being chummy with the murder victim wasn't the greatest start to a professional relationship with the man I hoped would lean the weight of his expert opinion against the wheel of the murder-accused's defence.

'I'd like your opinion on a line of defence,' I said.

'Accident?'

'I suppose you shooters get a lot of those,' I said.

'Not shooters who know what they're doing.' He pulled a tin of small cigars from his jacket pocket. 'Now if you don't mind…'

I followed him to the set of big glass doors and outside. The rain had stopped, but the wind had picked up and an impertinent ball of sun was attempting to shimmy its way past a scrum of grey clouds. 'Could I run a scenario past you to see what you think about it?' He looked over his shoulder at me as though I was a fart he'd let go earlier and was trying to disown. 'There'd be a fee of course,' I said.

At the mention of money, Derry stopped. He raised his chin, stared across the River Almond into the distance, closed his eyes and breathed deeply. 'Been stuck in that witness room since half-nine this morning. Good to get a breath of fresh air at last.' He removed a short cigar from the tin and stuck it between his lips precisely below the yellow stain on his greying moustache.

'It's a thousand for a consultation.' he said. 'Guineas.'

Guineas? A guinea was a pound and a shilling in old money, wasn't it? So that meant a thousand pounds and a thousand five pences – one thousand and fifty pounds. 'That's not a problem,' I said.

He lit up, took a puff and blew smoke skyward. 'Okay, fire away.'

'I thought it might be easier if we could inspect the shotgun together,' I said. 'It'll have been lodged in court, but, if not, I can arrange a visit at the police custodier's so that you—'

Derry coughed dramatically. He picked a loose piece of tobacco from his tongue, flicked it away and flapped his hand at me. 'Steady, old darling. Not so fast. The consultation. This is it. We're having it now. Right here.' He pointed at the damp tarmac path on which we were both standing in case I was unsure exactly where here was. 'I've no time to be traipsing all over the countryside looking at shotguns and reconstructing murders. Just tell me what you think happened and I'll let you know how plausible it sounds.'

'How much do you know about Armando Diaz's death?' I asked.

'Not a lot other than I understand he was shot dead in his own home.'

'You've heard of Dario?'

'Footballer isn't he?'

'Yes, his wife's been charged with shooting Armando. She's my client, and Dario's a man who avoids publicity. What I'm telling you must remain confidential.'

Derry grunted his assent through a billow of smoke.

The defence think—'

'Don't tell me. It was an accident? Can't see it. There's no way a responsible shooter like Armando Diaz is going to be wandering around the family home with a loaded shotgun.'

'But clearly he was. That's why I think Armando shot himself.'

'I've already told you—'

'Not by accident. I think he meant to kill himself.'

'Really? Didn't strike me as the suicidal type. Then again, I only met him the once. I suppose you never can tell. Anyway, I'm not a shrink. Tell me more about the gun.'

'I don't know much about guns, that's why I wanted you to see it.'

'For now, describe it to me.'

'It's a twelve bore.'

'Up and under or side-by-side?'

'The firearm report says it was a single barrel shotgun. Is that unusual?'

Derry shrugged. 'Not really. Not for an expert skeet-shooter, and if I remember correctly Armando was a champion DTL-er.' He looked at me through a haze of bluish smoke. 'DTL – mean anything to you?' It didn't. 'Down the line. It's a type of clay pigeon shooting. The clays are released one at a time at the same height, but from different angles. After a certain number of shots, usually five, the shooter moves to a different location—'

'Down the line?'

'Yes, it's a crescent shaped line with four stations. In most competitions competitors shoot at one hundred clays over the day, three points for a first barrel kill, two if it takes a second shot. The perfect score is three hundred. The top shooters, at least the ones who like to show off a bit, occasionally use a one-barrel gun to give the others a chance. I expect Armando would use a double-barrel when competition shooting, but a single barrel job is great for practising. Focuses the mind. Any more info on the make of gun?'

'It was an old one. Italian, I think. Something Lombardi.'

'Ivo Lombardi?'

I was sure that was the name. 'I'd be really grateful if you could take a look,' I said.

'No need.' One last drag and he stubbed the cigar butt out on the sole of his ox-blood brogue. 'I've got one myself. My father's actually. Don't make them anymore. Haven't since

180

the Fifties. Custom made jobs. Twenty-six-inch barrel, a lot shorter than they use today. Beautifully light and well balanced, easy to bring to bear. A fine gun if you've ten grand lying about to spend on it.' He pulled up the sleeve of his jacket, checked his watch and decided there was time for another smoke.

'The shorter barrel would make it easier to shoot yourself, don't you think,' I said, hopefully.

'You certainly wouldn't need such long arms,' Derry said, dryly, lighting up his small cigar. 'How are you saying he did it?'

'Single round to the chest.'

'That would make it more difficult. Then again, Armando was a tall chap and if he bent over sufficiently... Would probably have to have propped the gun against the floor. Newton's third law and all that. The angle of the blast would have been upwards. You'd need to see the chaps at the morgue about that.'

'The forensic pathologist I've spoken to reckons Armando was shot at close range. A couple of metres at most because they found the fibrous wadding from the cartridge in the wound. Closer than that he couldn't say. He felt it was something for a firearm's expert to give an opinion on.'

Derry tapped ash off to the side, watched it fall and tumble along the path, and took another drag. He looked at his watch again. 'Ideally, I'd need to test fire the weapon with the same type of cartridge and then compare the shot pattern with the wounds. That'll already have been done I expect. Happy to scan the reports you've received and see if there's anything they've overlooked or can be queried. Let's consult again once you're apprised of all the facts.' And he was apprised of another one thousand guineas I guessed.

'There's another thing,' I said. 'When they found the gun, the barrel was broken and the spent cartridge was on the floor not far away. How could that happen? Could the gun have broken open when it was dropped, and the cartridge ejected itself?'

'It's possible,' Derry agreed. 'Ivo Lombardi's are all ejectors. Helps for speed of reloading. The barrel breaking open would be quite likely if it fell onto a hard enough surface. The cartridge could easily have popped out.' I remembered the hardwood floor of Armando's study. Derry was getting into his stride. 'Like most pre-Sixties' models, Lombardi's don't have the same locking mechanisms as the modern guns. A lot of them don't even have safety catches, or, if they do, they rely on cross-bolt safety catches that prevent the trigger being pulled. Drop one of those old guns, even a modern one, and inertia can trip the sear and cause it to fire.'

I didn't know what a sear was, other than I assumed it was part of a shotgun's internal mechanism, but it didn't matter.

'Would you take a look at the shotgun and, if you're right about what you say, testify in court?' I asked. He wrinkled his leathery face. 'I know you're a busy man, and I'd make sure you were fully remunerated for your valuable time.'

He sighed. 'Look, Mr…'

'Munro.'

'I'm happy to consult, but sitting around in court… all the hassle of cross-examination. My reputation at stake…'

'What you've just told me could possibly save my client from going to prison for life, and her husband is an extremely wealthy man. If your evidence helped secure an acquittal, I know he'd be very grateful. I'd personally make sure you got… let's call it a win bonus.'

'And if I examine the gun and discover that it wouldn't break open and the cartridge eject itself. What then?'

'As I say, you'd be well paid for your time.'

'But I wouldn't be required for court?'

'No.'

'And the… What did you call it? Win bonus?'

'You'll appreciate that the suicide defence is dependent on the gun breaking open and the cartridge coming out. Armando could hardly have shot himself and then broken the barrel and ejected it.'

Derry's moustache twitched. He studied the glowing end of his small cigar. 'And what if...' Derry took a few rapid puffs and pinged the stub an impressive distance. 'Somebody else shot him?'

'What do you mean?'

'Have you heard of a snap-cap, Mr Munro?'

I hadn't. But I was a quick learner.

Chapter 31

I drove back to the office in buoyant mood, repeating over and over in my head my discussion with Laszlo Derry. The man was worth every additional five pence of his exorbitant fee. I could have hugged his tweed jacket and kissed his nicotine-stained moustache. To find a firearm expert prepared to back up one line of defence was the most I could have hoped for, and yet there had been Derry handing me a brace of them. My first instructions to Grace Mary were to lodge an additional witness list with his name on it and intimate it to the Crown.

When I got home from work that evening Joanna was on lifeguard duty with Jamie who was having a bedtime bath; something he tried to avoid as vigorously as he later defended his right to remain in the water when it was time to come out again.

'Oh good, you're back,' she said. 'Can you go and check on Tina to make sure she's doing her homework?'

She might as well have asked me to go check if Israel had laid down a welcome mat on the Golan Heights.

I knelt down beside her at the edge of the bath. 'What if someone else shot Armando?' I said.

'Someone other than himself you mean?' That was exactly what I meant. 'Oh, Robbie, make your mind up. First of all, we had the *he deserves it* defence then it was *oops it was an accident*, I thought we'd settled on suicide, and now you're suggesting what? Incrimination? Why not throw in an alibi too?'

I didn't see the problem. Surely the more potential defences the better? It wasn't our job to work out who done it. Our task was to raise a doubt that the person in the dock had done it.

Joanna was of a different mind. 'We want to present the jury with a single viable alternative to the Crown's position, not a selection of half-baked theories, and, when I say half-baked, some of your ideas haven't even seen the inside of the oven yet.'

'What's wrong with lots of possible scenarios?'

'It seems weak. Like we're clutching at straws. I like the suicide scenario. It's our best defence. And more importantly, it's the truth. Isn't it? What have you done about finding a firearms expert?'

'That's what I'm trying to say. I spoke to one today. As expected, he's more or less ruled out accident. He can't see any way Armando would have come into the house with a loaded weapon.'

'That's good for our suicide defence,' Joanna said. 'He obviously *did* come into the house with a loaded shotgun. I think that's our strongest point. What did the expert say about the problem of the shotgun being found with the barrel broken and the cartridge on the floor?'

'He thinks it could have happened when the gun was dropped. The gun could have broken open and the cartridge would have been ejected.'

'He's not even seen the gun yet and he's saying it's possible?'

'That's because he has a gun just like it.'

'Who is this expert?'

'Laszlo Derry,' I said.

Joanna placed the heel of a soapy hand against her temple. 'The guy from the telly who likes squirrels?'

I was pretty sure it was just red squirrels Laszlo Derry liked. I'd once heard him describe grey squirrels as the devil's oven mitts. I let it go. 'Derry is hugely experienced with shotguns, and just as importantly he's a great communicator.

A bit of star quality will impress the hell out of the jury. It was him who suggested someone else might have shot Armando.'

'Why would he say that?'

'Snap-caps,' I said.

'What on earth are they?'

'It's like this: with shotguns, especially old guns like the one Armando had in the study…'

'You mean the one he shot himself with?'

'Yes, but no, I'm talking about if he didn't shoot himself.'

'So… the gun somebody else shot him with?'

'No, nobody shot him with that gun. They shot him with their own gun and left unnoticed.'

'Then why was there a spent cartridge on the floor?'

'Just listen. Old fashioned shotguns have this… I can't remember what it's called exactly, the parts have all got weird names, but it's a trigger spring thing. And when you put them away for the night it's important to keep the pressure off —'

'The trigger-spring-thing?'

'Yes. So, what you do is fire the gun… But it's important not to fire an empty gun otherwise you'll damage something else inside it —'

'Something else you don't know the name of?'

'Yeah, or it might be the same thing.'

'The trigger-spring-thing?'

'Jo, I'm being serious here. This is a game changer.'

'Okay, sorry. Carry on.'

'Do you understand so far?'

'Don't worry. I'll stop you if you start getting too technical.'

'In order to stop damaging the… In order to stop any damage, you insert this thing that looks like a cartridge. It's called a snap-cap. Then you can pull the trigger safely. That takes the pressure of the spring-thing, and you can put the gun away. Derry thinks Armando, being an experienced shooter with a valuable old gun, would do that. In fact, he's willing to testify that Armando's most likely routine after he'd finished shooting for the day would be to insert a snap-cap into the barrel, fire the gun and then put the gun away in a secure cabinet, which as we know he had in his study. That's what he was doing when he was shot. That's why when the gun fell and broke open a spent cartridge was ejected onto the floor.'

Joanna hadn't interrupted me in a while and was now looking at me sympathetically, like I was Jamie trying to put together a two-thousand-piece jigsaw.

'But Robbie. It was a spent cartridge on the floor, not one of those snap-caps,' she said. Which was the very same thing I'd pointed out to Laszlo Derry.

'Yes, but, according to Derry, a lot of people don't bother buying snap-caps. Snap-caps are reusable. Some have a coating of oil on the exterior. They're good if you're storing the gun for long periods, but a regular shooter who's using the gun every few days, might simply use a spent cartridge, probably the last one he fired. For a one-off use it basically does the same thing.'

Joanna thought it over. 'It's an ingenious idea,' she said, absent-mindedly basting Jamie with soapy water. 'But if someone else did it, why did no one see them?'

I relayed my visit to West Hope House and the conversation I'd had with Rosemary Dow the karate cook.

'Are you saying there is a way into the house that isn't covered by the security cameras?'

I saw it for myself,' I said. 'Was given a guided tour and everything. You take a side road off the A904, jump a dyke, walk over a field, through a small, wooded area, over another wall and you're more or less in Armando and Bev's back garden. Once you've overcome the security of a couple of friendly golden retrievers, you can access the property through a kitchen door that's never locked during the day. From there it's a short dash to the study and... BLAM! Job done.'

Jamie laughed at my shotgun impression, splashed about a bit, and then went about the important matter of rescuing a drowning plastic dinosaur.

Joanna handed me a towel. 'If that did happen, and the person left undetected, it would look like the gun used was Armando's, leaving Salome, as the only person in the house at the time, to take the rap.' Joanna bent over and fished our squirming son out of the bath and into my waiting arms I wrapped the towel around him and carried him through to the bedroom.

'I'm not saying it wouldn't be better than the suicide theory, but the jury is going to want a motive. You're going to need to do some digging on Armando, and fast,' Joanna said. 'Find out if he had any enemies.'

'Well, someone couldn't have been all that keen on him otherwise they wouldn't still be picking pieces of him out of the Axminster,' I said.

'I wish you wouldn't say things like that,' Joanna said.

'Sorry Jo, but you know what I mean. The difficulty is going to be finding someone who knows if he did have enemies. You can't go and see Beverly, and I doubt if she'll talk to me again.'

Joanna thought about that while she pushed Jamie into his pyjamas. 'Set up a consultation with Salome. If she was good enough friends with Bev she might know if Armando was having problems with someone.'

'Why would she know that?'

'Because, Robbie, unlike men we women actually talk to each other and not just about football. It could be that Bev confided something in Salome that she doesn't realise the importance of. And then you should try to meet with Dario.'

'Do you think I haven't tried? I can't get near him. He's probably still annoyed about what happened at the wedding apart from anything else.'

'Maybe, but I've a feeling it will be easier now. Things have changed,' Joanna said. 'He's on Salome's side now.'

'Because she's pregnant? Pretty shallow, don't you think?'

Joanna didn't answer. Pyjamaed and hair combed, we took Jamie to the livingroom for supper and a story, catching Tina surfing Joanna's iPhone when she was supposed to be doing homework. I took the phone from her and replaced it with her homework sheets. Then Joanna sat me down on the sofa with Jamie on my knee while she went to put some bread in the toaster.

'We can arrange a meeting at Dario's place in the country,' Joanna said on her return with a cup of milk. Being forced to use one of the so-called unspillable versions, Jamie was determined to put it through its paces. 'I'll speak with Salome, woman to woman, and you can see if Dario will talk to you.'

'About football?'

'Very funny Robbie.'

'Tell you what,' I said. 'Why don't I speak with Salome, and you talk to Dario? After all you seemed to form a bond on the dance floor.'

'You know I can't speak to Dario. He's on the Crown witness list.'

She was right. My wife usually was. If the Crown got wind of the fact that she'd spoken to Dario about his wife's murder charge, they'd no doubt suggest she'd rehearsed his evidence. Something we didn't do in Scotland.

'Okay, I'll try and arrange a meeting with him,' I said. 'After all, I'm the one who should feel aggrieved. I mean, it was nice of him to try and intervene at the wedding, and it's a shame he fell over, but it was my wife's bum his pal was groping on the dance floor.'

Tina piped up, 'Was someone groping your bum, Mum?' The last I'd checked on my daughter she'd been sitting with a jotter on her knee dividing a mathematical cake into fractions. The longer her tongue stuck out the more difficult the sum.

'No. it's just a turn of phrase,' I said. 'And have you not finished cutting those cakes into pieces yet? You could have eaten the thing by now.'

But homework was furthest from my daughter's eight-and-a-half-year-old mind. 'Mum! Uncle Malky's just sent you a text asking if he can buy me a tracksuit from FastFreez for my Christmas!'

Joanna looked at me.

'Definitely not,' I said.

'But Flo's auntie's buying her one.' Sounded like Malky hadn't given up on his seduction idea and that Isabella Ewart had plans for spending her boxing winnings already. 'Flo says she's going to be in the Olympics when she's big. Mum, are you going to be in the Olympics?'

'No, I'm not,' Joanna said, firmly. 'Now, would you do as your dad says and please get on with your homework?'

'Not even for wrestling?'

The toast popped in the kitchen. 'What are you talking about, Tina? You'll do anything but homework, won't you? If you're stuck your dad will help once we've given Jamie his supper.'

'Why's Mum angry?' Tina asked, as Joanna went off to butter the toast.

'She's not angry,' I said. 'She's had a long day and just wishes you'd do your homework when you come in from school and not wait until the last minute and then start mucking about on her phone and asking all sorts of questions that have nothing to do with anything.'

'I only wanted to know if Mum was going to the Olympics. When you and Mum were wrestling in bed on Sunday morning—'

'Sunday? Oh, yeah, well, that was just for fun.'

'Flo says her aunt Isabella can throw the disc thing for miles, but the men can throw it even further. If Mum had you pinned down and you're a man she must be able to wrestle a woman and beat her.'

'I don't think your mum's quite ready for the Olympics yet.'

'But you said Mum was the best at wrestling.'

'That's because I am,' Joanna said, joining me on the sofa with a plastic plateful of PB&J toast squares. 'But I only like wrestling with your dad.'

'And look where your wrestling career got you,' I said, dumping Jamie on her lap. I beckoned to Tina.

She came over bringing her homework sheet; a page that showed a series of circles that represented cakes with questions alongside. Tina had divided them using a pencil that was blunter than a Yorkshireman. There was one left. 'I'm stuck, Dad. How can I cut it into pieces that are thirty-three and a third per cent?'

'It just means to cut it into three. Three, thirty-three-and-a-thirds make a hundred. And a hundred percent of anything means all of it. Try and keep them all the same size. Now off you go. And use a ruler.'

'Robbie?' Joanna said, feeding Jamie a square of toast. 'Where was Dario at the time of the murder? Does anyone know?'

'Who's Dario? Did he murder someone?' Tina asked. The girl had ears like GCHQ.

'Never mind,' I said. 'Go sharpen your pencil.'

'The rape,' Joanna whispered, after Tina had gone off to the kitchen with her pencil case. 'You don't think...'

In a split-second I was all over the idea like blue paint on Braveheart. 'Revenge? He found out about the rape, sneaked in the back door and shot Armando?'

I dropped into the sofa beside her.

'But he'd only know about…' I made sure Tina was still in the kitchen. 'The rape, if Salome had told him.'

'Maybe she did and she's covering for him. He owns shotguns,' Joanna said. 'And he'd know his way about West Hope House. She could have driven back with him, dropped him off in the country lane, and gone in through the front door while he was coming through the woods and in the back.' Joanna was on a roll. 'She waits in the car until Armando returns, then goes into the study because she knows he'll be coming in there to put his shotgun away. She stalls him long enough for Dario to come in and—'

Tina came back into the room with her pencil.

'Sounds plausible enough,' I said. 'But that's not a defence. That's art and part in a murder. Which was a better point than the one on the end of my daughter's pencil. The one she was now using to plough a furrow across her page. I laughed. 'It's going to be a bad enough result if we get one client convicted, but her husband as well? No, I doubt Dario's security team will let him out of their sight for five minutes far less allow him an unchaperoned day trip for a spot of murder on a Monday afternoon. He'll be alibied up to the ears.'

Joanna froze, a small square of toast in her hand and Jamie open-mouthed, looking like a hungry hatchling. 'Hold on a minute. If someone else did shoot Armando, and the cartridge on the floor was one he was using as a snap-cap thing, where's the actual cartridge that was fired? Wouldn't it come flying out?'

'They only come out if you break the barrel and then you have to pull the cartridges out if they don't eject themselves,' I said.

Joanna screwed up her nose. 'Without a possible motive or incriminee, I think we should stick with what we have - suicide. We've got Professor Bradley to say the fatal injury was close range. We've got Laszlo Derry to say it's physically possible, and why else would Armando have a loaded gun in his house? We've also got the psychologist to say Armando fitted the criteria for the type of person most likely to shoot themselves. What's more we have a client with a bombshell of a reason why he'd kill himself, one the Crown will never see coming, but which also ties in with Salome's injury and what she told the police about Armando deserving it. Salome would have no reason to say that if it was a stranger who killed him.' Joanna picked up a toastie square. Jamie had already been helping himself and was wearing quite a few of them. She popped it in my mouth. 'Suicide is the best defence, and it's all thanks to your efforts. With the trial just over a week away, all we need is to take final instructions from the client, and I'd say we were good to go.'

Chapter 32

It was a dreich, late-November morning when Joanna and I set off in the car; our destination the Great One's hunting lodge, just an hour or so's drive southeast of Edinburgh.

On arrival we were permitted entry by a man I recognised as the smaller of the two door stewards from Armando's wedding: the one who'd been very much against photographs. He revealed his diamond eyetooth in the practised smile of his that never troubled his eyes. I was half expecting to be frisked. Instead, he ushered us into a wood panelled room, the walls of which held shelves of books and hunting trophies. I looked at Joanna. She looked at me. Minus the shotgun and whisky cabinets, it was unnervingly like the study where Armando Diaz had met his end.

Our coats taken, coffee offered and accepted, we were joined by Salome and Dario as a silver tray of refreshments arrived via one of the staff. Before Dario sat down Joanna thought she should put him right on something.

'I'm afraid you're on the witness list... Dar... Mr—'

'Dario is fine,' he said.

'Well, Dario, because you are a potential Crown witness at Salome's trial you can't be here while we talk to Salome.'

Dario looked at Joanna as though he'd heard the phrase *"you can't"* somewhere before in a time long ago but couldn't quite place it.

Joanna clarified what should have been obvious. 'If it came out in court that you'd been at a consultation with Salome and her legal representatives, you'd be accused of colluding.'

'But we are living together. We are man and wife.'

'Doesn't matter,' Joanna said.

Dario sat down on a sofa next to his wife. He rubbed her stomach. 'We are in this together,' he said with the look of someone who was going nowhere. 'All three of us.'

'How about this for a suggestion?' I said. 'We leave Joanna and Salome to go over things, and me and you take a walk? This is a great place and I'd love to see more. Once Joanna's finished, we can come back and she can summarise anything she thinks you should know.'

'Why can't you summarise when I'm here with my wife?' He turned to Salome. 'I told you. My lawyers know other lawyers. Good lawyers, who—'

'Go with him,' Salome said softly, and the gentlest nudge from her was enough to have Dario rise from the sofa and trudge towards the door like a small boy who was being sent early to bed without any Xbox time.

I followed him into the hallway where a shout from my host was enough to have our coats brought to us by the larger of the two wedding bouncers, still as sullen-eyed as ever. Soon we were outside tramping along a rocky path that led from the rear of the house. I couldn't help but notice that diamond tooth was following at a discreet distance. Dario saw me glancing over my shoulder and called to the man to go back into the house. 'Emilio,' he said to me with a dry laugh. 'My agents insist he comes everywhere with me. He was once with Unidad de Operaciones Especiales, like your SAS. Emilio trusts no one. Not even you - unlike my wife. My agents have a great many lawyers, but Salome insists that you defend her.'

'I'm going to do my best to have her acquitted. We both are,' I said.

'Your wife is a good lawyer?'

'The best. And she knows the case against Salome inside out. To bring in someone else at this late stage would be a bad idea.'

He grunted. 'So you say. Me? I'm not so sure. How much?'

'I've already sent Salome our terms of business letter,' I said. 'Our fee structure is set out clearly.'

'I'm not interested in your fee structure. How much to leave the case and let me bring my own people in?'

It was a tempting offer. Walk away, avoid all the stress of a High Court murder case, and be paid for it. Why was Salome so keen to stick with me? Had I been overconfident when apprising my client of the strength of her defence? Or was she smart enough to know that bringing in a new legal team this close to trial was risky? Did she not realise that a motion to postpone for more time to prepare would most likely be met with some sympathy? After all, the court diary was always full, and there was no rush now that bail had been granted. Her case could easily be punted well into next year.

We walked on in silence, the path rising beneath us, a gentle mist swirling about our feet. I wasn't equipped for a walk in the wild and could feel the damp creeping into my clothes. Soon the path petered out, and frost on the ground squeaked underfoot as we tramped through the scrub.

'What makes you so sure you are the right lawyer for my wife?' Dario asked, clearly not for giving up.

'Dario, I like Salome and I'm convinced she's innocent. Joanna and I have prepared a defence which we think will see her acquitted. What we don't want is anyone else coming in and mucking that up.'

'Coming in and taking the glory. And my money.'

'Or the blame if things don't go according to plan,' I said.

'This plan. You don't think I could find a hundred other lawyers with one just as good or even better?'

I was getting just a little bit fed up with Dario. 'Maybe… Probably…' I said. 'But do you want to take that chance? I have almost a four-month head start on anyone coming into the case now. I've been working night and day building the best defence I can for your wife. What have you been doing? Shooting pigeons while Salome was doing pigeon.' I could tell that last remark flew over his head. I was also going to point out to him that it wasn't that long ago he'd been asking Joanna advice on divorce, but I knew my wife had been sworn to secrecy. 'What do you think was going through Salome's head while she lay in a prison cell for three months? It's not like you were visiting or bombarding her with letters. During that time she only had me to rely on. Maybe that's why she doesn't trust your choice of lawyers.'

He squared up to me. 'You don't understand.'

'Don't I? Suddenly Salome's having a baby, all is forgiven, and you want to bring in an A-team of lawyers to defend her, money no object. The more I think about it the more I'd be happy for you to pay me to step aside.'

'Then why don't you?'

Because I believed Salome innocent and because the case was so important to Joanna, was the truth of it. My wife was determined to conduct the defence and win. She had a point to prove to her biggest critic – herself.

'I'll resign from the case if that's what Salome wants. If not, I'll do the case anyway and you can keep your money,' I heard someone who sounded very like me say.

Dario stared hard at me. 'You remind me of your brother. In training we played small-sided games. Nothing at stake, but we could be three goals down with five minutes to go and he'd be determined he was still going to win. That's what this is to you, isn't it? It's not about the money. It's not even about Salome. It's about winning the game.'

It was possibly the nicest thing you could say to a defence lawyer, even though I was sure it wasn't intended that way.

'Salome won't change lawyers,' Dario said. 'She has faith in you. She says you were sent by God.' If I was the best God could come up with, the Big Man had gone down in my estimation. Then again, maybe heaven didn't have that many lawyers to choose from. Head down, Dario walked on with me at his side until we came to the summit of what couldn't be called a hill and was more of a rocky island in a sea of heather. He stopped, spread his arms wide and turned full circle. 'Five hundred hectares and by now I think I know each square metre. Every August I come here, one maybe two months, then onto Fuensauco for the partridge on the first of October. This year I don't go because of Salome. Do you shoot, Robbie?'

'Only pool,' I said. He didn't get it. 'You know, the game like snooker but in the pub.' He humoured me with a weak smile.

'What kind of shooting is it you do here?' I asked. 'Grouse?'

'Yes, but it is nearly the end of the grouse season. Still, there are plenty partridge, pheasant, even hare.'

'Don't you think it's a shame to kill all these animals for sport?' I said.

'I don't eat meat, but many of those who shoot with me do,' he replied. 'And people like you don't understand. Grouse shooting is good for conservation of wildlife. Good for the countryside. There is nothing more important to me than protecting this beautiful environment. I employ two gamekeepers and also a warden. There would be no grouse if it wasn't for me.'

'Sounds like an expensive hobby,' I said.

He smiled. 'It is. But then I have a lot of money. And my shooting parties. They help cover a lot of the costs.'

'Was it through shooting that you met Armando Diaz?' I asked.

'I was introduced to Armando by my agents when I moved to Madrid. He was to handle some of my investments. Armando was a good banker, but a great sportsman and a far better shot than me. He invited me to his estate in La Mancha and over one weekend taught me how to shoot. From then on it has been my hobby.'

'Not football?'

'Football was my work, my profession. Shooting is my joy.'

'Does Salome shoot?' I asked.

'Not the birds. She doesn't like to kill things.' That was good to know. Joanna could use that in cross-examination. 'She has tried a few times at the clay pigeons. She is quite good. Usually when she's here she is happy to relax with her books, have friends down to stay, take shopping trips into Edinburgh. I tell her it's only for one month or two. This year I am only staying longer because of her.'

'If you didn't visit her in prison, why did you not go shooting in Spain?' I asked. He didn't answer. 'I've read the statement you gave the police. You travelled to Scotland on the Thursday before Armando and Beverly's wedding the next day. You stayed at The Newberry because it was handy for the venue. On the Saturday you fell out with Salome, and she went to stay with Beverly and Armando. The statement doesn't say what the argument was about?'

Dario shrugged. 'About coming here, to this place, I think. This year she says it is too cold.'

I didn't believe him. He'd phoned Malky for Joanna's number that Saturday to set up a consultation about a divorce. Joanna had given me no details about that, and it seemed that Dario had faith that she would tell no one. Not even her husband. 'The evidence shows that on the Saturday night Beverly went to stay with her mum. According to the CCTV evidence, Monday morning Salome left in her car—'

'Yes, to come here and collect some of her belongings.'

'You we're splitting up?'

'She was staying with Armando and Beverly. She needed a few things.'

'When I met Salome at the Newberry on the Sunday morning before Armando was killed, she said she was there to collect her things.'

199

Dario laughed. 'My wife has lots of things. At Armando's house, here, at the Newberry. You wouldn't believe how many things she has.'

'No, there must have been more to it than that,' I said. 'Surely, you could easily have had her luggage sent on.'

Dario blew white air on his hands and rubbed them together vigorously, like he was trying to start a fire.

'She wanted to see you, didn't she? To try and patch things up. But you told her to leave. That you didn't want to see her anymore. That's right, isn't it?'

'I was busy. I was getting ready for a hunting trip. There were four members of my party in the storeroom with me. How could I talk to her? I told her to wait until I returned.'

'Did you? Or did you tell her to go?' I was sure that was what had happened. Salome getting the blame for killing Armando was the perfect excuse for him to get rid of her out of his life and move onto more fertile ground. Someone who could provide him with a footballing dynasty. Had it been his idea? Or had others been working away in the background?

Dario dug at the turf with the toe of his shoe. 'How bad is it? What do they have against her?' We were nearly four months down the line and only now was he asking about the evidence against his wife.

'The CCTV shows Salome arriving back from here not long before Armando returned from shooting practice, carrying a gun. He went around the rear of the house and out of camera shot. Salome went in through the front door. A short time later, Beverly arrived back from her mother's and found Salome coming out of the study where her husband was lying dead. The reason why Salome is in the frame for the killing is because there was no one else in the house at the time.'

'What else do they have against her?'

'Salome's fingerprints and DNA on the shotgun. She says she went to see if she could help Armando and touched the gun in the process.'

'What about the cook? Where was she when this was happening? She must have seen or heard something,' Dario said.

I told him how I'd spoken to Rosemary Dow, and that she'd left for the day around three o'clock. 'CCTV shows Armando was still alive at five-twenty.'

Dario looked up to find the late-November sun, suffocating under a blanket of cloud. He pulled his jacket closer, searched in a pocket, found a beanie and squashed it down over his head. 'Then Armando must have killed himself,' he said. 'He wasn't murdered, and it was no accident.' Dario seemed quite certain about that. 'If Armando had a loaded gun in the house, he meant to have it there.'

I couldn't mention Salome's rape allegation. She'd told me under no circumstance was Dario to learn of it. Not yet. He'd hear about it soon enough at the trial.

'But why would he do it? Was his business in trouble do you think? His investments? Your investments?' It was my meeting with Peter that had given me this thought. You heard of bankers throwing themselves out of windows. Had Armando been the one who advised Dario to get into shipping? Had he shot himself because of Salome's threat to report the rape or had shooting himself been his way of going down with the ship? Was it a case of better a shotgun than a meeting with Dario's agents and a Colombian necktie?

'What do you mean?' Dario said.

'If Armando had lost you or some other client a lot of money—'

'I was Armando's only client.'

'If he did, do you think he might have killed himself rather than face up to you?'

201

Dario didn't reply at first. He stamped his feet and took a last look around. 'It's cold. Let's go back,' he said, eventually. 'There are people I need to speak to.'

Chapter 33

For an accused person a criminal prosecution must be a lot like what I imagine having a baby is. Things happen very quickly at the beginning, followed by several months of uncomfortable waiting and anxiety. Then suddenly everything speeds up again, and, before you know it, you're in a room with a lot of strangers who are looking into things which in other circumstances you'd rather they didn't.

In the High Court a case never starts when you think it will. Salome Ramirez's trial had been declared a floating diet which meant that it could begin anytime over a four-day period. Naturally, it began on the fourth of those days, the Thursday, and not at ten o'clock because there was an IT problem. Certain of the Crown's video productions were incompatible with the court system and they had to bring in their own equipment. So it was that Salome Ramirez's trial commenced after lunch a mere six and a half court days before Christmas.

The Macer brought on the judge, Lady Carrick, and hooked the silver mace of office on the wall behind her chair beneath the coat of arms. A jury of eight women, seven men was empanelled; a procedure that took less than half an hour. Once they'd been allowed to divest themselves of their outdoor clothing and had returned to the jury box, I studied them. A few stood out more than others. Back row, second from the left, was a very attractive dark-haired woman in a low-cut blouse. Sitting to her right was a young man who looked like he'd won the raffle, which in a way he had. Apart from those two and a girl who I found it hard to believe met the age criteria of over eighteen, the others looked to be forties and above. Quite far above in most cases. Including an elderly gent, burly, with waves of white hair, and wearing a thick knitted pullover, leather patches at the elbows. I'd noticed him when his name had been drawn from the big glass fishbowl. He'd had on then a threadbare tweed jacket, flat cap folded and stuffed in one of the pockets, looking like he'd come straight from the fields and not had time to change. Generally, you don't want people on a jury who are delighted to be there, but this guy looked particularly disgruntled. If I could have objected to him, I would have. But in Scotland, unless there's a very good reason why not, you take whoever hasn't managed to dodge jury duty.

The public benches were heaving and the well of the court was busy too. A couple of cops loitered on the fringes. Two security guards sat in the dock either side of the accused. Then there was a court officer, the Macer, the Clerk of Court, and, at the big table in the centre, Joanna and me. Seated opposite us were the three lawyers for the Crown: the vampiric Cameron Crowe QC, beside him a well-fed junior counsel wearing too much makeup. She didn't look too pleased either. Perhaps because she'd had her hair done special for the occasion and then had to plonk a horsehair wig on top of it. Still, nothing promotes a progressive Scottish justice system quite like early 18th Century fashion. Making up this unholy trinity was Hugh Ogilvie the Procurator Fiscal, looking fuller of himself than a Russian doll.

From previous experience I knew Crowe's tactic would be to start strongly, finish with a bang and to try not to have too much information in the middle that might allow the defence to confuse the jurors. It was a strategy that had worked well for him in the past, and one of the reasons he was Scotland's most effective prosecutor.

Most murder trials start off with a witness who sets the scene. It's usually a Scene of Crimes officer, who is led through a series of photographs of the locus accompanied perhaps by a layout plan and more often than not a video walk-through and 360° panorama of the murder scene itself.

Cameron Crowe obviously felt that as an aperitif a SOCO droning on for an hour or so would be far too dry. Better to whet the jury's appetite for what was to follow by calling as his first witness Beverly Diaz. There's nothing like a weeping widow to bring home reality to a bunch of jurors who are probably inured to bloody murder from hours of Netflix and crime fiction paperbacks. After taking the best part of an hour to have Beverly walk us through the layout of the house, the courtyard, even the clay pigeon shooting range, Crowe moved her on to the day of Armando's death.

'I'd been at my mum's for two nights. She wasn't well. It looked like I might have to stay longer. I only came back to the house for a change of clothes.'

'I think we may see later from CCTV footage that your car arrived in the courtyard outside the house around about five-thirty that afternoon. Would that be correct?'

'Yes it would.'

'Please go on.'

'Before I came into the house, I noticed that Salome's car was still there.'

'And by Salome, you mean?'

'Salome Ramirez.'

'If you see Mrs Ramirez in court, could you point to her, please? You are pointing to the woman in the light blue dress seated between the two security guards. Is that correct?'

Beverly nodded.

'For the recording, please?'

'Yes, that's her.'

'And did it surprise you that her car was there?'

'Not really. She'd fallen out with Dario and come back to stay at our place on the Saturday night.'

'Come back?'

'Salome had stayed with us lots of times. She came to stay with us a few weeks before... before the wedding. She was a friend. Salome was always welcome to...' For the first time Beverly's until now stoic expression showed signs of cracking. She cleared her throat, lifted her chin and continued. 'She was welcome to stay for as long as she wanted.' Crowe paused to let the witness gather herself before asking, 'You mentioned Dario. Is that the accused's husband?' As if it might have escaped the jury's attention that the woman in the dock was married to one of the world's top footballers.

Beverly agreed that it was.

'Had you told Salome when you'd be returning that day?'

'No, I didn't know myself.'

'So, your arrival would have surprised her?'

Joanna stood. 'Don't answer that, please,' she said to the witness before turning to look up at the Bench.

Lady Carrick raised a hand and gestured for her to sit down. 'Mr Crowe, perhaps you could rephrase the question.'

But there was no time for that. 'Yes, I expect she would have been surprised,' Beverly blurted, her voice rising an octave as she stared straight at the dock. 'She certainly looked surprised when I met her hurrying out of the study where my husband was lying dead inside!' This time there were tears.

Crowe paused to ask the Macer to bring the witness a glass of water. 'Please, take your time and tell us what happened after you arrived,' he said, once Beverly had taken a sip and indicated she was ready to continue.

'I parked outside the house, walked through the front door and into the hallway.'

'Have before you please, Crown Production 1, a book of photographs, and turn to photograph A17.' As the Macer brought the thick book of photographs to the witness, Crowe nodded to his colleague in the wig. Normally the video display operator would be a bar officer, but on this occasion, possibly because of the earlier IT problems, Crowe had asked his junior to assist. She quickly scrolled to an image of the hallway that we'd been shown earlier. It flashed up on the screens around the court. 'And do we see different views of the hallway from different angles in photographs A18, A19 and A20?' he asked as in turn the various images appeared.

'That's right,' Beverly said.

'And does image A21 show the view of the study door as you would see it upon entering through the front door into the hall and looking right?' According to Beverly it did. 'What happened next?'

'I came in and could see that the study door was open. I heard someone moving inside.'

'Who did you think it was?'

'I assumed it would be Armando, and I called to say I was back.'

'And when you say Armando?'

'I mean my late husband, Armando Diaz.'

'Of course. When was the last time you'd seen Mr Diaz?'

'Late Saturday afternoon, just before I left for my mum's.'

'How did Armando seem to you at that time?'

'He seemed fine. Normal.'

'And in the days before that?'

'The day before was our wedding. We'd have been on honeymoon if my mum hadn't taken ill.'

'No signs of depression?'

Joanna could have objected on the basis that Beverly was hardly qualified to give a mental health diagnosis, but to do so would only have highlighted what Crowe was trying to do, which was puncture a suicide defence.

'I'd say he was very happy.'

'Who wouldn't be in his circumstances?' Crowe purred. 'Tell me, what did you call out as you entered the house?'

'I don't know exactly. I saw the study door open, heard someone inside and probably called, "It's me. I'm back," or something like that.'

'And when you did, was there any answer?'

'No, I continued walking, and when I got to the study door I was met by Salome, rushing out.' Beverly put a finger across her top lip and held it there for a moment.

'Image A26 please,' Crowe asked, and junior counsel scrolled down a couple of notches to an image of the inside of the study and a close up of the bloody corpse of Armando Diaz lying on his back on the floor of the study. Some of the jurors gasped and Beverly gripped onto the sides of the witness box.

'Mr Crowe,' the judge said. 'Some kind of warning should have been given.'

Crowe glanced down at his papers. 'I'm terribly sorry, M'Lady. My sincere apologies to the jury and, of course to the witness. My fault entirely. A slip of the tongue. I meant photograph A25. A close-up of the study door.'

Joanna gave me a sideways look. The stunt had clearly been rehearsed. Cameron Crowe was not prone to slips of the tongue. He always knew exactly what he was saying, and while his face remained its usual crypt-crawling grey, junior counsel's chubby cheeks looked like they'd been slapped. The judge turned to the jury. 'Members of the jury, it's almost half past eleven. I think now would be a good time for a short break. Court will resume in fifteen minutes.'

We waited for the courtroom to clear before asking one of the security officers to escort Salome to the toilet. While she was away Joanna and I discussed the evidence led thus far and agreed that there hadn't been too much to damage the defence, even although Crowe had guessed correctly and tried to spike our suicide defence.

'Poor Beverly, having to go through all that again,' Joanna said. 'She must have relived the moment she found Armando so many times, but to have to do it in court in front of all these people... The good thing is there's nothing that doesn't tie in with the defence. Salome says she heard a bang when she was in the bathroom and when she went to see what it was, discovered Armando's body. She was coming out of the door just as Beverly was coming in. Of course, she'd be hurrying out of the room where she'd just found a dead body. Who wouldn't? I'd say it's so far so good, wouldn't you?'

Yes, I would have, and that was what was worrying me. This was Cameron Crowe we were dealing with. He'd have wanted to start the prosecution with something memorable for the jury, and although he'd done that with the photo of Armando's corpse, I was certain there would be more to come.

'Did you notice anything peculiar about the accused when you saw her leaving the room?' Crowe asked Beverly after the restart.

'I saw blood on her hands. She got some on me when she tried to stop me going into the room.' Crowe called for a labelled production that turned out to be the jacket Beverly had been wearing. It had already been agreed that the blood on one of the sleeves had belonged to her husband. 'Yes, that's where Salome grabbed me.'

'And after that?'

'After I saw Armando and realised... and realised...'

Crowe gestured to the Macer who topped up the witness's glass of water.

'Mrs Diaz, it's difficult, I know, but what did you do?'

'I wanted to stay with Armando. I didn't want to leave him, but they wouldn't let me.'

'Who wouldn't?'

'Salome. And him.' Beverly pointed down at me like she wished she was pointing a pistol.

'You're indicating the accused's solicitor?'

'Yes, Robbie Munro. He and Salome took me upstairs to my bedroom.' She looked at me for a few seconds then turned her death ray stare on the accused and held it there.

'It's a matter of agreement that Mr Munro arrived shortly after six o'clock, and the police thirty minutes later. Do you know why that is?'

Joanna was about to object, but Beverly was quick off the mark. 'Salome obviously called him first.'

'And why do you think she would call a defence lawyer before calling the police?'

This time Joanna was on her feet, and again the judge waved her down. 'Don't answer that question Mrs Diaz,' she said to the witness, and then to the jury, 'Mrs Diaz is not an expert witness, members of the jury. Her opinion is not evidence, only what she saw or heard. Mr Crowe, you should really know better. If you can fairly reframe the question, please do.'

Crowe smiled up at the Bench. 'That won't be necessary, M'Lady. I'm sure the jury has the flavour.'

Chapter 34

Thursday night, the kids were in bed, and Joanna and I were back at the kitchen table discussing tactics. We'd been given a running order of the witnesses the Crown proposed to call next day and were going over possible lines of cross-examination together.

Joanna's cross-examination of Beverly had been short. The best cross examinations usually are. The Crown could inflate a large balloon of evidence during examination-in-chief, but it only took a jab with a pin to burst it. Joanna had started off by taking from Beverly that her husband's job was high-pressure and involved handling millions of pounds of other people's money. Beverly had played things down by stating Armando was used to pressure and in any case was semi-retired, newly married, and spending the summer doing what he liked best.

'If anything, Armando was more relaxed than ever,' had been Beverly's reply to Joanna's opening salvo, a signal, were it needed, that she would have to proceed extremely cautiously. Beverly would be doing her utmost to dispel any notion her husband had killed himself; she stood to lose too much financially. It was a tricky situation for Joanna. She had to lay the foundations of a defence of suicide, but without asking questions the answers to which would only serve to reinforce how unlikely it was the fatal shot had been self-inflicted.

Things improved for the defence thereafter. Beverly agreed that her husband was an extremely experienced shot, and she had to accept that his ammunition was stored in another part of the house while the guns were locked securely in the study. She couldn't give any explanation why he'd come into the house with a loaded weapon. With reference to the CCTV, Beverly had also to concede that while the video evidence showed Armando walking to the rear of the house carrying a shotgun, it also showed Salome entering the front door carrying nothing but a small handbag. At this I sensed a welcome, if almost imperceptible, stirring on the other side of the table. When Joanna asked Beverly if it looked to her like Armando had inexplicably brought into the house the loaded shotgun that later killed him, the stirring turned to rustling of paper and Hugh Ogilvie even dropped a pen on the floor, making a fuss of picking it up: a classic jury-distraction method.

Beverly hadn't answered at first, but, when directed to do so by the judge, had given such a grudgingly delivered confirmation of what seemed so bleedingly obvious, that Joanna thought it a good time to sit down.

'Saw you on the news,' my dad said, steaming in through the back door unannounced, Malky in his wake. You were going into court or maybe you were coming out. It was hard to tell with all the folk crowding round you. Tell me all about it.'

Malky shoved past. 'Never mind him on the telly dad, what about me *not* being on it?' Ever the optimist he checked the fridge for beer and came out empty handed.

'Aye, son,' my dad said to me. 'What about Malky? I thought you were going to have a word with that big beanpole Peter Falconer.'

Joanna gave me a look. Leaving my wife to her studies, I ushered father and brother from kitchen to living room.

'Stick the kettle on pet,' my dad shouted to Joanna as I closed the door behind us.

'I did have a word with Peter,' I said, once my dad was comfortably ensconced in my favourite chair and I was on the sofa with Malky. 'He's going to talk to Colin Lancaster and—'

'He *has* talked with Lancaster,' Malky said. 'That's the problem. He's talked him into signing one of his own clients into my slot for next season. And wait until you hear this. It's a woman. No offence, but…'

I find that people who say, "no offence" tend on the whole to be quite offensive. Malky went on to prove my point on the subject of female footballers.

'I hear what you say, Malky—'

'I was the captain of Rangers. I captained Scotland five times. I scored—'

'The winning goal in the cup final, I know, but it's all about diversity nowadays. Viewers need to hear from people with different viewpoints.'

'You mean the viewpoint of people who can play football and the viewpoint of people who can't? Why don't they make Joanna a judge on Masterchef instead of someone who can actually cook?'

'I heard that!' Joanna shouted through the closed kitchen door.

'Maybe they're looking for people who don't call other people Nancy-boys and big girls' blouses,' I said.

'No, they just give my job to someone who wears a blouse!'

'Give it a break, Malky,' I said. 'This isn't my fault. It was your idea that I go and speak with Peter. I could have told you that he'd stab anyone in the back if there was a few quid in it for him.'

Shortly, Joanna came through with three mugs of tea. 'Is that it?' my dad said. 'Just tea? Where are we? England?'

I got up, led Joanna to the kitchen, sat her down at the kitchen table with the trial papers, found a packet of Jammy Dodgers, went back through to the livingroom and lobbed the biscuits into my dad's lap. 'Joanna's busy. So am I supposed to be. We're in the middle of a big trial. We weren't on the news because someone chucked a firework up a close.'

213

Our talking had clearly alerted Tina's early warning system. 'Uncle Malky's buying me a tracksuit from FastFreez!' she yelled, bounding into the room and flinging herself on top of Malky. Fortunately, he managed to avoid spilling his tea over his niece. His groin region wasn't so lucky, and he leapt to his feet, jumping about the room in a manner not only my daughter found highly amusing.

While he was in the bathroom inspecting the damage, I put Tina back to bed. I returned to find Joanna had given up and joined my dad in the livingroom. He'd obviously been grilling her about the day's events in my absence. He wasn't enthused by what he'd heard.

'It's not a case of asking questions for the sake of it, Alex,' Joanna said. 'Cross-examination is as much about knowing what not to ask. No point the jury hearing something you don't want them to hear, or the same unhelpful answer twice that only reinforces the Crown case.'

'That's right,' I said. 'The secret to a good defence is to sail as close to the Prosecution case as you can. At the last-minute you take the jury on a reasonable doubt detour, letting the Crown crash into an iceberg while the defence sails onward to the land of not guilty.'

'I know what the Prosecution case is,' my dad said. 'Your client was alone in the house and shot her pal's husband. What detour were you planning on taking from that, Cap'n Munro?'

Joanna screwed up her face. 'Alex, we can't talk about—'

'It's okay, Jo,' I said. 'You know my dad won't say anything to anyone. Will you Dad?'

Having made a show of putting his right hand up and swearing an oath, he sat back expectantly.

Malky returned wearing, I noticed, a pair of my jeans, loose at the waist and short in the leg.

'Away and read Tina a bedtime story,' my dad said, aware, like we all were, that one should never tell my brother anything you didn't want the rest of the northern hemisphere to know. Tina appeared from nowhere and dragged Malky off.

'Suicide,' I said, once the two of them were out of ear shot.

My dad sat back, lifted his mug to his lips and noticed it was empty.

'More tea, Alex?' Joanna asked.

He thought about it for a while, staring into the mug and massaging his moustache. 'Malky's driving,' he said eventually.

Two minutes later, a whisky in hand, he sat back rolling his glass and taking occasional sniffs. It was a ten-year-old Benromach, and according to my dad a whisky needed a minute in the glass for every year in the cask.

'Suicide? Why?' he asked. 'He was what? Sixty?'

'Fifty-nine,' I said.

'That's not old. That's only about ten years younger than me. Was he not well?'

'Fit as a violin,' I said.

So, you've got a man nearing his prime of life, who's a millionaire and married to a young thing? Pretty is she?'

I let Joanna answer that one. 'Yes, Beverly's good looking. But, Alex, people intent on killing themselves aren't thinking rationally. If they were they wouldn't kill themselves. We've already got a psychologist on standby. He'll testify that most gunshot suicides are committed by middle-aged men, who own shotguns and have no previous history of mental health problems.'

'And I've spoken to Professor Bradley, Scotland's top forensic pathologist, who agrees that the wound indicates the shot was fired at very close range,' I said. Adding for good measure, 'We also have Laszlo Derry, that's right, the guy off the telly. He'll say that it would be physically possible to shoot yourself in the chest with the type of shotgun used and also some other helpful stuff.'

My dad wasn't convinced, but then he seldom was by arguments that might tend to show someone charged by the police was innocent.

'What about it being an accident?' He took a sip of his whisky having decided that five minutes was a long enough wait in the circumstances. The circumstances being that he was impatient. He considered his own proposition while swilling and chomping the single malt in a manner that I knew Joanna found immensely irritating. 'Then again, I suppose that would mean he'd have had to have made two mistakes: bringing a loaded shotgun into the house and then carelessly shooting himself with it.' For my dad, noticing holes in defences was second nature. Not so much finding the mote in the eye of a prosecution case.

I had to agree though. 'Laszlo Derry has more or less ruled accident out for an experienced gun-owner like Armando Diaz.'

'I still don't like the whole killing himself thing,' my dad said. 'Doesn't matter what your suicide researchers say. The folk on the jury are going to think, why would this guy kill himself for absolutely no reason when on the face of it he had everything to live for?'

I could have, but didn't think it right to mention Salome's rape allegation or her supporting black eye. The Crown no doubt thought my client's, *he deserved it*, reply to caution and charge was the icing on the Prosecution's cake. Personally, I felt the remark would look just as good atop the Defence's, and in case the Crown witness chose not to call karate cook Rosemary Dow, we'd insisted she remain available to the defence. Her accounts of Armando's wandering hands could only assist Salome's version.

Malky returned. 'I think she's asleep,' he said, and parting Joanna and me like Moses and the Red Sea, he plonked himself down on the sofa between us. 'Right, we need to talk about this plan Robbie and I have come up with to get me my

216

job back.' Before I could deny any involvement, he set out the idea in all its full horrific detail and reclined, an arm around each of us.

I shrugged him off. 'Can I just say that this idea is all Malky's,' I said.

Malky didn't seem to mind taking full credit. He looked around at his audience with the air of anticipation Einstein no doubt felt the first time he chalked E = mc2 on the blackboard of the scientific world. 'Well, what do you think?'

It took Joanna a moment to regain the power of speech. 'Malky, apart from that being the most stupid idea I have ever heard,' she said, escaping from under his arm. 'And remember...' she added, rather gratuitously I thought, 'I've been married to Robbie for four years.' She held a hand up in front of my brother's face to prevent possible dissent. 'It would also be an extremely horrible and cruel thing to do. And another thing. No one will be buying Tina that tracksuit. Not even her parents. Even though the wee girl's got her heart set on one.' She was really rubbing it in. 'Robbie's put his foot down. It's all blatant consumerism according to him.'

'Well, it is Jo,' I said. 'They shouldn't be encouraged. A hundred and fifty quid for a tracksuit you could buy anywhere else for a fraction of the price, simply because it's got a special pattern and some stupid logo on it. It's probably made in the same sweatshop as the one's you can get for twenty-nine ninety-nine down the market. Tina's eight years old. She eats like a plague of locusts. She'll have grown out of the thing by Easter, if it's not already out of fashion by then.'

'Why does that mean I can't buy her it?' Malky wanted to know.

'How would that look?' Joanna asked.

'It would look good for me,' Malky said. 'Cement me in as her favourite uncle.'

'Malky,' Joanna said, 'you're not going within one hundred miles of that shop or Annette Lancaster. It's a really stupid and mean idea. You and Robbie will just have to come up with a better one.'

'A better idea shouldn't be difficult,' my dad said. 'It's one that'll actually work you want.'

The room fell silent, and I thought I heard Malky's brain whirring. Though it could just have been the washing machine changing cycle. At one point he sat bolt upright, pumped with excitement, then after a moment or two deflated himself and slumped back into the sofa again. I didn't dare ask what idea had struck him, that, after just a few seconds reconsideration, he'd deemed worse than the great seduction scheme.

My mobile rang somewhere afar. Joanna escaped to answer it for me. She was gone some time. When she came back she looked worried. 'Robbie,' she said. 'That was Salome. We need to talk.'

Chapter 35

And talk we did, far into the night. Salome had called to say that she did not want there to be any mention of her rape in court. She wouldn't say why not but wouldn't be swayed.

Next morning when we met before court, Salome was still determined that nothing should be said about it and that were it put to her in the witness box she would deny everything.

'That leaves you in a very difficult position,' I said. 'Without the rape allegation that you were going to make against Armando, why would he kill himself, and why would you tell the police he deserved it?'

'I didn't. I said the opposite. Do you speak Spanish, Robbie?'

I didn't; however, the remark had been recorded. Even then, it could be argued that *'no se lo merecía'* sounded very like *'se lo merecía'*. I didn't think there'd be many Spanish speakers amongst an Edinburgh jury, and Crowe, for all his sharpness, hadn't included a Spanish interpreter on the Crown witness list.

'Is that right, Robbie?' Joanna asked. 'You were there when she said whatever she said. Could it have been *he didn't deserve it*?'

'It's all Spanish to me,' I said, but even if there was room for doubt, I still didn't like it. The threat that Salome would report the rape was the motive we wanted to put forward as the reason Armando had killed himself. It was the reason for Salome's minor injury and the *he deserved it* angle might have been attractive to some of the jury. When freedom or life behind bars could hinge on a single vote, every little helped. Now what could we say was his motive? Like my dad, I didn't think that even a university research paper would convince a jury that Armando had blasted himself in the chest with a 12 bore because he was a sad, married-to-someone-half-his-age, multi-millionaire.

When day two of the trial commenced, it was apparent that Salome's instructions would also cause problems for the defence when it came to Rosemary Dow, the karate cook. According to the Crown list, she was next to give evidence. I expected her to be called to say that she'd left for the day at around three o'clock, and that at that time Armando was not lying in pieces in the study. It was something the CCTV evidence would confirm in any case, but she could also testify that there was no one else on the premises at the time she left. With no one seen arriving other than Salome, it was implying guilt by a process of elimination.

What we had intended to take from the cook was evidence of Armando's wandering hands. It might not have been much, but it was an adminicle to support Salome's rape allegation. Now that we had instructions not to mention the rape, it would sound like we were speaking ill of the dead for no reason other than to blacken his character.

But as it turned out, the karate cook was not next up to bat. Instead, for the first part of the morning, we heard routine evidence from a series of police officers about their attendance at the scene and speaking to various links in the chain of evidence that had not otherwise been agreed by way of Joint Minute. The worst evidence to come out was that the shotgun had been found a distance away from the body, but we had an explanation for that, so there was no need to cross examine. By the eleven-fifteen coffee break, I was thinking that Cameron Crowe's estimation of a six-day trial with a following wind might have been right on the money. Someone else who was wondering about the length of the trial was the old guy in the front row of the jury. While the court officer was fetching the next witness, Elbow-Patches raised a gnarly hand. The Macer hurried over to him, but before he could reach the jury box, the old guy had stood up and called out to the judge, 'How long's this all going to last?'

The Macer tried in vain to have him sit down.

'That's all right,' the judge said, waving the Macer aside. 'I'm sure we'd all like an answer to the gentleman's question.' She looked down to her right. 'Advocate depute? Would you care to revisit your original estimation?'

'I believe at the Preliminary Hearing I thought six days all going well. I don't see any reason why I should change my view on that, M'Lady.'

Lady Carrick turned to the jury box and her fixed smile was enough to have the old guy sit down and fold his arms.

Next up was a police sergeant from the firearms unit. Athletically built, dark hair pulled back in a knot, she turned out to be one of those jazz-music people: they sound quite pleasant at first, but the more you listen to them the more annoying they become.

After he'd shown the expert the shotgun found at the scene, Crowe's line of questioning moved onto the peculiarities of shotgun cartridges.

'Have before you please, Crown Label Production 7. What is that Sergeant?'

The witness looked at the small, yellow object that had been brought to her sealed in a transparent plastic tube. 'It's a shotgun cartridge.'

'Have you signed the label?'

'Yes, Sir. The cartridge was delivered to me for examination.'

'Can you describe it?'

'It's a normal shotgun cartridge.'

'Anything unusual about it?' Crowe asked.

'Well, clearly it has been fired. This is nothing more than the outer casing. And then there's the colour.' She held up the tube. 'As you can see, this cartridge is yellow. Shotgun cartridges come in all sorts of colours depending on the brand: blue, black, white, even gold. Most commonly they are a reddy-orange.'

'Is there something written on the side?'

'Yes, Sir, the brand name Delta is printed in bold, and this is their Champion version. You can just make it out printed in smaller italic font.'

'Thank you. It's a matter of agreement that this was found on the floor of the deceased's study. Could you tell us a little more about shotgun cartridges officer?'

She could. A lot more. 'What is fired from a shotgun is different from what is fired from say a handgun or a rifle. The difference is that whereas pistols and rifles fire a single projectile—'

'You mean a bullet?'

'That's correct. Shotguns don't fire bullets as such. A shotgun is loaded with a cartridge.' For the benefit of the jury a close-up photograph of the cartridge found on the study floor was put up on the screen. 'And, while a shotgun cartridge is not entirely dissimilar to a bullet, when fired it doesn't produce one projectile, but multiple projectiles.'

The old guy in the front row of the jury box groaned and let his head flop to the side.

'I realise some of the jury members will have a knowledge of shotgun cartridges,' Crowe said, glancing at the man with the leather elbow patches. But for the rest of us, Sergeant, do you mean it fires a number of small pellets?' Crowe asked.

'That's correct. Years ago, they were made of lead. Now they're usually made of a non-toxic metal alloy or occasionally steel. When the trigger of a shotgun is pulled, the firing pin hits the primer located in the centre of the brass head of the cartridge. This ignites the gun powder at the base. When the powder ignites, it creates gases which expand and in turn propel the wad—'

'Wad?' Crowe was determined the jury understood the workings of a shotgun cartridge, not that they sounded particularly complicated.

'That's right,' the firearms officer said. 'There is a wad made of fibre or occasionally a plastic capsule, depending on the type of cartridge, that separates the powder from the pellets. It takes up around fifty-percent of the cartridge. The gases push this wad or capsule which in turn pushes the pellets out of the front of the shotgun. The further the pellets have to travel, the more they will spread out.'

'It's agreed that the post-mortem report states the wound sustained by the deceased was approximately ten centimetres, in diameter,' Crowe advised the witness.

'What's that in inches?' The voice came from the jury box. The old guy in the front row.

'Members of the jury,' the judge said, 'if you have any questions, please don't shout them out. Put your hand up and let yourself be identified by my Macer. I will do my best to assist. Thank you. Advocate depute, perhaps you could ask the witness to clarify.'

Crowe didn't need to. 'That's around four inches,' the firearms expert said.

'Does that tell you anything, Sergeant?' was Crowe's follow up question.

'The relatively small diameter of the wound would suggest that the pellets had remained grouped together. So the gun must have been fired from close range.'

'Within the confines of a large room?'

'Easily.'

Crowe looked over at his junior and then back to the witness. 'Sergeant, I wonder if you could have a look at the autopsy photographs and in particular B12, 13 and 14. Have you seen these before?'

'I have.'

Joanna was on her feet. 'M'Lady, unless the witness is an expert in forensic pathology as well as firearms, I don't think she should be asked to comment on the wounds sustained by the deceased.'

Lady Carrick was of a different opinion. She looked down at the witness. 'You say you've seen the photographs before, and according to your report I see you have carried out some test firings, Sergeant?'

'That's correct, Ma'am.'

'Very well, continue Advocate depute.'

Joanna sat down as Crowe went on. 'Sergeant, what impression did you form, if any, from your investigations as to the range the shotgun might have been fired from?'

'Normally, with a shot fired from anywhere over sixty centimetres to a metre...'

A woolly sleeve was hoisted in the jury box.

'That would be two to three feet,' the witness said, and the arm lowered. 'After that distance you'd expect the pellets to have started to spread sufficiently for there to be at least a few satellite wounds around the main wound. That doesn't seem to be the case here. Having examined the gun in question and carried out test firings, using the same type of cartridge, I'd put that down to the barrel of this shotgun having had a permanent choke fitted.'

'What does that mean?'

'It means the barrel was tapered at the end. It's very common. The narrowing of the barrel allows for greater accuracy because it tightens the pattern of the pellets.'

'And that means in simple terms?'

'That they don't spread out so quickly.'

'From your sight of the photographs and test firing have you formed any idea as to how far away the shotgun could have been fired from to produce a lack of these satellite wounds?'

'I'd say up to two or even three metres away.'

'Ten feet?' said Crowe.

'Or thereabouts,' the witness agreed.

I waited for Crowe to ask if the shot could have been self-inflicted, but he didn't. I wondered why not. He had to know what the witness was likely to say. He wasn't one to ask a question to which he didn't already know the answer. Did he know the witness would say yes, and strengthen the argument for suicide? Or did he know she'd say no, and wanted the defence to fall into the trap and ask the question?

'Another thing you could perhaps explain to the members of the jury, Sergeant. What does one do having fired a shotgun?'

'Do?'

'Yes. What is the next thing one does after having just fired a shotgun?'

'Reload it, I suppose. Is that what you mean?'

'And how does one do that.'

'There's a mechanism for breaking the barrel. A person would remove the spent cartridge, discard it and either carry the gun broken for safety reasons or else replace the spent cartridge with a live round.'

'And how would a person who has just shot themselves with a shotgun, go about breaking open the barrel and discarding the spent cartridge, Sergeant?'

The firearms officer snorted a laugh. 'Obviously, that would be impossible.'

With some further tidying up, Crowe left the witness to Joanna. 'We don't need to take anything from her,' I said. 'Our expert can explain about the gun breaking open when it fell, and the cartridge being ejected. '

Joanna wasn't listening. I could see she was determined to cross examine, and I was concerned at the way Crowe had left the witness with that one question simply begging to be asked. I also couldn't see a police witness in a murder trial voluntarily saying anything that might remotely assist the defence. The very best we could hope for would be a grudging agreement that suicide was possible, which we knew in any case we could take from Professor Bradley in due course. If, however, the answer was an unequivocal no, then we'd be in trouble. I felt sure Crowe wanted us to ask the question because a bomb like that going off to a question asked by the defence would make a far greater impression than if elicited by him. So why risk it? Much better to leave it hanging.

Despite my warning, Joanna rose to her feet. 'Sergeant, when you say that the fatal shot could have been fired from ten feet or three metres away, that would have been the absolute maximum from your test firings?'

'Correct.'

'So, it could have been a lot closer?'

'That's what maximum means.'

'The shotgun you've shown us seems unusually short. Is it?'

'The barrel length is sixty-six centimetres.'

Joanna turned to the jury as she spoke. 'That's only around two feet, am I right?'

'Two feet and two inches, to be precise.'

'Whereas most shotgun barrels are usually about eighty-three centimetres. That's about three feet, isn't it?'

'Eighty-three centimetres is approximately two feet eight inches.'

'But you'd agree the barrel of the gun that shot Mr Diaz, was around half a foot shorter than a normal barrel?'

'Yes, fifteen centimetres shorter or thereabouts. The shotgun in question was an older model.'

Joanna left it there, with the abnormal shortness of the barrel fixed in the minds of the jurors. Even if they tried to work it out for themselves in the jury room, we were satisfied that inquisitive jurors would come to the same conclusion we had when we'd experimented using a length of stick at home.

226

It was definitely doable, and for a tall man like Armando, easy. It was a clever move by my wife. Children always learn better if left to work out something for themselves rather than be told the answer. Juries were no different.

I thought that enough and we should get out while we could. Joanna had other ideas.

'You were never at the actual scene, Sergeant?'

'No, ma'am, the weapon was delivered to me with instructions to carry out test firings and prepare a report.'

'Then, this shotgun, what else can you tell us about it?'

'I'm not sure what you mean, ma'am.'

'Well, you've told us how unusually short the barrel is—'

'I said—'

'Just wait for the question please, Sergeant. You've told us of the short barrel, and that it's an old shotgun. Is there anything else of note about it?'

'It's got a single barrel. I suppose that's quite unusual, and… well… that's about it.'

'Nothing else?'

'No, not really.'

'I see from your report you have been through a great deal of training in various forms of firearms?' The witness modestly agreed that she had. Joanna read from the report. 'It says here that you have trained with pistols and revolvers, rifles, semi-automatics and SMGs. What are SMGs?'

'Sub-machine guns, Ma'am.'

Joanna flicked through the report and then tossed it onto the table in the well of the court, before looking at the witness again. 'Doesn't say anything about shotguns.'

'No, but—'

'Do you hunt game fowl?'

'No, I don't.'

'What about clay pigeon shooting?'

'I've tried it once.'

'Really? Once? I think we may hear later from a Mr Laszlo Derry…' I could see some interested faces on the jury. 'You've heard of Mr Derry?'

The witness had.

'And you'd agree, would you, that he's a man who knows a lot about shotguns?'

'I don't know Mr Derry's qualifications.'

Joanna didn't so much roll her eyes as give them a little flick at the jury. They knew Laszlo Derry's qualifications all right, and they now knew how unhelpful the witness was trying to be.

Joanna walked over to the production table and lifted the shotgun still contained in its thick plastic production bag. She laid it on the ledge of the witness box. 'We may hear later in this trial from Mr Derry that this shotgun is a mid-1950s custom-made Ivo Lombardi model, worth in the region of ten thousand pounds. What do you say about that?'

'I wouldn't really know, Ma'am.'

Joanna smiled condescendingly. 'No, you wouldn't, would you?'

Chapter 36

'Nice work,' I said to Joanna as she sat down. Not only had she planted the relative shortness of the barrel in the jury's mind, but she'd also given them a heavy dose of *our firearms expert is better than theirs.*

I could see Crowe was wondering whether to re-examine the witness. He could only do so on matters raised in cross-examination, and Joanna's cross had left no rough edges. He decided against any more questions. Re-examination can sometimes come across as an indication that the other side's cross-examination has done your witness some damage that you're desperately trying to repair. Often its best just to pretend things are fine and sit tight hoping your inaction will make the jury think you aren't the least bothered.

When the firearms officer stepped down it was twenty-five to one. I could see the clerk making eye signals at the Crown side of the table, inquiring if now might be a good time to break. Some of those packing the public benches had already drifted off. The third estate liked to lunch.

'I have one witness I think we could possibly fit in before one o'clock,' Crowe said, and with the judge's consent asked the bar officer to bring Dario into court. Word spread quickly and a lot of those who had drifted off for an early lunch, quickly drifted back in again to see Dario take the oath and confirm his identity.

Although Salome and Dario were reconciled and living together, strictly speaking she, as the accused, was not supposed to discuss the case with her husband since he was on the prosecution list. It was all very artificial, and Joanna had asked for him to be called early in the proceedings to save him sitting in a witness room while the trial went ahead.

The fact that Crowe was doing so as a courtesy to the defence was most unlike him. That's what I thought at first, until I realised that while the Crown required to call Dario to account for his wife's movements, his evidence would naturally tend to be more exculpatory than incriminatory. What better than to rush him through just before lunch?

Dario was in the box just over half an hour. He wasn't asked about any marital difficulties, only of Salome's movements on the day in question. The jury heard that Salome had been staying at the Diaz's home, although Crowe continually referred to Armando and Beverly as 'the newlyweds' and the locus as 'the family home'. Salome had driven to the lodge in the borders where Dario was hosting an afternoon shooting party. Dario had spoken briefly to his wife. What about, Crowe never asked. Salome had come to collect some of her belongings, and said she'd be staying at West Hope House for a while longer. Dario stumbled a little when asked why his wife would be staying with friends who were about to go on honeymoon, but recovered to say that Salome probably wanted to support Beverly while her mother was ill.

Crowe asked Dario for an approximate time for Salome's departure, something he was able to do with a degree of accuracy, since his chat with Salome took place as he and his small party of friends were already in his storeroom collecting guns and ammunition, and ready for the off at two o'clock that early August afternoon. From there it was possible to extrapolate that if Salome had hung around the lodge, packing, and stayed to have something to eat before driving back to West Hope House, her arrival would have coincided with the time recorded by the big house's security camera. It also matched the results of the phone analysis which had tracked her journey. The evidence had required to be led, and Crowe had done so quickly, without fuss and in the hope that the jury's rumbling stomachs had drowned most of it out, for none of it was at all harmful to the defence.

When Crowe sat down and the digital clock on the Bench moved to eight minutes past one, the judge would have stopped for lunch had Joanna not stood to say she had only the one question for the witness.

'Mr Ramirez,' she said, 'can you think of any reason at all why your wife would want to kill Mr Diaz?'

Even on a *well he would say that wouldn't he?* basis, with Dario's resounding 'no' still echoing around the walls of the courtroom, it was a good time to adjourn for food.

Salome and Dario were whisked away in a limo, Joanna took her brief and a sandwich to the robing room, and I took a banana and went in search of Peter Falconer. He was out on his daily circuit when I arrived, and so I waited until he returned. It didn't leave me a lot of time to discuss matters with him if I was to walk back up the High Street in time for the trial resuming at two.

'What do you want now?' Peter said, glowering down at me after I had accosted him on the pavement outside his offices.

'Malky asks you to help him out and you go and stab him in the back by landing one of your clients his job on Scotgoals? If that's doing him a favour, I'm glad you didn't want to do him a bad turn.'

The big man released a suitably big sigh. 'It wasn't like that, Robbie. I offered Lancaster some big names at cut price money, but it was Dario or nobody. I have to do the best for my clients, and if there's a juicy TV job going a begging it would be daft for me not to pitch for it.'

'Did you even try Dario?'

'He's not taking calls until after the trial. Anyway, I told you, we've signed an exclusive with SKY for his first interview.'

'So what? Scotgoals aren't going to be fussy if they get second dibs.'

'Look, Robbie. Dario doesn't do interviews. If he wasn't so skint, he would tell SKY to get stuffed.'

'Skint?'

'I told you about his disastrous shipping venture. It cost him millions.'

I didn't buy it. Dario might not know where his next five-hundred-hectare country estate was coming from, but he wasn't selling the Big Issue yet.

'You know where I've been today, Peter? The High Court of Justiciary.' I pointed up the Royal Mile for the sake of geographical accuracy. 'Sitting watching my wife rip the arse out of the Crown's prosecution of Dario's pregnant wife. When we get her off, Dario will do an interview for The Beano if I ask him nicely.'

'You mean, *if* you get her off.'

'Yeah, and *if* Dario gives that interview, Malky will get his job back. Let me tell you what's going to happen. You're going to tell Lancaster that he'll get his Dario interview.'

'What about—'

'You'll find your other client something else.'

'Never mind her. What about me?'

'Scotgoals will pay top dollar for the Dario interview. You can take your cut from that,' I said.

Peter had no immediate comeback and so I left him and his dazzlingly white trainers to begin the march up the High Street. With five minutes to spare, as I turned from pressing my nose against the window of Royal Mile Whiskies, I almost bumped into the bulky figure of Professor Edward Bradley. His usual crumpled three-piece suit had been surgically removed and a sombre dark blue affair transplanted. Beneath it, a crisp white shirt was set off by a burgundy tie, embroidered in gold thread with the motif of a man on horseback, or it might have been a centaur, firing an arrow.

232

His beard and moustache had been the subject of some fairly radical topiary. He was clearly dressed and groomed for the occasion, but too early for it.

'What are you doing here?' I said. 'We've not even finished the Crown case. I don't think we'll need you until Wednesday, Tuesday afternoon at the very earliest.'

'I was told to be here at two and here I am,' he replied.

'Told by who?' At the rates he was charging himself out at, I'd told Grace Mary to tell him not to come to court until he got a message from us. I wasn't paying him silly money to sit in a witness room practising his foot dangling. 'If you think we're paying you to hang around all—'

'Someone from the Procurator Fiscal's High Court Unit phoned me yesterday afternoon. Told me to be here after lunch today.'

He checked both ways at St Giles' Street and crossed the road with me trotting after him.

'The *Crown* told you to come?' Although defence and prosecution lodge and cite their own witnesses, in practice there is no such thing as a prosecution or defence witness. There are only witnesses. If someone's name is on a list, they're up for grabs.

'It wasn't entirely unexpected,' the Professor said. 'I met with some chap Ogilvie and a big-boned girl last week. They wondered why I hadn't lodged a report and wanted to go over a few things with me.'

I deliberately hadn't lodged Professor Bradley's report or that of our psychologist because, while they might take a good guess at it, I didn't want the Crown to know for certain that the defence case rested on suicide or the strength of the evidence.

We walked in the front door of the High Court. 'Tell me you haven't changed your mind?' I said, as we made our way up the slope towards the security desk. 'Not after we consulted in the Bow Bar when you said—'

'Professor Bradley?' Hugh Ogilvie took the last step down from the staircase leading to Courtroom 3. 'We're just about to restart, and you're next on.' He took the elbow of the navy-blue suit. As the Professor was led away, he flashed me an unrepentant smile, the wee golden men on his burgundy tie shooting arrows at me.

Chapter 37

'I really don't like this,' Joanna whispered to me when a few minutes later Professor Bradley crammed himself into the witness box and took the oath.

'You are Professor Edward Leopold Bradley?' Crowe began, and then proceeded to set up the professor as an expert witness by having him list his qualifications. Bradley was in full flow and enjoying himself until Lady Carrick interrupted. 'Members of the jury, I think you can take it from me that Professor Bradley is widely regarded as one of Scotland's foremost forensic pathologists...' I thought Prof B frowned slightly at the *one of* part of that remark. 'And as such you may regard him as an expert and listen to whatever opinion he may have on the matters presented to him.' I could feel the jury relax. Here was someone they could trust. Even the old guy in the woolly jumper and leather elbow patches seemed mildly impressed. Lady Carrick exchanged smiles of mutual appreciation with the witness, and allowed the Advocate depute to continue.

'You were present at the post-mortem examination of the late Armando Diaz, I think?'

An experienced witness like Professor Bradley was someone you stood in the dock, wound up with a single question and let them run like a clockwork train set.

'On the instructions of the accused's solicitor and the kind consent of my colleagues, I attended a post-mortem examination and dissection on the body of Armando Diaz at the Edinburgh City Mortuary along with certain others.' He then went on to list a veritable coach party of attendees, nine altogether consisting of himself plus two consultant forensic pathologists instructed by the Crown, a photographer, DS MacGillivray and DC Swan, a police constable and two mortuary technicians as well as a trainee forensic pathologist along for experience. 'The body was identified as being that of Mr Diaz by accompanying documentation…'

'Have Production 44 in front of you please. Is that Form 4-601 signed by DS Russell MacGillivray?'

'It is,' said Bradley, 'and there was also a body tag attached to the body bag.'

'Please have Production—'

'M'Lady there is no dispute that the body examined was that of Mr Diaz,' Joanna said.

Crowe gave her a polite nod of the head and allowed the witness to continue.

'A tissue sample was also taken, I presume for DNA identification purposes on the instructions of the Procurator Fiscal,' Bradley said.

'What did you know of this case before you attended, Professor?'

'Very little, though prior to the post-mortem examination I was aware Drs Strang and Parlane had attended a Forensic Strategy Meeting. They were kind enough to provide me with a copy of the Homicide Briefing Document.'

'From which you understood what?' Crowe asked.

'That the deceased had been found in the study of his home with what appeared to be a single shotgun wound to the thorax. A 12-bore shotgun and cartridge were found nearby. I also understood that the evidence indicated there to be only one other person present at or around the time of the fatal shooting, namely, the person I believe to be the now accused.'

Joanna leaned into me. 'They could have taken all this from the Crown pathologists.'

That was what worried me. Why press-gang the defence pathologist when the Crown had two of their own?

'I expect after, how many years Professor…?'

'Forty-two as a consultant pathologist.'

'Tragically, you'll have seen many such wounds?'

'Too many.'

'Then I wonder, Professor, if you would take the time to explain the hallmarks of such injuries.'

Professor Bradley took a deep breath and turned to the jury like it consisted of a bunch of undergraduates.

'Shotgun injuries have a completely different profile when compared to those inflicted by rifled firearms. This difference is determined primarily by the type of projectiles in the shotgun. Shotgun cartridges consist of multiple projectiles... What you'd call pellets. These disperse a short distance from the muzzle, leading to extensive damage. The penetrating power of each projectile is, however, reduced the further the distance from the target.'

'Having examined the fatal wound did you form an opinion as to the distance from which the shot may have been fired in this case?' Crowe asked.

'With a shot fired from close range, but over, say, two to three feet away, you'd expect to see a few satellite wounds around the central rat hole.'

'Rat hole?'

'Yes, sorry. That's an expression normally used to describe the main gunshot wound. Not very pleasant.'

'And were there any in this case?'

'Not that I could see. There was some crenation of the wound.'

'Crenation, Professor? For the benefit of the jury please?'

'Like nibbling around the... the rat hole. It's an indication that the pellets have begun to disperse.'

'We've heard from a firearms expert that the weapon in this case was choked, and that test firing suggested that there was limited dispersal over anything up to three metres. That's approximately ten feet for some of us,' Crowe said obsequiously, playing to the jury.

'I can't argue with that,' Bradley said. 'The dispersion of pellets from a shotgun is extremely variable and depends on the weapon and the cartridge. The practice of choking the barrel, intentional narrowing of the muzzle, decreases the dispersion of pellets, so it's essential to test each weapon for individual variations.'

Crowe came out from behind the podium and rested his back against it. He stared down at the defence side of the table before looking to the witness box again. There was a long pause before his next question. 'It's not a matter which has yet been raised in this trial, but what if I were to ask whether you thought Mr Diaz's fatal wound might have been self-inflicted?'

'Suicide?' Professor Bradley seemed to take an age to answer. In reality it was only as long as it took him to stroke his recently landscaped beard a couple of times. 'Not possible in my opinion.'

'And that's your opinion after *how* many years a forensic pathologist?' Crowe was now staring straight ahead. Not at the witness, but at the jury box.

'Forty-two.'

I hardly heard the answers to the final few questions, I was so angry. I heard enough though to realise Bradley had put the kibosh on the suicide defence.

Crowe gathered his papers and with a swish of his black silk gown, walked back to his side of the table. Before he sat down he had one last question for the witness. 'I understand you had a chat with Mr Munro, the accused's solicitor, about this case some time ago. Where did that meeting take place?'

'The Bow Bar on Victoria Street, as I recall.'

'Thank you, Professor.'

Crowe poured himself back into his seat.

'Miss Jordan?' the judge inquired. 'Do you have any questions for the witness?'

238

Chapter 38

'The pub! You consulted with Professor Bradley in the pub!'

Joanna had somehow managed to suppress her anger during the journey back home from court, right through tea and up until the children were in bed. After that, even my volunteering to do the dishes hadn't helped. That Friday evening my arms weren't the only things in soapy water.

'It wasn't like that, Jo.'

'Wasn't like what? Wasn't like a pub? The Bow Bar's running a forensic lab on the side these days, is it?'

'Okay, it was like a pub, but it was a proper consultation and he definitely said suicide was a possibility. He said there was debris found in the wound and when I asked him what kind of debris, he said it was the fibrous wadding from the cartridge which made him think the shotgun must have been fired from really close range. It's all in the post-mortem report.'

'But you didn't think to go back to him after we'd received the firearms report that said the shotgun was choked.'

'No.'

'Or the findings in the Crown autopsy results that reported no contact injury from the barrel…'

'Armando didn't have to hold the gun against himself. We experimented with the stick, remember? Even you could hold it a centimetre or two from your body, Jo. I thought you got somewhere when you crossed him about the wadding,' I said, scraping left over baked beans that were welded to the base of a saucepan. 'Prof Bradley admitted that—'

'He admitted the presence of wadding meant close range, and that, yes, in a suicide it would have been present—'

'There you are then.'

'But not in isolation. Not without skin burns, or singeing, or reddening of skin around the wound from escaping gases, or tattooing from unburnt powder… My cross-examination only made things worse!' Apparently, it wasn't what was contained in the Crown's autopsy report that had been important. It had been what was missing. 'I was made to look stupid because you hadn't prepared the case properly, Robbie.'

As one gets older it's important to realise and embrace your inadequacies. Getting married helps. I heard my phone buzz somewhere in the distance, dried my hands and went off to find it. 'If that's Salome, tell her we need to meet early tomorrow before court,' Joanna yelled after me.

But it wasn't our client. It was Peter Falconer.

'It's a no go, Robbie. I eventually got through to Dario and he actually said he'd think about it if the money was right. Then I phoned Colin Lancaster with the news, and he told me to shove it.'

'What are you talking about? It was Lancaster's idea in the first place,' I said.

'Well, he's right off it now. You could bring Dario into his studio leading a marching band and he'd have him slung out.'

'What did you say to put him off?'

'Nothing. Honest.'

'You must have said something.'

'I said that you had Dario on a string, and all he had to do was renew Malky's contract. That was it.'

'And?'

'He said there was more chance of him letting a zombie plague into one of his TV studios than your brother. I tried, Robbie. Honestly, I did.'

'Who was that?' Joanna asked on my return to the kitchen. I hardly heard her. I was too deep in thought. What had put Lancaster off what had been his own idea? It wasn't like he didn't need the viewers. According to Malky the ratings for the last few episodes of Scotgoals were well down since his departure. An interview with Dario would have undoubtedly raised the programme's profile and would also have been a great way to bring Malky back in without losing face. Everyone would be a winner. Even Dario. The TV appearance would earn him enough for a few more nights at the Newberry, where Mr Allegedly Skint and Salome were slumming it for the period of the trial.

I took the frying pan from the hob and took it over to the sink. 'Did you know that Dario's broke?' I asked Joanna.

'Who told you that?'

'Peter Falconer. I was wanting him to talk Dario into agreeing to do a TV interview.'

'About the trial? I don't understand. Why would you want to do that?'

'No, I'm not talking about the trial. It's to do with Malky. I'll tell you all about it later. The point is that Falconer says Dario, who never does interviews, could be persuaded if the money was right.'

'Robbie, people will do anything if the money is right.'

'Not Dario. Not interviews, except maybe now because he needs the money.'

Joanna took me firmly by the biceps. 'Stop and listen to yourself. Dario is one of the world's most famous footballers. He's got a private jet and owns a big chunk of the Borders. He's just put up half a million in bail money and he's staying at the Newberry. How can he need the money?'

'He doesn't *need* the money, Jo. Not like we need money. But he has lost a lot of it recently. Dario invested in some ships. Drugs were found and the whole fleet was confiscated. Plus, he had to pay out a fortune to keep himself out of the picture.'

Joanna was quick to make something out of this information. 'Armando Diaz was Dario's financial adviser, and—'

'And now he's dead. That's not all. Dario's agents, if you can call them that, they're seriously bad news.'

'In what way?'

'In a Colombian necktie, kind of way.'

'What! And you're telling me this now?'

I returned to the sink and put some clean water in the basin along with too much washing up liquid. 'Jo, I told you weeks ago there was a way you could get into West Hope House undetected via the back door.' I walked over to the hob and brought back the frying pan. 'You just park on a country road that nobody uses, climb a dyke, walk a few hundred yards through some woods, pass a couple of friendly golden retrievers…'

'Yes, yes, I know. Let me think. Someone enters the house that way, shoots Armando, Salome hears the noise, rushes into the study, sees Armando dead or dying, goes to his aid…'

'Touching the shotgun, and only the shotgun, which is why her prints weren't on the cartridge…'

'And seconds later Beverly appears,' Joanna said.

I rinsed the suds off the frying pan, left it on the draining board to dry and sat down at the table across from Joanna. 'Not sure what to do, but knowing how it looked, Salome called the only lawyer she knew in Scotland. The same one who just the day before had been bragging about his latest famous victory.'

'And all the stuff about being raped?' Joanna said.

'She must have thought *he deserved it* would be a defence, because of what I told her about Isabella Ewart's case. That's why she no longer wants it mentioned. It's a load of nonsense. Tomorrow, when the cook or housekeeper or whatever she is comes to give evidence, you don't ask her about Armando's wandering hands, you ask her about the route into the house via the back door and the fact that it's not covered by CCTV.'

'What does Salome know about Dario's financial affairs?' Joanna asked.

I didn't know if she knew anything. I suspected a lot of women married to rich men didn't, not in detail, not until it came time to divorce. 'Strange, isn't it?' I said. 'That just a couple of days after you consult with her husband, Salome is charged with killing his financial adviser. You never told me much about what you and Dario discussed at the Newberry. Only that he was thinking of divorce.'

'Dario and Salome are devout Catholics,' Joanna said. 'We didn't discuss divorce so much as annulment.'

I didn't even know we had those in Scotland. Which was because, as Joanna went on to tell me, we didn't. There were certain factors that could render a marriage void, but none applied to Dario and Salome.

'He wanted to know if he had a religious annulment whether he'd still have to go through court for a divorce,' Joanna said.

'What did you tell him?'

'I told him he would. I also thought a religious annulment was pushing it a bit after fourteen years of marriage.'

I wasn't so sure about that. Dario was one of the world's greatest ever footballers. I felt the Vatican might find a way to bend a free kick around that particular wall.

'It didn't for Henry the Eighth,' Joanna said.

'But Henry was just royalty. Dario is football royalty.'

'Anyway, I told him it didn't matter what the Church decided. He'd still need to go through the court for a divorce, and Salome would have certain rights.'

'You seem pretty confident about that for someone who went straight from Uni into criminal law.'

'I have remembered some civil law from University, Robbie.'

'At Edinburgh University what we called Civil Law was actually Roman Law.'

'Yeah, well I went to Glasgow and unlike you actually attended some family law lectures,' Joanna said.

'And it took you half an hour alone in Dario's bedroom to tell him that?'

'It was more like twenty minutes, and there's something else. He's got a pre-nup. His legal advisers insisted on it. If Salome cheats on him or hits thirty five without giving him a child, it's over. She gets a limited pay-out and they call it quits. He also wanted to know if the Scottish courts would recognise a pre-nup drawn up under Spanish law.'

'Will it?'

Joanna shrugged. 'I don't even know if the Scottish courts would recognise a prenuptial agreement drawn up under Scots law. I told him he'd be better consulting an expert. He said the reason he'd asked me for advice was because he didn't trust any of his lawyers. I said I'd look into it. He insisted that I wasn't to tell anyone about our conversation. Not even you. He said if word got out he'd know where it came from.'

'Well, you've told me now,' I said.

'That's because it doesn't make any difference. Salome's pregnant.'

'But at the time Armando was killed it made a difference,' I said. 'Two birds one stone. Revenge for Armando's bad investment advice and frame Salome at the same time so she gets nothing from the divorce.'

'Only two things wrong with those particular birds, Robbie. Dario was out on the heath with a shooting party sixty miles away at the time Armando was shot. And being convicted of murder wouldn't have affected any divorce settlement.' She patted me on the cheek. 'Keep thinking.'

'What's the plan on Monday morning?' I asked.

'All we can do is show that there was a way a third person could have entered the house.'

'And after that?'

'After that?' Joanna said. 'After that, we put Salome in the witness box and ask her to tell us who she thinks that person might have been.'

Chapter **39**

Friday night, dishes washed, children in bed, Joanna was looking to relax in the company of a bottle of white Zinfandel, a bar of chocolate and a Christmas movie. I was pretty much surplus to requirements, so I walked round to my dad's because I knew Malky would be dropping his car off there after his five-a-side game. I was hoping to share a taxi into town with him, or my dad might even give us a lift.

'What do you think of that then?' my dad said, when I walked in to find him sitting in an armchair admiring a shiny, newly hand-turned wooden bowl, pride of place on the coffee table in the middle of his livingroom. He had a cupboard full of them. This was clearly bowl-of-the-week.

'How many's that now?' I said.

'This one's special. It's made from an old piece of sycamore that Charlie Sneddon had lying about in his yard. He cut me a blank out of it.'

'What's so special about it?'

'Look at the finish. That's Danish oil with a coating of carnauba wax.'

'It's lovely,' I said. 'Should come in handy for keeping your fingers in.'

He grunted. 'What are you here for? Need some more advice on that murder case of yours?'

'No, I'm having a night off,' I said. 'Thought I might go for a pint with Malky. It's been a busy week.'

'Busy? You've spent half of it sitting on your arse in court letting your wife do all the work. He lifted a bottle of whisky and a glass from the floor beside his chair.

'How many of those have you had?' I asked.

'This is my first. Why? Who's counting?'

'I was hoping you'd give me and Malky a lift to the Red Corner when he gets back from five-a-sides.'

He started to pour. 'Malky's not coming tonight. He's having a quick pint at the Red Corner and then going through to Edinburgh. So, you can just sit yourself down and we'll have a nice wee chat about your murderer. I'll get you a glass.'

'What's Malky going to Edinburgh for?' I called to him as he left the room.

He returned with a tumbler and handed it and the bottle over to me. 'He's gone to see Peter Falconer. He thinks he can persuade him to have Dario do an interview to get him his job back.'

I started to pour myself a small one and then stopped. 'Dad, I've spoken to Peter about this already. Even if Dario is prepared to do an interview for Scotgoals, the producer's no longer interested.'

'Then why didn't you tell him instead of having your brother traipse all the way through to Edinburgh to some dinner or other? I think it's a fundraiser for women's football. Malky won't stand a chance with his good looks. Those girls will pass him round like a scud mag in the slammer.'

The clock on the mantelpiece told me Malky's five-a-side game had not long finished. The chances were he'd still be replacing lost fluids at the Red Corner bar before he went for the train. I tried phoning, but there was no answer. After some persuasion my dad agreed to put down his whisky glass long enough to give me a lift.

'Not seen your brother tonight,' Brendan the barman said. 'Usually comes in here on a Friday night with a few of his mates, but he's been a no-show. 'What'll you have?'

I ordered a pint and sat down on a stool at the bar. The place was quiet, but it was still early.

'Big Bella find you yet?' he asked. 'She's out of hospital.'

Concentrating on Salome's trial, I'd forgotten all about Brendan's boxing event and Isabella Ewart's debut last week. 'Hospital?'

Brendan went off to pour some drinks further down the bar and returned to run some of the money he'd taken in payment through the cash register. 'Yeah, she did all right though. It was quite close for the first two rounds. She gave it all she had - until the knockout in the third that is. All the same, the crowd loves a good KO.'

'How could she end up in hospital?' I said. 'This is women fighting. It's two-minute rounds. She must have been in the ring for less than six minutes.'

Brendan laughed. 'Don't kid yourself. Some of these girls are big hitters and six minutes in the ring can seem like a lifetime. It's just a shame I hadn't longer to train her. I reckon six months and she might have won a points decision. She threw most of the punches - just not the last one.'

'And when you say she's looking for me...?' Somehow, I didn't think it would be to hand over her loser's purse.

'She came in here last night and said she'd catch you at your office today.'

I'd been out of the office at court all day, thankfully.

'Probably best if I stay clear of her for a while,' I said. 'Let the bruises heal.'

Brendan trickled off to serve some under-agers who'd ordered Red Corner shandies: draught lager, hold the lemonade. I took out my phone and this time got through to Malky.

'Where are you?' I said. Wherever he was, there was a lot of noise in the background. 'I'm at the Red Corner looking for you.'

'I'm in Edinburgh with Pete,' he said. 'I never went to fives tonight. Pete's telling me that he told you Colin Lancaster's deal is off and that he's not wanting an interview with Dario anymore. Why didn't you tell me?'

'That's why I came to the Red Corner. To let you know.' I wondered about Peter Falconer. The first thing that had happened after I told him about the termination of Malky's contract, was that one of his own client's got the job. Then when I had the Dario interview more or less sorted, suddenly Colin Lancaster was no longer interested, even though it was all his idea. 'Is Peter with you just now? Put him on, will you?'

'What is it? I'm busy,' was Peter's opening line.

'Not too busy to shaft my brother,' I said. 'I'm onto you. First you stiff me for my fee—'

'That was over two years ago, and it was my client, not me.'

'And now you're back-stabbing my brother by scuppering the deal with Scotgoals.'

'I've no time for this, Robbie. You're delusional.'

'Am I? Lancaster was red hot on the Dario interview and now he's a polar icecap. Who's guest of honour tonight at your do? It's her, isn't it?'

'I don't know what you're talking about.'

'Your client. The woman footballer who's taken Malky's job. You spoke to Lancaster and made sure Malky would never get it back.'

'I'm sorry, Robbie, but this conversation is over.'

'Good, put Malky back on. I want him to know what you've been up to.'

Brendan came over. 'Try and keep the noise down to a riot, Robbie,' he said.

'You're not needing to speak to Malky,' Peter said, very calmly to me, as I left the bar to continue the call outside on the pavement. 'There's more to this than you know, and I'll explain everything to him, in confidence, just as soon as I get a minute. Now, if you don't mind, I'm going to hang up and give your brother his phone back.'

The number of social events Peter and Malky had been to together over the years; sportsman's dinners where risqué jokes abounded, Peter had to have a lot of dirt to shovel about Malky. What had he told Lancaster about my brother to make him change his mind? It seemed Peter was a great one for confidentiality, providing it didn't apply to him.

'Why would Dario's agents have Armando Diaz killed?' I said.

'What!'

'You heard me. Armando Diaz was Dario's financial adviser. Dario lost a lot of money. So, I presume, did his agents.'

'I said you were never to talk about that to anyone,' Peter hissed down the line at me.

'I'm not. I'm talking to you,' I said. 'Where can I find the name of the agency and details of the drug bust in Colombia?'

'You do not want to go there, Robbie. Seriously.'

But I was going there. My client was looking at a life sentence for murdering someone who Dario's agents had bumped off for whatever reason. Revenge? Or did he know too much? Was that why Dario couldn't face his wife when she was in prison? Ashamed because he knew who'd really been responsible for his friend's death, too scared to do anything about it. Diamond Tooth, an ex-member of Spain's SAS, recruited by Dario's agents. Who better to enter West Hope House and do the dirty undetected?

The phone line went dead. I went back into the bar, finished my drink and went home.

Chapter 40

Rosemary Dow was called as a witness on Monday morning. The Crown's intention was for her to confirm that when she'd left at three o'clock there had been no one else at West Hope House other than Armando who was on his clay pigeon range. That would tend to show that when Armando was seen walking to the rear of the big house at five-twenty, and Salome had walked through the front door just a minute or so later, there were only two people present. One of them ended up dead, and according to the traitorous Prof B it wasn't suicide.

Examination in chief took half an hour and afterwards Cameron Crowe sat down looking like the Vampire who had bought the blood bank. For her part, Joanna did just as we'd discussed. Karate cook agreed that a path could be beaten from a country lane, through woodland, all the way to the back door of West Hope House. She agreed the dogs were everyone's friends and that when she left for the day the door had remained unlocked as usual. Armando usually came in that way and left his shoes along with anything needing washed, before locking surplus ammo in the storeroom off the kitchen.

'From that would you agree, Mrs Dow, that a person could enter the house from the woods, make their way to the study and leave by the same route without anyone noticing, and without it being captured on security camera?' Joanna asked.

'Don't answer that question, please,' Crowe instructed the witness, getting to his feet as he did. 'M'Lady, that's a leading question of quite ridiculous proportions. I appreciate Miss Jordan's inexperience, but—'

'But it's your witness and this is cross-examination, Mr Crowe,' Lady Carrick said. 'I'd have thought someone with *your* experience would have realised that. Please answer the question Mrs Dow.'

Crowe sank back into his seat. The objection had been a double mistake. He must have known the answer to a leading question would be allowed under cross, but even worse for him it now made it look like the answer was a concern for the Crown.

'Yes, they could do that if there was nobody in the kitchen, I suppose.'

'But after three o'clock on the day Mr Diaz died, you weren't in the kitchen. Were you?' Joanna didn't bother for a reply. 'Tell me, do you think Salome Ramirez killed Armando Diaz?'

Cameron Crowe emitted a strangled sound, which Lady Carrick took as an objection, but not quickly enough to prevent the witness from answering.

'No, I don't. Salome would never do a thing like that.'

'Members of the jury,' the judge said, 'the witness's opinion on the character of the accused is neither here nor there, and I direct you to ignore it. Miss Jordan, I want no more questions of that sort put to the witness. Do you understand?'

But Joanna was already making her way back to her seat.

Crowe stood. 'M'Lady, I realise it's not yet eleven, but I have a matter of law I wish to raise. Perhaps now might be a good time for the jury's mid-morning break.'

The jury seemed quite content with that. All except the old guy at the front, still dressed in the same clothes, still looking like he'd rather be on the hills with the sheep or whatever. The jury duly sent off to their room for coffee, Crowe was about to hold forth when the judge told him to sit. 'Unless I'm mistaken, Advocate depute, you are concerned, as I am, by a potential line of defence Miss Jordan may be intending to lead.' Lady Carrick stared down at Joanna who rose to her feet to be addressed. 'Miss Jordan, your client's defence to the charge has not been clear from the outset of this trial. I accept Miss Ramirez is quite within her rights to put the Crown to the test; however, if you are about to embark on a defence of incrimination—'

'M'Lady—'

'Please don't interrupt. If you are now, without having given due notice, intent on a special defence of incrimination, then I'm afraid I can't allow it. You were specifically asked at the Preliminary Hearing if you had any special defences, and you indicated very clearly then that you had none. And yet judging by your cross-examination of the last witness, it seems possible you may go on to suggest that someone else was responsible for killing Mr Diaz other than your client or, indeed, the deceased himself. Would you care to explain yourself to the court?'

'M'Lady, the defence is a very simple one. My client did not murder Armando Diaz, and if Professor Bradley is to be believed, he didn't kill himself. That leaves only one possible avenue for the defence, which is that someone else killed him.'

Lady Carrick grunted. It was hard to fault the logic. She let Joanna continue.

'The essence of an incrimination is that you have an incriminee. Someone you can name and give the Crown notice of, so that in fairness they can make their own enquiries. The accused does not know who, if anyone, killed Mr Diaz, only that she was not responsible. What is the defence supposed to do in order to give the Crown fair notice of that? It can hardly lodge a special defence incriminating the seven billion other people on the planet.'

'Then it's not your intention to specifically name any person or persons?'

'The defence does not know who that person might have been, though inquiries are ongoing.'

'If you have ongoing inquiries into an incrimination defence, Miss Jordan, that should have been highlighted at Preliminary Hearing stage. If you had, the court would have looked sympathetically on any defence motion to postpone the trial. As I recall, both Crown and defence were extremely keen to fix an early date, which the court with no little difficulty managed to accommodate. We are where we are. There will be no incrimination, not of any person or persons in this trial known or unknown. No aspersions cast. No vague notions put forward. Do I make myself clear? If new evidence should arise at some stage in the future, then depending on the jury's verdict, that would be a matter for the Appeal Court to consider.'

Lady Carrick pushed her chair back. She looked like she was going to get up, something she seemed incapable of without the assistance of her Macer. The man in black robes and white dicky bow opened the hatch at the side of the bench ready to go to her aid.

'M'Lady,' Joanna said. 'With the greatest of respect...'

The judge looked down as though Joanna had thrown a stink bomb at her. 'I've made my decision. Court will reconvene in ten minutes.' She stood and waited for her Macer to lead her off the Bench to her chambers.

'Where does that leave you?' Crowe called across the table at us. 'I saw the suicide nonsense coming from a mile off, but this big boy done it and ran away thing, that is new. Shame her ladyship doesn't seem to like it. Can't wait to hear what you come up with next.'

I'd like to have known that myself. All I could do was blank Crowe and his smug prosecution team as I got up and followed Joanna out of the courtroom, down the stairs, out the front door and into a crisp and cold December morning.

A fair number of those who'd been spectating had come out for a smoke.

'The judge has been nobbled,' I said.

Joanna led me out of earshot of the nicotine addicts, many of them journalists, to the other side of David Hume and his big shiny brass toe. Christmas shoppers hurried by us. 'Don't be ridiculous, Robbie. Nobbled by who? She's perfectly right. We didn't formally lodge an incrimination, and she's not letting us do it at this late stage. It's the rules of procedure.'

'Don't tell me. And we have to play by them,' I said.

'Fact is Lady Carrick's taken away our last chance of leading a credible defence,' Joanna said.

'Not if you tough it out,' I said. 'What's the judge going to do about it if you merely imply someone else could have been to blame? It'll look bad if she starts interfering when Salome is giving evidence. It could make for an excellent appeal point. You were quite right in what you said. An incrimination is for when you are accusing a particular person. You should still be able to suggest that some third-party—'

'A mysterious, unnamed third-party? Who's going to believe that without some motive, anyway?' Joanna said.

'What if the jury heard how Armando had lost Dario millions of pounds? That Dario's agents are little more than a criminal cartel and capable of anything? Okay, here's what we're going to do,' I said. 'You go back into court. While you're there, I'll take Dario into one of the consulting rooms and tell him that if he doesn't want his baby born in prison, he'd better come clean about Armando losing them a lot of money and what kind of people his agents are.'

'Dario's testified. We can't call him again,' Joanna said.

'No, but he can brief Salome tonight and we can take it from her when she comes to give evidence.'

'Robbie, that's called coaching the witness,'

'Who cares so long as it's the truth?'

255

'What good would it do? You heard the judge. She won't let me start banding about the names of possible incriminees.'

'You don't need to. All you do is take from Salome that Armando was responsible for losing her husband and, by dint of that, his agents, a massive amount of money.' Surprisingly, Joanna was no longer objecting. 'Of course, you can expect some flak from Lady Carrick.'

Joanna steepled her fingers and put them under her chin, head tilted upwards, eyes looking up into the blue winter sky. 'Let me handle the flak from the Bench,' she said.

'You're beginning to sound like me in the Isabella Ewart case,' I laughed, though I was starting to get a little worried. I hadn't really believed my wife would buy into my gung-ho approach. Now that she had, I wasn't sure if I wanted her to. 'Just be careful. This is the High Court.'

'And this is nothing like Isabella Ewart's case. You knew she was guilty, but you bashed on with the *he deserved it* defence nonetheless. I'm convinced Salome is innocent.'

'You don't know that.'

'I don't care. I'm not standing back again and letting—'

'Joanna, you've got to let what happened to Marc Traynor go,' I said. 'His death had nothing to do with you.'

'That time, when we stood here with him after the Preliminary Hearing... I could have done more to reassure him. Given him some hope at least.'

'You weren't his mum, Jo. You were his lawyer and you told him what the law was.'

'Then I'm fed up with the law, Robbie. We weren't allowed to lead important evidence in Marc Traynor's case and now we can't blame somebody in a murder trial because we didn't lodge a piece of paper in court five weeks ago.' She was on the verge of tears. I didn't know what to do. At a signal from the front door, the smokers began to file back into the building. I let Joanna go on ahead while I took a moment to think how I was going to approach things with Dario. That's if his security team would let me anywhere near him.

I was about to head into the building when someone tapped my shoulder. I turned to be met by a familiar smile revealing a diamond studded tooth. Dario's minder didn't say anything, just held up to my face his mobile phone. On it was a photo of Tina, school uniform, running about the playground at what I assumed was morning break. 'Don't do it,' Diamond Tooth said. Then, still smiling, returned the phone to his pocket and walked back into court.

Chapter 41

'He wouldn't even speak to you about it?' Joanna asked.

Lunch time, and as usual Salome and Dario had been spirited away by their entourage. Joanna and I went next door to the St Giles Café for a coffee and something to eat. I'd already phoned the school to make sure Tina was all right. While Joanna had been finding us a table, I called Grace Mary to ask her to collect Tina from school at three twenty-five, rather than have her walk to the office as she usually did when Joanna and I were both working.

I crunched into a crispy bacon roll. 'He doesn't want his agents, or anybody associated with them, even mentioned in passing.'

'Not even to save his wife from a life sentence? Doesn't matter, I can still put the question out there.'

'The judge will slap you down,' I said.

'When did you start worrying about judicial disapproval?' Joanna said, popping a piece of a brie and cranberry croissant into her mouth.

I couldn't tell her about Tina, she had enough on her mind, but I couldn't let her start putting it about in a courtroom packed with journalists that Dario's agents were nothing more than a criminal cartel. 'It'll sound desperate to the jury if we change tack now, Jo. You were right when you said we should stick with the one defence and not go off on tangents. Without any hard evidence to lead as to why someone would want to kill Armando, we continue with the line that he killed himself.'

'What about Professor Bradley?'

'Who cares about him? So what, there was no scorching or tattooing or whatever? We've got the Crown's own autopsy report and firearm's expert saying the gun was fired close range. We've got Laszlo Derry waiting in the wings to say suicide was possible and a psychologist to speak to the fact that Armando fitted the correct suicide profile. It's not for us to prove anything, only raise a doubt. What we have is enough. We don't need strange people coming in shooting Armando and disappearing into thin air.'

Joanna wiped her hands on a paper napkin. 'You're probably right. If only we could use Salome's rape allegation. That would be a reason for Armando to have killed himself the jury might understand.'

'That's not down to you. That's Salome's decision.'

'And the black eye?'

'It's a wee scuff mark. Who doesn't get one from time to time? It was good for us in the rape scenario, but I can't see how it helps the Crown case any.'

'I think DS MacGillivray is the last witness for the prosecution,' Joanna said.

I should have known Crowe would be closing the Crown case with a bang. Leaving Salome's word's *he deserved it,* ringing in the ears of the jury.

'The only line of cross I can put to him is that he's mistaken. We've listened to the recording. It's not *all* that clear. Is it?'

It had sounded pretty clear to me, and I'd heard it both live and the recorded version. 'Crowe will lead MacGillivray through his involvement with the case, but it'll just be a build up to his big finale,' I said. 'When you get up to cross, let the stuff about the mark on her eye, calling her lawyer before calling the police, the blood on her hands… Let that all slide. We can have Salome clear it up when she comes to give evidence. The thing we have to nip in the bud is Salome's reply to caution and charge. What you should do, Jo, is ask MacGillivray this one question.' I produced a scrap of paper from my pocket and slid it through the crumbs of my bacon roll and across the table to Joanna.

'Buenas tardes, Sargento. Entiendo que habla espanol con fliudez?' Joanna said haltingly.

'It means, Good afternoon, Sergeant, I understand you are fluent in Spanish.' Or according to Google translate it did. 'Learn it off by heart so you don't have to look at the paper when you're asking the question,' I said. 'McGillivray won't have a clue. That's when you say: Sorry, I was asking if you were fluent in Spanish. I take it the answer is no. And then you sit down.

I sat back and took a sip of coffee. I could tell Joanna was impressed, or at least she wasn't voicing any objections. What better way to round off the Crown case than by removing the detonator from its last stick of dynamite?

I'd sat through the live edition of Salome's police interview and had no interest in listening again to the recorded version. It had been a no comment interview, and, although Crowe was intending to play the whole thing, it was only to highlight Salome's outburst at the end. While it was playing, I slipped out of court, found a bar officer and asked them to go into court and bring Dario to one of the nearby consulting rooms as a matter of urgency. Court officers aren't renowned for their cooperation, but this one seemed quite chuffed at the idea, and a minute or so later it was just me, Dario and a certain diamond -toothed individual in one small room.

'I need to speak to you in private,' I told Dario, once he'd alighted on one of the hard wooden seats designed for people with no nerve endings. He turned to look at his minder who was standing by the door and then back to me as if to say, that's about as private as it gets.

I went over and opened the door. 'There's a window you can look through if you get lonely,' I said. Diamond Tooth didn't budge.

'This is important,' I told Dario. He nodded at Diamond Tooth who walked out. I closed the door behind him and sat down.

'In case you haven't noticed, things aren't going too well in there,' I said, jerking a thumb at the courtroom across the lobby from us. 'Someone killed Armando and it wasn't Salome. Don't ask me how, but I know that you lost a lot of money on a certain investment venture. I know there were drugs involved and I know that you don't want anything said about that.' He was going to interrupt, but I didn't let him. 'What I don't know, but can assume, is that it was Armando who advised you on that investment and that the people who look after your interests wouldn't be very happy about you losing all that money.'

'You cannot say anything about this to anyone,' Dario said.

'I know. Your friend has made that very plain to me.'

'What do you want?'

'The same thing as you. Salome acquitted. Here's what I want you to do. The Crown is about to close its case. First thing tomorrow Salome will be called to give evidence. In the course of that evidence she needs to say something to give a reason why Armando might have killed himself. I want her to blurt out that Armando was involved with drug traffickers. She doesn't have to mention any names.' Lady Carrick wouldn't like such an outburst, but no blame would attach to Joanna if the accused's remark was unsolicited, and even if the jury were told to ignore what they'd heard - how were they supposed to do that?

'What if the prosecutor asks for names?' Dario said.

'She can say she doesn't know any.'

'Then how does she know about Armando and drugs?'

'Maybe she overheard something while she was living at his house. She seems to have been there often enough. Or he could have told her about it, and that he was worried there might be repercussions.'

261

'That would not be the truth,' Dario said.

I stood up and leaned over the table at him. 'It would be the truth about Armando being involved in a drug deal, wouldn't it?' I said. Dario looked away. Answer enough for me. 'So, it is the truth, just not the whole truth. There's no need for Salome to bring you or anyone else associated with you into this, but, Dario, this is the rest of your wife's life we're talking about. This is about your child growing up without its mother. If she's got to edit the truth a little in order to save herself, I think we can live with that.'

I opened the door to find Diamond Tooth standing arms folded outside in the corridor leading to the lobby. 'Remember,' he said to me as I brushed past him and onward into the courtroom.

By the time I had made my way to my seat beside Joanna, Cameron Crowe was finishing his examination in chief. 'Se lo merecía. He deserved it. You have no doubt that's what the accused said, Sergeant?'

'It sounded like that to me, Sir,' MacGillivray said. 'And you've heard the recording.'

'Yes, we've all heard the recording,' Crowe agreed, 'but it was in Spanish. How can you be so certain?'

Joanna was on her feet. 'M'Lady, I don't think Sergeant MacGillivray did ever say he was certain of what he'd heard. I think he said, it sounded like that to him.'

Lady Carrick looked down at her notes then over at Crowe. 'Miss Jordan is quite correct, Advocate depute. The witness didn't say he was certain the accused said, Se lo merecía. He said, *it sounded like that to me.*'

'A slip of the tongue on my part, M'Lady.'

'Another one?' Lady Carrick said.

Crowe smiled like a gangrenous wound. 'Let me ask the witness again. Sergeant MacGillivray, you were there at the time, and you've heard the recording again today. What is it you believe on oath that the accused said in reply to caution and charge?'

'She spoke in Spanish, and I believe the correct interpretation is, he deserved it.'

In hindsight I wouldn't have cross-examined the witness. Answers like, *it sounded like that to me* and *I believe she said* were hardly definitive. If Salome maintained she had said something slightly different in Spanish, who was to say who was right - the Scotsman or the Colombian?'

'Thank you,' said Crowe. 'If you'll wait there, I think my friend may have some questions for you.'

By the way Joanna was gathering her papers and heading for the podium, Crowe was tooting-sure his friend had some questions for the witness, one question in particular. Joanna took a breath and said innocently, 'Buenas tardes, sargento, entiendo que habla espanol con fliudez?' She'd clearly been practising.

Some of the jurors, realising what Joanna was doing, smiled. Most just looked confused. The only person whose facial expression didn't change was the old guy in the front row. His craggy features remained set in a permanent scowl. Someone, I felt sure, was going to pay for his wasted time.

MacGillivray asked Joanna to repeat the question. She did. 'Buenas tardes, Sargento. Entiendo que habla espanol con fliudez?'

The police officer shifted in the witness box, cleared his throat and replied, 'Buenas tardes, señorita Jordan. Sí lo soy. Mi abuelo es español. De niño pasé muchos veranos con él.'

Chapter 42

The standard routine when Joanna and I were at the High Court was that my dad looked after Jamie, and Tina pretty much looked after herself. First thing, we'd drop Jamie off at my dad's house, or he'd come to ours, and then we'd drop Tina off at school with a packed lunch. When school got out, she made the short journey from the Lowport Primary School to my office at the Cross. Once there she was all Grace Mary's until we arrived back from Edinburgh or Glasgow. Since court usually finished around four o'clock, catching the train from Edinburgh to Linlithgow and returning to the office before my secretary finished at five wasn't usually a problem.

Joanna was still reliving her cross-examination of DS Russell MacGillivray as we walked from the train station back to the office. 'Walked right into the trap. Now we know why Cameron Crowe didn't instruct an interpreter to listen to the police interview. He knew we'd try and pull a stunt like that. Just like he knew MacGillivray was fluent in Spanish.'

'Stop killing yourself about it. You did all right,' I said. 'In the circumstances.'

I'd long since stopped defending myself. The question in Spanish would have been a cracker, but for MacGillivray's Spanish grandfather and the fact that he'd spent most of his boyhood summers in Spain. When the old boy had died, MacGillivray had inherited a property in Andalusia, which he still used as a holiday home. He was practically a native.

'You did eventually get him to accept it was possible *no se lo merecía* could be mistaken for *se lo merecía*. That was good work.'

'He didn't say it was possible, Robbie. He said it was *possible*, but unlikely.'

We'd caught a slightly later train than expected, and by the time we reached the office door Grace Mary and Tina were already outside on the pavement. It was when I saw my precious wee girl standing there, wrapped up against the cold and waiting for me, that I wondered if I'd gone too far with what I'd told Dario to tell Salome to say. She was to blurt it out so it wouldn't seem like Joanna had intended her to say it. Nor was Salome to mention any names. Where was the harm, except to the Crown case?

When she saw us, Tina broke loose from my secretary's hand and came charging towards us. I swept her up and gave her a big hug. It was then that I made two decisions. The first was that I'd tell Salome when we consulted next morning not to say anything about Armando and drugs. We had the psychologist's evidence which was enough without an actual motive, and, anyway, if Salome wanted to keep the best and most believable reason for Armando killing himself a secret, that was her problem. Why should I put my family at risk? The second decision was just as easy.

'You know what?' I said, as with a parting wave to Grace Mary we went in search of my car. 'You've been so good, Tina, me and Mum have decided to buy you a FastFreez tracksuit after all.'

'We have?' Joanna said.

'Yeah, you remember, Jo. Tell me, what colour do you want, Tina? Didn't you say Florence was getting a blue one?' Once she's stopped hugging my neck and shrieking, I asked her, 'Did anything strange happen at school today?'

'Strange? What do you mean strange, Robbie?' Joanna answered for her.

'Sorry, did I say strange? I meant did anything funny happen?'

Tina filled us in with a blow-by-blow account of what sounded like an average school day all the way back home, where my dad and Jamie were in the livingroom in the

265

company of a set of Duplo bricks. My dad was into construction while my son was more on the demolition side of things.

'Word on the street is your girl's going down,' my dad said.

'Word on the street? Is that Sesame Street, Dad?' You've been watching Jamie all day. How would you know anything?'

He tapped the side of his nose.

'Don't tell me. Dougie Fleming?' Fleming, now DI Fleming, had been my dad's old police cadet.

'He likes to keep me in the loop.'

'What's he been saying?'

I could see Tina standing listening intently. 'Have you not got homework to do?' I said.

'How can I do homework if I can't find my pencil case?' My daughter's missing pencil case was a dilemma that had been troubling mankind since half-eight that morning.

'Go with Mum and she'll find you a pencil. A sharp one!' I called after her as she trudged off, following Joanna into the kitchen, hauling her schoolbag behind her like Jacob Marley's schedule of previous convictions.

My dad placed a final brick atop a three-foot tower with one hand while gently holding my son at bay with the other. 'Dougie was speaking to Russell MacGillivray. He was…' He got up and closed the door between kitchen and livingroom, allowing Jamie to knock down his building. 'He was saying about Joanna trying to catch MacGillivray out by speaking Spanish. Says everyone knows Russ MacGillivray has a place in Spain. Half of C Division used to have him bring them back cheap fags whenever he was over there. What made her ask such a daft question?'

I picked up some bricks and started in on the rebuild. 'What else was he saying?'

266

'That they've eliminated everyone else apart from your client being in the house at the time Diaz was shot. That your own expert has ruled out suicide. That your client's fingerprints are on the gun and…' he could hardly finish the sentence for laughing, his voice going squeaky at the funny side of it all. 'And she more or less admitted it - but in Spanish.' His hands were shaking so much with laughter that he was having trouble joining two pieces of Duplo together. 'When Dougie was telling me about it, I said, is that all you've got?' There were tears in his eyes. Even Jamie stopped trying to invade our redevelopment site and sat back wondering what was going on.

'Hilarious, Dad, but I'll tell you what they don't have,' I said. 'A motive. They haven't a clue why a friend of Armando Diaz, a woman who's stayed at his house many times, would shoot him for absolutely no reason whatsoever.'

My dad stopped laughing and wiped his eyes. 'When did women ever need a reason for anything, Son? So, what's the plan for tomorrow?' he said, having recovered himself by the time Joanna joined us, leaving Tina at the kitchen table.

'I'll come to that,' Joanna said, 'but first of all, Robbie, why the sudden change of mind about Tina's tracksuit?'

I couldn't tell her about Diamond Tooth's photograph. 'It'll do for her Christmas,' I said. 'Save us having to think of something.'

'Robbie, I've bought Tina's Christmas! Don't you member all those days I went shopping with my mum?'

If at all possible, I tend not to go shopping. It's not that I don't want to, it's just that I've found after around the forty-five-minute mark I begin to lose the strength in my limbs. It's a recognised medical condition. A congenital thing that comes down through the generations with the Y chromosome.

'It can be a wee extra, then,' I said.

'*A wee extra*? It'll be two hundred pounds if you include the special T-shirt that goes along with it. Still, I don't mind if you don't. But you'll need to be quick. Christmas is only six days away. The worst thing that could happen is for you to say she's getting one and then finding they're sold out.'

Sold out? Was that what I was doing to Salome? Selling her out because of the threat by Diamond Tooth? If we were going to leave a doubt in the jury's mind about Armando's suicide, did we have enough without Salome's rape allegation? With the drugs trafficking accusation, we'd at least have a reason, vague though it might be. All we needed was to get that motive out in front of the jury without blackening Dario's character in any way. What should I tell Salome to do tomorrow? What should she say when she climbed into that witness box, put her hand up to God and testified to save her liberty? Tell the world that Armando, the Great One's financial adviser and close friend, had been exporting drugs? Say that and possibly put my daughter at risk? Or should I tell her to say nothing about it, and hope for the best while fearing the worst? What was it to be? Risk my daughter or let my client go down for life? Daughter or client?

'Tell Tina we'll take her to FastFreez on Saturday,' I said.

Chapter 43

This close to Christmas it wasn't only the guy in the woolly jumper who wanted the case over with quickly. Lady Carrick had decreed that court should start at nine-thirty that Tuesday morning rather than the usual ten o'clock kick-off.

'This is it then. You have one shot at it,' I said to Salome. Joanna rolled her eyes at my choice of words. We were sitting in a small consulting room on the Mezzanine floor of the High Court building outside Courtroom 3.

Salome looked cool and calm wearing a dark blue ensemble, a familiar gold crucifix on a chain around her neck. She was wearing very little make up, her hair as soft and natural as a three-hundred-pound hairdo could make it look. Maybe Malky was right. Who in their right mind would want to put this beautiful woman behind bars for life?

'Okay,' I said, 'you'll be called into the witness box and after you've taken the oath, Joanna is going to lead you through your evidence. We've been over it. Take your time and answer the questions slowly. Got it?'

It seemed she had.

Joanna picked up where I left off. 'It might seem like a long time to you, but I won't have that many questions to ask. After me it will be the Advocate depute's turn to cross examine you. Be careful. He won't shout or bully you, but every question will be tailored to lure you into a trap. I can't advise you what to say. You know what happened. All you can do is tell the truth. If you don't understand a question or need time to think about it, that's fine. All you have to do is to ask for the question to be repeated. If you ever want a break, signal to us and we'll ask the judge for five minutes. Do you have any questions?'

She hadn't.

'Good,' Joanna said, collecting her papers. She stood up and walked to the door expecting me and Salome to follow.

'Go on ahead, Jo,' I said. 'I just want to firm up on some things with Salome.'

Joanna hesitated. 'All right, but the court's starting in two minutes. Don't be long.'

'Did Dario say anything to you last night?' I said once Joanna had left, closing the door behind her.

'About what?'

'About what you were to say today?' She looked puzzled. 'About blurting out something to do with Armando and drugs?'

She looked even more puzzled. 'Armando and drugs? I don't know what you're talking about.'

Dario hadn't bothered telling her. Despite my conversation yesterday when I laid it on the line for him. He'd chickened out. Diamond Tooth or whoever was pulling his strings had got to him. At least it saved me some trouble.

'Forget it,' I said. 'Just remember this. You had no reason to kill Armando. You must say that as often as you get the chance. All you know is that you drove back to West Hope House, waited in the car listening to something on the radio. What was it you were listening to?'

'A discussion programme.'

'About what?'

'I'm not sure.'

'Then if you can't remember just say so. Don't go guessing. What happened after that?'

'Robbie, we have been through all this. The court...' She looked at the tiny face on her wristwatch and stood up.

'After that?' I repeated.

She sighed and sat down again. 'After that I went into the house, into the bathroom, heard a loud bang and went downstairs to the study. I saw Armando and rushed to try

270

and help him. I picked up the shotgun, threw it to the side, but he was dead. I was hurrying out of the door when I met Beverly coming in…'

And that's more or less how it went. Salome allowed Joanna to lead her through her version of events. No foot was put wrong, and she remained poised and composed throughout. Never nonchalant, sad at all the right times and with no fake tears or melodrama. When Joanna sat down again, I felt things couldn't have gone any better.

'Advocate depute?'

In response to the judge's invitation, Cameron Crowe rose like a black cloud and drifted behind the podium.

'Mrs Ramirez, what was being discussed on the radio that so grabbed your attention that you stayed in your car a full fifteen minutes before entering the house?'

Salome looked to me. It always looks dodgy to a jury when a witness does that, so I pretended not to notice and busied myself scribbling notes.

'I can't remember. I think it may have been something to do with Brexit.'

'You like to keep up with foreign affairs, do you?'

'I don't consider Britain to be a foreign country. My husband and I have visited very many times.'

'And I must say your English is excellent,' Crowe said with a slippery smile. 'And, of course, you have a property here. I think it's twelve hundred acres down the borders somewhere. Is that right?' Salome agreed. 'Good game shooting land. That's why you and your husband come here, isn't it? The shooting?'

'My husband likes to shoot, yes.'

'And you?'

'I have tried.'

'Quite successfully, I think?'

Salome didn't answer.

'Come now Mrs Ramirez, don't be modest. Did you not win the Lammermuirs Women's Skeet Shooting Competition a few years ago?'

I kept writing. Joanna toyed with an earring carelessly. Rule one when the other side is cross-examining: never show any reaction to a direct hit.

'I was lucky.'

'Not so lucky when you turned up at Armando Diaz's study to find him dead and no one else in the house.'

'That's not a question Mr Crowe,' the judge said, saving Joanna the need to object.

'Why did Mr Diaz deserve to die?' Crowe asked, not letting the judge put him off his stride.

'He didn't and I never said that. I had no reason to kill Armando. He was my friend,' Salome said with just the right amount of anger in her voice. She was doing great, and she continued to do great. Despite his best efforts for over two hours either side of coffee break, Crowe couldn't even chip the paintwork on the accused's version of events. The mark on her face, the lack of anyone else in the house, her fingerprints on the weapon, she had answers for them all. The mark was caused on the corner of the car door. She couldn't say who else was in the house because she'd been in the bathroom when she'd heard the shot. She'd handled the gun when going to Armando's aid. As for Professor Bradley's evidence, all she could do was look at the jury and say how we all knew doctors didn't always get things right.

It was half-twelve when Crowe sat down. Joanna advised that there would be no re-examination necessary. As she did so a hand shot up in the jury box. 'How much longer is this going on for?' the old guy in the front row asked.

I could tell that Lady Carrick's patience was wearing thin with Elbow-Patches' continual interruptions. With a pained expression she looked down at Joanna. 'Miss Jordan does the defence intend calling any more witnesses?'

272

'Two, M'Lady,' Joanna said. 'If your ladyship allowed us to sit on a little later, my next witness should take us up to lunch. That will allow my defence's final witness to be called and the defence case closed this afternoon.'

The judge turned once again to the jury box. 'There you have it, members of the jury.' It seemed Cameron Crowe had been extremely accurate with his estimation of the length of the trial. 'With speeches and my directions to you in the morning, I would hope to be in a position to ask you to retire and consider your verdict after lunch tomorrow.'

The judge sat back, Joanna called our next witness, and the jurors seemed happy with the judge's prediction of a finish tomorrow. Or at least fourteen of them did.

Chapter 44

It's a long way to the top if you wanna rock and roll. It's also a long drop from an ivory tower into the witness box at a High Court murder trial.

Professor Philip Dankworth was a tall man, with a wide forehead and the rumour of a moustache, who, for all his academic success, was a failure in the witness box. At least as a psychologist he should've known why that was.

When I'd cited Dankworth in Salome Ramirez's defence, I'd done so thinking he was an expert witness. He wasn't. He was a witness who was an expert. There's a difference. It's handy if an expert witness has a host of qualifications, but they don't need them. To be expert as a witness one only needs to be a good communicator or a good liar or, occasionally, both. The individual Dario's legal bill had brought all the way from Cambridge University to Edinburgh, was a witness who was an expert, but someone with the communication rating of two bean tins and a piece of string. Even with Joanna leading him by the nose, Dankworth stumbled his way through examination-in-chief, unable it seemed to give a straight answer to even the simplest of questions. There must have been politicians of all stripes, doffing their expenses-paid caps to him.

It took Joanna a full twenty minutes to drag from the witness that he'd led a research team studying the causes of suicide and methods of prevention. It took the same again for her to draw from Dankworth that his inquiries had shown shooting suicides to be most commonly committed by middle-aged men with no prior history of mental health issues and by use of a shotgun. It was all we wanted him to say and were paying handsomely for it. But he just mumbled a lot, muddying the waters of his testimony even further by lobbing in words like epidemiology and aetiology.

Watching Cameron Crowe rise to his feet as Joanna sat down, was like watching a cat come to babysit the budgie.

'You're telling us, Professor Dankworth,' Cameron Crowe, began his cross-examination, 'that your years of research conclusively revealed that the people most likely to shoot themselves are the people with guns?' One or two of the jurors found that amusing.

'Fascinating stuff,' Crowe continued. 'But you'd agree it's not so easy to shoot yourself without a gun?' More of the fifteen began to see the funny side.

'We found the guns involved were predominantly shotguns,' the witness stuttered.

'Ah,' Crowe raised a finger, then scratched the top of his wig with it. 'And do you think that has got anything to do with the fact that just about every other type of gun, apart from shotguns, is currently banned in Scotland? I mean you're not going to do much damage with an air rifle, or a paintball weapon, are you?'

Professor Dankworth was prepared to concede that, when compared to a shotgun blast, loss of life was reduced with a ping from a small lead pellet or a paintball pellet.

'And you'll also agree, Professor, that people who do have known mental health issues are seldom seen as prime candidates to be the possessors of shotguns?'

'It's true the UK licensing laws are strict,' the witness replied.

'And so, it stands to reason that the owner of a shotgun would need to be of sound mind in order to own the licence that allows him to keep such a weapon in the first place, wouldn't you say?' The witness could do nothing other than agree. 'I was also wondering about your definition of middle-aged?' Crowe said, continuing to lay waste to the years of research. 'The victim in this case was fifty-nine-years-old.

How many one-hundred-and-eighteen-year-olds do you know, Professor?'

'Well, of course, when I say—'

'Did you ever meet Armando Diaz?'

Professor Dankworth hadn't.

'Therefore, you can't comment on the man's mental health?'

Professor Dankworth couldn't.

'For all you know, Mr Diaz may have been a depressive or the life and soul of the party? He may have been an extrovert, an introvert, bipolar or for all you know a polar explorer.'

'That's quite enough, Mr Crowe,' the judge said, stepping in like a boxing referee at a mismatch.

Crowe inclined his head at Lady Carrick, obviously thought that apology enough, and asked the witness, 'Did your team of psychologists carry out any research into how many people were murdered by people with shotguns?'

Dankworth cleared his throat. 'That was beyond the remit of our studies,' he conceded.

'Then I'm afraid, Professor,' Crowe said, wringing his hands, 'you wouldn't appear to be of much use to us. You see we're here to find out if Armando Diaz, a recently and happily-married, multi-millionaire, was shot at close range and in cold blood…' he swivelled at the hip, the better to point to the dock. 'By this woman. And yet for all your research, that's really something you can't help us with at all, is it?'

The bright lights of the courtroom bounced off the witness's shiny forehead, as he twitched, cleared his throat and answered softly. 'No.'

'No? No! What did he mean no?' Joanna ripped off her gown and hurled it onto a chair. Lunch time. We were on the third-floor, in Counsels' Robing Room, which sounds a lot grander than a room with a long table, a coffee maker and some dusty

276

old lawyers sitting around reading newspapers and eating sandwiches actually is. Two weeks before Christmas and the Faculty of Advocates tribute to the festive period was a plate of supermarket own brand mince pies and a scrap of tinsel taped to the wall that someone had forgotten to take down last year.

The robing room assistant poured me a black brew from a glass jug into the sort of canteen cup you can hurl at a tank and only risk damaging the armour-plating. I took a gulp. There's never any risk of burning yourself on court coffee. 'Come on, Jo. It could have been worse,' I said, without specifying exactly how.

'Where did you get him from, Robbie?' Joanna said.

'Chill out, dust yourself down and have a mince pie,' I replied. 'We've still got a few cards up our sleeves. How is the prosecution going to get around the fact that in order to shoot Armando with his own gun, he'd have had to have brought a loaded weapon into the house? Why would he do that? Who or what was he going to shoot in the study if not himself? Laszlo Derry's our trump card. Everyone knows him. He's a national treasure. If he says suicide was possible with that shotgun, and, remember, he owns one just like it, who's going to disagree?'

Not entirely placated, Joanna snatched a mince pie from the plate and told the robing room assistant I was paying.

I walked over to the table with her, standing as she sat to drink her coffee and eat her mince pie. 'Okay Jo, with Derry there's no need for any fancy stuff. Keep it simple. He met Armando once, and, as you know, he's already ruled an accident out of the question because Armando was such a responsible gun-owner. Have him agree with you that a responsible gun-owner doesn't bring a loaded shotgun into the house. After that, take from him the fact that he owns the same type of shotgun Armando had, and how in his expert opinion it could be used to commit suicide by way of a shot

277

to the chest. Job done, sit down and sit back. I guarantee he'll not be swayed in his testimony by Cameron Crowe. There's too much at stake for him.'

Joanna put the last of the mince pie in her mouth. 'What do you mean, he's got too much a stake?' she asked, with her mouth full.

'I might have promised him a win bonus.'

She coughed and took a drink of coffee. 'Robbie…'

'What? These experts all get paid far more than they're worth. Do you know how much Professor Dankworth was hiring himself out for? The man could hardly string two words together and when he did it wasn't English. I understood Russell MacGillivray's Spanish better. I mean aetiology – what the hell's that?' I nicked a morsel of mince pie. 'Trust me. When Laszlo Derry struts his stuff in the witness box, you'll be the first to agree he's worth a wee sweetener.'

Chapter 45

Laszlo Derry sashayed into the witness box after lunch. He was wearing a chequered sports jacket that could best be described as sudden, and beneath it a yellow and blue-striped shirt set off by a knitted, green tie. It was certainly an eye-catching combination even if it occasionally made one's eyes go in and out of focus.

As a witness for the defence, Derry was everything I'd hoped he would be. Charming and confident, he came across as knowledgeable, and I could tell the jury adored him. Most of them anyway. Nothing other than an early finish was going to lighten the mood of Elbow-Patches, sitting arms folded, face set like concrete.

'You're familiar with this model of shotgun?' Joanna asked, once the routine evidence was taken. It was important to cut to the chase as quickly as possible because, even if there is a TV personality in the witness box, a juror's mind can start to wander after lunch. She had the Macer bring over the shotgun and place it in front of the witness. 'Is it true you own one exactly the same?'

Derry smiled as he lovingly caressed the plastic production bag. 'No two Ivo Lombardi's are exactly the same. Each gun is similar in design, but customised, perhaps by the choice of wood in the stock, engraving on the receiver…'

'The barrel lengths are the same, though?'

'Yes, twenty-six inches.'

'That's sixty-six centimetres, isn't it?'

'If you say so. I'm a foot and inches man,' Derry said, his smile at the jury box being reciprocated by some of the older members.

'Could a person shoot themselves in the chest with one of these?' Some of the jurors shifted in their seats at the bluntness of Joanna's question. If any minds had been wandering before, they weren't now.

'Using my own...' he looked across at the jury, 'unloaded gun, I tried to reconstruct such a scenario and found it possible if one bends over at the waist sufficiently. It's a bit of a struggle, but I knew Armando Diaz,' he said anticipating Joanna's next question. 'He was a much taller man than I, so it would have been a lot easier.'

'We've heard that the shotgun was found on the floor not far from Mr Diaz's body, broken with the spent cartridge nearby. Can you explain how that could happen?'

'Easily,' Derry croaked a laugh from a throat grizzled by years of tobacco. 'Mr Diaz could hardly have shot himself and then broken the barrel and ejected the cartridge.' Which was a point I knew the Crown would have hoped to make hay with. 'If you take a look at the top of the gun above the trigger, you'll see there is a small, metal tab. Push that to either side, and the gun breaks. Drop it the right way on to something solid...'

'Like a hardwood floor?' Joanna asked.

'That would certainly do it. The correct angle of impact and the gun will break open.'

'And the cartridge inside?'

Derry took a breath. 'I don't know if many of the ladies and gentlemen of the jury are familiar with shotguns...'

The general mumbling and muttering from the jury box suggested a distinct lack of knowledge but willingness to learn. Elbow-Patches groaned and looked at his watch in a how-long's-this-all-going-to-take kind of a way.

'Would it be all right for me to demonstrate using this?' Derry asked, tapping the plastic wrapped shotgun. There being no objection, the weapon was removed, and Derry left the witness box keeping the muzzle pointed at the floor. 'The small tab I mentioned earlier, it can be used left or right-handed. I'm right-handed so if I push the tab with my right thumb like so, the barrel breaks open. He looked down the barrel to make sure the gun was unloaded. To prime the shotgun, I would insert a cartridge here.' He demonstrated pushing an imaginary cartridge into the breech and snapping the gun shut. 'The weapon is now ready to fire.' Directing the muzzle to the floor again, he pulled the trigger and produced a soft click. 'The gun having fired I now want to reload. Some shotguns are extractors, others are ejectors. With an extractor, I break the gun, the cartridge pops out maybe a quarter of an inch and I use my fingers to pull it out completely, allowing me to dispose of it and insert a new cartridge. That's fine if you're not in a hurry. This particular shotgun, like my own, is an ejector. All Ivo Lombardi models are. That means when I break the barrel, the spent cartridge ejects itself onto the ground and I can immediately reload, close the gun and fire again. As most shotguns are double-barrelled, it's even more important to be able to reload quickly if you are using a single barrel model like this one.'

'I wonder please, if you would consider a possible set of circumstances,' Joanna said, once the witness had returned to the witness box and the shotgun was restored to the production bag. 'That is: Mr Diaz shoots himself with the shotgun, as you have already suggested is physically possible. Naturally he drops the gun. It falls on to the hardwood floor of his study, the barrel breaks and the cartridge ejects.'

'A perfectly reasonable scenario,' Derry replied, glancing around the courtroom as though Joanna had asked him his views on the wetness of water.

Joanna paused to let the answer sink in, then leaned forward, both elbows on the podium. 'Finally, Mr Derry, before I sit down. Can you think of any reason why a responsible gun-owner would bring a loaded shotgun into his home?'

'I cannot,' came the immediate reply. I couldn't help but think Laszlo Derry was already mentally spending his win bonus. 'Not unless he intended to shoot someone or, indeed...' He looked at the jury, 'Shoot himself.'

I pulled Joanna's chair out for her as she returned to the table beside me. As she sat down, Cameron Crowe rose like steam from a dung pile and wafted himself over to the podium. He set his papers in front of him and squared them up. 'Mr Derry, the jury has heard from a forensic pathologist that the signs you'd expect to be present on the deceased's body, had he shot himself from extreme close range, are absent. What have you to say to that?'

'If the quacks never got things wrong there'd be a lot of medical negligence lawyers out of business, don't you think?' He gave the jury a sideways smirk. Derry was living up to all my expectations. 'Not exactly a precise science, is it?' he said.

'And you're not exactly a man of science or of medicine, are you, Mr Derry?'

'That's perfectly true.'

'But you do know about shotguns?'

'I do.'

'And you're happy to give us all the benefit of your opinion?'

Derry spread his hands. 'That's why I'm here.'

'Then, since you've given an opinion on one scenario, would you consider another?'

'Of course.'

'Excellent,' Crowe said, in a way that sent a rush of ice-water through my veins. 'Please have before you Crown Production 1, a book of photographs. These will also be available on the screens. Crowe's junior went over to operate the laptop on which the images were stored and scrolled down. 'This is photograph A56, Mr Derry. The jury were

282

shown these images earlier in the trial to better understand the layout of the locus. What do you see?'

'It's a large room, with bookshelves, windows, a wooden floor, is this the —?'

'Yes, it's the study where Armando Diaz's body was found. What do you see in the corner?'

Derry lifted the book of photographs closer, then put it down and strained his eyes to look at one of the court screens. 'It looks like a cabinet.'

'Photograph A57 please. Is that a close up of the same cabinet?'

'It certainly looks like it.'

'And what do you see?'

'Well, it's obviously a gun cabinet with the doors open and I can see various shotguns inside. I think four altogether.'

'Does it look to you like someone has been either taking something out of the cabinet or replacing it?'

'Clearly. The doors to a gun cabinet would be locked otherwise.'

'You'll see there is a shelf above where the guns are held in some kind of rack. Do you see something on that shelf?'

'I do. It looks to me like a small, yellow, cardboard box.'

Like the rest of the courtroom, I was squinting hard at the screens to see where Crowe was going with this.

'Can you read what is written on the side of the box?'

'I'm sorry, I can't.'

'Then I'll ask my junior to magnify the image for you.'

As the computer-generated image zoomed in on the box, it became pixelated, but the printing on the side of the box was clear enough.

'Can you read what's written there now?' Crowe asked.

The witness could. The whole courtroom could. 'It says Delta Champion.'

'Does that name mean anything to you?'

'It's a make of shotgun cartridge, I believe. Not one I use personally.'

'Have before you Crown Label Production 7.'

A plastic tube containing what we'd seen during the Crown's firearm expert's evidence was brought over by the Macer and placed on the ledge of the witness box.

'We've heard that's the spent shotgun cartridge found on the floor of Armand Diaz's study. You'll see it's yellow. Can you read what's printed on it?'

Derry held the tube close to his face then laid it back down on the ledge. 'It says Delta.'

'And below that?' Crowe enquired innocently.

Derry lifted the tube and read again. 'I think it says Champion.'

Crowe came around from behind the podium and leaned an arm against the dock as he spoke. 'I said at the beginning of my questions that I had a certain scenario I'd like to put to you. If you don't mind, I will ask it in two parts. Firstly, do you think it likely the cartridge found on the floor of Mr Diaz's study came from the box of the same brand in Mr Diaz's wide open shotgun cabinet?'

'How could I possibly know that?' Derry was a man now fighting for his win bonus.

'Let me put it this way. You enjoy a cigar.' As ever Crowe's homework was spot on. 'What's your favourite type?'

'I suppose I'm especially partial to a corona gorda.'

'Then let's say you've been given a box of Montecristo Whites for your birthday. There's a box of them in your sitting room. One evening you come home to find the box open and me sitting in an armchair puffing away on nothing less than a Montecristo White. Are you telling me that not for a moment would you think it likely I'd helped myself?'

'If you put it like that…'

284

'Mr Derry, it's not a difficult question. There's a box with Delta Champions in a cabinet in a room where a spent Delta Champion cartridge is found a few metres away.'

'Yes, well, I suppose it does seem quite likely,' said Derry.

'Good. Then, the second part of the scenario I'd like you to consider is this: that Mr Diaz, the multi-millionaire, who is about to go on honeymoon with his delightful new bride, does not suddenly contort himself sufficiently, the better to shoot himself in the chest, but instead someone else waits for him to enter his study and open his shotgun cabinet. Then, as he is putting his gun away, that person...' Crowe paused, turned from the witness and looked directly at the accused, 'takes the gun from him, loads it with a Delta Champion cartridge and blasts him with it from short range!' It was more of a speech than a question, but it stunned the courtroom. Crowe drew closer to the witness box and cupped a hand to his ear. 'Sorry, what was that?'

His win bonus flashing before his eyes, the confident, chummy, expert witness of a few minutes ago was gone. Even Derry's moustache appeared to have withered. 'I don't think... I suppose... It's difficult to—'

Crowe smiled mockingly. 'Yes, I thought that's what you said.' And with that he revolved on a heel and floated back to his seat.

Chapter 46

'Don't blame me, Jo. You perused those photos as much as I did.' Day five of the trial, and, as we strode up the High Street towards the Lawnmarket, it was beginning to look a lot like chaos. 'There's nothing for it. You're going to have to do some pretty fancy re-examination of Laszlo Derry, but at least you'll be pushing at an open door.'

'I suppose so, but I always think re-examination is a sign of weakness. The jury will realise we've been badly damaged,' Joanna said, mistress of the understatement.

'Badly damaged? Jo, if this defence was a car it would be a write-off.'

'Then we need to focus, and it would help if you didn't stop to look in the window every time we passed a whisky shop.'

I could understand my wife's irritability. A defence that had been galloping along just fine twenty-four hours earlier, had fallen at the final fence and was all but ready for the knacker's yard. Still, looking on the bright side, we were being handsomely paid, and I thought we might nip down to Princes Street after court and buy Tina's tracksuit.

'It would save us a trip on Saturday,' I said. 'Edinburgh on Christmas Eve - talk about the nightmare before Christmas?'

It was Joanna's turn to stop. Coincidentally, right outside Royal Mile Whiskies. 'Oh, no. Do not think for one minute you are ducking out of this one, Robbie. We're not forking out two hundred pounds on a designer tracksuit for Tina to open the parcel on Christmas morning and discover it's the wrong size. She'll need to try it on. And it being your idea that we get her one, you can bring her into town for it.

There's no point us both going. I'm not taking Jamie on a shopping trip if I can help it. You know what he's like.'

I did. My son, like his father, could turn tetchy if subjected to prolonged exposure to retail outlets.

'There could be none left on Christmas Eve,' I said. 'Maybe we should wait until after Christmas. Get one in the New Year sales.'

'You're going on Saturday,' Joanna said. 'I'm not having Tina disappointed on Christmas morning. Also, I phoned. There's no danger of them running out of stock.'

My fate sealed, we walked on, and nearing the High Court spied a familiar figure pacing up and down smoking a hand-rolled cigarette. It was his back I saw first, but straightaway I recognised the shapeless tweed jacket over the baggy knitted jumper. Elbow-Patches turned and dropped his cigarette butt in the gutter just as we were passing. I gave him a smile. Every little helped.

'Is this definitely going to finish this morning?' he called to us.

'Sorry,' I called back, 'I'm not allowed to speak to you.'

'But I'm taking my granddaughter to the pantomime this afternoon!' he shouted at our backs as we entered the building.

Salome, Dario and the ever-present Diamond Tooth were waiting for us at the top of the flight of stairs leading to the mezzanine floor and the lobby outside courtroom 3.

'I never knew anything about a box of shotgun cartridges in Armando's gun cabinet,' Salome said, before we'd taken the final step. She was sobbing, Dario at her side an arm around her waist, Diamond Tooth fixing me with a stare. While we were doing our best to console our client, the Macer came out of court to say that the judge was coming on the bench five minutes early to speak to accused and counsel only. He didn't say what about. We were soon to find out.

'It's been brought to my attention by my court officer that one of the jury would like to be excused.' There were no prizes for guessing who. 'The gentleman states that his granddaughter is unwell and in hospital. She's not gravely ill, but he's worried and would rather not be here. What are parties' views of letting him go and proceeding with fourteen jurors?'

'Sick granddaughter? I thought he was taking her to the pantomime?' Joanna whispered to me.

'Maybe she took ill when she heard she wasn't going,' I whispered back. 'Who cares? It's fine by us. We don't need some old grumpy guy who looks like he'd convict Santa of housebreaking.'

Cameron Crowe was first to his feet. 'M'Lady, while I appreciate the juror's grandparental concerns, if the child isn't at death's door, and as he has sat through five days of evidence so far, I'm sure he could stay for what would be one more day, two at most. While I anticipate there may be some re-examination of their final witness, I understand there are no others for the defence. The issues are in short compass, and I would not have thought speeches would require to be unduly long. The jury could hear Prosecution and Defence before lunch, after which, were your ladyship to charge the jury, I wouldn't be surprised if we had a verdict this afternoon or tomorrow at the latest.' He sat down again. It wasn't difficult to see why Crowe fancied Elbow-Patches as one of the fifteen who held my client's fate in their hands.

Joanna was about to stand, but the judge waved her down. 'I agree with Mr Crowe, and unless you have some extremely cogent reason why the juror should be excused, I see no reason why having come this far he can't remain for one more day. They have evening visiting hours in hospital, don't they?'

Without waiting to see if Joanna did have any counter argument, Lady Carrick gestured to her Macer to have the jury brought in. When they were duly ensconced, Laszlo Derry returned to the witness box.

Joanna began as we'd discussed overnight. 'Mr Derry, look again at Crown Production A57. Can you see if there are any cartridges in that box?'

'I'm afraid I don't have x-ray vision,' Derry said with a dry chuckle.

'But there'd be little point in keeping an empty box securely locked in a cabinet, wouldn't you say?' Lady Carrick intervened, unhelpfully.

'Tell us about snap-caps,' Joanna said.

'Did snap-cap arise in the course of cross-examination, Miss Jordan?' the judge enquired.

Joanna turned to the bench. 'As I'm sure Mr Derry will explain much more capably than I could, M'Lady, a spent cartridge can be used as a snap-cap, and the Advocate depute had a fair number of questions in cross-examination on the subject of shotgun cartridges.'

Allowed to continue, Joanna took from the witness all about snap-caps.

'Then would you agree it is perfectly feasible that if Armando Diaz had put a spent cartridge in the breech to protect the mechanism of the gun before storing it, the shotgun could have broken, and the dud cartridge ejected after he'd fallen?'

'I see no reason why not,' said Derry.

His answer caused some dissatisfied muttering as the jurors looked at one another. At least it showed they'd been paying attention. The inevitable leather-patched arm rose from among the fifteen. Lady Carrick cleared her throat. 'I think what many of us are wondering Miss Jordan, is why Mr Armando would fall at all, far less end up dead on the floor of his study, if, as you suggest, his shotgun had been armed only with one of these snap-cap things and not a live round?'

289

This was the moment I'd known would arise. It was the situation we'd discussed most in the hours since Cameron Crowe's cross-examination. I'd counselled against Joanna trying to blame a third-party. I didn't want to mention Diamond Tooth's threat, and so had harked my wife back to the lecture she'd given me following Isabella Ewart's acquittal: *There are laws and we're lawyers. We're supposed to abide by them. That's how it works.* Adding what she'd told Marc Traynor in the shadow of David Hume's statue: *These are the rules of the game, and we have to play by them.*

As I was at pains to remind her, the rules of the game had been spelled out by the judge quite clearly the last time she'd tried this line of questioning. There was to be no incrimination of any person or persons in this trial. No aspersions cast. No vague notions put forward.

'If I might make one final attempt to clarify, M'Lady,' Joanna said, with a polite smile to the bench before turning to the witness. 'Mr Derry, I think it's accepted that an experienced and responsible gun-owner like Armando Diaz would not be expected to bring a loaded weapon into the house?'

'Out of the question.'

I glanced over my shoulder to the public gallery, where Dario and Diamond Tooth sat shoulder to shoulder. Dario looking worried. Diamond Tooth looking directly at me.

'And assuming for a moment,' Joanna said, 'that in order to keep his expensive shotgun in good condition Mr Diaz had inserted a spent cartridge as a snap cap...'

There were certain rumblings coming from the Crown's side of the table, and I was sure it wasn't through lack of breakfast.

Joanna paused for her words to sink in.

'I'm with you so far,' Derry said.

'Can you honestly say it's impossible that someone other than the accused might have entered the house undetected and shot Mr Diaz with their own shotgun, as he was putting his away?'

It's uncommon in Scotland's highest criminal court for lawyers to shout out in the middle of proceedings. This isn't America, with lawyers in casual attire and judges with gavels. A gentle clearing of the throat or a pretence at rising to one's feet is usually indication enough to the judge that exception is being taken to your opponent's line of questioning. Not so on this occasion. Crowe's chair was thrown back, and he was on his hind legs, his normally midnight pale complexion almost as brightly hued as the Judge's own. 'Objection!'

'Don't answer that question, Mr Derry,' Lady Carrick said. 'Miss Jordan, you were warned earlier in this trial about presenting lines of defence that had not been properly intimated to the Crown. If you insist on doing so, I will have to consider the question of contempt. Now are there any more questions for this witness?' Her tone suggested that there'd better not be.

'Nothing further, M'Lady,' Joanna said.

'What are parties' views on how we should proceed?' Lady Carrick asked, once Laszlo Derry had been thanked for his attendance and Joanna had closed the defence case. 'I'm minded to follow Mr Crowe's suggestion that we hear speeches now, which should allow me to charge the jury after lunch. That would mean the members of the jury would have the rest of the day, as well as tomorrow to consider their verdict.'

Someone had other ideas. That someone was wearing a woolly jumper. Before Joanna could agree or disagree, he raised a leather, elbow-patched sleeve, and said, 'I want to see the cartridge box.' He had a peculiarly stubborn look on his face, as if to say, 'if you're going to keep me here all week, then I'm going to keep you all here too.'

'M'Lady,' Crowe said. 'I appreciate the jury is entitled to view the productions, but the cartridge box was not lodged as a production in this case.'

Why not? I wondered. It was hard to believe a box of live ammo wouldn't have been seen as an important piece of evidence. Did Crowe know it was empty? Or had he only noticed the existence of the box in the photograph during the course of the trial? Was he objecting because he had no idea if the box was empty or stuffed full of shotgun cartridges, and didn't want to gamble? If it did hold ammo, it could only help the Crown case. But if it was empty, it would negate the damage done by his cross examination of Laszlo Derry. Better for the Prosecution to stick with the hand they had than twist and go bust.

What did the defence have to lose by taking a look? I nudged Joanna. 'We need that box.'

The court adjourned for mid-morning coffee break, and afterwards Lady Carrick heard legal submissions on the subject of the cartridge box.

Crowe continued to object, stating that it could reasonably be inferred that a cartridge box inside a secure firearms cabinet would contain live ammunition, especially as the name on the box was the name on the spent cartridge found on the study floor.

When the judge looked down at our side of the table, Joanna rose to meet her stare. 'M'Lady, while the item has not been lodged as a production, a photograph of it has been produced and referred to as an integral part of the Crown case. I strongly suspect the Advocate depute may intend to rely upon its presence at the locus when he comes to speak to the jury. I think it only fair the jury has before it the best evidence.'

Lady Carrick thought about it for a while. 'I agree,' she said, eventually. 'I understand the locus was sealed in the event that the jury might wish to carry out a site inspection. I

292

take it the cartridge box in question will have remained in situ.' She glanced up at the clock. 'As it is now nearly twelve there is no guarantee we would have time to hear speeches, charge the jury and put the members out to consider their verdict at a reasonable hour. It's better to start afresh in the morning. Advocate depute, you said six days and we are still on course. I'll ask you to reserve your remarks until nine-thirty tomorrow, and meantime please have your office instruct the collection of the cartridge box in question – and any contents, so that they are here when court resumes.'

The jurors were brought back, the situation explained to them, the Macer called, 'Court!' Lady Carrick was escorted off the bench, and Salome Ramirez was allowed one more day of freedom.

Chapter 47

'What am I going to say, Robbie?' Joanna asked, later that night when we were home and sitting at the kitchen table. The kids had been in bed until uncle Malky arrived unannounced bearing sugary gifts. He was now playing with them in the livingroom. It seemed my brother was practically living with us these days, always dropping in wanting to know what I was doing about his employment predicament. What I was doing was absolutely nothing. It was case closed so far as I was concerned. Colin Lancaster had made his mind up. Even if Dario could have been tempted to give Scotgoals an interview, Lancaster was no longer interested for some reason. A reason I put down to Malky trusting Peter Falconer to do him a good turn, and not take advantage of the situation by landing one of his own clients a plum job.

We'd been trying to draft Joanna's closing remarks for about an hour when Malky came through drying his hands on his jeans. 'Sorry about that,' he said. 'I think I've dropped a dress size after that one.'

'What is it with the Munro men that they have to debrief the rest of us on their bowel movements?' Joanna said. 'And talking of the rest of us, where's Tina and Jamie?'

'The wee man's in bed. Tina's watching telly,' Malky said, pulling up a chair alongside us.

'Did you brush their teeth?' I asked.

He wafted a hand at me. 'They're kids. They lose them and then they get new ones.'

'Tina's already got some new ones.' Joanna got up and went in search of our daughter.

'So, what's the big plan?' Malky said after she'd gone. 'You don't want me to hook up with Lancaster's daughter, and you say he's gone cold on the Dario interview idea. Where do we go from here?'

I thought where *he* went, as opposed to where *we* went, was out looking for a new job.

'You're baling out, are you?' Malky said. 'That's fine, but how am I supposed to eat?'

Though my brother had given it his best shot, he had not yet managed to exhaust the vast amounts he'd made playing professional soccer, even if his illustrious career had ended prematurely. Not only that, but there were blue-tinged public houses and restaurants in Scotland where he never needed to put his hand in his pocket. I didn't see immediate starvation on the horizon.

'I think I'll maybe have to go and see a real lawyer,' was Malky's considered opinion. 'Have them look over my contract. Who do you recommend?' The answer to that was anyone with a law degree, so long as it wasn't me. He lifted the draft from the table. 'How's the speech writing going? Shouldn't be too difficult to talk the jury into a not guilty. Who's going to send a honey like Salome Ramirez to the jail? What a waste that would be.'

'It's not a beauty contest, Malky,' I said. 'There's no swimsuit round. If the jury think she's guilty, and I don't see why they wouldn't, she'll go to jail just like the ugly people do.'

'And this is it?' he said, waving the single sheet of A4 in front of my face. 'I've been entertaining your offspring all evening, and so far your combined efforts have come up with half a page of scribbles?'

I snatched the sheet of paper away from him. 'Those are bullet points.'

'All four of them? Haven't exactly been spraying the page with shotgun pellets, have you?'

He alone found that amusing. But it was true. Four jury points was all we had. There was Salome's testimony, which, if believed, was enough in itself. Then we had Professor Dankworth's suicide research, for what it was worth, and, of course, Lazlo Derry's *it's possible to shoot yourself in the chest with a shotgun, but it helps if you've got rubber arms* theory. Our fourth and best point was, or at least, had been: why would Armando bring a loaded shotgun into the house? Now according to the Crown, he hadn't. He'd brought in an unloaded gun. An unloaded gun that Salome had primed with a live cartridge from his gun cabinet before she shot him. We'd know tomorrow morning, when the cartridge box was brought to court, whether we still had that fourth bullet point. Hopefully the box was empty and had been used for storing dusters or something.

'She'd need a reason to do it though, wouldn't she?' Malky said. 'Why would she grab a shotgun and come out blasting?'

Salome's original rape explanation had given an understandable reason. If not a defence, it would have been excellent mitigation. Why hadn't I tried harder to go for a culpable homicide? She couldn't use it now. Not after swearing that she'd been in the loo when the shooting took place.

Malky shrugged. 'Time of the month. That could explain it. Isn't having the painters in a defence these days?'

Just in time to miss Malky's jurisprudential take on the menstrual cycle, Joanna came back into the kitchen with Tina who wanted a pre-teethbrush drink of milk. When it came to going to bed, my daughter could stall like a spitfire in a dogfight.

Milk drunk, bedtime hugs and kisses administered, we sent Malky off with Tina to read her bedtime story, though we knew he'd never open a book and instead regale her with his old football tales. At least it would keep him out of the way for a while.

Joanna picked up the piece of paper. 'Not much to go on, is there?'

She was right. But it was all that we had. In fact less, if that cartridge box turned out to be crammed with live ammo.

Chapter 48

The yellow cardboard box was sitting front and centre on the production table by the side of the jury box when court resumed next morning. I noted that seated on a chair beside the Macer was the firearms officer who'd given evidence earlier in the week.

'Members of the jury, as you can see, the item in question has been delivered and you will be permitted to view this and any of the other productions during the course of your deliberations. I must point out, though, that when you view the cartridge box you will require to do so in the presence of a firearms officer, and when that happens you must do so in silence and under no circumstances speak to her. All the evidence in this case has been led. The officer is here for your safety, not to answer your questions. Do you understand?' They understood all right. So did I. You didn't need a firearms officer to stand guard over an empty cardboard box. The judge looked down from on high. 'Advocate depute?'

Cameron Crowe took up his position at the podium. 'Good morning,' he said, and gave a good imitation of a smile, considering his lack of practice. 'I'll not keep you long, in the same way that I don't think it will take you very long to consider your verdict and come to the conclusion that Salome Ramirez, with premeditation, cold-bloodedly murdered Armando Diaz. The very man under whose roof she was sheltering. The man who, along with his bride of just a few days, had allowed her to share his table.

Now, you may ask, why would she do such a thing? Why repay the hospitality she'd been so generously given in this way? Who can say? But it's not for you to speculate. Not for you to wonder why she had a bruise on her face or why she told the police that Mr Diaz deserved to die. No, it's for you to look at the cold hard evidence and to base your verdict on that and that alone. So, what is the evidence? Well, we know that the accused came back to West Hope House around 5.10pm on the day in question and remained in her car a full fifteen minutes. To listen to a discussion on the radio? You may think rather she was waiting so as to enter the house at the same time Mr Diaz was returning from the shooting range with his gun. Ten minutes later Mr Diaz was dead.' Crowe turned to his right to look at Salome, dressed in a sombre, two-piece outfit over a white high-necked blouse. He held his gaze there for a moment before returning it to the jury box. 'The accused's fingerprints and DNA are on the shotgun. Mrs Diaz arrived only minutes after Mr Diaz and the accused had entered the house, albeit by different doors, to find the accused rushing out of the study and her husband inside, shot dead. What was the first thing the accused did? Call an ambulance? No. Call the police?' Crowe croaked a laugh. 'No, she called a lawyer.'

Crowe let his words sink in for a while. 'You've heard a number of scenarios bandied about in this trial. What do the defence say? That by some act of contortion and for no possible reason, Mr Diaz shot himself in the chest with a shotgun on the eve of his honeymoon. And when Professor Bradley the forensic pathologist ruled that out, what did they try and do? They changed tack completely and tried to suggest, before her ladyship rightly put a stop to it, that some mysterious third-party must have entered the house undetected while their client was indisposed, shot Mr Diaz with yet another shotgun and left the building undetected. It would be funny if this matter were not so serious. The defence scenarios are a pick-n-mix. The Crown has only one. The accused waited in her car until Mr Diaz returned from the shooting range. She knew from her many stays at his residence that he would enter via the back door to store his ammunition, and from there return his shotgun to the secure cabinet in his study. So that's where she met him. And that's where, with the usually locked cabinet wide open, she took this cartridge...' Crowe stepped to his side and lifted the clear plastic tube housing the yellow shotgun cartridge and held it up. Then he replaced it and slowly lifted the newly arrived, yellow cartridge box and shook it gently. It rattled. 'From this box and loaded it into this weapon.' It was the turn of the plastic wrapped shotgun to be hoisted. 'Salome Ramirez shot Armando Diaz from such close range that the very fibrous wadding from the cartridge was found amidst his horrendous and fatal wounds.'

Crowe was taking a breath when another hand was hoisted, this time from the jury box. 'No, it wasn't,' Elbow-Patches announced. He looked in a happier mood today. Thanks to yesterday's early finish, he must have made it to the pantomime after all.

Crowe looked to the judge. The judge scowled. 'Jury members may I remind you not to ask questions until you have heard from both Prosecution and Defence, and I have charged you on the law. Please continue, Advocate depute.'

'But I'm not asking a question,' the man in the woolly jumper replied. 'I'm telling you. Delta Champions don't have fibre wadding. They're plastic wads, and not the biodegradable ones either. Leave a terrible mess around the place.'

This time it was the judge who looked at Cameron Crowe. It wouldn't take a person endowed with Crowe's undoubted forensic skills to work out that if the fibre wadding found in Armando's chest wound hadn't come from the spent cartridge, it must have come from somewhere else. He blinked a few times, his face an even whiter shade of pale than its usual default setting. His confident expression of a few seconds ago, now the look of a general who'd thought he was in for a quiet evening at the officers' mess, and instead received orders to march on Moscow in winter.

'If it please the court,' he said, having cleared his throat. 'I wonder if I might pause my address to the jury in order that the court can adjourn for, say, fifteen minutes to allow me to consult with the firearms officer?'

'A very good idea,' Lady Carrick replied.

Chapter **49**

The firearms officer duly confirmed that, while the spent cartridge matched those from the box in the gun cabinet, they were a type with a plastic capsule as opposed to fibre wadding. Had it been used to shoot Armando Diaz, not only would there have been no fibrous wadding in his wound, but the plastic capsule would have also been found on the study floor, unless it had embedded itself in Armando's body; something which would have been hard to miss during the post-mortem examination.

The honourable thing would have been for Crowe to seek no conviction, have Lady Carrick thank the jury and send us all home. So it wasn't a complete surprise that it didn't happen. When court resumed and the puzzled jurors had taken their seats, the Advocate depute merely invited the jury to convict and withdrew, whereupon all eyes turned on Joanna. I squeezed her knee as she was getting up from the table. 'Give them both barrels,' I said. And that's exactly what she did.

'Salome Ramirez gave her evidence frankly and honestly. She was in the bathroom when she heard a bang and rushed to the study to find Armando Diaz fatally wounded. She did what any of us would have done. She went to the aid of her friend, getting blood on her hands and fingerprints on the shotgun in the process. The same shotgun which, when Armando dropped it, broke, ejecting the spent cartridge he'd used as a snap-cap to protect the trigger spring. Salome was leaving the room when she met Mrs Diaz. Uncertain as to what to do, she stayed to comfort her friend, but, in a panic and realising how things might look, did the right thing and sought legal advice.'

From there Joanna went on to remind the jury of the karate cook's evidence about the unlocked back door, the lack of security cameras and the unhindered access from there to the study.

'Members of the jury, the Crown can give you no motive for Salome Ramirez to have killed her friend. They tell you not to speculate. That's all very well, and yet somebody did shoot Armando Diaz, that is for sure, and that person must have had a reason. My client didn't have one. All I can say to you is that...' It was Joanna's turn to hold up the Crown productions one at a time. 'Whoever entered West Hope House that afternoon and whoever did murder Armando Diaz, they didn't do it with this shotgun, and they certainly didn't do it with this cartridge.' With thanks to the jury, Joanna replaced the weapon and ammunition on the production table, paused to tap the lid of the yellow box of cartridges and sat down.

The jury was out for only an hour and a half. When they returned it was to return a verdict of not guilty by a majority. Salome Ramirez was released from the dock and, shielded by her husband and their diamond-toothed minder, left the court to an awaiting limousine and a hoard of disappointed journalists. The media hate an acquittal.

'I wonder how many voted to convict,' I said, as we gathered our bundles of paper and waited until things quietened down. It was always annoying after a majority verdict that you were never told the result. It always pained me to think that a person in Scotland could be sent to prison for life despite 46.67% of the jury thinking the case hadn't been proved.

'And who was the old guy in the woolly jumper? I'm thinking a gamekeeper or a farmer or something,' I said to Joanna as we meandered our way down the Royal Mile rather than take the News Steps or those at Advocates Close. 'Obviously, someone who knew about shotguns.'

We were toying with the idea of stopping off for a celebratory drink when Joanna's phone buzzed. She read the screen and put the phone away again. 'That was Beverly,' she said. 'She's heard the verdict and wants me to give her a call. I think I'll wait a while before I reply.'

Next it was my phone's turn to go off. It was Grace Mary. 'Tell Joanna well done. When will you be back?'

'We're going for the half-three,' I said.

'Good, I'll put Isabella Ewart in for a quarter past four.'

'Did she say what she was wanting?' I asked. 'Phone her back and say that if she wants to settle her bill she can hand in a cheque or do a bank transfer. I'm going to be busy for the next wee while.'

'Doing what?'

'Anything except meeting her,' I said. If Isabella had been on the end of such a beating that she'd been hospitalised, all thanks to my idea as to how she could pay my fee, I was happy to indefinitely postpone any face-to-face with her.

Fate had other ideas.

Chapter 50

Christmas Eve, I left for Edinburgh with Tina, leaving no word of our shopping expedition with Malky in case he pitched up at FastFreez looking for Annette Lancaster with flowers and tickets to the theatre. When we arrived at the store on George Street there was a long queue outside, and we had to stand being whipped by the kind of icy, winter wind the capital can conjure up any day of the year.

Eventually, we were allowed into the hallowed interior. It might have been winter outside, but in the heart of pre-teen fashion it's always spring, and we were met by a posse of young and excruciatingly cheerful assistants wearing tight shorts and T-shirts with the FastFreez logo. As we entered, the staff seemed to be everywhere, speaking to the children, telling them all about merchandise in excited, high-pitched voices, though the tight shorts may have had something to do with that.

'What's up with the lighting in here?' I asked Tina, after one particularly annoying sales assistant had showed us to yet another queue. 'Have they not paid the electric bill or something?'

Children can learn a lot of things from their fathers. Patience is just one of them.

'Shoosh Dad,' Tina said, staring around at the other children who were standing in line; the cooler, older ones keeping a distance from their parents.

When at last we were permitted to browse, Tina was straight over at the tracksuits. She knew exactly what she was looking for: the ones with the special stitching, or pockets or flashes or a badge or something. Something so vitally important it meant me forking out a wad of my hard-earned.

I didn't care. I'd have bought my darling daughter the whole shop if she'd wanted, and if I had the money, which I didn't, though with the fee from Salome's trial, Munro and Co. was destined to enter the new year in a better financial state than it had started the last.

'There's Flo!' Tina yelled, above the sound of Christmas music. 'Look, she's in the queue for the changing rooms. She's trying on a red tracksuit. I thought she was getting a blue one.'

'The red one's nice,' I said, which decided matters for Tina, and she opted for an electric blue number. It looked just her size, but I knew if we didn't try it on, and it didn't fit when we got home, I'd have to come back. I wasn't about to let that happen. Already, thirty minutes in, I was feeling my life-force diminishing with each passing second.

Coveted tracksuit clutched in my daughter's hand, we joined the queue for the changing rooms. It was then that I noticed young Flo was also accompanied by an adult. A large adult, dressed in jeans and black leather jacket, who was browsing, head and shoulders above everyone in the near vicinity.

While Isabella Ewart was busy examining the merchandise, I was trying my very best to be invisible. Unfortunately, the same couldn't be said for Tina. When she caught her friend's attention, Flo shouted to her to come down and they'd share a changing room. Tina was off before I could do anything about it. Rather than stand by myself in a queue of predominantly wee girls and their mothers destined for the female changing rooms, I tagged along, explaining as I went why I was skipping the queue, and not receiving too many festive greetings as I did. I waited with Tina and Flo until we were next but one in line for the changing rooms. That was when Isabella came over and stood in front of me, thankfully making studious attempts to give me the cold-shoulder.

'Hello Isabella,' I said, when I thought I'd really have to say something. 'I heard about the fight.'

'Did you?' she replied not turning around.

'I didn't mean for you to get hurt. I thought maybe—'

This time she did turn around. There were fading yellow bruises beneath both her eyes. 'You thought maybe I could beat the women's English Amateur Champion after a few weeks training? Somehow, I don't think so, Robbie!'

'Okay, keep your voice down. I didn't know who you were fighting. I thought a few weeks with Brendan would be enough. He won a gold medal at the commonwealth games after all, and a big girl... I mean a powerful woman like yourself... Over how many rounds was it? Five?'

'Six.'

'Two-minute rounds though. I mean how much damage could be done?'

In answer, Isabella pointed to her face.

'But you got paid, didn't you? The loser's purse was fifteen hundred.'

'Oh, I got paid all right,' Isabella said. 'Brendan took five hundred for training expenses, I'm buying Flo a tracksuit for her Christmas, and the rest I'm keeping for myself. You got a problem with that?'

Isabella's fists were clenched at her sides. The muscles in her jaw, albeit already slightly swollen on the left, were protruding. I had a feeling she might put Brendan's training into practice and suddenly two minutes did seem like a very long time. All the same, a deal was a deal.

'That money was for me, Isabella. That was our arrangement. I'm sorry you got bashed about a bit—'

'I had a suspected fractured cheek.'

'How was I to know that would happen? I mean, twelve minutes in the ring—'

'It was only five.'

'There you are then. Five minutes is a lot better than five years in the jail.'

Isabella had started breathing heavily through the nose like a bull that's just seen a lot of red FastFreez tracksuits running across its favourite patch of meadow. In the circumstances I was prepared to negotiate. 'You've a thousand left. You buy Flo her Christmas present, that leaves eight hundred. We'll split it down the middle. That's me making a loss of eleven hundred, but, hey, it's Christmas. What do you say?'

Isabella didn't say anything. Instead, she decided to let her right hand do the talking. She threw a punch at me that would have connected if only she hadn't so much as telegraphed it as taken it to the post office and sent it second class. I dodged the blow, and, while onlookers may say that I tripped Isabella up, my leg just happened to be there. Big Bella's momentum was carrying her forward in any case, so a wee shove in the back was almost an involuntary action on my part. Almost. The couple, a woman and her child, behind us had just skipped in front and been allowed into the changing rooms. There was no one to break Isabella's fall. She landed heavily. I reached out, and the three of us, Tina, Florence and I hoisted her to her feet, hair dishevelled, face on fire. I showed Isabella the palms of both hands. 'You're obviously upset,' I said. 'I can understand that, but you need to see things from —'

'*Excuse me.*'

I looked to my right to see a woman, mid-twenties, in lime green FastFreez T-shirt and shorts, hands on hips and staring up at Isabella and me as though we were about to be the latest additions to Santa's naughty list. The T-shirt had a badge on it that said, Annette - FastFreez Manager.

'I'm afraid you'll both have to leave,' she said.

Isabella drew herself up to her full height, towering over the woman in the lime green T-shirt. 'I've stood in this queue for the best part of an hour, Petal. And if you think you're going to throw me out now, maybe you should give it a try.'

Lime Green took a step back. 'You're Isabella Ewart, the Olympic shot-putter.'

'It was the discus actually, but—'

'Is this man bothering you?' Lime Green asked, looking at me as though the jury was happy to return a guilty verdict without all the bother of hearing the evidence.

I switched seamlessly into plea in mitigation mode. 'Just a small misunderstanding. No harm done. Isn't that right, Bella?'

'No, it's not right, and it's Isabella to you, or better still Miss Ewart.'

'Hold on—'

'Stop talking Dad,' Tina said, tugging at my jacket, whether out of embarrassment or because we were so near and yet so far from the changing rooms, and with a queue of people behind us already pretty miffed we'd jumped ahead.

'I'm sorry, Sir, Lime Green said, 'I have to ask that you leave.'

At this Tina and Flo began to protest.

'I'm not going,' I said.

'Yes, you are,' said Lime Green.

Ignoring her, I ushered my daughter and the electric blue tracksuit towards the changing rooms.

'I said do not go in there!'

Realising how upset my, and therefore Tina's, imminent ejection was making young Flo, Isabella had a sudden change of heart. She enveloped the lime green T-shirt with a friendly but restraining arm around the shoulders. 'It's okay. Let the wee girl try on her clothes. *Then* you can chuck him out.'

I didn't hear the rest of the exchange. Nor did my daughter and I make it as far as the changing rooms, because someone tapped me firmly on the shoulder. I assumed it would be an irate parent. I suppose in a way it was. I turned to see the face of Colin Lancaster, lips pursed like the rear end of a hotdog, eyebrows in a tight V formation.

'When Peter Falconer told me about this, I almost never believed him,' he said. 'And yet I might have known.'

Maybe Lancaster's confusion over identification was fuelled by his paranoia, aided by the fact that my brother and Isabella were both around the same height. Maybe it was that they both had brown collar length hair. Maybe it was the dim lighting and because Lancaster could only see Isabella from behind; whatever, he reached out, grabbed Isabella's collar and pulled her away from his daughter, making Isabella stagger backwards. She spun around. Perhaps the adrenalin from her recent fall had speeded up Big Bella's reactions. Perhaps during her weeks of boxing training she'd concentrated more on left-hooks than right-crosses. Undoubtedly, it was the shock of being confronted, not by Malky, but by Isabella Ewart, that caused Lancaster to, ironically, fast freeze. The blow struck him squarely on the jaw and sent him careering backwards, scattering shoppers and almost squashing some of the smaller children.

I'm renowned for leaving my mobile phone behind when I go places, and often accused by my wife of doing so on purpose. On this occasion it was with me in case I had to phone home for some shopping advice. It was out of my pocket, in my hand and a video taken of the sprawled Colin Lancaster in less time than it takes to write a tabloid headline.

His daughter jumping in between him and Big Bella, Lancaster struggled to his feet. Angry didn't come into it. Keeping a safe distance from Isabella, he put one hand to his jaw and held the other out to me. 'Give me that,' he demanded, making a grab for my phone.

I pulled it out of his reach. 'Perhaps between us we could reach some sort of a compromise over Malky,' I said.

310

Chapter 51

Christmas came and went. Malky made a comeback on Scotgoals' annual football round-up along with a newcomer to the show: a female professional footballer. They hit it off big time, and I could see the two developing into the sort of bantering double-act that could only boost the programme's viewing figures. Tina's tracksuit was hardly off her back, she even slept in it on Christmas night, and Jamie's third Christmas was a happy one, though, like all three-year-olds, one he'd not remember when he was older. Much the same could be said about my Dad's Christmas. But that had more to do with cask strength Glenburgie 1997 than infantile amnesia.

On Boxing Day Joanna announced we'd received an invitation from Beverly to join her and a few friends for drinks the following evening. We couldn't not accept, and when we arrived at West Hope House, the halls of which were fittingly bedecked for the season, discovered that by 'a few friends' Beverly meant more people than I'd ever seen in one place at the same time; major sporting and music events excluded.

'I just wanted to say thank you,' Beverly said, when she'd managed to drag herself away from other guests. 'I know I was… Well, I was very—'

'There's no need to say anything,' Joanna said.

'But I want to. What's done is done. I don't suppose I'll ever know the truth about what happened to Armando, but you were quite right, Jo.' She took a hold of Joanna's hand. 'I think it's because despite my law degree I've never actually dealt with any proper law. You know, appearing in court.'

It was strange to hear her say that. I'd never thought of court work as proper law. A lot of the time it could be quite improper. I'd always viewed proper law as solicitors in big city offices, sending contracts to each other that nobody but they could understand, full of notwithstandings, hereinbefores and without prejudices.

'And Robbie. I can't forget you, can I? Wait there,' Beverly said, and left us for a few minutes. I was pleased that Armando's widow seemed to be coming to terms with his death. Her mourning eased no doubt by falling heir to a patriarchal wealth that included a large death in service payment, now that the insurers were satisfied her husband's death hadn't been suicide. She returned clutching a key. 'I know how much you appreciated Armando's whisky collection.' I'd appreciated about a quarter-bottle's worth of it as I recalled. 'He was very fond of Salome, and I'm sure he'd be happy if you were to take... Well, we'll call it a New Year bottle. The study has been locked since Armando's death. I can't bring myself to go in there. I don't know if I ever will. But, please, help yourself.'

'No, Beverly, the bottles in Armando's whisky collection are worth far too much. I couldn't possibly.' Was what I managed to stop myself from saying just in time, and instead allowed her to press the key into my hand.

My head was still spinning as Beverly led Joanna away, saying that Salome would want to thank her in person.

I hadn't heard from Salome or Dario since that last day in court. One of the things you learn after a very short time in criminal defence work, is that clients are generally very ungrateful, the innocent ones especially. I could understand why. To them the defence solicitor, although on their side, is just another cog in the wheel of a justice system that has ground down the innocent accused over many months if not years. Not that I'd expected to be carried shoulder high from court by the world's former best centre-half and his pregnant

312

wife. Okay, it would have been nice, but payment for services rendered was thanks enough. On that front, I'd had no concerns. Munro &Co.'s bill was settled immediately upon presentation. It included a handsome win bonus for Laszlo Derry. I would have liked to have sent an even larger bonus to the man in the woolly jumper and leather elbow patches if I'd known who he was and didn't mind being struck off for contacting a juror.

I looked around for my former client, and could only catch the glint of a Diamond Tooth grinning at me from a distance. I let Joanna and Beverly merge into the crowd, made my way to the study door, unlocked it and went inside. The room smelt musty, almost damp, and there was a layer of dust on the furniture. Someone seriously needed to throw a window open. I don't know why, perhaps to prolong the pleasure of it all, before I reached the whisky cabinet, I stopped to look at the bookcase, heaving with volumes. The titles of most were unsurprisingly in Spanish. One in particular I recognised. But I couldn't put it off any longer. I don't know how long I studied Armando's whisky collection that night. Some of the bottles were older than me. Which bottle to take was an impossible choice. I thought I had managed to narrow it down to several dozen possible contenders, when I heard someone come in and turned to see Salome in a tight-fitting, white evening dress trimmed with gold that did nothing to hide her bump. She was glowing and positively stunning.

'You like the whisky?' she said.

'Just a little,' I replied.

Salome took a small gold cylinder from her clutch bag, and, studying her reflection in the glass front of the whisky cabinet, refreshed her lipstick. 'Dario doesn't drink,' she said, smiling. 'His body, what is it you say? It's a temple.' I smiled back at her. My body was fast becoming something the Building Preservation Trust might want to take a serious look at.

She stood beside me as I continued to consider my options, breaking my concentration. Beautiful women are all well and good, but not when you're trying to choose a rare single malt.

'When is the baby due?' I asked, when she showed no sign of leaving. 'I don't expect Dario cares if it's a boy or a girl, so long as it can play attacking mid-field.'

Salome laughed politely. I returned to deliberate the attributes of a Rare Old St Magdalene over a 38-year-old Brora, while carrier of the Great One junior wandered over to the bookcase.

'I see your book is still here,' I said, over my shoulder. 'El Amor en los Tiempos del Cólera.'

I thought she'd laugh some more, this time at my pronunciation. She didn't. I turned around to see her hand on the very book I'd been talking about, only to see her pull it away when she saw me watching. I walked over and reached out to pull the book from the shelf. Salome put her hand on mind. I continued to tug at the book. When I'd managed to unwedge it from where it was tightly squeezed amongst the many others, I saw something in the space left behind: a small red ribbed cylinder with brass casing at the end. Salome took her hand off mine and laid it on her stomach, rubbing it. Caressing as it were the unborn child. The child that would save her marriage. Dario's child. Wasn't it?

'He did rape me,' she said softly, as I removed the spent shotgun cartridge. 'Not only that day, but before the wedding when Beverly invited me to come help with the preparations. I don't know… Maybe I led Armando on in some way. After their wedding, when I fell out with Dario, Beverley said I could come to stay with her for a few days. I didn't know she was leaving to be with her mother and that I would be alone with him.'

'Why come back here at all?' I said. 'And why didn't you tell Beverly what had happened before she married him?'

Salome shrugged. 'What could I say? Sorry, Beverly. I can't come to your home because your husband-to-be is a rapist?'

'Might have been the friendly thing to do,' I said.

'Do you think Beverly would have believed me?' Salome looked around. 'Given up all of this?'

I thought back to the trial, and the security camera showing Salome returning to West Hope House on the day of Armando's murder. Returning after a talk with her husband that had taken place in his gun store, just as he was tooling up and readying himself for an afternoon's shooting. Plastic wadding? Somehow, I didn't think Dario would use any cartridges on his land that weren't environmentally friendly. He'd prefer the fibre, biodegradable kind. The kind found embedded in Armando's fatal chest wound. And where were the belongings Salome had gone to collect? She was seen on CCTV carrying only a small handbag, but then a seven-centimetre cartridge was as easily concealed as a lipstick.

I could hear the chatter and laughter from the crowd beyond the study door. Judging by tonight's turnout, Beverly had no shortage of friends. What was so special about Salome that she'd invited her to come help six weeks before the wedding? Had Salome invited herself? Was Armando a rapist? Had he deserved it? Strange, but I hoped so. Better that than he'd merely served a purpose. Been an unwitting means to an end. A loose end that Salome thought needed to be tied off before her husband found out the truth.

I looked at her. She looked back at me. Salome didn't appear quite so beautiful anymore. I walked away, over to the whisky cabinet and stared for a long moment at the riches inside. Then I walked out of the room empty handed, closing the door behind me.

More in the Best Defence/Robbie Munro Series:

#1 RELATIVELY GUILTY

Follow the trials of Scots criminal lawyer Robbie Munro as he joins battle in the fight for truth and justice - hoping truth and justice don't win too often because it's terribly bad for business.

A policeman with a caved-in skull, his young wife found clutching the blood-stained murder weapon; it all looks open and shut until Robbie detects the faint whiff of a defence and closes in on a witness who might cast a precious doubt on proceedings.

So why is it, the nearer he gets to the truth and a possible acquittal, that Robbie's murder client becomes more and more eager to opt for a life sentence?

Short-Listed for the Dundee International Book Prize

#2 DUTY MAN

Do your duty and leave the rest to heaven

Continuing the trials of Scots defence lawyer, Robbie Munro.

Local lawyer Max Abercrombie is gunned down in cold blood, and the historic town of Linlithgow is rocked by its first assassination in five hundred years. Robbie, Max's childhood friend, is duty-bound to act in the accused's defence, and when investigations reveal a link between his friend's murder and that of a High Court judge many years before, he wonders if his client might actually be an innocent man.

The more Robbie digs into the past, the closer he gets to the truth and the more the bodies pile up.

#3 SHARP PRACTICE

Scotland's favourite criminal defence lawyer, Robbie Munro, is back and under pressure to find a missing child, defend a murdering drug-dealer and save the career of a child-pornography-possessing local doctor.

Add to that the antics of his badly behaving ex-cop dad, the re-kindling of an old flame and a run-in with Scotland's Justice Secretary and you'll discover why it is that, sometimes, a lawyer has to resort to Sharp Practice.

#4 KILLER CONTRACT

'It's the trial of the millennium: Larry Kirkslap, Scotland's most flamboyant entrepreneur, charged with the murder of good-time gal Violet Hepburn. He needs a lawyer and there's only one man for the job – unfortunately it's not Robbie Munro. That's about to change; however, more pressing is the contract out on the lives of Robbie and his client, Danny Boyd, who is awaiting trial for violating a sepulchre.

Who would anyone want to kill Robbie and his teenage client?

While Robbie tries to work things out, there are a couple of domestic issues that also need his urgent attention, like his father's surprise birthday party and the small matter of a marriage proposal.

#5 CRIME FICTION

If the ink is in your blood...

Desperate for cash, criminal defence lawyer Robbie Munro, finds himself ensnared in a web of deceit spun by master conman Victor Devlin. What is Devlin's connection with the case of two St Andrews' students charged with the murder of a local waitress? Enter Suzie Lake, a former-university chum of Robbie's, now best-selling crime fiction author, who is especially interested in the St Andrews' murder and looking for some inside information. How can Robbie refuse the advances of the gorgeous Suzie, even if she threatens his pending nuptials? Is it merely coincidence that the more he tells Suzie, the more Robbie finds himself in a murky world of bribery, corruption and crime fiction publishing?

#6 LAST WILL
Blood is thicker than water - but it's not as hard as cash.
The trial of Robbie Munro's life; one month to prove he's fit to be a father. No problem. Apart, that is, from the small matter of a double-murder in which Robbie's landlord, Jake Turpie, is implicated. Psycho-Jake demands Robbie's undivided attention and is prepared to throw money at the defence - along with some decidedly dodgy evidence.
Robbie has a choice, look after his daughter or look after his client. Can the two be combined to give the best of both worlds? Robbie aims to find out, and his attempts lead him into the alien worlds of high-fashion, drug-dealing and civil-litigation. It's what being a father/lawyer is all about. Isn't it?

#7 PRESENT TENSE
Criminal lawyer Robbie Munro is back home, living with his widowed, ex-policeman dad and his newfound daughter, Tina. Life at the practice isn't going well, neither is the love life he regularly confesses to his junior, Joanna. Then again, on the subject of Joanna, Robbie may be the last to know... When one of his more dubious clients leaves a mysterious box for him to look after, and a helicopter comes down with two fatalities, events take a much more sinister turn, and all of this is complicated by the rape case he has to defend.

#8 GOOD NEWS BAD NEWS
Life's full of good news and bad news for defence lawyer Robbie Munro. Good news is he's in work, representing Antonia Brechin on a drugs charge – unfortunately she's the granddaughter of notorious Sheriff Brechin. His old client Ellen has won the lottery and she's asked Robbie to find her

husband Freddy who's disappeared after swindling Jake Turpie, but he's not willing to bury the hatchet – unless it's in Freddy's head. Robbie juggles cases and private life with his usual dexterity, but the more he tries to fix things the more trouble everyone's in.

#9 STITCH UP
The truth is out there - sometimes it's better to leave it alone.
Everything is coming up roses for Robbie Munro, newly married and living in the country with wife and child. That is until his wife takes up employment abroad just as old flame, Jill Green, asks him to investigate the unexplained death of her partner. Suspecting foul play, Jill insists Robbie turns poacher to gamekeeper and does whatever it takes to find the killer – with no expense spared. Another killer on the loose is child-murderer Ricky Hertz, whose twenty-year-old conviction is under scrutiny. Was the evidence at his trial fabricated? Suspicion falls on Robbie's father who now faces a criminal prosecution. The only way to prove ex-Police Sergeant Alex Munro's innocence is for Robbie to show there was no miscarriage of justice.

#10 FIXED ODDS
There's no such thing as a safe bet
On the home front, defence lawyer Robbie Munro is looking forward to the birth of his second child, while at work he's called to defend George 'Genghis' McCann on a charge of burglary, and Oscar 'the Showman' Bowman, snooker champion, on one of betting fraud. Genghis has stolen – and lost – a priceless masterpiece, while Oscar doesn't seem to have a defence of any kind. With another mouth to feed and promises of great rewards if he finds both painting and defence, Robbie has never been more tempted to fix the legal odds in his favour.

#11 BAD DEBT

Defence Lawyer Robbie Munro's wife has been stalked by a witness in a trial she is prosecuting. When the stalker is killed, and Robbie is charged with murder his friends are only too willing to come up with schemes to prove his innocence. In the end though, will it be his enemies who make the difference?

ABOUT THE AUTHOR

William McIntyre is a criminal defence lawyer. Over the years William has been instructed in many interesting and high-profile cases, and now turns fact into fiction with his string of legal thrillers, The Best Defence Series, featuring defence lawyer, Robbie Munro.

Based in Scotland and drawing on William's thirty years as a criminal defence lawyer, there is a rich vein of dry humour running through the series, which he describes as an antidote to crime fiction that features maverick cops chasing serial killers, and in it he emphasises that justice is not only about convicting the guilty, but also about acquitting the innocent.

The books, which are stand alone or can be read in series, have been well received by many fellow professionals, on both sides of the Bar, due to their accuracy in law and procedure and Robbie's frank, if sardonic, view on the idiosyncrasies of the Scots criminal justice system.

William is married with four sons.

Printed in Great Britain
by Amazon